Josef pressed his palm to his forehead as Eli resumed shoving his way forward. Thankfully, no one else seemed to have heard the thief's remark. The bounty hunters were all loudly clamoring for copies, shouting over each other while the bounty officer tried to shout over everyone that no one was getting posters until the official copies were up.

Eli vanished into the fray only to reappear moments later with a scroll tucked under his arm.

"They get better with every likeness," Eli said, proudly unrolling his poster. "If it wasn't black and white, I'd say I was looking in a mirror."

Nico nodded appreciatively, but Josef wasn't even looking. Eli turned to berate his swordsman for his shocking lack of attentiveness, but Josef was just standing there, staring at the bounty board like he'd seen a ghost. Eli followed his gaze, glancing over his shoulder at the bounty wall where the Council men were hanging one last poster, just below Den's and just ahead of Eli's. As the Council men tacked the poster's corners up, a familiar, stern face glared down at the room, and below it, in tall block letters, was the following:

JOSEF LIECHTEN THERESON ESINLOWE.
WANTED ALIVE, 250,000 GOLD STANDARDS.

"Josef," Eli said, very quietly. "Why is your bounty larger than mine?"

BY RACHEL AARON

The Legend of Eli Monpress

The Spirit Thief

The Spirit Rebellion

The Spirit Eater

The Spirit War

Spirit's End

The Legend of Eli Monpress:
Volumes 1, 2 & 3 (omnibus edition)

THE SPIRIT WAR

AN ELI MONPRESS NOVEL

RACHEL AARON

orbit

www.orbitbooks.net

Orbit
Hachette Book Group
237 Park Avenue, New York, NY 10017
www.HachetteBookGroup.com

First Edition: June 2012

Orbit is an imprint of Hachette Book Group, Inc. The Orbit name
and logo are trademarks of Little, Brown Book Group Limited.

The Hachette Speakers Bureau provides a wide range
of authors for speaking events. To find out more, go to
www.hachettespeakersbureau.com or call (866) 376-6591.

The publisher is not responsible for websites (or their content) that
are not owned by the publisher.

The characters and events in this book are fictitious. Any similarity
to real persons, living or dead, is coincidental and not
intended by the author.

Library of Congress Cataloging-in-Publication Data
Aaron, Rachel.
    The spirit war / Rachel Aaron. 1st ed.
        p. cm.
    ISBN 978-0-316-19838-7
    I. Title.
PS3601.A26S65 2012
813'.6—dc23

                        2011029884

        10 9 8 7 6 5 4

RRD-IN

Printed in the United States of America

For Peggy, without whom this book
would not have been.

PROLOGUE

The old swordsman was kneeling in the dirt, blowing on the embers of last night's fire when he saw the boy approaching. He paused, keeping low to the dusty ground as he watched the boy start up the hill toward his campsite. The boy was a tall one, skinny and fair but with the large shoulders and wide ribs that spoke of the man he'd become once he finished growing into them. The swordsman pegged him at seventeen, maybe a little younger, but he wore the two short swords at his hips like he knew how to use them.

The swordsman sat back with a long sigh and glanced at the great black sword stabbed in the sand beside him.

"They never give up, do they?"

"No," the sword answered. "Thank the Powers. I think we'd both die of boredom if they stopped coming."

The swordsman sighed. "Speak for yourself."

The sword didn't answer, but the ground creaked as it settled itself deeper. The old swordsman shook his head and sat back to wait.

It took the boy the better part of an hour to climb to the top of the old swordsman's hill. At last, he pulled himself over the final boulders and stepped panting into the circle of dusty brush outside the cave where the swordsman made his home. He caught his breath and straightened up, fixing his eyes on the swordsman with a challenging glare.

"I'm looking for Milo Burch," he announced. "You him?"

The old swordsman frowned. "Why would a boy like you be looking for an old has-been like Burch?"

The boy stepped forward, planting his feet in first position. "I've heard he's the greatest swordsman in the world, wielder of the legendary Heart of War. I've come to challenge him."

"Really?" The old man rubbed his graying beard. "How did you get here?"

The boy paused, thrown for a second. "I walked."

The swordsman looked at him, and then looked out over the scrubby, flat desert that stretched as far as he could see in all directions. "You walked?" he said. "Alone?"

"Yes, alone." The boy's voice was growing frustrated. "Are you Milo Burch or not? I was told he lived out here. If you're not him, then I'll be going."

"Let's say I am," the swordsman said. "Who would be asking?"

The boy straightened up. "I am Josef Liechten, and I demand a duel for the title of greatest swordsman."

The swordsman started to laugh. "You demand it, do you?" he choked out at last, wiping his eyes. "I'm afraid you'll be a little disappointed. 'Greatest swordsman' isn't a hat you can pass around, and it's not like there's anyone out here to see your victory over an old man." The wind blew as he spoke, its lonely whistle a sharp reminder of the vast emptiness around them.

The boy set his jaw stubbornly. "Doesn't matter," he said. "Are you going to fight or not? I didn't walk all the way out here to stand around talking."

The old swordsman stood with a deep sigh and walked over to the scrabbly tree that grew just beside the little space he used as his fire pit. "You certainly sound determined, Josef Liechten," he said, reaching up to break off a dry branch. "I'm too old to go tumbling around with kids, but I can see that trying to talk you out of this duel nonsense would be nothing but a waste of breath."

The boy, Josef, nodded.

The swordsman turned, holding up the branch he'd just taken from the tree. "How about we make a deal? If you can break this, I'll fight you."

Josef stared at the stick in the man's hand. It was a sad thing, knobby and dead, its ends already cracking under the force of the old man's grip.

"I think it would be a greater challenge not to break it," he said, his voice turning cautious. "Is this some kind of trick?"

"If it was, I certainly wouldn't tell you," the old man said, his tanned, leathery face breaking into a grin. "Then again, the greatest swordsman in the world would hardly have to resort to tricks, don't you think?"

Josef glowered and shifted his feet. "All I have to do is break the stick," he said slowly. "Just break it, and you'll fight me for real?"

The old swordsman nodded. "That's it."

Josef scowled, and then he drew his swords. They were good work, the old man noticed. Well balanced and a good size for Josef's reach. It seemed the boy knew something. That was good. He was too old to waste energy on idiots.

"Come at me whenever you're ready," he said, lifting his stick.

With one final, annoyed look, Josef charged.

It was a good assault, a straight-on rush and then, three steps in, a feint to the left. Milo Burch stayed still just long enough to let the boy think he'd fallen for it and then quietly ducked out of the way.

The boy charged past him and stopped, boots skidding on the loose dirt. He turned around, panting. Milo smiled at him, resting the stick on his shoulder.

"That was good," he said. "Perhaps you should try—"

Josef was running before he could finish, cutting around to Milo's left. Again, Milo let him get just close enough to commit to the blow before ducking down. Josef's sword whistled over his head, and the boy stumbled past him. Josef cursed loudly, and Milo stepped right to avoid the second sword that thrust from below. He spun around as Josef carried the thrust through, bopping the boy on the head with the stick as he passed.

Josef yelped in surprise and stumbled, falling to the ground. Milo sighed.

"If I'd taken your duel, that would have been the end, you know," he said, swinging his stick. "I won't think less of you if you want to give up."

He'd barely finished when Josef dropped the sword in his left hand. The knife came a second later. Milo opened his hand, letting the stick drop in his grip just before the knife sliced through the air where it had been. As soon as the knife was past, he sidestepped again as Josef followed through with a lunge at his legs.

"Again, not bad," Milo said, grinning. "Why don't you—"

"Shut up!" Josef shouted, grabbing for the stick with his now-empty left hand.

Milo stepped neatly out of his reach, making Josef stumble as he overbalanced. The boy was panting now, his face red from the sun and slick with sweat.

"You're not a bad fighter, you know," Milo said gently. "Surely you're good enough to see the difference between us. You know you can't win. There's no point in pushing yourself."

Josef scowled at him, breathing hard, and then flicked another knife right at Milo's hand.

This went on all afternoon. Josef would attack and Milo would step out of the way. Josef never attacked the same way twice, but the end result never changed. As day wore into evening, Josef's lunges grew slower, but he did not stop until finally, as the sun sank below the horizon, he tripped and fell and did not get up again.

Milo leaned on his stick. "Are we done?"

Josef didn't answer. He just lay in the dirt, panting. Milo sighed and set the stick on the ground beside the fire. He walked over, shoved his hands under Josef's arms, and began dragging him toward the cave.

"What are you doing?" Josef gasped.

"Keeping you from dying of dehydration," Milo said. "I also imagine you would like some food."

Josef stared at him. "But I'm your enemy," he said, the words wheezing.

"You're the only one who said that," Milo said. "I was sitting here minding my own business." He dumped Josef unceremoniously on the floor of the cave. "Do you want some water or not?"

"Yes, please," Josef said, lying flat on his back. "Thank you."

"Polite," Milo said, handing him the water skin. "I like that."

Josef was too focused on drinking to answer.

He drank the entire water skin and half of another, and then ate the five loaves of bread that were meant to keep Milo the next week. He was still chewing when he fell asleep. When he was sure the boy was out, Milo tossed his blanket over the boy and walked out to sit beside the great black sword that was still staked beside the fire.

"What do you think?"

"He's stubborn as a rock," the sword said. "He's slow, his movements lack subtlety, and he has no grace."

Milo arched a white eyebrow. "Since when do you care about grace?"

"A minimum is required," the sword grumbled. "Still, he lasted five hours. That's the best yet."

"It is, isn't it," Milo said, rubbing his aching arms. Dodging all day was harder than it used to be. "He's spirit deaf, you know."

He felt the sword's ambivalence brush over him like a shrug. "I've had many deaf wielders. Hearing isn't what matters. It's everything else."

"Well, you'll have to stop being so picky," Milo said quietly. "We don't have much time left."

"I have all the time in the world," the sword answered. "Still, we'll see. Tomorrow, maybe."

"Tomorrow," Milo said, lying back to watch the moon rising over the desert.

Josef woke with the sun in his eyes and the old man standing over him, poking him in the shoulder with the hated stick.

"Morning," Milo said, grinning.

Josef smiled back, and then, fast as he could, rolled to grab the stick. For a second it was in his grasp before the old man snatched it away.

"Nice try." He sounded genuinely impressed. "Shall we begin?"

Josef pushed himself up, wincing as every muscle in his body protested, and reached for his swords.

"Ready."

They fought all morning with nothing to show. Everything Josef tried, the old man countered. The desert sun was brutal, burning Josef's skin through his shirt. Sweat soaked everything he owned, but he did not let himself stop. The old man had yet to admit it, but there was no more question in Josef's mind. He was fighting Milo Burch, the greatest swordsman in the world, famous across all the Council Kingdoms. It had to be him; no one else could be this fast. This was the reason he'd traveled all the way to the desert, why he'd walked through the heat and the burning sand for two days. It didn't matter if Burch was toying with him; he could not lose now. Not when he was this close.

Noon came and Josef kept going. His movements were jerky, and he could scarcely see through the burning sweat in his eyes. His limbs were so tired he actually dropped his sword a few times, but he pushed on until, at last, there was simply nothing left to push.

He didn't realize he'd fallen until he saw Milo standing over him, pressing a water skin to his cracked, dry lips.

"You know," he said softly, "there's a fine line between being determined and being an idiot. If you keep this up, I won't have to lift a sword to kill you. You'll kill yourself."

Josef choked on the water. He tried to sit up, but he had no strength left in his back. In the end, he settled for lying back and letting the water trickle down his throat.

"Josef," Milo said. "Give up, would you? When you're as old as I am, you've seen enough of the world to recognize its patterns. You think you're unique, but I've seen you dozens of times. Let me guess: You were the best swordsman in your village, or wherever you came from. Sword work came as easy to you as breathing, and soon there was no one who could give you a challenge. You took to wandering, fighting whoever was strong enough to teach you some-thing. You've probably defeated a hundred men, haven't you?"

"More," Josef croaked.

Milo shrugged. "Your problem is you're young. Impatient. You think that by beating me you can somehow jump to the top, but you can't. You can't beat me, and you can't jump ahead. The sword must be earned, Josef. Strength that comes easily is no strength at all."

Josef opened his eyes, squinting in the bright light. "I know that," he whispered. "But I'm not fighting for strength."

The old man's face was too far away for him to focus on, but Josef felt him frown. "What are you fighting for?"

7

"I hurt a lot of people when I decided to be a swordsman," Josef wheezed. "Let a lot of people down. That's why I have to be the strongest."

"Do these people care if you're the strongest?" Milo said quietly.

Josef shook his head. "But they will," he said. "I have to show them—"

His words broke into coughs as he choked on the water again. It didn't matter, though. Milo finished for him.

"You have to be the strongest to give meaning to their suffering," he said, tilting his head.

Josef nodded, breathing deeply as the coughing subsided. "I was the one who left. If I'm not the best, then I hurt her for no reason."

"That's a dangerous way to think," Milo said quietly. "There's a good chance you will never be the best. That you will die alone and forgotten, remembered only as a disappointment."

"I don't believe in chance," Josef whispered. He looked at Milo and raised his sword. His hand shook as he lifted it, the sword sliding in his weakening grip. Josef forced himself to be calm, to be strong one last moment. The shaking slowed, and then, for one breath, stopped. That was when Josef moved.

He tossed his sword into the air, over Milo's head. The old man's eye went wide, but Josef grabbed the old man's wrist where he was holding the water bottle, pinning him in place. Trapped, the old swordsman could only watch as Josef's short sword flew through the air, spinning in wobbly arcs, and landed behind him, on top of the stick he'd laid aside when he knelt to help Josef. The blade landed sideways, bouncing away the moment it stuck, but the branch was old and brittle, and it was enough. The stick cracked with a soft pop, breaking into two ragged halves.

For a moment, all Milo could do was sit there, watching the broken remains of his stick rocking in the hot desert wind. Then he turned and looked at Josef with a strange, bemused expression on his weatherworn face. Josef grinned back.

"I never stop fighting," he said. "I'm holding you to your word, Milo Burch."

"And I never go back on my word," Milo said with a sigh. "Tomorrow, then. At dawn."

Josef nodded and released the old man's hand. He grabbed the water skin and drank until he drained it. When he was finished, he crawled across the baked ground and collapsed on a blanket just inside the cave, falling asleep instantly.

Milo picked up the broken pieces of his stick. When he had them both, he sat down with his back against the broad slab of scarred black metal that stood rooted in the sand and began feeding the pieces into the fire.

When Josef woke the next morning, the cave was empty. He took a long drink from the water barrel and helped himself to a breakfast of bread and dried apples from the swordsman's supplies. When he finished, he grabbed his sword from where he'd dropped it and walked out onto the hilltop.

Milo Burch was already there, sitting beside the now cold fire pit with his back against the massive, black metal shape that dominated the open space. As Josef stepped into the sandy ring around the fire, Milo held out the sword Josef had thrown to break the stick. Josef took it, sheathing it opposite its brother on his hip. When they were both ready, he took his stance and waited for Milo to begin.

The old swordsman stood with a sigh, rubbing the small of his back as he straightened. But his hands were empty as he turned to face Josef.

"Wait," Josef said. "Where's your sword? I'm here to fight the master of the Heart of War. Let's see it."

Milo shook his head and laid his hand on the wrapped handle of the great metal monster in the ground beside him. Josef's eyes widened. The black slab was enormous. He couldn't even think of what it must weigh. A man Milo's size shouldn't even have had the muscle to lift something that heavy, and yet the old swordsman pulled it up as easy as a farmer pulling a weed out of new-tilled dirt.

"I thought we agreed, no more games," Josef said. "What is that thing? Where's your sword? Where's the Heart of War?"

"This is the Heart of War," Milo said, swinging the black blade in front of him.

Josef almost laughed out loud. "*That* is the Heart of War? That… that *iron post* is the greatest awakened blade ever made? You're kidding. It doesn't even have a sharp edge. It couldn't cut paper."

Milo smiled. "A sword cuts whatever its swordsman wants it to cut. The Heart is no different."

Josef scowled. "We'll see."

They took their positions on either side of the dead fire. Josef readied his blades, keeping the man's movements from their earlier fights clear in his mind. He almost thought the old man should have stuck to the stick. There was no way he could move fast enough carrying that enormous weight. There had to be a trick or something. Maybe the sword was hollow? Something that large couldn't be solid metal, not if a human was meant to lift it. Still, the few awakened blades he'd beaten had all had their own oddities. He'd just have to push and see what happened.

"You know," Milo said. "You don't have to go through with this. I meant it when I said you were a good swordsman. Give you a few years and you could very well become the best, but not yet. The Heart won't let me hold back. You should stop now, while you still can."

"I told you before," Josef said. "I never stop. I can't stop." He raised his sword. "Guard yourself."

The words had barely left his mouth when he lunged. He pushed forward, slamming his feet down faster than he ever had before. He would get only once chance. He'd learned the first day that he couldn't beat the old man in speed, but yesterday he'd proven he could still trick him. He'd seen the strain in Milo as he stood up. The days of fighting had taken their toll on his old body. Now, weighed down with that enormous sword, especially after so long fighting with a stick that weighed nothing, there would be a hesitation in his first swing as his body got used to the weight difference. That was when Josef had to strike.

He rushed forward, boots pounding on the sand, watching the old man's arm for the moment he lifted the sword to parry. He had to parry. What else could you do with a sword that big? But the old man didn't move. He just stood there, watching as Josef came closer and closer. When he was one step away, Josef realized he might have been wrong. The old man might be too slow to catch him. There might be no need to wait for the hesitation in the parry. Already his swords were racing for the man's torso, one high, one low, and for one shining moment, Josef thought he might actually land the blow before Milo could move.

One moment, that's all it was. And in that moment, Milo Burch attacked.

It happened so fast Josef couldn't see the blows, but he felt them. There were three in the space of a second. The first shattered his left sword, the second broke his right, and the third hit him dead across the chest. That last blow knocked the breath from his lungs and sent him flying backward. He hit the side of the hill like a stone hurled from a catapult. For a moment, all he could feel was the rough ground on his back and the strange sensation of air against his chest through his sundered shirt, and then pain like he'd never felt before slammed down and he hit the ground with a sound that would have been a scream had he still had breath.

He floundered in the dirt, his whole body convulsing. Somehow, he ended up on his back again. That was when he saw it, though it took him several moments to realize that the bloody mess he was looking at was his own chest.

A deep, perfect cut ran from his left shoulder to his right hip. It was perfectly straight, as though he'd been cut by a razor, but so deep he had to look away. When he turned his head, he saw Milo crouching beside him, leaning on the Heart of War as he bent down to whisper in Josef's ear.

"Worst pain you've ever felt, isn't it?"

Gasping, Josef could only nod.

"This is the pain of defeat," the old swordsman said. "You are dying. I have defeated you utterly. Even if I were to bind your wound right now, there's no saving your life. This is the end. So now I'll ask you: Was it worth it?"

Josef looked at him and wheezed, "Yes."

Milo paused. "And if you'd known this was how it ended, would you still have broken the stick?"

"Yes," Josef said, his voice little more than a grating of breath. "I would rather die trying than ever give up."

"Is that so?" Milo said. "Then prove it. Take another breath."

Josef grimaced and looked down at his sundered chest. He tried to talk, but he had no air for the words.

"I can't," he mouthed.

"If you can't, then all your struggles to this point, all the pain you've caused, it's all for nothing," Milo said, his voice taut. "Take another breath, Josef Liechten."

Josef closed his eyes and focused on his lungs. For an eternity, nothing happened. His body was going stiff. Nothing would obey him. He concentrated, pouring every speck of his consciousness into that one action. The pain was so intense now he could barely think, but he felt his chest rise and fall, and suddenly he had air again.

His eyes popped open just in time to see Milo's face break into a grand smile. The old man held out his hand, offering something. Josef blinked, it was dark and heavy and, he could see now, larger than it looked.

"If you walk the path of the swordsman, you will feel this pain hundreds of times," Milo said. "You will never know a moment's peace, even if you move to a hill in the middle of the desert. Your life will be brutish, violent, and most likely short but it will also be glorious. This is what it means to live your life on the sword. You said you would rather die trying than give up. Now you must try living, or die. If you want to live, Josef Liechten, then reach out as far as you can and take your sword. Rise a swordsman, the master of the Heart of War, or do not rise at all."

His words fluttered against Josef's ears. The world felt very far away now. Even the pain was going, but Josef could still see the black shape of the sword hovering high above him. With the last of his will, he lifted his arm. He saw his hand moving above him, his fingers stretching up to clutch the wrapped handle. The moment his fingers made contact, a voice deeper and broader than any voice he'd ever heard spoke through him.

Welcome to your rebirth, swordsman. The words were more vibration than sound, but they were clear as carvings in his mind. *As you gave your life to become a swordsman, so did I give my life to become a sword. We are the same, you and I. Will you fight with me?*

Josef could not speak, but the answer echoed in his mind.

I will.

It is done, the voice said. *Welcome to your mountain, master of the Heart of War.*

As the voice faded from his mind, so did the pain. Strength like

13

Josef had never felt flowed into his body. All at once he could breathe again. His eyes were clear and open to the world. His arms moved without pain, and he was able to stand enough to let Milo guide him back to the cave and wrap him in the blankets, all the while dragging the massive black blade behind him.

He fell asleep the moment Milo lay him flat, the Heart of War clutched to his chest. How long he slept, Josef never knew, but when he woke it was night and Milo Burch was gone. The cave was empty except for the bloody blankets Josef lay on, the water barrel, and a large supply of food. A loaf of bread and a water skin lay on the ground beside his head, and Josef ate greedily before falling asleep again. When he woke next, it was evening. This time he was strong enough to stand. He went looking for Milo, but the old swordsman was gone. There was, however, a message scratched in soot on the cave wall.

After fifty years as a swordsman, it read, *I think I've earned the right to live my last few as just a man. Remember why you fight, Josef Liechten, and the Heart of War will never forsake you.*

That was it. No name, no date, no direction. Josef smiled. Nothing else was needed. He read the note twice and then rubbed it out with his palm. He gathered the food and as much water as he could carry. Then, tying the great black blade across his back with strips torn from the blood-ruined blankets, Josef Liechten, master of the Heart of War, set off into the desert to become the world's greatest swordsman.

CHAPTER

1

Den the Warlord, unknowing owner of the highest bounty the Council of Thrones had ever issued, was bashing his way through a jungle. He ripped out the waxy green plants in wet handfuls, kicking the rotten ground whenever it tried to trip him. Insects whizzed by in the humid air above his head, flying at his eyes whenever they dared, biting and stinging and all the while buzzing, "Go away! Go away!"

Den smacked them out of the air and kept going.

He knew by this point that the jungle was another dead end, but he had nowhere else to go but through it. So through it he went, smashing the undergrowth with mechanical efficiency until he spotted something white through the trees. Den slowed at once, sliding into a stance as he pushed the last of the broad leaves back. There, hanging directly in his path between two large trees, was a hole in the world. The hole was rectangular, an inch taller than himself, which was to say very tall indeed, and easily wide enough for him to walk through. Its edges were smooth and white, and they shone brighter than the noon sun reflected off water, which explained the flash he'd seen earlier. But strangest of all was that the jungle he saw through the opening was not the one he stood in. It was as thick as his jungle, just as green and overgrown, but the wind that drifted through the white-edged hole was hotter than the humid air around him. The soil on the other side was sandier, the trees denser and older. Though he'd been following a ridge in this jungle, the new jungle was flat, the land unremarkable save for a knot of trees directly ahead, their roots tangled around the entrance of what looked to be a small dirt cave.

Den frowned and took a moment to consider. He'd seen such a portal once before, the only time he'd ever managed to corner a League man. His face broke into a grin at the memory. That had been a good fight.

If he hadn't already decided his jungle was a dead end, that thought alone was enough to decide for him. Smiling in anticipation, Den stepped forward, ducking through the portal. When his feet hit the ground on the other side, he took up a defensive position, looking for his opponent. But the new jungle was as empty as the old one had been, its trees tossing in the lonely wind. Feeling cheated, Den turned back only to find that the portal was gone, leaving nothing but a fading white line in the baking air.

Den snarled. It wasn't that he was angry to leave the first jungle. When you were searching blindly as he was, one place was as good as the next. But he didn't like unknowns, and he certainly didn't like having fights taken from him. He closed his eyes and listened, ears straining, just on the off chance the League man was waiting for an opening, but it was no use. If the League had been here, they were long gone. Den was working himself into a foul mood over this when he caught a faint sound on the wind, almost like a sob.

All at once, Den's smile returned. Seemed this jungle wasn't so empty after all.

He turned on his heel until he was facing the dirt cave below the tree roots. It was a wretched thing, a black hole in the mud held together by tree roots. The entrance crumbled a little as Den pushed his way in. The inside of the cave was dim and low, forcing Den to stoop almost double until he'd climbed down to the bed of mud and leaves that served as the cave floor. When he reached the bottom, he straightened as best he could and gazed through the dark at the woman hunched against the cave's far wall. Den's smile split into a toothy grin. Not a League man, true, but a better prize, the one he'd been walking through jungles for almost ten years now in search of.

Despite his noisy entrance, the woman didn't appear to notice Den for several seconds. Finally, she shifted against the mud, glancing at him through slitted eyes.

"Oh," she said, looking away again. "It's you."

Den crossed his arms. "It's me."

The woman didn't answer, and Den, tired of crouching, sat down. Normally, he would have just knocked the roof out, but he'd been looking for her a long time and, much as it irked him, a little tolerance was a small thing compared to the hassle it would take to find her again if she ran, miraculous portals notwithstanding.

When it was clear Den wasn't leaving, the woman pressed her face against the cool dirt as though she could somehow ignore him. It was a futile effort, for the cave was very small and Den was a large, large man.

"What do you want?" she grumbled at last.

"What you promised me," Den said.

The woman laughed, a harsh, joyless bark. "Is your life so dull you'd search all across the Empire to collect a bad debt?"

"You promised me a war," Den answered calmly. "I crossed half the world for that promise. Does it really surprise you that I would cross the other half to hold you to it?"

She glanced sideways at him, her dark eyes sharp and almost as he remembered them. "I suppose it doesn't," she said. "My apologies, Bloody Den, but you'll have to find someone else to stage your fights." She turned away, pulling herself against the wall again. "I have no more care to rule."

"No!" Den's shout rattled the earthen walls. The woman jumped, flinching as Den leaned in, towering over her despite his seated position.

"You promised me," he whispered, low and deadly. "Twenty-six years ago you promised me a war. Twenty-six years I've waited, fought your warriors, and prepared your troops. I've held up my end of the deal tenfold, and you owe me. If you want to lie in the mud and feel sorry for yourself, do it on your own time, but right now you need to finish what you started. You will honor your pledge, or I will test your famous immortality for myself, Nara." The name rolled off his tongue like a curse.

The woman leaped up from the mud and turned to face him, staring him down like he was a cockroach. "You will not speak so informally to me, barbarian."

Den leaned back against the cool mud. "I'll treat you like an empress when you start acting like one."

For a moment, the rage burned in her eyes, and she was nearly herself again. Her authority radiated through her mud-stained rags, dismissing her long, matted hair and wretched surroundings until he could almost see the Empress he remembered, tall and dark and terrible in her rage. But then, between one second and the next, it crumbled, and she sank to the mud floor in a broken heap.

"What does it matter?" she whispered, letting the dirty mass of her dark hair fall over her face. "The Shepherdess has abandoned me. Everything I did, my entire life, it was all for her. I gave her everything—my soul, my love, my service—but she doesn't even look at me anymore. All she cares about is that *boy*."

The ragged, naked hatred that trembled through her voice when she said the word *boy* shocked even Den, and he seized his chance. "Of course she doesn't want to look at you," he said. "I can hardly stand to see what you've let yourself become."

The woman hissed and turned on him, lashing out with her fist. Den caught the blow with one hand. "Who could love such a self-pitying, wretched hag?" he said, letting his disgust ring clear through the words. "You were the favorite of creation. The unquestioned ruler of half the world for twelve generations. Now look at you, a rat hiding in a cave, and all because your White Lady found a new pet."

She snarled and the ground began to rumble, but Den held on, pulling her forward until they were eye to eye. "If you want your Shepherdess to love you again, become something worth loving. Even if her boy died tomorrow, she'd never look at you while you're like this. Who would? No one loves a failure, Nara."

Her eyes went wide and she wrenched herself free. Den let her go, watching her with a sneer as she stumbled back to her rut in the mud. She stayed there for a long time, not speaking, not moving. Den matched her silence, waiting to see if his gambit played true. If it didn't, he was in for another long walk. But it seemed he was in luck, for at last she sat up.

"You are a horrible man, Den," she whispered, pushing the filthy hair out of her face. "But you are also a keen one. Fine. My years of begging have earned me nothing. Perhaps it is time to see what action can do. We shall see who is called favorite when I rule all the world. After all..."

She closed her eyes, and the air in the cave rippled like water. Den flinched as her spirit opened over him. It rolled out of her, a roaring wave of power, and everywhere it touched, the world began to change. The cave walls shook like leaves, the spirits crying in obedient awe as they reshaped themselves to please her.

The roof of the cave vanished, replaced by clear, blue sky. The mud Den sat on flattened, drying and hardening and spreading until he sat in the middle of a court pressed with spiraling patterns of impossible beauty. At the edge of the clay circle, the jungle trees lifted their roots and began retangling them into walls of beautifully knotted shapes. Then, as quickly as it had started, the changes stopped, and Den found himself sitting in a beautiful open court as grand as any he'd ever seen. At its center, seated on a raised throne of living wood, was the Immortal Empress. The dirt had fallen from her skin and hair, leaving her radiant, her body almost glowing beneath a sheath of beautifully patterned silk, the ends of which were just finishing weaving themselves from the remnants of her rags. Her glossy black hair was piled on her head, each hair holding itself of its own accord in an impossible arrangement that seemed to float over her ageless face, now as stern and as proud as he remembered it.

"After all," she said again, leaning back on her throne, "I am the Immortal Empress still, a star of the Shepherdess, and I will be victorious."

She held out her hand, and a white line appeared in the air. Den blinked in recognition as it sank silently through the empty space, glowing like the full moon. Through it, Den could see the interior of the throne room at Istalirin, her war palace, and the chaos of the panicking staff as they realized what that glowing line meant.

A wide grin broke over Den's face and he hopped to his feet. "So it was you then," he said. "Suits me. Let's go."

"I have no idea what you're babbling about," the Empress said. "But this is for me. You're walking."

"What?" Den roared.

"You were very disrespectful toward your Empress," she said with a cutting look. "Your punishment is that you must walk back to Istalirin. Your commission will be ready when you arrive."

Den frowned. "And you will honor your promise at last?"

The Empress gave him a cruel smile. "Beyond your wildest dreams, Bloody Den."

And with that, she was gone. The white line shimmered and faded, leaving Den alone in the beautiful court under the sky. He stood a moment, grinding his teeth until he could feel the pain shooting down his neck. Finally, he turned and stomped out. That had been petty, even for her, but he should have expected it. The Empress was a woman, and women were always petty, especially when their pride was bruised. Still, it didn't matter. He'd just spent almost fifteen years walking the breadth and width of her cursed land, what was another few weeks? What mattered was that he'd done it. He'd found her, and better, he'd won. He would have his war.

A great smile broke over Den's scarred face, and he began to walk faster, jumping into the jungle at the clearing's edge. This time the trees parted for him, whispering apologies. Now that he was in the Empress's favor again, the world was bending over to make his life easy. His walk became a run as the forest opened for him, and Den began to laugh. A war at last. Finally, after so long, he would reclaim his paradise.

Still laughing, Den fell into a mile-eating jog, running through the now-genteel forest. He didn't know where he was still, but it didn't matter. The spirits had their mistress again, and they would make sure he got where she wanted him to be. Grinning at the thought, Den picked up his pace, running full out along the path the trees made him, following the setting sun west toward the war palace of the Immortal Empress.

Two Months Later

"Are you sure?" Queen Theresa of Osera leaned forward, frail fingers tightening to white-knuckled claws on the velvet arms of her chair. "Absolutely sure?"

The fisherman looked almost insulted. "I can tell you only what I saw with my own eyes, your queenship," he said, lifting his head to look at her for the first time. "For years now, my crew has sailed the roughest ocean in the world to be your eyes on the Unseen Coast, and I'm telling you the shipyards are active again."

"But why now?" The queen shook, though with fear or rage even she could not tell. "She built like mad for twelve years after the war, and then fifteen years ago, everything stopped. Now you're telling me she's building again? Why? Why ships? Why now?"

The fisherman flinched and gave no answer.

None was expected. The queen had already hauled herself to her feet and was now pacing the length of the small stage at the end of her private-audience chamber, muttering under her breath.

"What changed?" Her whisper was tight and raspy. "Did we show some weakness? Or perhaps I was the fool to think she had given up." Her jeweled heels clicked faster on the glossy wood floor. "How many ships?"

The fisherman jumped. "Too many to count. I took the time to spy on only one of the yards before coming to you. Was I wrong?"

"No," the queen said, shaking her head so sharply that she knocked loose one of the carefully pinned curls of her once famous golden hair, now mostly white. "Without your information we wouldn't have a candle's chance in a storm. Tell me, though, in your hurry, did you see what kind of ships was she building?"

"I did," the fisherman said, licking his chapped lips. "They was palace ships, lady. Every single one."

The queen stopped walking and pressed a bony hand to her forehead. "Lenette?"

A strikingly beautiful woman in an elegant dress of stiff black silk appeared from a side door. "Yes, my queen?"

"Pay him. Double."

Lenette nodded and walked across the room to the strongbox.

22

She took a fist-sized bag from the bound chest and walked to the fisherman, holding it out for him with both hands. He took it with a blush and opened the bag at once, eyes bulging when he saw the pile of gold it contained. But the smile slipped from his face when the queen looked at him with a glare that could have cut iron.

"Spend it quickly."

The captain swallowed loudly, but the queen's attention was already back on her pacing. Lenette took the man's arm and led him back to the doors, gently pushing him into the hall. Thus dismissed, the fisherman bowed several times before the guards shut the doors in his face. The moment they closed, the queen collapsed into her chair with a pained sigh.

"And there's the other shoe," she muttered. "Twenty-six years after her first invasion, the immortal sow finally rouses herself to finish the job."

"The man was a fisherman, my lady," Lenette said gently, walking over to kneel beside the queen's chair. "Not a trained spy. He could have been mistaken."

The queen gave an unladylike snort. "I'm not sending the fleet into the Unseen Sea to check his story. The deep trawlers are the only ones who dare that crossing. Fortunately for us, the same reckless greed that sends them chasing leviathan spawn in the deep current spurs them to take my money to spy for their country. Anyway, without that 'fisherman,' the old harpy would have caught us naked as a cheating lover." She nodded at the closed door. "The captain is Oseran born and old enough to remember the war. If he says they're palace ships, they're palace ships. It's not something you forget."

"But we only know that she's started building again," Lenette countered. "Those ships might not even be for us. She could have a new target."

"Where?" the queen said with an exasperated huff. "The

woman rules half the world. There's nowhere left for her to conquer save the Council Kingdoms, and our little island is dead in her way. Her army will roll over us without even a pause. When I think of all—"

A racking cough stopped her midsentence. The queen doubled over, pressing a lace handkerchief to her mouth as her body convulsed. Lenette was with her in an instant, rubbing the queen's back with her small, delicate hands until the attack subsided.

"You shouldn't think about such things, lady," Lenette whispered. "You'll only worsen your condition. Remember, Osera and the Council have pushed the Empress back before."

"Yes," the queen wheezed. "Two and a half decades ago, when I was young." She looked at her blood-streaked handkerchief with disgust. "When I wasn't sick. When I could stand to look at myself in the mirror. Back when I was truly queen."

She raised her gaunt face and gazed across the chamber at the portrait that took up most of the wall. It was enormous, large as life and set in a gilt frame that touched both floor and ceiling. On it, a steel-gray sea pounded the rocky eastern shore of Osera. The stony beach below the cliffs was filled with soldiers raising their swords in salute, or perhaps taunting, for the choppy sea was scattered with the Immortal Empress's warships, some crashing on the reefs, some ablaze, all fleeing defeated back across the Unseen Sea. In the painting's foreground, a young woman dressed in the heavy black armor of the Eisenlowe stood with her feet in the sea. She faced the fleeing ships with her head held high, hair flying behind her like a pale gold banner. Her hand was stretched out toward the ocean, the gloved fingers tangled in the long, black hair of the enemy general's severed head.

Queen Theresa smiled. That was not how it had ended, but it was the way she wanted the war to be remembered—bloody, glorious, an absolute victory. The way it should have been and, she closed her eyes, the way it could never be again.

"Osera has always been ruled by the strong, Lenette," the queen said quietly. "We've grown wealthy and civilized thanks to the Council, but it will take more than these few generations to tear us away from our bloody past. Were we a softer kingdom, more deeply rooted in law and nobility, perhaps I could re-create the miracle I stumbled onto all those years ago. But we are not. The Empress is coming, and an old, sick woman cannot lead Osera to war."

Lenette stiffened, her face, still so lovely despite her advancing years, falling. "Will you abdicate, then? Give the country to your cousin?"

"Finley?" The queen made a disgusted sound. "He'll get his soon enough, much as I hate to think of it. But he's no Eisenlowe. Much as he hated to, father entrusted our line to me after my brothers died. I've spent the last thirty years fighting to stay on my throne. I do not intend to meekly hand it over now."

Lenette shook her head. "But what will you do, lady?"

"Crisis demands stability, Lenette," the queen said grimly. "I'd thought I could give him a little more time, but circumstance has left us little choice. The Throne of Iron Lions must follow the proper succession, whatever the cost." She settled back into her chair with a pained sigh. "Wake up the Council wizard and have him bring me the Relay point. We must warn the Council tonight. I'll need to speak with Whitefall personally, and then I'll need that cousin of his, the one who runs the bounties."

"Phillipe Whitefall?" Lenette said.

The queen waved her hand dismissively. "Whoever. I never could keep all the Whitefalls straight. Just get me the head of the bounty office. Also, get Adela in here. Your daughter is a sensible girl, and she has a larger stake in this business than most."

Lenette pursed her lips. "It's time then, is it?"

"Long past," the queen said, patting her friend's hand. "If the Immortal Empress is on her way, then we have no time left for patience. That boy is out there somewhere, and I don't care if I have to hand over every scrap of gold in Osera, he will come home and do his duty."

Lenette nodded and bent to kiss the queen's hand. "I will bring Adela to you, lady," she said, rising to her feet. "And send someone to fetch the Relay keeper. Meanwhile, I'll have the maid bring up your medicine."

The queen smiled. "Thank you, Lenette. What would I do without you?"

Lenette smiled and stepped off the little stage. She walked to the door, her heels clicking delicately across the polished floor, and vanished into the hall with a curtsy.

When she was gone, Queen Theresa lay back in her padded chair, staring at the picture of what she had been. As her eyes struggled to focus on the familiar brushstrokes, she remembered not the gory glory of the artist's rendition, but the real morning, twenty-six years ago, standing on the windy beach, too large for her armor at nine months' pregnant, weeping in relief at the retreating ships while her guard made a square around her so that no one could say they'd seen the Lioness of Osera cry.

When the maid arrived a few minutes later with the medicine tray, the queen dabbed her eyes with her handkerchief and took the cup that the girl offered, drinking the bitter concoction without so much as a grimace.

CHAPTER

2

The Perod bounty office was packed with the usual riffraff. Dozens of men and a few scowling women lounged on long benches stolen from the tavern across the street, boredly polishing a startling variety of weaponry and trying to look like they weren't waiting. It was a farce, of course. It was criminally early on a Monday morning, and the only reason bounty hunters ever came into a regional office before noon was to get their hands on the weekly bounty update from Zarin.

The only person who didn't try to hide his anticipation was a young man toward the back of the crowd. He stood on his bench, hopping from foot to foot and ignoring his dour-faced companion's constant attempts to pull him back down, an anxious scowl marring the boyish face that everyone should have recognized, but no one did.

"Honestly," Eli huffed when Josef finally managed to drag him down. "Are they walking from Zarin?"

"It's not even eight," Josef said, his voice low and annoyed as he nudged the wrapped Heart of War farther under the bench with his foot. "The post isn't due until eight fifteen. And can you at least pretend to be discreet? I love a good fight, but we walked all night to get here. I'd like some breakfast and a few hours of shut-eye before I have to put down an entire room of bounty hunters, if it's all the same to you."

Eli made a disgusted sound. "Go ahead. I could wear a name tag on my forehead and these idiots still wouldn't notice. No bounty hunter worth his sword goes to a regional office for leads. There's not a soul here who's good enough to see what they don't expect." He slouched on the bench. "Sometimes I think there's no pride in the profession anymore. You were the last of the bounty hunters worth the name, and even you got so bored you took up with the enemy."

"Not bored," Josef said. "I just learned that working with you got me better fights than trying to catch you. Anyway, Coriano was perfectly decent, and what about that man who attacked you at the hotel? Gave you quite a scramble for a dying profession, didn't he?"

Beside him, Nico did her best to stifle a laugh, but her coat gave her away, moving in long, midnight waves as her shoulders shook. Eli rolled his eyes at both of them.

"Well, too bad you killed them, then," he said with a sniff. "Knocking over the best of a dying breed without even leaving a calling card—it's such a waste. No wonder your bounty's only ten thousand."

Josef shrugged. "Unlike some people, I see no need to define myself by an arbitrary number."

Eli bristled. "Arbitrary? I earned every bit of that bounty! You should know; you were there for most of it. My bounty is a reflection of our immense skill. You should take some pride in it. After all," he said, grinning painfully wide, "I'm now the most wanted man in the Council Kingdoms. Two hundred and forty-eight thousand gold standards! That even beats Nico's number. My head is worth more than a kingdom—no, two kingdoms! And to think, just last

year I was struggling to break thirty thousand. This is an achieve-
ment no one else in the world can touch, my friends. You are sitting
beside a *national power.* Tell you what. When they hand out my new
posters, I'll sign them for you. How's that?"

Josef looked decidedly unimpressed and made no comment.

"It *is* a large number," Nico said when the uncomfortable silence
had gone on long enough. "But you're not the highest. There's still
Den the Warlord with five hundred thousand."

"Den doesn't count," Eli snapped. "He was the first bounty,
made right after the war. The Council hadn't even decided on a
valuation for its currency yet. If they'd made the bounty properly
with pledges from offended kingdoms rather than just letting old
Council Daddy Whitefall pull some grossly large number out of his
feathered helmet, Den would never have gotten that high. Anyway,
it doesn't matter. I'll be passing him soon enough, just you watch.
This time next year I'll be at a million, and see if I offer to auto-
graph your poster then."

"I'll take my chances," Josef grumbled, eyeing the crowd. "Look
lively. I think the post is here."

Eli was on his feet in an instant, elbowing his way through the
crowd that was no longer even pretending to look bored. The hunters thronged around the door as a sleepy-eyed bounty officer and
two harried men in Council uniforms with piles of paper under
their arms attempted to push their way in.

"No shoving!" the officer shouted. "Stand back! Individual posters can be purchased after the official notices are hung!"

The crowd took a grudging step back as the Council postmen
began tacking up the latest posters under the bounty officer's direction. First they hung up the small-fry, lists of names with tiny
descriptions and even tinier numbers beside them. Next came the
ranking bounties, criminals with a thousand or more on their heads
whose notoriety had earned them a sketch and a small poster of

their own. These were all pinned between the floor and waist level. The top of the wall was reserved for the big money. Here, the Council men hung up the famous names.

Izo was gone. The men stripped his old poster down with minimal fanfare, moving those bounties below him up a notch. The old, yellowed poster offering two hundred thousand for the Daughter of the Dead Mountain was left untouched, as was Den's large poster at the top of the board. Between these, however, the men tacked up a fresh, large sheet featuring a familiar face grinning above a rather astonishingly large number.

Eli stopped shoving the men in front of him and gazed up at his poster, his eyes glowing with pride. "It's even more beautiful than I imagined," he whispered. "Two hundred and forty-eight thousand gold standards."

Josef pressed his palm to his forehead as Eli resumed shoving his way forward. Thankfully, no one else seemed to have heard the thief's remark. The bounty hunters were all loudly clamoring for copies, shouting over each other while the bounty officer tried to shout over everyone that no one was getting posters until the official copies were up.

Eli vanished into the fray only to reappear moments later with a scroll tucked under his arm. Josef raised his eyebrows and began easing the knives out of his sleeves, just in case, but the bounty officer was too busy screaming at the bounty hunters to get in line to notice that one of his carefully protected posters was already missing.

"They get better with every likeness," Eli said, proudly unrolling his poster. "If it wasn't black and white, I'd say I was looking in a mirror."

Nico nodded appreciatively, but Josef wasn't even looking. Eli turned to berate his swordsman for his shocking lack of attentiveness, but Josef was just standing there, staring at the bounty board like he'd seen a ghost. Eli followed his gaze, glancing over his shoulder at the bounty wall where the Council men were hanging one last poster, just below Den's and just ahead of Eli's. As the Council men tacked the poster's corners up, a familiar, stern face glared down at the room, and below it, in tall block letters, was the following:

JOSEF LIECHTEN THERESON ESINLOWE.
WANTED ALIVE, 250,000 GOLD STANDARDS.

"Josef," Eli said, very quietly. "Why is your bounty larger than mine?"

Josef didn't answer. He just stood there, staring. Then, without a word, he turned, pushed his way through the crowd to their bench, grabbed his bag and his wrapped sword, and stomped out the back door.

Eli and Nico exchanged a look and ran after him.

"Josef," Eli said, running to keep up with the swordsman's ground-eating strides. "Josef! Stop! What's this about? Where are you going?"

Josef kept walking.

"Look," Eli said, jogging beside him. "If you're worried I'm upset that you have a higher bounty than I do, you shouldn't be. I mean, I am upset, but you shouldn't be worried. I'm sure it's just a mistake. If you'll stop walking for a second, I can go nick your poster and we'll take a closer look. Maybe they added an extra zero by accident or—"

"I don't need a closer look."

Eli stumbled a little. Josef's voice was quivering with rage. Quick as he'd taken off, Josef stopped and turned to face them. Eli shrank back at the cold, white anger on his face, nearly falling into Nico.

"It's no mistake," Josef said. "That bounty is her last card. I can't let her do this."

"Her who?" Eli said.

"Queen Theresa."

"I see," Eli said, though he didn't. "Well, if it's not a mistake, then I'm stumped. What did you do to this queen to earn a number like that?"

The side of Josef's mouth twitched. "I lived."

Eli arched an eyebrow. "Could you try being a little less cryptic?"

"No." Josef pulled his bag off his shoulder and tossed it to Nico. "I have to go away for a while. There's food enough for the next day in there. Nico, I'm counting on you to keep Eli from doing anything stupid. I realize it's a tall order, but do your best."

Nico scowled at him and tossed the bag back. "I'm going with you."

"And I'm with her," Eli said, straightening up. "You can't just walk out on us now."

Josef crossed his arms. "And I suppose my opinion in this doesn't matter?"

"Not in the least," Eli said. "Where are we going?"

For a moment, Josef almost smiled. "The port at Sanche. We can catch a ferry from there to Osera."

"Osera?" Eli made a face. "You mean the island with the carnivorous yaks, endless rain, and zero-tolerance policy toward thieves? Why?"

"Because," Josef said, setting off down the road. "I've been called home."

Nico fell in behind him, her feet kicking up little clouds of yellow dust as she hurried to catch up. Eli stared at their backs a moment longer, and then, cursing under his breath, he shoved his new poster into his bag and ran down the road after them.

Alber Whitefall, Merchant Prince of Zarin and Head of the Council of Thrones, was having a terrible morning. Actually, considering he hadn't slept since yesterday, morning was a misnomer. What he was having was a terrible night that refused to end.

There were two others sitting in his office on this terrible morning. Sara was there, of course, and Myron Whitefall, his cousin and director of Military Affairs for the Council. As usual, Sara looked equal parts miffed at being called away from her work downstairs and intrigued by their new problem. Myron, however, looked like a man who'd just learned he's dying from plague.

"Is there a chance she's overreacting?" Myron said, pulling at his stiff military collar. "The queen is getting older."

"Theresa is younger than I am, Myron," Merchant Prince Whitefall said flatly. "She's hardly to the age of senility."

"And this is Osera we're talking about," Sara added with a sniff. "They're not people who'd ask for help unless things were desperate. *Especially* Theresa. Shouldn't you know that?"

Myron gave the wizard a disapproving look. Sara stared right back, daring him.

"Be that as it may," Alber said, bringing the conversation back to himself before things could get any worse. "Osera's borne the brunt of the Empress before, and they've never forgotten. If Theresa says the Empress has reactivated her shipyards, then I believe her. The only real question is, how much time do we have left to prepare?"

Sara looked away from Myron with a dismissive huff. "A decent amount, I'd wager," she said. "Unless she's spent the last twenty years making upgrades, palace ships are slow and the Unseen Sea is wide and treacherous. Even if she set sail tonight, we wouldn't see her fleet for two months. Maybe three, if she's bringing a larger army this time, which I assume she would."

"Three months is hardly a 'decent amount,'" Myron snapped. "Even if we called in conscripts today, I can't raise an army on such short notice."

Alber scratched his short beard thoughtfully. "It doesn't make sense," he said. "Why is she moving now? Her initial attack was the disaster that birthed the Council. She was the only thing scary enough to finally convince the kingdoms to stop fighting each other and stand together. And stand together we did, but anyone in the know understands that the only reason we survived was because we had the Relay and the Empress didn't. That, and the fact that her fleet was too far from home to maintain a supply line. Still, it was hardly what I would call a decisive victory. Were I the Empress, I would have renewed my attack the very next year while the Council was still unstable. Even five years later we couldn't have turned back any sort of invasion force, but now? We're stronger than ever. She has to know that. So why did she wait?"

"Maybe she was rebuilding?" Myron said. "The combined Council forces sunk nearly a hundred ships before her fleet retreated. Maybe even the Empress can't pull that kind of firepower out from under her skirt."

"This is the Empress, Myron," Sara said, exasperated. "If our reports are anywhere close to right, she has enough people and resources to bury us in boats without batting an eye."

"So why hasn't she, then?" Myron said. "How do we know this resurgence is even aimed at us? There's been no declaration of war. All we have is some fisherman's tale about palace ships."

"Where else is she going to go?" Sara said. "There are three continents in the world: hers, ours, and the icy wastes in the north sea. You don't build a fleet of palace ships to go ghosthound hunting, so I think we can safely say she's coming for us."

Myron's face went scarlet, but Sara seemed to have forgotten him entirely. She leaned back in her deep-cushioned chair, thin arms crossed over her chest as she met Alber eye to eye. "It's a bad position any way you look at it. Forgetting the issue of whether or not the Empress is actually immortal, her empire has been a stable ruling power for as long as we've known there was another continent across the Unseen Sea. We know she has wealth, resources, and a troop capacity we can't even quantify. Considering this, the force we sent running twenty-six years ago was likely little more than a small excursion."

"*Small excursion?*" Myron cried.

"Yes," Sara said calmly. "I wrote as much in my report at the time, which, by the way, you should read."

Myron looked away with a sniff. Sara ignored him, focusing on the Merchant Prince.

"I believe it was a test," she said. "An opening strike to reveal the strength of the opponent. That said, I don't know why she's waited so long to strike again. Maybe she truly is immortal and twenty-six years is nothing. Even so, now that she knows what we're capable of, her course is simple. If our strength is our ability to communicate instantly through the Relay and move our troops to counter her attacks with our full strength at a moment's notice, all the Empress needs to do is send enough soldiers that it doesn't matter. Move, counter move. This time she will overwhelm us, plain and simple."

"So what would you have us do?" Myron growled. "Roll over? *Surrender?*"

"I'm only being realistic," Sara said. "The Relay was our trump last time, but that card's been played."

"So make us another," Alber said, leaning back in his chair. "If she knows how to counter our advantage, make us a new one. That's why you're here."

Sara clenched her jaw. "I'm working on it."

"Well, it's not going to be enough," Myron said. "We can't beat the Immortal Empire with wizard tricks. The Relay was fine and dandy, but it was our soldiers who fought and won. Talking tables and carts that roll themselves don't sink ships."

"Yes, Myron, thank you," Alber said before Sara could snap back and make things even worse. "Your opinion is noted. Now, if you're done antagonizing my wizard, what have you got for me?"

With one final, dirty look at Sara, Myron reached into his jacket and pulled out a packet of folded papers.

"We have five thousand soldiers on active duty across the Council," he said, spreading out the stack of figure-covered papers on the table. He pulled a map from the satchel beside him and laid that out as well. "I think we can safely assume that any attack will begin as before, at Osera." His finger tapped a long island just off the Council's eastern coast. "As well as being geographically in the way for an invasion from across the Unseen Sea, Osera is the Council's greatest naval power. Ignore them, and the Empress will have Oseran ships at her back while she's fighting us on the mainland. Go far enough to get around them, and she lands in the mountains." His finger traveled north, tapping the wild mountain country that formed the Council's northern border. "Or the jungle." His finger went south to the lush, tropical nightmare that covered the Council's lower tip. "There's no way around it. She has to take Osera first. Now, I can have our current forces to the coast in a month. With reserves, country-by-country conscripts, and heavy recruitment, we can probably field another ten thousand in the next two months. Training will take another four."

"That's six months," Sara said. "We don't have—"

"*I can't pull soldiers out of the air!*" Myron roared, standing up so fast that his chair toppled behind him. "I'm talking about men, wizardess, not spirits! Men take time. I have to move them, equip them, train—"

"*Myron.*"

The general stopped. Alber Whitefall was sitting at his desk as before, calm as ever, but his eyes were narrow and his mouth was a thin, clamped line.

"Myron," he said again in a soft, measured voice. "Do your best. Don't worry about Sara. Just get me as many soldiers as you can. Understood?"

"Yes, Merchant Prince," Myron grumbled.

"Excellent." Alber gave him a smile. "You'd better go get started. Time is wasting."

Myron Whitefall did not look pleased by the dismissal, but he gathered his papers and stomped into the hall without comment.

"Why is he in charge of our army again?" Sara said the moment the page closed the door.

"Because his mother was very insistent," Alber answered, standing up with a sigh. "And because he's not a bad general. He did secure the northlands, if you'll recall. You're seeing him at his worst. He was never one for politics, but he's quite good with the soldiers."

Sara glanced at the door and gave a dismissive snort. "*I* could have told you the Empress would go for Osera."

"Yes, well, you have the benefit of experience, don't you?" the Merchant Prince said, pouring himself a finger of brandy from the bottle on the table behind him. "And the day you feel like marshaling our army, I will be more than happy to let you. Until then, Myron will have to do." He paused. "It would also help if you didn't treat him like some idiot child."

"I treat him as he shows me he deserves to be treated," Sara said, pulling her pipe out of her coat pocket. She lit it with a spark from a tiny ruby, one of nearly a dozen she kept on a chain in her pocket, and took a deep drag, pointedly ignoring Alber's glare.

"He's right, though," she said softly.

Alber sipped his drink. "About what?"

"I don't have a trick to beat the Immortal Empress."

Alber lowered his glass. "Then why am I paying for your little playground downstairs?"

Sara grew very still. "The Relay was the idea that started my career, Alber. If I could have flashes of genius on call, I wouldn't be working for you. But brilliant as the Relay was, we were fighting the Empress's army, not the Empress herself."

"Come now," Alber said. "You don't actually believe all that malarkey about the Empress being an unkillable, magical queen, do you? Everything we know came from captured soldiers who knew they were going to die. Of course they'd tell us the Empress is our doom incarnate."

"There's something going on with her," Sara said. "Maybe she's just a powerful wizard who's good at selling herself, but one thing's certain, Alber. I have a dozen different projects going right now, all with good potential, but I don't have a miracle. Not this time, and not like we're going to need."

"Sara," Alber said, swirling his drink. "I am an old man who has been up for nearly thirty hours. If you have a point, get to it."

Sara took an angry puff from her pipe. "My point is that no matter how many poor farmers Myron shoves into Council uniforms, it's not going to be enough. The Empress's army isn't just men. In the last war, the Empress's forces used spirits on a scale I've never seen before. She had amalgam spirits, blends of fire and metal better than even Shaper work, specifically created for war and directed by trained teams of wizards."

"How could I forget?" Alber said dryly. "And I suppose you're going to say we can't field something similar?"

Sara nearly choked on her smoke. "Powers, no. Even forgetting the combination of spirits for war, I would have written wizards working in teams off as impossible if I hadn't seen it with my own eyes. I've tried for years to duplicate it, but individual wizard's wills are simply too different to..." She trailed off when she saw Alber's bored look. "Never mind. The point I'm trying to make is that we caught a very lucky break last time. We can't count on that kind of lightning striking twice. If we're to have any real hope of keeping our lands, we're going to need a different sort of army than Myron's putting together. A wizard army."

"You have wizards," Alber said.

"A hundred, maybe," Sara answered. "And that's counting the idiots I give Council kingdoms to mind their Relay points. A hundred's not an army. I'm talking about a large-scale, organized, combat-ready force."

The Merchant Prince's eyebrows shot up. "You can't seriously be suggesting what I think you are."

"I am always serious," Sara said. "The Spirit Court accounts for almost every wizard born in Council lands. We cannot do this without them."

Alber sighed heavily, shaking his head slowly from side to side. "Banage is going to be a problem."

"Who's talking about Banage?" Sara said. "Banage hates the Council. Has for years. The only reason he goes along with us is because we're too powerful for him to openly antagonize if he wants his Court to have any say on the continent. The second you go to him hat in hand asking for help, he's going to try and shove his doctrine down our throats."

"I am well aware of Banage's low opinion," Whitefall said. "He's never bothered to hide it, after all. But the years have made you too jaded, Sara. Even Banage can't stand around on his principles doing nothing while the Immortal Empress destroys everything he's built."

"Banage will stand on his principles until they gnaw his legs off," Sara said with a puff of smoke. "But we don't need Banage to get the Court. There are several Spiritualists, especially among the Tower Keepers, who would have no problem working with the Council."

"Sara!" Whitefall said, shocked. "We are on the verge of a perhaps unwinnable war. I will not cause a schism in what might be our only salvation just because you don't want to work with your former husband."

"The Spirit Court's already broken," Sara countered. "Banage's constant hard line has driven many of the more moderate members away. He almost tore the Court apart last year when they put his apprentice on trial. If Hern hadn't gotten himself tangled up in that Gaol nonsense, the Court would already be ours."

"Put it out of your mind," Whitefall said. "You don't win wars by ripping up your allies. Not if there is any other hope." He turned away, looking out over the city. "I'll send Banage an invitation to talk. Compromise is always possible, and who knows? Maybe this Empress thing will make him see we're not actually that bad."

Sara chuckled. "Want to wager on that?"

"I already am," Whitefall said, looking at her over his shoulder. "I'm wagering our survival on the hope that Etmon Banage likes being Rector Spiritualis more than he dislikes working with you. After all, if we can't find some way to work together, the Empress will crush us both, and you can't be Rector when there's no more Spirit Court."

Sara bit her pipe between her teeth. "I wish you wouldn't group the rest of us in on your impossible wagers."

Whitefall set his empty glass on his desk. "We're all going to have to do the impossible before this mess is done. Now, get downstairs and start working on that miracle. I'll take care of Banage."

Sara stood and walked out without a word. When she was gone, Alber called his pages in. One he sent to the Spirit Court, and the rest he set to opening windows. When his office no longer reeked of smoke, he poured himself another glass of brandy and lay down on his silk couch to contemplate the wreck his carefully cultured plans had become.

CHAPTER

3

So," Miranda said. "One more time. The demon under the Dead Mountain is sealed, but he can sneak out shards of himself, called seeds, that bury themselves into host bodies, who become demonseeds."

"Correct," Slorn said. "Demonseeds are tiny slivers of the demon itself. Each seed has the potential to grow into a new demon, given enough time and food. The stronger the host and the longer the seed is able to incubate, the stronger the resulting demon is at awakening."

Miranda shuddered, blinking her eyes against the memory that refused to vanish—the hideous black shape standing over the woods outside Izo's bandit city, its black wings blotting out the sky as it ate the screaming world.

"How do we stop it?" she said quietly. "Stop the seeds from coming out?"

"I don't know," Slorn said. "Unawakened demonseeds constantly travel through the shadows in and out of the mountain, bringing their master new vessels. There is a human cult that serves there, presenting wizards to the demon in hopes of becoming demonseeds themselves. The League has cleared out the mountain several times—killing the human followers, setting up a perimeter, but the seeds always get through. All demonseeds can hear the demon's voice in their heads, and he moves them like pieces on a board that only he can see the whole of. This makes them very hard to block completely, especially as the League can find them only when they cause a panic. Alric gave up trying to blockade the mountain years ago. Staying on the mountain for any length of time is dangerous, even for the Lord of Storms, and the reward wasn't worth the risk. They now focus on the eradication of seeds that cause problems."

"Well," Miranda said with a huff, "it doesn't seem to be working."

"It works," Slorn said, looking at her with his black, calm, bear eyes. "We are still alive."

Rebuked, Miranda shut her mouth and focused on the path ahead. Seeing that the lesson was at an end, Slorn leaned back on the roof of his walking cart to stare thoughtfully at the wispy clouds flowing like silk across the pale blue sky.

They were high in the mountains, riding north. It was slow going, even for Gin. The constant wind kept the ground clear from snow, but the stone itself was icy and treacherous. The ghosthound kept his eyes on his feet, delicately picking his way across the steep slopes, his dappled silver coat shifting with the wind. Still, they could have gone faster if not for Slorn's wagon. The wooden cart climbed at a snail's pace, rattling and scraping as its carved wooden legs scrabbled on the ice despite the metal hooks Slorn had attached. Sometimes they barely made ten miles in a day, but the pace didn't bother Miranda. She'd learned more from Slorn in the two weeks since they'd left Izo's camp than from all three years she'd spent training to begin her apprenticeship with the Spiritualists. Gin, however, didn't seem to be enjoying himself.

"I don't like him," the ghosthound growled when they stopped for lunch.

"You don't like anyone," Miranda said, smearing a sliver of cold butter across her hard baked bread as best she could. "And keep your voice down."

"He asks too many questions," Gin said, loud as ever. "And he looks at the sky too much."

Miranda glanced at Slorn. He was standing beside his cart, talking to it softly as he checked the wooden legs. "What does that have to do with anything?"

Gin made a *harrumphing* sound. "He shouldn't be doing it, is all. Or talking about the Dead Mountain like he does. I've never understood you humans and your constant need to know things. You're the nosiest spirits in creation."

"And you're the biggest curmudgeon in creation," Miranda said, smacking him across the haunches. "You saw that thing at Izo's the same as all of us. I'm a Spiritualist, but that thing, demon or demonseed or whatever, makes the usual Spirit Court worries look like children's games. It's not something I can just ignore, and until I find out what I can do to stop what happened at Izo's from happening again, even if that turns out to be nothing, I can't go back to Zarin. Not while still calling myself a Spiritualist."

Gin flattened his ears. "Not everything's a crusade, Miranda. The bear man's leading you places you shouldn't go, and you're going to get hurt if you keep following."

"I'm a big girl," she said, reaching out to scratch his nose. "I won't get in over my head."

Gin moved away from her hand and shook himself, sending dirt and ice everywhere. "Just watch yourself," he said, trotting away.

Miranda frowned. "Where are you going?"

"Hunting," Gin growled, stalking off down the frozen path.

Miranda started to remind him that there was dried meat in Slorn's cart, but the ghosthound had already vanished into the frosty landscape, his shifting fur blending into the white mist rolling down from the peaks.

"I'm starting to understand why they call them ghosthounds."

Miranda turned with a start. Slorn was standing behind her, smiling in a way that was probably meant to be reassuring but never quite made it, thanks to his sharp teeth.

"Sorry about that," she said. "Gin doesn't have a lot of tact."

"Don't worry about it," Slorn said, sitting down on the large, flat rock that sheltered their little fire from the wind. "It's a ghosthound's nature to be protective and wary of outsiders, and I never fault a spirit for following its nature. Besides, he's not exactly wrong. Spirits have learned over countless centuries that some things are better left alone."

Miranda frowned. "You mean the demon?"

Slorn shrugged. "The League, the Dead Mountain, demonseeds, these are all things that spirits, even Great Spirits, have learned to ignore. Must learn to ignore. You can't have a life worth living when you're constantly worrying about things you cannot fight or change. All they can do is trust the system that has worked for thousands of years and go on with their lives."

Miranda's frown turned into a scowl. "And where does the thing we saw at Izo's fit into that system?"

"It doesn't," Slorn said. "That's why we're going to the Shaper Mountain. If the League will not listen, then I must make my case to an outside party. If I can find even one voice to speak for me that the Shepherdess will heed, Nivel's death won't have been in vain."

Miranda bit her tongue. Slorn spoke his wife's name with such sadness that words felt pointless. But there was so much of what he said that she still didn't understand and she could not keep quiet.

"The Shepherdess," she said. "I've heard of her, of course, but never in any detail. Most Spiritualists are lucky if they ever get to talk to a Great Spirit." Mellinor found that amusing, but Miranda ignored his bubbling laughter and pressed on. "She's the greatest spirit, isn't she? The one at the top of the spirit world."

"Assuming she's a spirit at all," Slorn said. "Which I don't think she is. The Shepherdess is the force that guides the world and commands the spirits. She also controls the League and keeps the demon locked beneath the mountain, among other things."

"How can she not be a spirit?" Miranda said. "Everything has a spirit."

"I don't know the answer precisely," Slorn answered. "But I do know her control is nothing a spirit could manage. No spirit except a human's can control another, and humans can't touch the spirits of other humans. But, so far as I understand it, the Shepherdess can command everything. Therefore, she's not a spirit. Or, at least, not a spirit like we are familiar with."

Miranda slumped down. "I feel so ignorant," she muttered. "You'd think I'd have at least heard more than a passing mention of something so important." A tremor of reproach went through her before she could stop it, and deep in her mind she felt her rings twinge.

"Don't blame your spirits," Slorn said. "Nothing talks about the Shepherdess unless they have to. It took me decades to piece what little I have together, and even I don't know for certain. All I have are theories. Suppositions based on years of asking too many questions, as your dog would say. It may be that the Shaper Mountain can do nothing and this journey is little more than a waste of time."

"But we have to try," Miranda said.

"Yes," Slorn said quietly. "We have to try." He leaned back, looking up at the snow-covered slope they'd been following all day. "If we keep this pace we'll make Knife's Pass by sunset. From there it's a straight shot to the Shaper Mountain. We'll reach the gate by noon tomorrow, weather permitting. After that, there's no turning back."

Miranda laughed. "There's been no turning back for a while now. Remember, I was the one who asked to come along."

"I have not forgotten," Slorn said, standing up. "Let's go. We have more miles to cover than we can make if we dawdle."

Miranda took his offered hand, and he helped her to her feet. They had almost everything together by the time Gin returned with a scrawny mountain goat in his jaws.

It was late when they reached Knife's Pass and Miranda was too tried to look at anything besides her bedroll. When she woke at dawn, Gin was still sleeping, his body curved to shelter her from the icy winds. She smiled and packed her blankets, and then, stepping softly so she wouldn't wake the ghosthound, she tiptoed to Slorn's wagon. As always, Slorn was already awake. He was sitting on the fold-out steps, staring up at the clear morning sky. There were two steaming mugs of tea on the step beside him, one half empty, the other full. Miranda took the full one.

"How much farther?" she said, blowing on the steaming liquid.

Slorn looked at her with an incredulous expression and pointed north. Miranda's eyes followed his gesture and she nearly dropped her tea. The sheltered pass they were camped in wasn't a pass at all, or at least not a natural one. It was a road cut between the mountains, running due north in a perfectly straight line between two sheer cliffs, and at the end of that road stood the largest mountain Miranda had ever seen. It was impossibly tall, soaring above the surrounding mountains like a spire. Its steep sides were snowbound and blinding white in the morning sunlight, but the mountain's peak was too sheer and tall even for snow. It loomed far, far overhead, naked and gray-white, a porcelain knife set against the pale sky.

"That's the Shaper Mountain?" Miranda said when she could speak again. "How does anyone live on a slope like that?"

47

"Not on," Slorn answered. "In."

Miranda frowned and looked again, squinting against the glare. Sure enough, the tiny dark spaces beneath snowy overhangs that she had first taken to be shadows were now clearly windows. There were balconies as well, each placed so elegantly along the mountain's natural cliffs that Miranda would never have spotted them if not for the faint glimmer of the icy railings. Panes of glass flashed between the snow banks, and at the end of the pass she could just make out the unnaturally straight edge of what looked like a door set deep in the mountain's base.

"The upper body of the mountain is given over to the Shapers for their work," Slorn said. "In return for its protection, leadership, and instruction, the Shapers serve the mountain and work in its name."

Miranda shivered. "And what kind of work does a mountain need done?"

"All kinds," Slorn said with a toothy smile. "Though only the Great Teacher understands how it all fits together."

"Great Teacher?"

"You'll see soon enough," Slorn said, standing up. "Let's get moving. We have far to go."

Miranda looked back at the mountain. It didn't seem that far away. But she obeyed and walked back across the camp to wake up Gin. The hound was already up and waiting when she reached him, his orange eyes narrow and guarded as he watched Slorn's wagon pack itself. He answered her "good morning" with a gruff snort, and though Miranda tried several times as they packed their camp, that was all the comment the hound would make.

Though the mountain looked like it was only a few miles away, the distance was deceptive. Knife's Pass was an endless corridor between the lesser peaks, a straight, flat slab of rock large enough to march a legion down walled in by two featureless stone walls.

Ahead, the Shaper Mountain rose over everything else, filling the end of the pass, but no matter how fast they ran along the smooth road, it never seemed to come any closer.

The sun was high overhead when the end of the road finally came into sight. Gin was panting hard, his feet swollen after running full out for miles on the hard stone. Slorn slowed the pace, and Miranda started to thank him on Gin's behalf when she realized that Slorn had not slowed for them.

Just before the towering spire of the Shaper Mountain took over everything, the mountains fell away. The ground simply stopped, leaving an enormous gap of empty air between them and the Shaper Mountain. As they got closer, Miranda saw that it was a canyon. The divide cut between the rest of the mountains and the Shaper's peak like a sword stroke. At the very bottom, a deep blue, freezing cold river glittered in the noon sun, but it was so far away that Miranda couldn't even hear the sound of the water, only the endless wind howling between the cliffs.

The road, however, did not stop. A bridge of arching stone just wide enough for two carts running side by side spanned the enormous divide, linking Knife's Pass to the mountain on the other side. The bridge was all one piece, a great length of curved rock that sprouted like a branch at one end from the stone under their feet and on the other from the roots of the Shaper Mountain itself. There were no railings, nothing to save a careless traveler from plummeting into the ravine, but the bridge itself was free of ice, and Slorn's wagon stepped onto it without hesitation.

With a nervous swallow, Miranda followed, leaning with Gin into the wind that threatened to toss them both into the canyon below. She was so focused on not falling that she didn't notice Slorn had stopped until she was past him. She turned around, nudging Gin back until they were pressed against the wagon.

"What's wrong?" she shouted over the wind.

Slorn looked down at her from his seated position on the wagon's roof, his small bear ears blown flat by the wind. "Things might get a little tense in the mountain," he said. "No matter what happens, I need you to stay calm and follow my lead."

Gin began to growl. "What do you mean 'tense'?"

"You'll see soon enough," Slorn said, starting his wagon forward again. "Just stay with me and everything will be fine."

Gin snorted, sending a poof of white vapor into the air that was instantly snatched by the wind. "If he thinks we're just going to roll over—"

"Gin!" Miranda said sharply.

The hound shut his mouth, and Miranda pushed him forward. She didn't like this any more than he did, but they'd come too far to stop now. All she could do was press herself flat against the ghosthound's back and follow Slorn's wagon across the final half of the ravine.

The bridge ended at a sheer wall in the mountain's side, the smooth stone road butting up against an unnaturally straight, unnaturally square cliff. The wind here was stronger than ever, buffeting them against the cliff face. Miranda kept low on Gin's back, her eyes darting up the mountain for another path, but there was nothing, just the bridge and cliff. She was about to ask Slorn where to go next when a loud crack sounded over the wind. More cracks followed until the ravine sounded like a breaking glacier, and then, all at once, the cliff opened.

An enormous slab of stone twice as wide as Gin was long swung into the mountain with a long scrape, revealing a cavern larger than anything Miranda had seen before, including the Relay chamber below the Council. For a moment, she just stood, gawking at the sheer size of it, the perfect smoothness of stone so white it seemed to glow as it arched up to the domed ceiling. It was only when Gin began to growl that she realized they were not alone.

Just inside the stone door, a sternly handsome older man with a long, white beard stood with his arms crossed, as though he'd been waiting. Two younger men flanked him on either side. They were all strangely dressed. The two younger men wore what looked like work shirts and simple trousers, but the cloth was nice enough to take the front window in the best Zarin shops. The old man, however, was dressed in a padded silk robe finer than any Miranda had ever seen.

It was the old man who broke the silence. He lifted his chin, eyes narrowing as he looked Slorn over from boots to ears. "Heinricht."

"Guildmaster," Slorn answered, his deep voice strangely flat.

The old man's expression wavered, and for a moment he looked almost heartbroken. Then the stern frown was back, and he flicked his fingers. At the signal, the two men stepped forward, each carrying a pair of iron cuffs. Slorn held out his hands as the men lay the cuffs on his arms, one at the wrists, one farther up at his elbows. They held the cuffs in place as the iron rings fastened themselves with a dull clank.

"Wait just a moment," Miranda said, sliding off Gin's back. Forget staying calm, this was ridiculous. "What's going on? What are you doing?"

"They're arresting me," Slorn said, lowering his bound arms.

"As you knew we would," the old man said, his voice as deep and solid as the mountain beneath their feet. "You knew the punishment for leaving, Heinricht. Why did you return?"

"Nivel is dead," Slorn answered. "I've come back to honor my duty as a Shaper and return our knowledge to the Teacher."

One of the men who'd cuffed him looked at Slorn with a sneer. "What knowledge could a deserter have for the Teacher?"

"Knowledge has no faction, Krevich," the Guildmaster said.

The young man blushed and bowed his head, but the Guildmaster didn't look at him. His eyes never left Slorn. "You may bring your knowledge to the Teacher. As for the outsider you've brought"—his eyes flicked to Miranda—"leave. This is no place for Spiritualists."

"Spiritualist Lyonette brings knowledge as well," Slorn said before Gin's growling could get any louder. "My story would be incomplete without hers."

The Guildmaster's face darkened, but he turned and walked away without another word, his beautiful silk robe moving with him. The men grabbed Slorn and marched him inside, the sound from their boots echoing through the beautiful cavern. After a moment of hesitation, Miranda followed, guiding Gin into the Shaper Mountain as the enormous door swung closed behind them.

"And there they go."

Sparrow slid down the icy rock and tossed the spyglass to Tesset. "I told you this was going to end in tears."

Tesset caught the spyglass and stowed it carefully in his belt pouch. "No one's crying yet."

"Sara will when she hears that her sea on a leash and pet bear are gone for good," Sparrow said. "Assuming she could do something so human as cry."

Tesset didn't reply. Sparrow shook his head and pulled his now-ratty coat closer. It didn't help. The wind on the cliffs above Knife's Pass was cold enough to freeze his bones. "No point in dragging it out," he said, fishing the Relay link out of his pocket. "Let's face the music."

He twirled the Relay link until it turned bright blue. Since Sparrow didn't have enough spiritual presence to wake up an awakened sword, Sara had created his link to activate when it was shaken. She'd given him a huge lecture about this when she'd handed it over. Fortunately, Sparrow hadn't wasted his time listening.

It took Sara an uncommonly long time to answer the Relay.

When her scratchy voice finally did speak, she sounded harried and annoyed.

"Well?"

"No luck," Sparrow said. "Papa bear and Banage's darling were swallowed by the mountain. We couldn't catch them, which should come as no surprise, seeing how you failed to provide us with either a walking cart or a ghosthound."

Sara's voice grew thoughtful. "So they *were* going to the Shapers."

"Of course they were," Sparrow snapped. "Where else would they be going up here?"

"With Slorn, you never know," she said. "Anything else to report?"

"Yes," Sparrow said. "We're coming home. I'm sick of being poorly dressed and freezing. And since there's nothing left for us to—"

"Don't be stupid," Sara said with a puff from her pipe so vivid Sparrow could almost smell the smoke. "The job's not done. This Empress situation is getting out of control. I need Slorn and the Spiritualist girl's sea more than ever. Actually, Tesset, are you there?"

"Yes, Sara," Tesset said, straightening up.

"I want you to come back to Zarin. I'm headed down to the desert for a few days and I need someone here whom I can trust to deal with Myron."

Tesset arched an eyebrow. "Myron?"

"The Whitefall in charge of the army," Sara said, yawning. "He seems to think I'm made of Relay points."

"Isn't there someone else?" Tesset said, scratching his stubbly chin. "It's a long walk back to Zarin just to run interference on a Whitefall."

"No one he'll like," Sara said. "He's a military man. He'll like you. And that's an order, so stop questioning it."

Tesset furrowed his brows, giving the matter careful consideration.

"It will take me a few days," he said at last. "I'm not as young as I used to be."

Sara sighed loudly. "Just do your best."

"And what am *I* supposed to do?" Sparrow said. "Surely you have more members of the Whitefall family who need corralling."

"I do," Sara said. "But you've got your orders."

"Sara!" Sparrow cried. "The bear man I get, but Miranda? I understand she has fantastic powers or whatever, but you and I both know you only pulled her into this to make Banage steam. Why should I have to risk my neck just so you can stick it to your—"

"Sparrow."

Sparrow snapped his mouth shut. He knew that tone in her voice.

"That's better," Sara said. "Tesset, report to Zarin. Sparrow, your orders stand. Secure the Spiritualist and the Shaper and bring them to me."

"And how am I supposed to do that without Tesset?" Sparrow said. "In case you forgot, Miss Lyonette doesn't feel too kindly toward our office at the moment. Even if I get to her, she's not going to just come back. What do you want me to do, arm wrestle the ghosthound?"

"You're charming," Sara said. "Figure it out."

Sparrow flopped back against the icy rock in disgust, but the link's light was already fading. Sara had severed the connection.

He shoved the orb into his pocket with an exasperated huff. "Can you believe this?"

"That Sara is being unreasonable?" Tesset said, buttoning his coat. "Of course. What Sara have you been working for that this behavior comes as a surprise?"

"And you're just going to abandon me?" Sparrow said, his voice pathetic.

Tesset didn't even have the decency to look hurt. "I'm going to do my job, as are you. I couldn't help you in the Shaper Mountain anyway. It can see me, remember? Just make sure you get a good look around or Sara will never forgive you."

"Right, right," Sparrow said, rubbing his eyes. "She must be distracted not to mention that angle. This Empress thing really has her on edge."

"If the Immortal Empress doesn't put you on edge, you're a fool," Tesset said, lacing his boots tight. "Good luck."

Sparrow nodded, but when he looked up, the older man was already gone, jogging down the path and picking up speed with every tireless step. With a frustrated groan, Sparrow pushed himself up from the rock. He shrugged off what was left of his brocaded coat and tossed it on the ground. Then, dressed only in his drab pants and shirtsleeves, he began to walk along the ledge toward the Shaper Mountain, fading instantly into the gray landscape.

CHAPTER

4

Eli sat on the prow of the schooner, sulking at the blue ocean that spread out in all directions. Ahead of him, the shadowy peaks of the islands of Osera dominated the horizon. Eli sulked at them too. They'd made record time to the coast, thanks to him. Not an hour after Josef had announced they were suddenly and inexplicably going to Osera, Eli had found an express carriage. After a little excessive bribery, the driver somehow found time in his schedule to take them from just south of Zarin to the port at Sanche in a little over a day and a half. At the port, Eli had found a private fishing schooner willing to take them to Osera the very next morning, well before the commercial ferries. It was nothing short of a miracle that they were on the ocean at all right now, but Eli might as well have saved his miracle making for all the thanks he got.

Josef had been in high dudgeon since they'd left the bounty office. He hadn't said more than a syllable at a time the whole trip. This wasn't remarkable in and of itself, but considering that Eli was bending over backward to get them to Osera for as yet unknown reasons, the swordsman's silence irked him more than usual.

Eli sighed and fought the urge to scratch under his wig. They were deep in civilized lands now, where people actually read bounty posters, and he didn't have the luxury of running around like he usually did. The golden wig wasn't enough to fool anyone who was actually looking for him, but it was fine at throwing off the casual glances. It was also unbearably hot. Even sitting on the prow with the sea wind in his face and the slightly fishy shade provided by the lofted nets, Eli could feel the sweat crawling down his scalp. But no matter how bad it got, he kept his hands on the railing. The ship wasn't big, and the sailors had enough to talk about with Josef's swords. The last thing they needed was for bored, curious fishermen to start wondering why the blade-covered man's business partner was wearing a wig.

He was just starting to work himself into a really foul mood when something soft touched his arm. Eli jumped and nearly fell off the boat. He grabbed the railing and turned to see Nico standing beside him.

"Don't do that!"

"I said hello," Nico said, sounding a little hurt.

Eli took a deep breath. "Sorry. What can I do for you?"

Nico shrugged and sat down beside him. Eli shifted uncomfortably. They'd never really talked about what had happened in the valley, but he liked to think that he and Nico were square these days. Still, it was hard to tell where you stood when the other party in the relationship never said more than five words together under the best of circumstances. After several awkward moments, he tried again. "I don't suppose Josef has told you why we're rushing to Osera?"

"No," Nico said, looking down at the water. "He hasn't said anything."

Eli was immediately sorry he'd asked. The girl looked heartbroken. He glanced over his shoulder toward the back of the boat where Josef was standing with the Heart in his hands, practicing his stances. He looked so calm as he brought the enormous sword around (narrowly missing a tied-off line, much to the crew's displeasure) that Eli wanted to strangle him.

"Who does he think he is?" Eli growled, turning back around. "We're supposed to have a plan when we enter a new country. We *would* have had a plan three days ago if I'd had my way, but *no*. I don't know what he expects us to do when we land in Osera. Powers forbid he actually tell us anything."

Nico shifted uncomfortably. "I'm sure he has his reasons."

"Oh, I'm sure he does," Eli said. "I just wish he'd share them. We're *supposed* to be a team."

For the first time in days, Nico smiled a little. "Well, we were the ones who decided to come along. I suppose we can't complain if he doesn't share plans that he didn't want us along for in the first place."

"I can complain about anything," Eli said, straightening up. "And if you ever quote that back at me, I'm never speaking to you again."

Grinning at her arched eyebrows, Eli spun on his heel and walked off to find the captain to ask, yet again, how much longer this unbearably long boat ride was going to take.

Nico listened to Eli's light footsteps until they were lost in the crashing waves. Fifteen steps, she noted to herself. Fifteen steps from a famously light-footed thief on a rocking ship in the middle of the sea. She gripped the railing until her already-white fingers were the color of bleached bone. It wasn't her imagination. Her hearing was getting better.

And it wasn't just her hearing. Ever since she'd taken back her body from the demon, her strength had grown as well. Her night vision was now better than her normal sight, and she could smell the tiniest traces of scents lingering days after whatever had made them was gone. She could hear the turning of the sleeping spirits and the laughter of the winds as they rushed overhead. But all this she could accept. It was reasonable that her senses would get better now that she was her own master. What didn't make sense, what she couldn't accept, was that she wasn't just seeing the world more clearly. She was seeing things she'd never seen before, things that were not there.

Nico tilted her head back, squinting up at the clear sky overhead. At first, she saw nothing but the sky, deep blue and cloudless. Then her eyes adjusted, and she saw them. High overhead, great *things*— she had no other name for them—streaked through the air. They were as faint as shadows, but they were always there, swimming through the sky in great colorless coils, turning and flashing so quickly it made her nauseous.

The snakes in the sky weren't all she saw, the strange things were everywhere: in the boat, in the sails, in the nets. Unlike the things in the sky, these were stationary, twitching only slightly, mostly when Eli walked by. The sea, however, was roiling with half-seen shapes. They flowed with the waves, thousands of millions of little sparks swimming in and out of each other.

The first time she'd seen the shapes was the day after she'd beaten the demon. They were so dim then, barely more than shadows, that she'd dismissed them as a trick of the light. But the trick never went away. Day and night she saw them like a second world over the real one. As the days passed and it was clear the things weren't going away, she'd finally decided to talk to Eli. Other than Slorn, he was the only person who might know what they were. But just when she'd finally worked up the courage to ask him, Josef had declared they were going to Osera. Nico decided to keep her mouth shut after that. Whatever Josef needed to do in Osera, he had enough to worry about without her adding more.

Nico closed her eyes. When she woke up on the valley floor, it hadn't occurred to her that she might be different. How stupid. You couldn't be torn apart and rebuilt and expect to still be what you were. What had happened in Izo's valley had changed her. Was still changing her. But whatever was different, whatever changed, she was still the master of herself. The demon was still buried. She could feel the rock in her mind keeping him down as clearly as she felt her own arms. The shadows weren't his doing, but that almost made things worse. The demon she could deal with, but these new visions were alien and frightening. Every time she saw them, which was all the time now, she couldn't help thinking that maybe she hadn't been truly rebuilt that day. Maybe something was still missing, something important.

Maybe she really had gone mad.

Against her better judgment, Nico opened her eyes and looked up again, past the coiling snake creatures that streaked through the air and up to the sky itself. It was hard to make out under all the movement, but if she stood very still and focused on one spot, there was no mistaking it. There, at the very top of the world, something was moving. Something enormous, something sharp, dragging across the other side of the sky's dome.

Fear closed over her like ice, and she slammed her eyes shut. It made little difference. From the moment she'd first seen the things clawing the sky, she could not unsee them. The dread followed her waking and sleeping, eyes open or closed, and through it all a thought went round and round and round her head, like a marble rolling around the inside of a bowl.

Only mad people saw shapes against the sky.

She stayed like that for several minutes, eyes shut, forcing her breath to remain calm. Finally, when she'd worked up the courage to open her eyes again, Nico looked over her shoulder at Josef. He was standing at the back of the boat with the Heart in his hands, moving through his stances. His face was blank, eyes half closed.

To an outsider, he probably looked bored, a man going through a routine, but Nico had been watching him all her life that she cared to remember. She could tell he was upset as well as if he'd screamed it. It was written all over him: in the tenseness of his footing, the way his hands folded white-knuckled around the Heart's hilt, the clench of his jaw. Something about this trip to Osera bothered him deeply, and until she found out what, and why, she could not add her fears to that burden, no matter how desperate she got. Whatever had changed in her that day in the valley, nothing could change the fact that Josef was the center of her life. He was her partner, her savior, the one person who had never done her wrong, who had always believed in her even when there was nothing to believe in. Whatever he needed out here in the middle of the sea, she would help him reach it, and no madness, no bizarre other world that crept across the real one would keep her from being whatever he needed her to be.

That thought alone drove the fear back, and Nico gripped it like a lifeline as she turned again to face the islands rising like swords from the sea.

Seen on a map, the kingdom of Osera looked like a wall separating the Council's eastern seaboard from the wild waters of the Unseen Sea. Though even those who lived there called their land "the island," the kingdom of Osera was not one island, but dozens, a long line of mountaintops rising vertically from the ocean along the Council coast. Most of these islands were uninhabitable, their sloping sides too steep for anything other than sea birds, but at the center of the chain the islands grew wider, and there was room for people, especially on the island of Osera itself.

Even on its largest island, Osera was like a wall. Over fifty miles long, the main island Osera measured barely twenty miles at its widest point. Dominated by the peak at its center, the island was constantly sloping. This slope was long and gentle on the Council side, but steep and short on the side facing the Unseen Sea. Because of this quirk in geography, and the fact that the face the island turned to the open ocean had borne the brunt of the Empress's attack, the eastern side of the island had been left to ruin. After the war, Osera had turned its back on the sea and the Empress, embracing the Council's new prosperity by covering its gentle western slope in city.

"Covering" was the right word. Buildings on the island's western slope crowded every inch of land that was flat enough to lay a foundation. Tiny streets ran seemingly at random, following the flattest paths upward or sideways along the mountain and sometimes changing into stairs without notice when the island's geography took a sudden turn for the vertical. The farther up the mountain the buildings climbed, the shorter and narrower they became, clinging to the mountain's rising cliff like barnacles. But down by the water, the buildings were tall and broad, a busy tangle of workshops, warehouses, and shipyards spilling out onto Osera's pride and greatest source of wealth: the marina.

The marina ran nearly unbroken for thirty miles along the island's western edge. Docks jutted far into the calm water of the protected channel that ran between Osera and the Council coast. Endless lines of moored ships waited their turn to be unloaded and reloaded by the armies of barefoot dockworkers while captains did business on the large, permanently moored barges that served as mobile offices for the hundreds of trading companies that called Osera home.

Eli's ship tied in at one of the long sloops jutting from the floating tangle of deepwater docks at the center of the marina. Josef hopped off the moment they stopped moving, and by the time Eli had worked out a payment for the schooner captain that was large enough to make sure the old man didn't remember them should anyone ask, but not enough to send him bragging in the taverns and drawing unwanted attention, the swordsman was halfway to the island. Nico trailed behind him, a black blot in the bright sun.

With a final, frustrated sigh, Eli pressed the gold coins into the captain's hand and jogged down the planks after his companions.

"Well," he said, raising his voice over the squawk of the sea birds. "Here we are. Do you have further directions to find your queen, Mr. Cryptic, or shall we just turn ourselves in at the local bounty office?"

Josef didn't even honor that comment with a sneer. "We're going to the palace," he said, boots clattering on the wooden boards.

"The palace?" Eli fell in step beside him. "Of course. Brilliant. Where else do you find queens? Out of idle curiosity, what's your plan for getting into said palace?"

"We're going to walk up to the front gate and ask the guard."

Eli nearly tripped. "Are you out of your bleeding mind?"

He would have said more, but Nico elbowed him hard in the back. He grunted and gave her a hurt look over his shoulder. She didn't even have the good grace to look apologetic, just pressed her finger to her lips and glanced pointedly at the sailors crowded on the dock beside theirs, most of whom were now unloading their cargo suspiciously slowly with their ears turned toward Eli.

Eli shoved his hands in his pockets. "The question still stands," he said, albeit more quietly. "All you had to do was say, 'Eli, I need to get into a castle' and I could have done it in a heartbeat, but *no*. You've apparently taken too many hits to the head to remember that you're traveling with a master thief. And since you never thought to share any of your *magnificent* plans, I don't have anything ready. No false papers, no aliases, no nothing. That kind of throws a kink in the whole front door plan."

"Really," Josef grumbled.

"*Really*," Eli grumbled back. "I never saw a palace that just let random people in off the street, especially not when one of them was carrying enough blades to open his own armory, but maybe I'm just being negative."

Josef stopped and turned to face the thief. "Are you done?"

Eli opened his mouth and then snapped it shut and threw out his arms for Josef to lead the way. Shaking his head, Josef resumed his march down the wooden dock and into the packed, tangled streets of the city itself.

Put out as he was, Eli enjoyed the walk. For a country burned to the ground by the Immortal Empress, Osera looked remarkably well. Narrow streets merged into large courtyards strung with vines that shaded merchant stalls of every sort. The buildings were brightly painted and cheery, and though their upper stories loomed over the streets, the vertical nature of the island made it impossible to feel claustrophobic. Every corner came with a grand view of the port below, and, narrow as they were, the streets were impeccably clean, probably because of the constant wind tunneling down them from the mountain above.

Nothing in the city looked old or dilapidated. Everywhere Eli looked he saw new construction, most bearing the clean architecture and ornate accents that had come into style with the Council's rise. Every building had glass windows, tiled roofs, and iron window grates that grew only more ornate as they climbed away from the docks. Storefronts showcased impressive displays behind large picture windows. In the space of two blocks, Eli saw clothes, fabrics, cheeses, pastries, and metal goods as fine as any in Zarin. Tastefully painted signs advertised restaurants that, this close to noon, were full of well-dressed men and a few women. Eli could almost smell the money in the air, and he was beginning to wonder why he'd never come to Osera before.

Josef led the way, forging a path upward through the busy streets and toward the top of the island. He kept his eyes ahead and said nothing, and Eli, thoughtful friend that he was, took the opportunity to do a little digging.

"So," he said, pushing through the crowd until he was walking beside Josef. "You're from here, right?"

"Yes," Josef said without looking at him.

"Not what I expected," Eli said, smiling as they passed through another of the vine-shadowed merchant squares, this one with a large, ornate, bronze fountain done in a fanciful representation of a whale gushing water from its enormous mouth. "I'd always heard Osera was an island of barely reformed pirates, terrible weather, and fish smokehouses. This place rivals Zarin."

Josef stopped to let a cart go past. "Being burned to the ground leaves a lot of room for improvement."

"But all this?" Eli said. "In twenty-six years?"

Josef shrugged, picking up the pace again. "Osera bore the brunt of the war so the inner kingdoms didn't have to. In return, the Council waived most of our sea-trade tariffs. That's the kind of thing that can make a small country rich enough to build just about anything."

Eli grinned. "So I see. My only question now is what to steal first."

"Nothing," Josef said.

Eli's smile faded. "Why not?"

"Because we're not going to be here long enough for you to steal anything," Josef snapped. "We're going to the palace, hearing what the queen has to say, and then we're leaving."

"What?" Eli cried. "Wait, wait, wait. That's it? That's why you dragged us all the way out here? Powers, Josef, if we're just going to tell this queen to shove off, why did we even come?"

"Because even I feel guilty sometimes," he said. "Now come on. And shut up. The last thing we need is more attention."

Eli stopped, affronted. The street was packed with people on their own business. No one so much as glanced their way. Still, when Josef was this prickly it never did any good to push him further. So with great difficulty, Eli kept further opinions to himself as he stomped up the hill after Josef and Nico.

The sun was high and hot overhead when Josef finally stopped them. Eli fell against a building, panting. "Please tell me we're there," he said, fanning himself. "We've been walking for years."

Josef rested his hands on the swords at his sides, infuriatingly untouched by the heat or the long climb. "Almost," he said, nodding across the street. "There's the palace."

Eli looked up. The road ahead opened into a large square. It was the most open space he'd seen since arriving in Osera, and the flattest. They were on the mountain's shoulder, a long stretch of relatively flat land before the final assent to the peak. The buildings surrounding the square were as rich as any Eli had seen in any country, but the square itself looked old and almost shabby. There were no shady vines, fountains, or merchant carts, just open stone baking in the noon sun. The crowds were thinner here as well, mostly men in formal dress carrying leather cases and looking very important.

They were very high now. To the west, Eli could see the whole of the city stretching down the mountain like a mushroom forest made of red-and-yellow-tiled roofs, but looking east, the view was entirely different. At the edge of the square, the mountain's sharp peak rose dramatically, and wrapped around it was a building unlike any Eli had seen in Osera. The palace of Osera was a hulking mass of rough-cut, weatherworn stone wrapped around the mountain like an ugly scarf. What windows it had were narrow as arrow slits, and its roof was tiled with stone shingles worn white by time and rain. There was no proper gate or guardhouse. Instead, the palace's face fronted directly onto the square, its tiny windows glaring down on the lovely modern buildings below like the squinty eyes of a disapproving old man.

Staring up at the old, ugly, ungainly mess, Eli felt crushingly disappointed. If the brightly colored city below had been modern and inviting, the building in front of them was gloomy and aggressive, more like a lonely fortress on an embattled front than the royal palace of a prosperous, modern nation. Just the sight of it was enough to kill any joy left lingering from the beautiful climb up, not to mention Eli's fledgling dreams of a glorious heist.

"Lovely," he said at last, fiddling with his wig.

Nico shot him a nasty look, but Josef didn't even seem to hear. The swordsman wiped a spare bandage across his face to clean off some of the day's grime, and then, tying the bandage tight around his wrist, started across the square like a man beginning his death march. Eli and Nico exchanged a final, worried glance before falling in behind him.

The front entrance to the palace was protected from the main square by a guard box, a wooden structure slightly larger than a shed, attached to the castle wall beside the narrow main gate. There were two guards on duty that Eli could see, and they came out to stand at attention only when Josef had cleared the center of the square and was obviously headed their way. The guards wore minimal equipment, just a simple chain jerkin under their uniform jackets and a short sword like the ones at Josef's hips, but they carried their swords like they knew how to use them, which was more than Eli usually expected of gate guards. The men kept their faces blank as Josef approached, but their hands were on their sword hilts when he stopped in front of them.

The older guard gave them a long, disdainful glance. "Business?"

Josef pulled himself straight. "I am Josef Liechten Thereson Eisenlowe, here to answer the queen's bounty."

Eli gritted his teeth. Trust Josef to find the baldest way to say anything. He eased his feet carefully, ready to jump if the soldiers made a move to arrest his idiot swordsman. But, to his surprise, the guards didn't budge.

"Josef, you say?" The older guard looked at his companion, who seemed to be smothering a laugh. "And do you have proof?"

"What proof do I need?" Josef was starting to sound annoyed. "Show me to the queen and that should be proof enough."

This time the younger guard did laugh. "If I had a silver for every time I'd heard that one..."

"We wouldn't be working here," the older guard finished. He grinned and turned back to Josef. "Listen, idiot, the queen doesn't have time to go over every two-bit con who says he's Josef Liechten. If you're going to try and impersonate a long-lost prince—"

"Prince?" Eli said before he could stop himself.

The guard gave him a funny look. "Aye, prince. As I was saying, if you're going to try and impersonate a prince, at least have the decency to clean up a bit. Look at you—knives head to foot, scars, worn boots, you look like a highway bandit." The guard snorted. "At least the last fool who claimed to be Josef Liechten had a crown. That was a nice touch. 'Course, it got all bent when we sent him packing, but you can't complain when you're scamming, can you?"

"But I *am* Josef Liechten," Josef said, his voice tight with anger. He pointed inside the guard box, where his wanted poster was prominently displayed. "Look at the picture."

The guard didn't turn around. "I seen the picture," he said, crossing his arms. "Drawn by some Council hack off the account of some witness who probably didn't witness anything. I've been working at the palace for close to twenty years. I saw the prince plenty of times when he was a boy. He was a handsome lad. I find it frankly insulting, you coming up here saying Queen Theresa's son'd grow into something like you."

Josef took a deep breath. "You won't take me to the queen?"

"No," the guard said. "Now shove off before I do it for you." And with that the guard spat on the ground by Josef's foot.

Josef didn't move. He just stood there with his hands clenched so tight on his swords that his arms were beginning to shake. Beside him, Nico was easing into a fighting stance, preparing to back Josef the second the swordsman moved. It was clear things were about to get bloody, and bloody was not how Eli liked to start his jobs, planned or not. Clearly, it was time to step in.

"Well," he said cheerfully. "I guess that's that."

Nico, Josef, and the two guards all turned to look at him.

Eli gave them a large smile. "Can't fault a fellow for trying, can you, gentlemen?" he said, his voice bright as the noon sun. "I don't suppose you'd believe I was Eli Monpress, would you?"

The guards stared at him for a moment more, and then they burst into laughter.

"Powers," the older one said, wiping his eyes. "No offense, friend, but you three look like beggars. Monpress is stinking rich. Wasn't even six months ago he robbed Gaol blind, so I hear. You do look like him, though. I'll give you that. 'Cept for the hair, of course." He eyed Eli's blond wig. "Tell you what." The guard reached into his pocket, pulling out a silver coin and tossing it at Eli. "Take this and get out of here. Go get a haircut and some better clothes, and then you come back and try that line again next shift. I'd love to see Wallace handle Eli Monpress at his door, the old stuffed shirt."

"Next shift," Eli said, catching the coin neatly. "I may just do that. What time?"

"Eight o'clock even," the guard said.

"Much obliged," Eli said. With a final, farewell grin, he grabbed Josef's arm and began to steer the swordsman back across the square. "Thank you, gentlemen. You've been exceedingly kind."

The guard waved. "Shove off. And if Wallace guts you later, you got none to blame but yourself."

"I'll bear that in mind," Eli called. "Good afternoon."

The guards started laughing again and walked back into the guard box. Eli kept grinning the whole way across the square. When they were safely out of sight around a building, he dropped the smile and slammed Josef against the wall.

"*Prince?*" he shouted. "You're a prince and you *never told me?*"

Though he could have broken Eli's hold easily, Josef let it stay, leaning in to the wall at his back. "Not anymore."

"Well, your mother's a queen," Eli said. "That sounds like a prince to me."

"Eli." Nico's hand closed on his shoulder. "Stop it. Now. I'm sure Josef had his reasons." She looked at Josef. "Didn't you?"

Josef glowered at them. "Do I need reasons?"

"Oh *come on!*" Eli cried. "What kind of a question is that? I thought we were partners. I thought we were *friends*. How do you just go hiding something like that? Never mind all the times before, how do you justify hiding it when you're bringing us back to your own country to turn yourself in?"

"Because I'm not a prince anymore," Josef growled. "I told you before. And I am your friend. That's why I let you come along."

Eli let his look say exactly what he thought of that logic, and Josef lay back with a deep sigh. "You know what? Never mind. This is all wrong."

Despite his anger, despite how hurt he was, Eli couldn't help laughing at that.

"Of course it's all wrong, idiot," he said, letting Josef go. "You didn't have a plan. You just expected to walk right in and then walk right out. This is what you get for not clueing us in, you know. If you'd just told me what you wanted to do, I could have made a plan that would have had us in your mother's throne room enjoying your embarrassing childhood stories at this very moment."

Josef shook his head. "All right then, Mr. Greatest-Thief-in-the-World, I give up. How would you do it?"

Eli straightened up and casually tossed the silver coin the guard had given him in the air, catching it in his palm. "I thought you'd never ask."

He gave Josef a final I-told-you-so sniff and started down the alley, tossing the coin as he went. Josef pushed himself off the wall with an enormous sigh. "Now I've done it."

"You should have done it days ago," Nico said, crossing her arms.

"Right as usual," Josef said. "Shall we?" He nodded down the alley.

Nico gave him an exasperated look and they started after Eli, walking side by side down the clean-swept alley.

CHAPTER

5

In the stinking swamp that would one day become the richest soil in the Empire, a girl ran through the muck. She ran wildly, arms flailing as she scrambled over clumps of grass and sticky clay. Behind her, men with lanterns were giving chase, the lights bobbing in the dark. The girl was quick and desperate, but the men knew this swamp better than she did. By the time she realized she'd gone the wrong way, they had surrounded her.

She cowered in the mud as their circle tightened. When the men were an arm's length away, the largest held up his lantern to get a good look at her face.

"This is the one," he said. "Gutted the captain proper, she did."

"'Swhat the old coot gets," said another. "Messing around with trash." He grabbed the girl's hair, yanking her up. "Mountain monkeys are for working, not sleeping with."

He spat in her face, and they all began to laugh. The girl hung by her hair, kicking wildly. And then, from nowhere, silver flashed in the lamplight. The man dropped her with a scream to clutch his arm. The girl landed hard and rolled to her feet, brandishing her small knife, its tip bright red.

"Filthy animal!" the man shouted, clutching his bloody arm. "We'll string your carcass up for the birds! Get her!"

The men charged her. The girl lashed out, swinging her knife, but the men were too many, too large. They grabbed her hand and pinched the nerve until her fingers went slack. The knife fell to the ground and was quickly trampled into the mud. She gasped for breath as their hands gripped her throat. The long, cold blades of their machetes pressed against her chest, and the girl realized that she was going to die. She was going to die in this swamp miles from her home. Die under the boots of the slavers with nothing to show for her suffering but an old, dead captain who would probably be replaced with someone even worse. But as despair swallowed her mind, something even deeper suddenly snapped, and her spirit ripped itself open.

Years ago, before the invaders had come, she'd learned spirit talking from the village elder. The old woman always said that spirit talkers may only ask, never demand. To demand was to lose the world's respect, and thus lose everything. But now, with the machetes pressing into her ribs and the fingers crushing her throat, what did she have left to lose?

She reached out with the roar of her open spirit and stabbed her will into the mud. The dirt screamed as she touched it, but her will was absolute, and it had no choice. The blades vanished from her chest as the men were yanked off her. Their laughter turned to terrified screams as the ground beneath their feet turned against them. They flailed as they started to sink, screaming in panic, but the girl dug her now-freed hands into the mud and tightened her grip, snarling as she slammed her will down. The moment it landed, the men vanished into the swamp, the sticky mud closing over their heads without a trace.

The swamp fell suddenly silent, empty except for the droning of distant insects. The girl crouched in the mud, her dark eyes bright in the flickering light of the toppled lanterns until the mud took those, too, and everything fell dark. Sensing its chance, the mud began to buck against her Enslavement. She let it go, staring dumbstruck at the bloody knife in her hand. What had she done? Killing the captain had been bad enough, but now she'd killed the foremen as well. They would slaughter the camp for this. They would find her and kill her, kill her brothers, kill her people, all to make an example for the other camps. They would all die and it would be her fault.

Bleak despair filled her mind, drowning out even her panic, and she began to weep. The sobs shook her until her bones ached, but the more she cried, the worse she felt. There was no escape, no hope. Nothing.

Finally, her crying subsided, and she realized something was different. The swamp was silent. Not just night silence, true silence. There was no rustle of water, no insects chirping. Even the gentle wind had stopped. Her body went tense, and the girl edged her head up, peeking cautiously through her tangled hair. The dark swamp was bright as noon, but that was impossible. Dawn was still hours away, and in any case, this was no golden daylight. The light was white, stark, and cold as fresh snow. She would have called it moonlight, but no moon had ever shone this bright. She raised her head to stare, and that was when she caught sight of a woman's white foot resting delicately on the surface of the swamp.

The girl jumped and scrambled back. The woman stood less than a foot away. She was naked, her skin flawless and alabaster white. White hair fell in a cascade across her white shoulders, and her white eyes were sparkling as she looked down at the muddy girl at her feet.

Hello—the woman's voice was like cold silk—*Nara*.

"How do you know my name?"

The question was out before the girl could stop it. Nara was her tribe name. Ever since the invaders took them to the camps, she'd shared it with no one. She should be furious that this woman, this obvious outsider, knew it, but she could not be angry with her. The woman was simply too beautiful.

The White Lady knelt, and Nara couldn't help noticing that the mud did not smudge her perfect skin. The woman extended her hand, cupping Nara's dirty cheek in a burning grip.

I know everything about you, the woman said. *I am your Shepherdess. I have been watching you since you were born. You are a brave girl, Nara. Brave and beautiful.* The white fingers stroked her cheek, leaving burning trails that made Nara tremble. *So beautiful. More beautiful than anything else I've created.*

"Created?" Nara whispered, the word little more than a feathered breath.

Well, the Lady spoke and smirked, as though this were some long-standing joke, *not fully. I am not the Creator. But I shaped you, you and all humans, in my image.* Her beautiful face fell. *For all that, you always were ugly, ridiculous creatures, fitting for the ugly job I made you to do. Even so, every now and then I catch a glimmer of something more.* The fingers slid down to brush Nara's lips. *Like you. You are beautiful, Nara. From the moment I saw you, I knew I had to have you. Knew that you and you alone of all the ugly, blind humans were worthy of being my star.*

Nara's eyes widened as the White Lady leaned down and pressed a burning kiss to her lips. It was the briefest touch, but the proximity alone was enough to send her reeling. Still, Nara had never been quick to trust, and, though it went against every instinct she had, she pulled away, putting space between her and the woman who called herself Shepherdess.

"Your star?" she said with as much strength as she could muster. "And what is that?"

The White Lady looked at her with a smirk. *My servant.*

Nara scowled. "I'm done being a servant."

I am not like your human masters. The Lady laughed. *Those deaf sacks of meat. I am Benehime, a Power of creation. I am the Shepherdess, all spirits serve me. But my stars are different. They are raised above all others, and answer only to me. As my star, there will be no want you can think of that I cannot provide. No wish I cannot grant.*

"Any wish?" Nara said, her throat dry.

Anything at all, the Shepherdess answered, spreading her arms. *All you have to do is worship me. Fear me. Obey me. Love me more than any other. Become my star, beautiful girl, and whatever you desire will be yours.*

She must have seen the hunger in Nara's eyes, for the White Lady smiled. *You have a wish, don't you? Speak it.*

Nara had never told her wish to anyone, but it came tumbling from her lips before she could think of denying the White Lady.

"I've been a slave for ten years," she whispered. "I and my people and all the peoples I met when I was a child, we all were made slaves when the invaders came because we could not fight back. They crushed the spirits of the forest and forced the stone to vomit its riches into the mines. The Enslavers turned our lakes into swamps and our mountains into open pits that we were forced to work. But that's how the world is. The strong step on the weak, and the weak can do nothing but weep. I want to change that. You said you could give me anything I wish—that's it. I want to stop the cycle of war and Enslavement. Can you give me that?"

The White Lady's face broke into a brilliant smile. *So noble,* she said, running her white fingers through Nara's dark, tangled hair. *So determined. I like you even better now, little darling. You might even become my favorite if you keep it up.*

"So you can grant my wish?" Nara said.

The Shepherdess leaned back a bit, her lovely white mouth pursed as she made a show of thinking about it.

I won't just give it to you, she said at last. *That would be no fun. But I will give you the power to take it for yourself.* She leaned in until her lips were a breath away from Nara's own. *I will give you power unlike any-thing you have ever seen. You will bear my mark, speak in my name. I will give you dominion over all spirits great and small and the life span to see your wish come true.*

Nara's stomach clenched. She still wasn't sure if this was a dream or not, but the Shepherdess was there in front of her, white and cold and more beautiful than anything her mind could make up. And in that realization, she knew her answer.

"If you give me the power to make the world what it should be," she said, trembling at the beautiful woman's closeness, "I will love you above all others until the day I die."

Though the shameful truth was, Nara already did. The woman was so beautiful, so powerful, Nara was already lost. But the Lady expected a wish, and Nara would give it to her. She would give her anything, Nara realized with a sinking feeling, and from the look on the Lady's face, the Shepherdess knew it.

The White Lady smiled and leaned in to kiss Nara gently on the lips. It was a bare brush, but the connection that opened between them nearly made Nara faint. Power burned through her, pouring into the well of her soul until she feared she would burst. Light seared her body from the inside out, burning her away until Nara was sure that she had died and her spirit simply hadn't realized it yet. And then it was over. The Shepherdess pulled away, catching Nara's falling body in her arms.

It is done, she whispered, cuddling the girl to her chest like a kitten. *You bear my mark forever, now. You are mine, mine alone.*

"Yours alone," Nara said, looking up into the Lady's white eyes. Eyes she now knew as well as her own. The white fire was still burning through her as tears rolled down her cheeks. "I will love you forever," she swore, leaning into the Lady's embrace. "Forever and ever, beautiful, beloved Benehime."

The Shepherdess laughed in delight as Nara said her name. She stood, taking the girl up with her. As they rose, the dirt fell reverently away, leaving Nara clean and perfect in the Shepherdess's glory. A white slit opened in the air in front of them, and Benehime carried her through, away from the swamp, away from the mud and the pain of slavery, into a perfect, white world.

When the sun rose the next morning on the slave camp, an unknown woman in golden armor carrying a gleaming sword strode into the master's tent and began killing the officers. She killed them quickly and efficiently, leaving only one alive to bring the word of what had happened to the other camps. After she'd sent him running, the woman turned to the buildings that held the cowering slaves. The stones barring the doors rolled away at the barest touch of her will, desperate to do what she ordered, for the mark of the Shepherdess was plain on her soul. The people cried in fear as the doors opened, but the woman held up her hand for silence. When the silence came, she told them they were free. Some of the people fainted, some ran in terror, but others raised their arms in praise, swearing their lives to the woman who'd won their freedom.

This was the Immortal Empress's first conquest.

Eight hundred years later, the Immortal Empress treasured this memory. By the time she'd conquered her first kingdom, Benehime had named her favorite, the soul beloved by the Shepherdess above all others. Many joys had followed in the centuries after, but that first night was still dearest in Nara's heart. Even now, the smell of mud brought a dreamy smile to her face.

"Empress?"

Nara opened her eyes and turned to face her commander. The old man winced, but he did not shrink back. He had been her general for many years before she'd vanished, and he knew her well. Now, however, he looked as though he had something to say, and so, regretfully, she let the memory go and returned to the bitter present.

"Report."

"Empress," the man said again, bowing. "Your return could not have come at a better time. The storm has been blowing for weeks now without weakening. Tidal waves have devastated your southern coast. Those who survived the initial flood escaped to higher ground, but they are now stranded and running low on food. I ordered your army to aid in the evacuation, but the storm is too dangerous. Now that you are with us again, however, I am sure—"

He fell silent as the Empress stepped up to the edge of the balcony. They were standing on the observation tower of her southernmost fortress, the one she'd left to remind the desert tribes who had conquered them. That was two hundred years ago now, but the fort was still one of her largest. From its tower, she could see clear across the sandy desert to the coast, miles away, but even if she'd been on the ground, she couldn't have missed the storm. It loomed off the edge of her continent's southern coast, a wall of black clouds and forked lightning stretching as far as she could see in any direction. Great winds blew in the smell of rain and sodden mud, and though the smell triggered her memories again, Nara did not smile. The storm chewed at the edge of her lands, destroying everything in its path beneath a rain of lightning and the endless booming thunder she knew too well.

The Empress shook her head. "I cannot banish this storm."

The general's eyes widened. "But surely," he began. "You are queen of everything. The spirits would not dare—"

"You question me?" the Empress said coldly.

The general froze. "No, Empress," he said, bowing so low that his helmet slipped off. "Forgive me, Empress. Your voice is the only law."

She nodded and held out her hand, letting the storm-tossed winds sweep over her fingers. When she felt a particularly strong one, she closed her fist. The wind squealed at first but grew still when it realized what will had caught it.

"Hail, Empress," it whispered.

Nara glanced pointedly at the enormous storm. "What is *he* doing here?"

"The Lord of Storm is in disgrace," the wind said, wiggling in her hand.

"I can see that," the Empress snapped. "He's been in disgrace for weeks, apparently, and wrecking my shore in the process. What did he do that Benehime would impose such a harsh punishment?"

The wind jerked. Lesser spirits were so obedient that even the mention of the Lady's name was enough to send them into a fit of reverential terror.

"He raised his blade against the favorite," it whispered at last. "The Shepherdess's wrath was swift."

White-hot fury roared through Nara's mind and, for a moment, she forgot everything. Forgot the storm, the general standing beside her, even the wind in her hand. Time seemed to flow backward, carrying her back to that hated day when everything in her life had fallen apart. The day the Shepherdess brought that boy into her white world.

She could see him clearly in her mind even now, a skinny, dark-haired thing sitting smugly on Benehime's beautiful lap as the Lady doted on him. The memory made Nara tremble with rage. That spoiled brat had stolen the Shepherdess's love from her, and with it everything Nara cared for. All the things that had given her pride—her victories, her legions, her unified country, the fairness and efficiency of the government she had built, the peace she had brought to her people, her loyal spirits, even her great wish of a fair and peaceful world—none of it meant *anything* when Benehime, her beautiful, beloved Shepherdess, was ignoring her in favor of that hateful, conniving, selfish child.

Nara bared her teeth at the enormous waves washing over the ruins of her sea towns. How could the Shepherdess love that brat enough to punish the Lord of Storms this severely just for raising his blade? He'd raised his sword to Nara several times, and the Lady had never done anything like this. Was she finally sick of his disobedience? Or was it because she loved the boy more than—

The Empress stopped that line of thought dead. She could not believe it. The Lady's love was for Nara alone. The boy was nothing more than an infatuation. He'd beguiled the Shepherdess. What else would explain Benehime's abandoning her Empress after eight centuries of Nara's ceaseless devotion? Her undying love? Nara clenched her fists. Den had been right. For eleven years she'd lived in her misery, waiting for the Shepherdess to remember who truly loved her, and all she had to show for it was the suffering of her own lands. She was through hiding, through crying. If the Lady loved her as an Empress, then Empress she would be. She would rebuild her army as never before. An army fit to conquer the rest of the world. And when all the lands of creation were united under her good rule, her wish would be fulfilled. She alone would rule a world without war, without unfairness, a world that was guided by her wisdom alone. And then Nara would take this perfect world and throw it at the Lady's feet. There, she would say, who is your favorite now?

Just the thought of it brought the smile back to Nara's lips. With such a grand offering, the Shepherdess would have no choice. She would cast the thief aside and return to her true favorite. Benehime would take Nara in her beautiful embrace once again, and together they would laugh at the memory of the boy called Eli, when they thought of him at all.

She was still savoring that thought when a high-pitched squeal brought her back to the present. The wind was writhing in her clenched hand. The Empress eased her grip, letting the wind slide gratefully through her fingers.

"Go to my war palace at Istalirin," she said. "See if Den has arrived yet."

"Yes, Empress," the wind panted, flitting gladly away.

Nara nodded and turned to deal with the mess the Lord of Storms had made. Without a word of warning to her general, she walked to the edge of the balcony and jumped off. The desert winds caught her fall, setting her down gently on the fortress's stone yard. The soldiers dropped to their knees when they saw her, pressing their heads to the ground in reverence. She ignored them, focusing instead on the stone beneath her golden boots.

"You," she said, stomping on the ground. "Wake up."

The stone rumbled as it woke, and then lowered itself in obedience.

"Yes, Empress?"

"Form a wall along the coast. This storm is no concern of ours. We will protect our borders and wait it out."

"Yes, Empress," the stone said again.

The Empress nodded and slammed her foot on the ground a second time. The stone obeyed instantly, and a pillar of rock shot up beneath her feet, lifting her back to the edge of the watchtower balcony. Her general ran forward to help her over the railing. When her footing was solid again, she turned to watch as the bedrock spirit followed her orders.

All along her coast, a great wall of stone exploded out of the sandy beach, forming a barrier between the water and the land. The stone wall ran as far as she could see, following the snaking coastline until her continent's entire southern tip was cut off, safe from the storm surge behind a fifty-foot barrier.

Nodding in approval, the Empress turned back to the waiting wind, who had just returned from the north.

"Den has arrived," the wind said. "He's demanding to see you."

"He would," the Empress sneered. "Well done. You are released."

The wind bowed and fled, vanishing into the clear, desert sky.

"General," Nara said, turning to face the old man who was still bowing in reverence. "You will leave five hundred men here to resettle those misplaced by the storm. The rest of your army will march to my war palace at Istalirin. I want everything: support, supplies, siege troops, the full panalopy. March them hard, I want my armies gathered by dark tomorrow."

The old man paled. Istalirin was miles away. Such a deadline, even on the Empire's awakened roads, would be nigh impossible. But the Immortal Empress expected the impossible from all her subjects as a matter of course, and her general knew better than to complain.

"Yes, Empress," he said, bowing lower than ever. "Is it war then?"

"War indeed," the Empress said. "It is time at last to bring the entire world into the light of my Empire." And to show Benehime who was truly worthy of her love.

The general eyed her nervously. "Permission to speak, Empress."

"Granted," the Empress said.

"Your army marches wherever you command," he said. "But the man Den is not to be trusted. While you were gone, he did nothing but wander your Empire, terrorizing your towns and challenging every strong fighter he could find. We lost several of your best to him. He has no discipline or loyalty, and he does not follow orders. You are the chosen of the land, Empress, and I would never question your judgment, but can such a man truly be a servant of the Empire?"

"No," the Empress said. "Den is a traitor. He betrayed his homeland to join our invasion as soon as the tide turned. He is a monster who thrives on conflict with no loyalty to anything but his own lust for battle. I know full well that he will never be my soldier, but I do not need another soldier, general." She looked west. "Soldiers I have in plenty, but the other half of this world is a barbarous, unciv- ilized, lawless place. If I am to bring such lands into my enlightened peace, soldiers won't be enough. If my control is to be complete, I must conquer swiftly, completely. We must devour their land before they realize they have lost it, and for that, I need a monster." She turned and smiled at her general. "Have no fear, this is the last war. When we are done, the whole world will be under my law, and there will be no more need for monsters. If Den is still alive when we reach that glorious end, I will see that he meets a monster's death."

The general bowed, his eyes shining. "As you command, Empress. Your soldiers march for Istalirin and the endless glory of your Empire."

"As they should," she said. "I will expect you there."

With that, she waved her hand, and a white line appeared in the air, twisting open to reveal the ornate map room of her war palace. Her officers stopped what they were doing and stood at attention as she stepped through the hole in the world. They murmured praises in her name, but the Empress paid them no mind. She marched straight past the table to the great window and looked out over the bay.

All she saw was ships. Her fleet spread to the horizon, her palace ships filled the great bay of Istalirin until no glimpse of water was visible between the hulls. Pride welled up in her chest. Twenty-six years ago, when she was the favorite and the world was as it should be, she'd sent a handful of ships to test the strength of the other half of the world. They'd returned defeated, but that was to be expected. She'd conquered close to a hundred countries since becoming Empress, and she'd learned early to use a small force to sound out the enemy's strengths before attacking in earnest. What had surprised her were her generals' reports of the enemy's ability to talk across distance. That had caught her for a moment, but the counter proved easy. If they could gossip about her movements and pile all their troops to meet her at full strength wherever she hit, then she would simply build so many ships that such a small advantage wouldn't matter.

The Empress enjoyed such simple, effective plans, but even for her, it took time to raise that large a force. But again, she was the Immortal Empress; time wasn't an issue. As soon as she'd heard her defeated generals' report, she'd put her shipyards to work and sat back to wait. For eleven years, everything went as planned. But then, just as her army was nearing completion, the boy had appeared and ruined everything.

Nara took a deep, shamed breath. When the boy first took Benehime away from her, she'd gone a little mad. She'd abandoned her lands, abandoned her nearly finished fleet, abandoned her people, abandoned her wish to hide in a cave like an animal. Fifteen years she'd lost to worthless misery, and then to be rescued by Den, of all people. It was her greatest shame. One she meant to undo with the fleet that lay before her.

Satisfied, the Empress turned away from the window and took her place at the head of the table as her generals began to arrange the battle maps for her inspection. As the papers were laid in place, she spotted Den himself entering the war room. Her officers stiffened visibly as he stepped up to the table, but Nara motioned for him to stand beside her. Mindless of the great honor, Den walked up and sat on the table by her elbow, his hard face sullen and bored.

"I'm here," he said. "Can we go?"

"Soon," Nara promised, nodding for her generals to begin their presentations.

Den sneered and walked over to the window overlooking the bay. As the generals began to speak, Den paid them no attention. His eyes never left the ships, and he stared at them with the ardor of someone witnessing the birth of his heart's desire. That look alone set Nara's mind at ease. Confident that her monster would be loyal for now, she turned to hear the greatest military minds of her Empire outline their plans to crush all who stood in her way.

Just beyond the bay at Istalirin, at the outskirts of the Empress's control, an enormous wind flew over the growing fleet. It blew through every ship, taking note not only of the mountainous hulls and cavernous crew quarters but of the great war spirits that slept deep in the ships' bellies. The wind looked as long as it dared, skirting the edge of the Empress's awareness. When it had seen enough, the wind turned west, flying as fast as it could back to its lord who waited on the far western edge of the world.

Far across the Unseen Sea, Tesset sat on the plush window seat in the Merchant Prince of Zarin's office, watching his employer pace a rut into the fine silk rug.

"Whitefall's an idiot if he thinks this is going to work," Sara muttered around the pipe she clenched between her teeth. "Compromises don't work with men like Banage."

"It's my impression that he doesn't have much choice," Tesset said. "Council and Court must stand together or face mutual destruction."

"Which is exactly why it won't work," Sara said, walking faster. "Mutual destruction loses its teeth when one party is willing to die for his beliefs."

Tesset leaned against the window. "If the Merchant Prince is showing any lack of judgment, Sara, it's not trying to compromise with Banage, but inviting you to attend."

Sara shot him a look that would have frozen the Whitefall River. Tesset settled his shoulders against the cool glass and stared back.

"There's no point in leaving me out of things," she said, resuming her pacing. "Whitefall may fancy himself the shadow king of the world, but this is as much my Council as it is his. He can't make a decision involving wizard matters without my say-so, and Banage knows it. Etmon won't agree to anything without me there for him to gloat over." She puffed on her pipe, adding more smoke to the haze that already filled the room. "This is ridiculous. I got back from the desert not an hour ago. I don't have time for this farce. Not if Alber wants his miracle, anyway."

Tesset started to comment, but a soft sound outside the door caught his attention. "Well," he said, "here's your chance to tell him so yourself."

The words were scarcely out of his mouth when the door opened and Alber Whitefall swept into the room. He was dressed in full regalia, with the white suit and golden medals of the Merchant Prince of Zarin as well as the maroon sash of the Council of Thrones, which the prince's valet was still attempting to tie as he followed his harried master through the doorway.

Tesset smiled approvingly. A clever move, playing to Banage's pride by greeting him with full honors as an equal. But Whitefall was a subtle, clever man, and Tesset never got tired of watching him maneuver. Pity he was spirit deaf. With the right training, he could have made a dangerous fighter.

"Banage is on his way," Whitefall said, holding out his arm so the valet could fasten his cufflinks. "Remember, let me do the talking. If you antagonize him, he'll just leave."

"It's what he's going to do anyway," Sara said, blowing an enormous puff of smoke at the ceiling.

Whitefall smiled. "We'll see. Our dear Rector is about to run out of options."

Sara eyed him curiously, but the Merchant Prince's face was all politeness as he glanced at the enormous clock on the wall. "Time to take our places."

He turned and walked out of the room, valet trailing in his wake. Sara followed, handing her pipe to Tesset, who tamped it out and placed it carefully in his pocket.

They walked through the citadel and into the large room at its heart, the Council Hearing Chamber. The chamber was empty this late in the evening, and Tesset got the feeling Whitefall had planned it that way. Another clever move. He was robbing Banage of his audience, hoping that the lack of witnesses would help the Rector compromise his principles. Tesset wasn't sure if that hope would pan out, but Whitefall was wise to seize whatever advantage he could.

They took their places, Whitefall at the head table, Sara beside him with Tesset standing at her back. Moments after the valet had finished pinning the final length of gold braid to Whitefall's shoulder, the doors at the opposite end of the chamber opened and Banage swept in. The Rector was in full regalia as well, the red robes of his order smothered beneath the heavy chain of his office. The enormous rings on his fingers glowed brighter than the lamps on the walls as he strode proudly across the polished marble to the table that had been prepared for him, but he did not sit. Instead, he stood, hands crossed at his waist, and waited.

Tesset bit back a smile. Banage had come ready to fight. This might prove more interesting than he'd hoped. For a moment, the two parties simply stared at each other, and then Whitefall made an almost imperceptible gesture with his fingers. The servants took their cue, closing the chamber door with a soft crack, leaving the three most powerful people in Zarin alone.

"So," Whitefall began politely. "Would it be a waste of my breath to ask you to sit?"

"It would," Banage answered, his blue eyes flicking from Sara to the Merchant Prince. "Let's not dance about, Whitefall. What do you want?"

"It's less what *I* want and more what *we* need, Banage," Whitefall said, lacing his fingers together. "I'm sure you've heard by now, but I'll tell you formally: War is coming. Twenty-six years after we drove her fleet back to the ocean, the Immortal Empress is on the move again, and we have precious little time. If our continent is to survive this assault, we must stand together. All of us. Even you."

Banage's eyes narrowed. "The Spirit Court is a peaceful organization dedicated to the protection of the spirit world. We do not go to war."

"And I am head of a trade coalition dedicated to beneficial coexistence and mutual profit," Whitefall said with a shrug. "These are times of extraordinary threat. We must all reach outside our normal parameters."

"And you're demanding my help?" Banage sneered.

"I'm asking for it, yes," Whitefall said. "I'm *asking* for everyone's help." He leaned forward, cool affection gone. He was staring earnestly at the Rector Spiritualis, and when he spoke again, his voice was full of real emotion. "I shouldn't have to explain this to you, Etmon. You fought with us in the last war against the Empress, you know how bad things could get. We may never have seen eye to eye on everything, but I know you care about what we've built. This war could destroy all of that—the Council, the Spirit Court, everything. The Empress isn't coming to expand her borders or seek a treaty. She's coming to conquer. If we're going to stop her, we must find a way to work together."

He ended with his hands on the table, eyes locked on Banage. On his side of the room, the Rector Spiritualis sighed.

"I understand what you're saying, Alber," he said quietly. "But the Spirit Court is not a political organization. We have worked together with the Council many times to our mutual benefit, but war is different. We serve the spirits, the land itself, and the land does not care who rules it. I cannot ask my Spiritualists to violate their oaths and put their spirits in danger to defend your borders."

"This isn't about borders," Whitefall said, his voice growing heated. "Do you think the Immortal Empress is going to let the Spirit Court continue to operate? You were with Sara and me on the beach at Osera when her wizards dropped their flaming war spirits on our heads. Do you think a woman who uses that kind of force is going to sit back and let you keep running your towers as you see fit?"

Banage lifted his chin. "Perhaps."

"*Perhaps?*" Whitefall repeated sharply. "That wasn't how you felt last time."

"It is because I fought then that I cannot ask my wizards to fight now," Banage said. "How many times must I say it? Our duty is to our spirits, not your Council. Our oaths are built on a trust deeper than anything your spirit-deaf mind can imagine. I lost two spirits in the war with the Empress. I will not make my Spiritualists go through that pain as well."

"We all lost friends in the war," Whitefall said. "I lost an entire legion in one night alone when Den the Traitor turned against us. Every single one of those men had a soul, had a mother, had a family. Are you saying your spirits' lives were worth more than theirs?"

"Men fight for countries," Banage said. "They choose to risk death in the name of their cause. But spirits have no countries or causes. This is their world, we are the interlopers. We have no right to drag them from their sleep into our petty conflicts. You are a leader of men, Alber. It is right for you to be concerned with their struggles. But I am a custodian of the Spirit World. If I compromised that position for human interests, I would be unworthy of the name Spiritualist."

Whitefall heaved an enormous sigh and collapsed back into his chair. "What will it take, Etmon? What can I do to bring you over?"

Banage tilted his head, and his eyes took on a gleam that Tesset knew well. He'd seen it on every fighter: the look that came just before the finishing blow.

"The Spirit Court exists to ensure the greatest good for all spirits," Banage said. "I was very young when we first fought the Empress, and I thought, as young people do, that the enemy was evil because she was our enemy. That we were right and she was wrong. But I am no longer young or naive, and I'm no longer sure that I am on the right side."

"That is very close to treason," Sara said, but she fell silent when Whitefall put out his hand.

"We are the right side, Banage," Whitefall said earnestly.

"Are you?" Banage said, his eyes flicking to Sara. "Then why does the Council hide its business with spirits down in its bowels? Why is its head wizard allowed to do as she pleases without Spirit Court oversight?"

Sara shot up from her seat. "I knew it!" she shouted. "I knew this was all just a ploy to—"

"Sara!" Whitefall's voice echoed through the chamber.

Sara flinched and shut her mouth. Across the room, Banage looked positively triumphant. Whitefall, on the other hand, looked dogged.

"Sara's achievements support the Council," the Merchant Prince said, picking his words carefully. "The Relay is what keeps the countries tied together. It's what makes them *need* us. Therefore, we need her, and she needs the freedom to innovate."

"Then it's time to weigh which need is greater," Banage said, crossing his arms. "Sara's secrecy or my Court. I know you are a man who plays with words, Alber, so I will say this as plain as possible. If you want our help, you must change your ways. I will lead the Court toward whatever end supports its purpose. Black as you paint the Empress, her crimes against the spirits are as yet only possibilities. Sara's crimes are far closer to home. You need my Court?

Prove you are worthy of it. Tear down the wall of secrecy Sara has built. Allow my people to inspect the Relay and all other works of Council wizardry, and swear to fix whatever abuses we find. Show the Spirit Court that you deserve our loyalty, and we will follow the Council wherever you need us."

Sara's face was scarlet with rage as Banage finished, yet she said nothing. Tesset could see why. Whitefall's hand was at her wrist, his long fingers pressed into the pressure point. The Merchant Prince was calm, his eyes half lidded as they regarded Banage. Tesset leaned back, watching the old man with interest. When Whitefall had nearly lost his temper earlier, Tesset had been worried he'd misjudged the man. Now he saw with satisfaction that the earlier bluster had been a feint, a ruse to draw out Banage's real objective just as a swordsman feigns injury to trick his enemy into revealing his finishing strike. But now that he knew what Banage really wanted, Whitefall didn't seem quite sure what to do with it. Tesset watched him carefully, waiting to see how he would counter. However, when the Merchant Prince finally did answer, even Tesset didn't see the blow coming.

"I'm afraid you leave me no choice," Whitefall said, drawing a folded piece of paper out of his pocket. "Give this to him."

Tesset stepped forward and took the paper. He walked across the chamber to Banage, who accepted the note with a suspicious glare before dropping his eyes to read.

"What is this?" he asked as Tesset returned to his position behind Sara.

"It's a conscription notice," Whitefall answered.

"*Conscription?*" Banage roared. "What is the meaning of this?"

"You've put me in a bind," Whitefall said, his voice growing cold and sharp. "I would like nothing more than to throw open the Council and let the Spirit Court scour every inch of it, but I don't even need to ask to know Sara's response. You know as well as I do that her word is final when it comes to Council wizardry, and yet you bring me this impossible request. If I didn't know better, I'd think you wanted this to fail."

Banage stiffened. "I want only what I have always wanted," he said. "Humane treatment for all spirits. If you will not let my Spiritualists inspect the Council's practices, then I no longer have suspicions. I now *know* that the Council of Thrones is abusing spirits, and you can't possibly think I would ally my Court with such a shameful organization."

"Be that as it may," Whitefall said. "Take a closer look at that paper in your hand. Like it or not, every member of your order is also a citizen of this 'shameful organization,' and it is my right, as written under section three of the Council edict, to order citizens of the Council to war for our mutual defense. If you and your wizards do not comply in full, then, by Council law, I have no choice but to declare you traitors."

Banage's face grew very pale, and Whitefall leaned forward. "Don't be a fool, Etmon," he hissed. "It doesn't have to be like this. Join me willingly and I will do everything I can to keep your spirits from harm. I swear it."

Banage looked the Merchant Prince directly in the eye, but he did not speak. Instead, he raised the conscription notice in the air between them and ripped it cleanly in two.

Whitefall watched tight lipped as the torn paper fluttered to the polished floor. "You realize you've just committed treason."

"One cannot commit treason against an authority he is not part of," Banage answered. "The Spirit Court was doing its duty centuries before you even imagined the Council of Thrones. We do not answer to you."

Whitefall let out a tight sigh. "As you like," he said. "Tesset, arrest the traitor."

Tesset stepped out onto the smooth marble, watching Banage

warily as the attack played out in his head. The tall Rector had reach on him, but the man was not a hand-to-hand fighter. The hardest part would be taking him down before he could call his spirits. Quick jab to the stomach should be enough. Decision made, Tesset dropped and began to run. But fast as he was, Banage was faster. Just before his fist landed, a wall of wind sent Tesset flying.

He turned in the air and landed on the Merchant Prince's table, catching an ink pot just before it blew into Sara's face. Across the room, Banage stood in the center of a small tornado, his robes flying like flags.

"Keril," the Rector said, and the pale blue stone on his index finger flashed like a small sun. The wind intensified, forcing Tesset to a crouch as he shielded Whitefall and Sara.

Tesset squinted against the wind. Banage was moving his other hand now, bringing a green cabochon of glowing jade to his lips.

"Duesset," he said, his deep voice clear over the roar of the wind.

The entire hearing chamber rang like a bell, and then, with a roar that cracked the windows, an enormous creature exploded through the stone floor. Tesset's eyes widened. It looked like a warhorse carved from jade, but it was larger than any horse Tesset had ever seen. The creature lowered its head, and its stone mane fell into easy steps for the Rector to climb onto its back.

Banage looked down on Sara, Tesset, and Whitefall from the creature's back, his face a stone mask.

"I am the voice of the Spirit Court," he announced, his words booming through the room. "I speak for us all, and I say this: The Spirit Court exists for the spirits. Just as we will never allow them to be coerced, so shall we never allow ourselves to be ordered to war by an outside authority. Fight the Empress with your own blood, Alber, for you shall have none of ours."

With that, the wind gave one final howl, shattering the large glass windows that looked out over the city. As the glass fell, the stone horse leaped, carrying Banage through the broken window. It landed with a crash in the courtyard below, but when Tesset ran forward, all he saw was a crater in the paving stones and the flick of the jade horse's tail as it charged the citadel gate. The iron bars crumpled like paper as the creature galloped through them, its stone feet striking the cobbles like smithy hammers on new iron as it vanished down the street and into the city below.

"Well," Whitefall said, pulling himself up. "That could have gone better."

"Could it?" Sara said, reaching out her hands for Tesset to help her up. "How many times have I told you? You can't speak sense to Banage. The nerve of that man, forcing his morals on the whole world. Spiritualists poking their noses into my workshop, can you imagine?" She shook her head. "You were right to turn him down, Alber. If they discovered the truth of the Relay, we'd have a full-out rebellion on our hands."

"I'm not sure we won't as it is," Whitefall said, his voice tired. "But I had hoped to avoid breaking the Court."

"It was already broken," Sara said with a sniff. "Banage is a fanatic. There's no place for him in an order as old and vested in its power as the Spirit Court. Forcing him to reject conscription was the best thing you could have done. Some of the old guard will stick to Banage's banner of high morality, but the majority of Spiritualists won't risk treason just to keep their hands clean, especially not when they can say they were only fighting for their country."

Tesset had to agree. In one move, Whitefall had taken Banage's ultimatum and turned it around, forcing the Rector Spiritualis into the weakest position possible. If the Merchant Prince had simply let him leave the first time he refused, or worse, threatened him with force, Banage could have stood on his principles, turning himself and his supporters into moralistic objectors. But with the conscription notice, Whitefall had backed Banage up against his own ultimatum. He could no longer stay aloof. It was give in and go with the Council as a conscript or be declared a traitor. Of course, Banage had still refused, but in refusing he'd doomed his own chances at keeping the lion's share of the Court. After all, while there were plenty of Spiritualists who would have jumped at the chance to avoid the war by siding with their Rector, only the true fanatics would be willing to be branded traitor for him. Tesset grinned. He loved a good turn-about.

"Get the message out to your contacts among the Tower Keepers, Sara," Whitefall said. "The Council will welcome any Spiritualists who wish to fight for their homes. Those who join Banage will be declared traitors, and their property and lands will be seized."

"Consider it done," Sara said. "But what are you going to do about Etmon? He'll only muck things up if you leave him to run loose."

"I don't think you'll have to worry about that," Tesset said, glancing out the crashed window. "Look."

Across the city, the Spirit Court's tower was moving. The white stone walls, clearly visible even at this distance, rippled like water. Windows vanished beneath a wave of stone, and the great red doors of the Tower fell like trees as they watched, crashing to the ground as the entrances they guarded vanished beneath a wall of stone. One by one, every escape to the outside world vanished beneath the rippling white stone until the Tower was completely sealed, an impenetrable, unblemished spire of pure white.

"Well," Sara said softly. "I suppose that takes care of that."

"What was that?" Whitefall said.

Sara held out her hand and Tesset handed her her pipe. "Banage's sealed the Tower," she said, tapping a measure of fresh tobacco into the bowl. "Took his toys and went home. Typical." She made a scornful face as she lit her pipe and took a long draw. "If you're done with me, Alber, I'm going to get those messages out

before Banage can convince the Spiritualists they're being perse-
cuted. The last thing we need is a bunch of self-righteous wizards
fighting us instead of the Empress."

Whitefall nodded, still staring. Sara turned on her heel and
marched out of the room. Tesset fell into step behind her, still smiling. Whitefall watched the sealed Tower a moment longer, and
then, shaking his head, he walked to the door and called the servants in to start cleaning up the mess Banage had made of his hearing chamber.

CHAPTER

6

Five hours after their failed frontal assault, Eli had everything he needed to get them into the castle. Business finished, they were now sitting at a tucked away table in one of the large inns overlooking the palace square, washed, dressed, fed, and killing the last hour before the guard change with a few hands of Daggerback. Josef was winning, which might have been the only reason he was still at the table.

"I don't understand why you wasted your money," Josef grumbled, picking up his cards as fast as Eli dealt them. "There's no point. I told you, we're just going to leave."

Eli pursed his lips as he turned over his bid card, a knight. "It wasn't a waste," he said. "We have to look at you, too, you know. And the guard was right. You were starting to come off a bit terrifying."

Josef made a *harrumphing* noise, and Eli grinned. Despite the swordsman's scowl, he was looking very well. They'd found a barber to cut his hair and give him a proper shave, and while nothing could be done about his scars, Josef had looked almost civilized when he got out of the chair. Eli had also bought him a new shirt, a white one, with no bloodstains or suspicious holes, as well as some nonpatched trousers. Small changes, really, but the overall effect was a wonder. With a pressed shirt, blond hair cut short and neat, and his chin shaved clean, Eli could almost believe that the man sitting across the table really was a prince. Provided, of course, he looked past the belts of blades Josef refused to take off.

"Five to open," Eli said, tossing his coins on the table. "Stop complaining, you look lovely. Nico thinks so, too. Don't you, Nico?"

Nico jumped and peeked over her cards. "He looks nice," she said, placing her ante next to Eli's. "But he looked nice before, too."

Josef gave Eli a "there, you see" smirk as he dropped his money onto the pile.

"There's nice that's fit for gutting people and nice that's fit for palaces," Eli said pointedly. "Besides, boys shouldn't visit their mothers in shirts that have stab holes, or with hair that looks like he cuts it with a throwing knife."

"Skinning knife," Josef corrected. "I use my skinning knife."

"Moving on," Eli said. "We are all agreed that you look quite well now. Looking well is universally useful, so the money wasn't wasted. I bet two."

Josef slapped two coins on the table without looking up. "Match."

Nico glanced at Josef, then at Eli. "Fold."

"One down," Eli said, grinning as Nico lay her cards on the table. "Two again."

Josef matched his bet with a nasty look. They went back and forth for another minute, trading coins until the pile was quite impressive. Finally, Eli called it, and they showed their hands. Josef won with a pair of kings. He scooped up the money with a satisfied smile while Eli watched glumly. When it was all gone, the thief stood with a resigned sigh.

"I think I've lost enough for one day," he said. "Josef, since you have all our gold at the moment, would you settle the tab?"

"Since it's your money, sure."

Josef set the Heart in the corner and made his way to the bar. When he was gone, Nico turned to Eli.

"Why did you keep betting?" she asked quietly. "You knew he had a better hand."

"That I did," Eli said. "But there's more to the game than gold, and Josef's always in a better mood when he wins."

He gave Nico a brilliant smile as he grabbed his bag and made his way toward the back door. Nico watched him with a puzzled expression until Josef returned.

The swordsman paused. "What?"

"Nothing," she said, rubbing her eyes.

Josef shrugged and motioned for Nico to lead the way to the alley where Eli was waiting.

At eight o'clock precisely, the guard changed as scheduled. Five minutes later, a carriage pulled into the palace square. The carriage was a fine one, with a matched pair of bays and a liveried footman who jumped down the moment the wheels stopped. The footman opened the door and flipped the folding stair out with a clack. From the shadows inside the shuttered carriage, a gloved hand reached out, and the footman hurried to help the gentleman down.

The passenger was a genteel figure in an old-fashioned long coat, fitted pants, and short boots cut from two shades of black leather. His face was obscured by a full, gray beard trimmed to a neat point, but his blue eyes were magnified by the silver spectacles that sat on the bridge of his nose. The old man moved slowly, leaning on the footman. He looked so fragile as he climbed down that the junior guard started forward to help him, but the senior guard stopped him with a shake of his head, and they held their position as the footman helped the old man down to the street.

As soon as the gentleman cleared the carriage door, another man exited almost on his heels. The second man was dressed similarly to the first, same old-fashioned coat and two-tone boots, but he was younger, much larger, and armed with two swords at his side as well as a long, sword-shaped-wrapped bundle on his back. He had a silver-tipped cane and a leather-wrapped satchel tucked under his arm, both of which he handed to the first man as soon as he reached the ground. The older man took the cane and the satchel gratefully, leaning on the first while he undid the straps on the second.

The younger man paid the footman without comment. From the way the footman began to bow and scrape, it must have been an impressive amount. After much groveling, the footman climbed back onto his perch and the carriage pulled away, leaving the two men alone with the guards.

The senior guard eyed the way the armed man rested his hands on his sword hilts and stepped forward, putting himself between the new arrivals and the palace gate.

"May I help you?"

"One moment, if you please," the older man said, still digging through his satchel.

The guard relaxed just a fraction. The expensive clothes had been a good hint, but now he was sure these were men of import. No one with an accent that refined could be up to trouble.

After much digging, the old man pulled a small book out of his bag and began thumbing through it. "Here we are," he said, stopping somewhere in the middle. "I'm looking for a Mr. Wallace." He glanced over his spectacles at the older guard. "That would be you?"

"Yes, sir." The senior guard, Wallace, stood at attention. "Are you expected?"

The old man sighed and adjusted his spectacles. "I shouldn't think so, Mr. Wallace. My name is Velsimon Whitefall and this is my bodyguard, Officer Fuller. We're with the National Obligation Audit Division of the Council Tax Bureau."

The man with the swords nodded, but Wallace didn't see him, the gate guard was too busy turning a pasty shade of grayish pink. He didn't know much about the inner working of the Council of Thrones, but he knew the name Whitefall, and he knew that anyone from an office with "Audit" in the title was no one you wanted at your gate.

"I apologize for our late arrival," the old man continued. "We were delayed leaving the mainland, but our business here is of the most pressing urgency. There was a bit of a miscalculation on Osera's last payment and I need to speak with your treasury officer, Mr...."

"Lord Obermal?" Wallace suggested.

"Ah yes, Obermal." The old man closed his little book with a sigh. "There are so many countries now, they all start to"—he waved his hands in a circle—"roll together." He finished with a shrug. "Would you be so kind as to take us to him?"

"I'm afraid Lord Obermal is at dinner," Wallace said carefully.

"Then I think you should fetch him," the old man said. "As I said, this is a matter of some urgency. I wouldn't be wasting my evening begging at gates were it otherwise, would I, Mr. Wallace?"

If possible, Wallace went paler still. "I—"

"Perhaps you could show us to his office and we could wait for him there?" the old man suggested helpfully. "So Lord Obermal doesn't have to come all the way to the gate?"

He punctuated this last bit with pointed lean on his cane. Wallace took the hint. "Of course, Lord Whitefall, of course." He looked over his shoulder. "Higgins!"

The younger guard snapped to attention.

"Take our guests to the treasury office. I'll go and fetch Lord Obermal."

The younger guard saluted and ran to open the gate for the Council Auditor and his guard. "This way, please, Lord Whitefall."

The old man smiled his thanks and hobbled into the palace, his cane clicking on the cobbles. His bodyguard went next, followed by Wallace, who walked with them just long enough to make sure Higgins was taking them the right way. When he saw the younger guard leading them up the stairs toward the treasury office, he grabbed a pair of guards from hall patrol and sent them to watch the gate. His duty satisfied, he ran to find Lord Obermal before things got any worse.

Fifteen minutes later, Lord Obermal, Keeper of the Treasury of Osera, excused himself from dinner with the Crown Secretary and the Officer of the Queen's Horse and set off for his office at a dead run.

"You're *sure* they said the National Obligation Audit Division?" he said, panting at Wallace, who was jogging beside him.

"Positive, my lord," Wallace said.

The treasury keeper made a noise like a mouse getting stepped on. "Audit officers, and a Whitefall no less, here at eight in the evening! Oh, there must have been some terrible mistake. I don't know how. I reviewed all the numbers myself. Did he say what payment he was here to inspect?"

"No, my lord," Wallace said. "But he made it seem deadly urgent."

"It's always urgent when it comes to the Council and money," Lord Obermal said, voice trembling. "The queen will have my head if we get audited now, what with everything going on."

Wallace jogged ahead to open the door to the treasury office. "I had Higgins put them in the receiving room," he said as Lord

Obermal rushed past him. "Anything else I can do for you, my lord?"

"Yes," Obermal said, grabbing a stack of ledgers from his assistant's desk. "Don't tell anyone about this until I've had a chance to talk to the queen. We can't afford a panic."

"Understood, sir," Wallace said, stepping back into the hallway. "Good luck, sir."

Obermal nodded and took a deep breath. Then, hugging the ledgers to his chest, he walked through his office and into the receiving room.

"Lord Whitefall," he said, trying his best to sound like he wasn't panicking. "I'm sorry to have kept you waiting. I have all of Osera's payment records right—"

He stopped, the account books slipping as his fingers went slack.

The receiving room was empty. Obermal stood frozen for a moment as his brain switched from one panic to another. When he could move again, he turned and ran for the hall as fast as his old legs could go, shouting for Wallace.

"There," Eli said, peeling the fake beard off his face as they walked briskly through the back halls of the palace. "What did I tell you? Not even ten minutes."

"Fine, you were right," Josef said, unbuttoning the stuffy longcoat. "How did you know it would work?"

"Have you ever been through a Council audit?" Eli said, taking off his spectacles. "Nasty, expensive business, and the auditors are the last people you want to be out of sorts. That's actually the third time I've pulled that scam. Works every time."

Josef rolled his eyes. "Uh-huh, and why do I always have to be your bodyguard when we do these things?"

"Because, my dear Josef, you are a fighter, not an actor," Eli said with a smile. "The only expressions your face can produce are surly and murderous, so I have to cast you in rolls that highlight those particular aspects. Also, since I have about as much chance getting you to leave your swords behind as you have of convincing me you're lead soprano at the Zarin Opera, it seemed the most prudent course of action."

Josef shook his head. "Why do I even bother?"

"I haven't any idea," Eli said, grinning wider. "Where's Nico?"

Josef glowered at the convenient subject change, but let it slide. He was wondering the same thing. "She should be somewhere around—"

A brush on his shoulder stopped him, and he turned to see Nico stepping out of a deep-shadowed corner.

Eli bundled his somber coat together with Josef's and put them, along with his false beard and spectacles, into the leather satchel, which he then stashed in the nearest closet. He made a mental note of the door just in case they ever got a chance to come back. The Council Audit scam was a sure bet, but it was horrendously expensive to set up. He didn't want to abandon the coats unless he had to.

When he was satisfied he could find the closet again in a hurry, he turned to Josef. "Well, my lord prince, where now?"

"Don't call me that," Josef snapped, setting off down the hall. "And this way. We're going to see the queen."

"Just like that?" Eli said, frowning.

Josef nodded. "Just like that. Nico, you're on scout. I've got point. We're headed for the north wing. Keep the guards away."

"Right," Nico said, vanishing into the shadows like smoke.

Eli whistled, impressed. "Nice to see she's got it back."

Josef stomped off down the hall without comment. Eli sighed and fell into step behind him.

They took a convoluted path through the servant passages, though any route would have been twisty, considering how the old palace wrapped around the mountain peak. Eli had been disappointed to see that the palace's outward shabbiness continued on the inside. The whole place seemed to be nothing but oppressive stone walls and wooden floors hollowed by centuries of feet. The narrow halls would have made avoiding people difficult, but, fortunately, most of the palace seemed occupied with after-dinner entertainment. Eli heard voices through doors and around corners, but they never encountered another person, servant or guard, even when they entered what was obviously a private wing. He was just starting to feel a little unsettled by this when Josef turned a corner and stopped.

They were standing in a long gallery. One wall had sets of narrow windows paned with leaded glass; the other was lined with portraits of stern, fair-haired men. At the end of the gallery, directly across from where they stood, two guards were slumped on the floor. Nico stood beside them, rubbing her hand.

Eli sighed. Of course.

"Nice work," he said flatly as Josef went to help Nico roll the soldiers aside.

"They'll be fine," Josef said. "I taught her how to do it. Right, Nico?"

Nico nodded. "Clean strike to the neck from behind," she said, looking at Eli. "What? It's never bothered you before when we knocked out guards."

"But these are his *mother's* guards," Eli said, pointing at Josef. "It feels rude."

Josef's lip curled into a dark smile. "They're guards in Osera. If they can't take a little hit to the head, they shouldn't be here." He turned away from Eli's grimace to face the closed door at the end of the gallery. "Let's get this over with."

He strode down the hall and opened the door with a shove. The first thing Eli noticed about the royal chamber was that, for the home of the monarch of a wealthy nation, it was remarkably cramped. The room was as narrow as the gallery, and the dark tapestries depicting battles and hunts that covered most of the stone walls made it feel only smaller. Same for dim light coming from the half-lit candelabra that hung from the high, but not impressively high, ceiling. There was a raised, wooden dais at the far end of the room, obviously meant for receiving guests in royal fashion, but the ornate chair at its center was empty and the gold-plated lamps were dark. For several seconds, Eli thought they'd come all this way for nothing, but then his eyes drifted to the small fireplace in the corner. There, a low couch was pulled up to the feeble fire, and on it, lying buried under a large blanket, was an old woman.

The firelight dug deep shadows below her eyes, painting her wrinkles in long black gouges. There was a stack of papers on her lap, but she wasn't looking at them. Instead, she lay back on the pillows with her eyes shut and her thin mouth pressed in a tight line, as though she were biting her teeth against some long-running pain. Her hair, a thin, brittle mix of pale gold and white, lay spread out on the pillows behind her, freshly washed and combed, though Eli saw no one who could have combed it. The three of them hung at the door, hesitant. The room was so dark, the scene of the old woman sleeping by the fire so private, Eli felt almost guilty stepping inside. Even Josef seemed to have lost his urgency. He stood hovering beside Eli, his scarred face strangely blank as he watched the old woman sleeping.

It was the woman herself who broke the silence. One second Eli would have bet his bounty she was deep asleep, the next her voice rang clear and cold through the room.

"I gave strict orders I was not to be disturbed," she said, pale eyes cracking open under her narrow, furrowed brows. "If this is not a matter of national emergency, I..." Her voice trailed off when she spotted Josef, and her whole, skeletal body went white as chalk.

Josef stiffened, and Eli leaned back to watch. He loved family reunions. He rather hoped the old woman would cry, if for no other reason than to see how Josef's stony swordsman routine would hold up under a mother's tears. But when the queen spoke again, her voice was even colder than before.

"Home at last," she said. "Why am I not surprised to find you sneaking in like a thief in the night, Thereson?"

"You put the bounty on my head," Josef said. "How else did you expect me to arrive when you made me a criminal, mother?"

The anger in Josef's voice made Eli wince, but the woman, whom Eli now knew was Queen Theresa, seemed unmoved.

"You left me little other recourse," she said. "It is a sad lot for Osera when her prince requires such drastic measures to bring him back to his duty."

Josef crossed his arms over his chest. "I'm not here to relive old fights," he growled. "I came only because you made it clear that you were willing to bankrupt Osera to get me home. So here I am. Now tell me what you want so I can tell you no and we can be done with this idea that I'm still yours to command."

Theresa's pale lips curled in a long, slow smile. "But you are, child. You've proved it, just now. You came back. It is but a tiny shred of the responsibility my son should hold, but it is a shred more than many thought you had."

Josef gritted his teeth. "Get on with it."

Slowly, with great effort, Queen Theresa sat up. She pulled her thin, bony hand from beneath the blanket and held it out, pointing out the tiny window east, toward the Unseen Sea. "The Immortal Empress has returned."

Josef's shoulders tensed, but his voice remained insultingly casual. "So? What do you want me to do about it?"

Theresa's eyes narrowed. "Your duty," she spat. "After fifteen years of silence, the Empress's shipyards are active again. My spies report a fleet of palace ships nearly finished. You are Oseran; you know what that means." Her voice began to quiver. "She is coming, Thereson. If we are to stand against her, Osera must be strong."

"Osera is strong," Josef said.

"But I am not," Theresa said, her bony hand clenching into a shaking fist.

Josef sighed. "You don't look that bad."

"Really?" the queen snapped. "Look at me again." She raised her hand to her face, pressing her thin fingers into the deep hollows of her cheeks. "Look."

Josef looked, jaw clenched. "Fine, you look terrible. Is that what you want me to say? I'm sorry you're sick, but—"

The queen's gray eyes grew stony, shutting Josef's mouth with a single look. "Sick?" she said softly. "*Sick* is what I've been for the last five years, not that you would know. But I'm no longer sick, Thereson. I am dying. Even my doctors have stopped pretending I will see another year."

Eli could hear Josef's teeth grinding, but the queen didn't flinch. For the first time, Eli could see the family resemblance. The queen looked like Josef did right before he threw his sword away and grabbed the Heart.

"Disappointment that you are," she said, "you are my only child, the only full-blooded heir remaining to the Throne of Iron Lions. If our line is to continue, you must—"

"Must what?" Josef said with a bitterness Eli had never heard in his voice before. "Maybe you've forgotten in your old age, mother, but you were the one who told me I would never be king. That you would disown me if I continued my 'swordsman nonsense.'" He laid his hand on the Heart of War's wrapped hilt. "My sword has stood me better than your throne. I won't abandon it just because you've changed your mind."

"My mind remains as it ever has," the queen said through clenched teeth. "So does your stubborn ability to hear what you want instead of what I say. Listen closely, boy. I'm not asking you to be king."

Josef froze. "You're not?"

"Of course not." Theresa lay back on her lounge with a huff. "Do you have any idea how hard I fought to inherit when my father died? How hard I fought to stay queen when my own cousins said a woman could never lead Osera? Do you think I'd leave that hard-won legacy to a selfish, violent, shiftless brat who doesn't have the presence of mind to be a prince, much less a king?"

She tilted her head, waiting for an answer. When none came, she continued. "Your cousin, Finley, will become king when I pass."

"Finley?" Josef roared. "Powers, woman! If you had an heir, why did you drag me all the way out here?"

"Because Osera has no heir!" the queen roared back. "Finley's not an Eisenlowe. He's blood enough to take the throne in an emergency, but not to pass it on to his son. Honestly," she huffed, "after all I spent on your tutors, I'd have hoped you'd remember something of Oseran law."

Josef shook his head, but Theresa held up her hand, cutting him off before he could get a word in. "I'm not asking you to be king, Thereson," she said coldly. "But I am asking you to do your duty to the family. There is only one royal blood line in Osera, and, tragically, that line runs through you. We have no other options. You must give Osera an heir."

Josef recoiled in horror. "An heir? You mean—"

"A baby, yes," his mother said. "I'm sure even you can manage that much. I know the princess can."

This was enough to make Eli break his uncharacteristic silence. "Wait, princess?"

"Yes," the queen said, raising her voice. "Adela!"

Josef pressed his hand to his forehead as the door to the queen's chamber burst open and a squad of guards marched into the room.

There were a dozen of them at least, but Eli's attention was on the woman who led them. She was shockingly lovely. As tall as Josef and clad in shining silver armor with an ornate short sword at her hip. Her hair was deep brown, almost black, and braided tight against her head. Her skin was the warm, healthy tan of someone who spent most of her time outdoors, but her brown eyes were narrowed in the cold stare of an absolute professional as she marched toward them.

Eli raised his hands without prompting, but the woman brushed past him, going straight for Josef. Eli felt Nico stiffen, and he put a warning hand on her arm. The other guards were fanning out around them, cutting off the exits. Nico glanced at him, then at Josef, and then at the door, but Eli shook his head. Josef hadn't moved yet.

Now that the door was open, another woman, older but also shockingly lovely despite her simple black dress, walked briskly into the queen's chamber and hurried to Theresa's side. Eli tilted his head, watching as the woman began to fuss over the queen. But Theresa shook her head and gently pushed the woman's hands away.

"I'm fine," she said. "Thank you, Lenette."

The woman in black nodded and fell back, surrendering her place beside the queen to the young, armored woman. The circle of guards tightened, and Eli glanced at Josef, but the swordsman still hadn't moved. He simply stood there, staring at the queen. For her part, Theresa was leaning back on her pillows, enjoying the turned tables.

"Thereson," she said, placing her hand on the lovely young woman's arm. "You remember Adela, don't you?"

"How could I forget?" Josef grumbled. His mother arched an eyebrow, and he adjusted his tone. "Good evening, Princess Adela."

"Prince Thereson," the woman said with a nod.

Eli looked from the lovely woman to Josef and back again. There wasn't much resemblance, but...

"Your sister?" he guessed.

"No," Josef said. "That's my wife."

Utter silence descended. Even Eli was speechless. But it wasn't Eli who recovered first. The voice that broke the silence was Nico's.

"Wife?"

Eli groaned inwardly. Nico was staring at Josef, eyes wide with a look of complete betrayal.

"Wife?"

"It's not what it looks like!" Josef shouted, stabbing his finger at the queen. "*She* married me in absentia last year. I didn't even know about it until a few months ago."

Eli took a deep breath. He *knew* he shouldn't rise to it, that now was not the time, but for once his tongue was faster than his good sense. "*Months ago?*" he cried. "And when exactly were you planning on sharing this bit of important social news?"

"Never," Josef said. "Because it's *not* important. It wasn't like I had a say. I can't control what my mother does without my knowledge."

Nico took a step back. She was still staring at Josef, her eyes so wide Eli could see the whites all the way around.

"Nico," Josef said, his voice warning.

She took another step.

Josef looked at her, his face as close to panic as Eli had ever seen it. "Nico, listen—"

Before he could say anything else, Nico vanished. There was no sound, no flash. She simply snuffed out like a candle.

After that, everything happened at once.

Josef roared curses as the startled guards rushed forward, swords drawn. Eli put up his hands as a blade pressed into his back, but when a guard tried the same to Josef, the swordsman whirled around, grabbed the sword out of the guard's hand, and threw him to the ground so hard the man bounced. The guard's sword followed a second later as Josef, still cursing, threw it hilt first at the man's head.

With that, Josef straightened up, rolled his shoulders, and started for the door. Started, and then stopped cold. Eli blinked in surprise. He hadn't seen her move, hadn't heard her, but the princess was suddenly right behind Josef, the tip of her short sword pressed into his right shoulder.

"That's enough, Prince Thereson," she said quietly. "One more step and I sever the ligament that moves your sword arm. Hands where I can see them, please."

Josef put his hands out slowly, and the princess turned him around to face the queen again.

"What was that?" the queen said in a low, angry voice. "What have you gotten yourself involved with, Thereson?"

Eli gritted his teeth. Things were rapidly falling apart. It wasn't so much the sword at his own back. He could duck out of that easily enough. But he could see Josef's hands shaking as the queen questioned him. The swordsman was pale with rage, the kind that took some good old-fashioned violence to pull him out of, and the queen wasn't letting up. It was up to Eli to act fast before Josef did something they'd regret.

"Your majesty," he said, stepping past Josef and the princess with a florid bow, much to his guard's surprise. Josef whipped around, but Eli stomped on his toes before the swordsman could say anything and smiled his best smile at the queen. "I believe we've started this on the wrong foot."

The queen looked down her nose at him, quite a feat, considering he was standing and she was sitting. "And who are you? What makes you think you have the right to speak in my presence?"

Eli's smile grew even more charming. "Because I am the son of one of your oldest allies." He reached into his coat pocket and drew out a creased slip of paper, which he handed to the queen with a flourish. "Eliton Banage."

"Banage?" The queen frowned, confused. "You are Etmon's son?"

"The very same," Eli said as she took the paper from his fingers. "And every bit as much of a disappointment to him as our dear Josef is to you."

The queen glanced at the paper. "This is a Council identity paper for a child," she said. "And it's almost two decades out of date."

"I don't get home much," Eli said, his voice deepening to a tragic note. "My father and I don't get along, as you can see. But he always spoke very highly of you and his time fighting for Osera against the Empress."

Queen Theresa arched an eyebrow. "I sincerely doubt that," she said, handing the slip of paper to the lovely lady in black. "You won't object if I ask Lenette to check the validity of your statement? I will admit there is a family resemblance, but I must be sure. Still"—her eyes narrowed—"you are the right age."

Eli gave her his best innocent look. The queen didn't seem to buy it.

"Well," Theresa said, sitting back. "If you are indeed Etmon's son, then I welcome you, but this is a family matter. You'd do best to stay out of it."

Eli's face clouded with a look of deep pain. "I understand your reticence, your grace," he said gently. "But your son and I have been thick as thieves for a while now. I know him as I know myself, and, if I may be so bold, I don't think you have things quite by the right end." He clasped his hands, and his voice shook with earnest emotion. "Whatever terms he may have left you on, your majesty, Josef dropped everything to come here when he saw those posters.

Even I was inspired. He's trying to do the right thing, but it's not easy. He's been living his life moment to moment as a mercenary for years, and now, to suddenly hear that he's expected to father a child with a wife he's known about for only a few months, that's a bone for any man to swallow. As you saw, the mere mention was too much for our other companion."

"Yes," the queen said, leaning forward. "What about your companion?"

"Oh, Nico does that all the time," Eli said, waving her words away. "She's quite the escape artist. Some people swear she disappears into thin air, but I'm sure your majesty is not one to be fooled by such cheap tricks."

The queen glared at him. "I don't care for your quick tongue, Mr. Banage. Get to the point."

Eli's smile faltered just a hair. "My point, majesty, is that we've been traveling for a week solid to come into your presence, and we're tired. Surely you would not begrudge your son a night to think things over before he's forced into the marriage bed?" He turned his smile to the princess, who still had her sword pressed into Josef's back. "Lovely as this young lady is, it's a big change for our Josef, and he takes to change about as well as a rock takes to floating. I'm sure that in the morning, once he's had time to think about what he owes his family, he'll be much more tractable."

The queen tilted her head, considering. "The young Banage makes a good point," she said. "Adela, release him."

The sword vanished from Josef's back, and the princess stepped aside to stand next to the queen once again. The other soldiers stood down as well, and Eli breathed a sigh of relief.

Josef lowered his arms and turned around, glaring daggers at his mother. The queen met him in kind, glaring so hard Eli was afraid the air between them would start to boil.

"Your friend has bought you a night of reprieve," she said at last. "You will stay in the palace tonight. The guards will take you to your rooms, but before that, I want you to look at me."

Josef's jaw clenched, but the queen cut him off before he could get a word out.

"No," she said quietly. "Do not speak. Look."

And with that, the queen tossed aside her blanket with a bony hand. Lenette and Adela both moved to help her, but the queen pushed them away. Slowly, painfully, Theresa pulled herself to her feet, standing by her own power before the fire.

It was a sad sight. The silk nightgown hung from the queen's bony shoulders. Her arms were so thin, Eli could have wrapped his hand all the way around her bicep. If her back were straight, she might have been as tall as Josef, but the queen was bent with age, her spine curved in an unnatural arc that forced her to lean forward. Even so, she straightened as well as she could before holding out her arms.

"Look at me, Prince Thereson," she said, her voice as hard as the stone around them. "Look at what is left of Osera's queen. The Empress's hammer falls on our shores, and this weak, dying body is all that stands to face her. You've been stubborn as a pig all your life, but if I ever did my duty as your mother, as your queen—if I ever instilled even a stirring of love for you homeland in that bitter, guarded heart of yours, then, just this once, listen to my command. Do your duty. Be Osera's prince, if only to pass on the blood of our ancestors, and I will never bother you again."

She stood a moment longer, and then fell back onto her couch. Lenette was at her side immediately, fussing and pressing the queen's blanket back across her legs. The queen paid the lady no mind. Her eyes never left Josef's, daring him to defy her again. Josef didn't say a word. When the guards moved to lead them away, Josef let them, but he never stopped watching his mother until the guards closed her doors behind them.

In Eli's experience, "room" was a royal euphemism for prison cell, and his suspicions proved correct. The guards led them up a flight of stairs to a nondescript hall lined with heavy wooden doors, not barred but not exactly inviting either. They stopped at two doors right next to each other. Josef went through the first, Eli the second, stumbling in as the guards locked the iron bolt from the outside with a solid click.

Eli sighed at the barred door and then took a moment to consider his situation. He'd been in nicer cells, but not many. There was a feather bed, a porcelain washstand, an ornate wooden table with books, cards, and a lamp turned low. The wooden floor was carpeted, and the bars on the narrow window were tastefully obscured behind thick curtains. It was all very well done and, for a lesser man, very secure. Eli, however, was the greatest thief in the world. Five minutes after the guards left, he was hanging off the palace's outer wall, banging on Josef's shuttered window.

The swordsman opened the shutters on the third knock, and Eli wiggled through the bars to land in a heap on Josef's rug.

"Well," he said, brushing himself off. "That was exciting. Ready to go?"

Josef sat down on his bed and didn't answer. Eli stood up, casing the room as he did. It was identical to his own, but Josef had pushed the writing table into the corner and was using the chair to prop up his weaponry with the Heart leaning against the wall. Eli grimaced, glancing from swords to swordsman. Josef bladeless was always a bad sign. Nico was also still conspicuously absent, despite the dozens of shadows available. Very bad indeed. He would have to tread lightly.

He walked over and took a seat on the bed, sinking down beside Josef.

"Listen," he said. "Remember the plan? We made it. We talked to your mother. She told you what you were going to do, and then you told her what you were going to do. So that's it. We're done."

Josef stared straight ahead and said nothing.

"I've been thinking about finding a nice job down south," Eli continued. "Big money, exotic locals, lots of good fights. If we leave tonight we can probably catch the pirate king's fleet before he goes back to sea. He's supposed to employ some of the nastiest swordsmen on the continent. What do you say?"

He turned to Josef with a bright smile, but the swordsman didn't even look his way, and Eli's smile fell into a scowl.

"*Powers*, Josef," he said, kicking the bed. "Snap out of it. We're thieves, remember? No one expects anything from us. The queen makes a nice speech, but no country teeters on the presence of one man. You already have a cause, remember? You swore to become the greatest swordsman in the world, the worthy wielder of the Heart of War. That's a noble goal, and you can't achieve it here." He stood up, tugging Josef's sleeve. "Come on, get your things. I'll call for Nico and we'll all get out of here together, tonight, just like we planned."

He walked to the window and was getting ready to climb out when Josef finally spoke.

"I can't."

Eli closed his eyes and cursed silently. When that was done, he turned, keeping his face cheerfully neutral. "Why not?"

Josef made a frustrated sound and ran his scarred hands through his newly trimmed hair. "Do you know why I became a swordsman?"

"Because you're good at it?" Eli guessed.

"Because it's the *only* thing I'm good at," Josef said. "I was a miserable failure at everything else, being a prince, being a son, being a politician. I hated it, all of it. Swordsmanship was the only thing that made life livable. The only thing I wanted to do."

He stopped, and Eli shifted awkwardly. This was the most Josef had ever told him about his past, and he wasn't sure what the swordsman expected him to say. Finally, he settled for putting a comforting hand on Josef's shoulder. Josef didn't seem to notice.

"I made my choice when I was fifteen," he said, his voice low. "In Osera, everything's about the queen. You live for the queen, fight for the queen, die for the queen. I didn't want to live for her, didn't want to live for anyone. I wanted to be a swordsman, to fight for the sake of getting better, not because I was ordered to. So I took my swords and I left. Just walked out. I swore that I would return only when I had become the greatest swordsman in the world." He clutched his fists together with an intensity that made Eli flinch. "The *best*," he said again. "Don't you see? If I falter, if I take even one step back, then all the problems I caused by leaving—my mother's suffering, the messed-up succession, Osera's shame at having a runaway prince—it will be for *nothing*."

"Josef," Eli said. "It's not—"

"That's why I never came home before when she tried to make me," Josef rolled right over him. "But as soon as I saw the poster, I knew this time was different."

He looked up, and Eli saw with a shock that his eyes were red.

"She's dying, Eli." Josef's voice was so soft Eli could barely make out the words. "My mother is dying. Believe me, I want to dive out that window with you, but I can't. Not now." He took a deep breath and leaned back, staring up at the ceiling. "Her telling me she didn't want me to be king was the final straw, you know. If she'd been unreasonable and demanded that I give up swordsmanship and take the throne, I could have told her to shove off. But all she wants is an heir, a child of the blood to preserve the family. How can I deny her such a small request?"

Eli didn't think a child was a small request, but he said nothing. They sat for a long while, letting the silence hang like a dead thing in the air between them. Finally, Eli heaved an enormous sigh.

"Bugger all," he grumbled, pushing himself off the bed. "You picked a really bad time to have a fit of responsibility. Nico's back on her game, we finally have the chance to pull some real heists, and you have to get all prodigal son on me, *Thereson*."

"Don't start, *Eliton*," Josef snapped. "You must be feeling suicidal, posing as the Rector Spiritualis's son. What made you think of that?"

"It was the best trick I had," Eli said, keeping his voice casual. "Queen Theresa's debt to Banage is well known. The name gave her cause to think twice at the very least, and if I hadn't given her a compelling reason not to throw me out, you'd be spending tonight with the lovely Adela. Of course," he said, glaring down at Josef, "if I'd known you were going to get all noble prince on me, I wouldn't have bothered."

Josef let the barb roll off with a shrug. "You're being thicker than usual if you think it isn't going to come back around," he said. "This isn't some idiot guard you're bluffing. You know the queen is going to check. I'd bet money the Spirit Court is here tomorrow morning, hunting for your hide."

"Really?" Eli said. "How much money?"

Josef arched an eyebrow. "You have a good reason why they wouldn't be?"

Eli folded his arms behind his back. "Let me come at this from another angle for you. Anyone who pays attention to bounties knows that Josef Liechten pals around with Eli Monpress, right? So think, what happens when you show up out of nowhere with a handsome young man who looks even a little like the posters? Queen Theresa hasn't hung onto her throne as long as she has by being an idiot. She'd figure things out real quick. By giving her another trail to sniff, I bought us time to escape. Which, of course, is wasted now."

Josef rolled his eyes. "Yeah, yeah. Still doesn't explain why you chose Banage. Seems needlessly reckless to me."

Eli smiled grimly. "I wasn't lying when I said the Rector Spiritualis was ashamed of his son. Let's just say that Banage has more on the line than most in making sure that any Eliton appearances stay uninvestigated. Your mother can send messages all she likes, but if we see so much as an apprentice come down to investigate, I'll eat your sword."

"Now that I'd pay to see," Josef said, tugging off his boots. "Get out of here, I'm going to bed. If I have to be home, I'm not doing it on no sleep."

"Bridegrooms do need their sleep," Eli said sagely.

The look Josef gave him wiped the smile clear off Eli's face, and the thief wisely decided it was time to leave his friend alone. He stood up and wiggled out the window as easily as he'd wiggled in. He had time for one last wave before Josef slammed the shutter behind him. Duly rebuked, Eli hung on the stone ledge momentarily, searching the shadows for Nico. He knew she was there. He could almost feel her watching. He called her name softly, but there was no answer, nothing but the wind blowing up the mountain and the sound of the city below.

Feeling defeated and more than a little angry, Eli pulled himself along the ledge and through the bars into his room. He landed on the carpet and picked himself up, snuffing out the lamp with a wave of his hand. He crossed the dark room and collapsed facedown on his bed. He rolled around awhile, wiggling out of his clothes and tossing his wig over the bedpost. Finally undressed, he flopped onto the pile of pillows, turning his head from side to side in a futile attempt to cut off the massive headache he could already feel forming. Fifteen minutes later he was still awake, his head throbbing full force. Eli sighed in a drawn-out curse, grinding the heels of his palms deep into his eye sockets.

It was going to be a long night.

CHAPTER

7

Miranda stomped five steps across her cell, hit the stone bars, turned on her heel, and stomped five steps back to the wall. She slapped her hand against the smooth, featureless stone before turning around to start all over again. Five steps, slap. Five steps, slap. Miranda gritted her teeth. The endless stomping was stupid, a waste of time and energy, and yet she could not stop. If she didn't do something with all the rage inside her, she would explode.

Across the hall, Gin shoved his nose through the stone bars of his cell, orange eyes narrowed to slits against the constant white glow that seeped from the mountain's stone. "Do it," he snarled. "It's past time for patience."

Miranda shook her head and glanced at Slorn. He was sitting as he had been since they'd arrived, cross-legged at the center of his cell. His dark bear eyes were closed against the whiteness, his breathing was deep, and his face was slack, as though he were asleep. It was his ears that gave him away. They stood taut on his head, shifting to follow every sound Miranda made.

He'd been like this since the Guildmaster had locked them in here two days ago, completely silent, no matter how many questions she asked. It was his silence that made her angrier than anything else. She'd followed him here like a little dog, licking up every bit of information he'd thrown her, but now that he'd landed her in prison, he wouldn't even talk to her. Just thinking about it made her shake with fury, but as much as she wanted to follow Gin's urging, Miranda held back. It wasn't the bars that kept her in. Gin could have broken them, she was sure, or any of her spirits could have, for the Shapers had not taken her rings. Once she was free, she was pretty sure that she could find her way out of the mountain if it came to that, but she didn't try to leave. She couldn't. Angry as she was, she'd followed Slorn to this mountain to help right whatever was going wrong with the world. Now that they were finally here, she wasn't about to give up and leave just because things weren't going like she wanted. Of course, that didn't mean she was going to forgive Slorn for clamming up on her when she needed him most.

Across the hall, Gin pressed his nose against the stone bars, his tail lashing across the wall behind him. Miranda shook her head again, more firmly this time. Gin snorted and looked away, grumbling to himself. Miranda just took a deep breath and went back to her stomping. It might not help anything, but at least it gave her something to do. So she walked, watching her worn boots slap against the glowing white stone, five steps forward and five steps back.

She was still going two hours later when Slorn finally spoke.

"He's coming," Slorn said.

Miranda nearly tripped over her own feet. "What?"

On the other side of the stone lattice, Slorn was getting up. Gin was on his feet as well, his quivering nose pressed against the stone bars. Miranda ran to the edge of her own cell. They'd gotten their food an hour ago, so it couldn't be time yet for the guard to return. But if she strained she could hear the distant sound of footsteps. One person, coming this way.

Miranda pushed away from the bars and started waking her rings, stirring each spirit. Mellinor was already awake when she touched him. He waited at the bottom of her consciousness, a deep, quiet pool, ready if needed. Gin was pacing in his long cell, his patterns shifting in tight swirls. He kept his head down and his teeth bared, ready to jump the second Miranda gave the signal. Only Slorn was calm. He stood at the door to his cell, arms folded behind him, waiting patiently as the steps came closer.

By the time the footsteps reached them, Miranda was ready. She clung to the barred door, rings flashing, but when the person came around the corner, she blinked in surprise. She'd expected another guard, but it was the Guildmaster himself who walked into view.

He wore a silk robe even finer than the one he'd worn the first time Miranda saw him. He did not look Slorn in the eye when he stopped in front of the bear-headed man's cell, but his voice was the essence of calm as he addressed them, opening the cells with a wave of his hand.

"The Teacher will see you now."

And with that, the Guildmaster turned on his heel and marched back the way he'd come. Slorn stepped out of his cell, falling into pace behind the old man. A moment later, Miranda did the same. Gin brought up the rear, stalking along with his head down and his ears flat, growling deep in his throat.

When they'd first entered the mountain, the Guildmaster had taken them down to their cells through a maze of white glowing tunnels. This time, he led them up, following a wide, inclined tunnel that seemed to curve in on itself in a tightening spiral. He did not speak. Neither did Slorn. Miranda had several things she would have liked to say, but she kept her mouth shut as well. After all, it wasn't like she was going to get an answer.

After ten minutes of climbing, the curving tunnel ended at a wide, circular platform. Miranda looked around, confused. It looked like a dead end, but even as she started to bring this point to the Guildmaster's attention, the high ceiling slid away with a soft scrape, revealing a long tunnel up through the mountain. Forgetting her dignity for a moment, Miranda gaped openly at the enormous hole that had suddenly appeared above her. It seemed to go up forever, a curved tunnel of pure, glowing white stretching as far as she could see.

She was still gawking when she heard Gin take a hissing breath. A second later, the floor began to vibrate under her boots, and then it started to lift. Miranda gasped and flung out her arms for balance, but it was Slorn who caught her hand and kept her from falling. The bear-headed man held her eyes just long enough for a small, subtle wink before letting her go as the stone platform under their feet rose smoothly into the glowing tunnel. The platform picked up speed as they went, moving faster and faster until Miranda could feel gravity pulling on her bones. Then, as quietly as it had started, the platform slowed. A new, stronger light flashed overhead as a door opened in the side of the tunnel as their platform slid to a gentle stop before the largest, most beautiful hall Miranda had ever seen.

The sheer size of it took her breath away. The hall stretched out forever, larger than the Spirit Court's hearing chamber, larger than the throne room at Mellinor, larger than the cave below the Council, larger, in fact, than any room she'd ever seen. The stone was the same glowing white as the lower levels, but where it had been smooth down below, here the rock was carved in subtle patterns that played with the stone's light. Fat pillars dozens of feet across sprouted like trees from the polished floor at regular intervals, rising up to meet the arc of the carved ceiling high, high overhead. The walls curved as well, following the natural slope of the mountain. There were several large doors leading to smaller halls that branched into unseen rooms, but the largest of all was at the other end of the hall, directly across from where they stood. There, a great door pierced the wall of the mountain itself, opening out onto a large, circular balcony that looked down on the sleeping mountains, their snow-covered peaks glittering in the light of the full moon.

Miranda caught her breath. Locked in the mountain, she hadn't even realized it was night. She also hadn't realized that the moving platform had taken them so high. They must be close to the mountain's peak.

The Guildmaster stepped off the platform and into the hall, walking briskly across the carved, glowing stone. Miranda pulled her coat tight around her shoulders and followed. The hall was nearly empty, but those few Shapers who were milling between the great stone pillars stopped to stare as the Guildmaster led his prisoners past them and through the middle of the great, white hall.

Miranda stole glances at Slorn as they walked, but the bear-headed Shaper's face was carefully neutral. Still, the Guildmaster was far ahead, and she decided to risk it.

"What is this place?" she whispered, careful not to look at him.

"The Hall of the Shapers," Slorn answered, just as quietly. His muffled voice sounded almost wistful.

Before Miranda could ask what that was, the Guildmaster stopped. They were standing directly in the center of the hall, between the moving platform that had brought them up here and the balcony door. The hall's center was marked with a circle of raised stone carved in looping patterns that made Miranda's head swim. The Guildmaster stepped into the circle and motioned for them to do the same. When they were all inside, the Guildmaster stepped out again.

"I don't know why the Teacher bothers," he said. "I only hope you do not disappoint him, Heinricht."

Though he hid it well, Miranda could hear the lingering resentment in the Guildmaster's voice, and she got the feeling he wasn't used to being excluded from whatever was about to happen. Slorn, however, looked almost relieved.

"I am already outcast and imprisoned," he said. "What more can he do?"

The Guildmaster's face darkened. "Do not take these things lightly. The Teacher's decision is final, but even he is not without mercy." The old man leaned in, dropping his voice. "For once in your life, Heinricht, bow your stubborn head and ask the Teacher's forgiveness. Let me welcome my son home once again."

Slorn met the Guildmaster's gaze. "I will do what I have to, father. Just as I always have."

Miranda's eyebrows shot up, but before she could comment, the Guildmaster made a sharp gesture and the floor below their feet began to move. She scrambled for balance as the entire circle of stone began to rise upward, taking them with it. She caught one last glimpse of the Guildmaster as the old man's face fell, collapsing from anger to a look of deep sadness. Then he was gone, hidden by the rim of the rising stone pillar.

She turned to Slorn. "Father?"

"Yes," Slorn said.

She gave him a look of disbelief. "Your own father locked you up?"

"He is Guildmaster first," Slorn said. "There will be those among the Shapers who will say he is being too lenient with me, letting me see the Teacher. I am an oath breaker, after all. Shapers are sworn to the Mountain for life, but we ran when Nivel became a demonseed. It doesn't matter that they would have killed her if we stayed; we both broke our oath as Shapers."

Miranda folded her arms across her chest. "You could have told me."

"I could have," Slorn said. "I could have told you a lot of things, but anything I told you in the cell I would also have told the Teacher."

"What do you mean?" Miranda said. "There was no one there but us."

"This is the Shaper Mountain," Slorn said. "It is always listening."

Miranda frowned. "Who is the Teacher, then?"

"You'll know when you see him," Slorn said.

Miranda bit her lip. She was getting pretty sick of these half answers, but Slorn would say nothing more. In the end, all she could do was watch in silence as the stone above them lifted away, and the rising pillar vanished into the hall's ceiling with a soft scrape.

They were in another vertical tunnel. Glowing stone surrounded them on all sides, filling the air with cold, white light. The pillar of stone under their feet seemed to have no end. It rose slowly, pushing them farther and farther up into the mountain. Miranda arched her neck, trying to see where they were going, but she saw nothing except the endless white. Still, things were changing. The air was growing colder and thinner, the light brighter.

Just as Miranda was starting to feel light-headed, the platform began to slow. Stone scraped overhead and the white walls of the tunnel fell away, leaving them standing in a brilliant white glare. Miranda covered her face, blinking furiously. Slowly, her eyes adjusted to the brilliance, and she saw that they were standing in another enormous, white chamber.

It was smaller than the Hall of the Shapers below, but there were no pillars here, no supports of any kind. Just a perfect circle of stone, white and brilliant as the morning sun on fresh snow, and nothing else.

"There's no one here," Miranda whispered. "I thought you said we were going to see the Teacher."

"Just wait," Slorn said. "He likes to make an entrance."

Miranda didn't see how. The white chamber had no doors save

for the stone platform they were standing on. But as she opened her mouth to ask Slorn what he meant, the light went out.

She gasped and nearly fell into Gin. For a heartbeat, the chamber was pitch black. And then, as suddenly as it had vanished, light returned, and everything changed.

Color flooded the walls, a wave of brilliant green, brown, and blue that washed over the stone, leaving mountains, forests, and sky in its wake. The floor underfoot came alive with pinks and yellows, blues, whites, and soft greens, all flowing together in a wash before separating out into thousands of flowers. Suddenly, they were standing in a high mountain field. A stream sprung to life a few feet from Gin's tail, bouncing merrily down a bed of smooth white stones. Mountains loomed in the distance, their peaks taller than any Miranda had ever seen. Clouds drifted across the perfectly blue sky overhead, and the bright sunlight turned her hair fiery red, but when she held her hands up to the light, there was no warmth in it. The rushing stream threw off no spray and, despite the waving flowers under her feet, she could still feel the cold stone through the soles of her boots.

She looked at Slorn for some explanation, but he was staring across the valley at the mountains beyond. Or, rather, at the one mountain that rose above all others. Almost half again as tall as the next tallest peak, the Shaper Mountain stood before them in all its majesty. Its summit scraped the clear blue sky like a white knife. Its snowy slope was the same as Miranda had seen from Knife's Pass, but there was no sign of the windows and balconies of the Shapers, nor was there any sign of Knife's Pass itself. The road should have been directly below them, but it wasn't. The ravine and the bridge were also missing, leaving the smaller mountains whole and uncut all the way to the Shaper Mountain's feet. The little mountains were dotted with high mountain meadows just like the one they stood in, little verdant patches, peaceful and blooming in the golden sunlight.

Miranda blinked and turned to Slorn, waiting for some sort of explanation, but Slorn said nothing. He just stood there, staring at the sky, his brown bear eyes open as wide as they could go. Frowning, she turned to Gin, but the ghosthound wasn't any better. He was crouched at her feet as close to her as he could get, his orange eyes wide as dinner plates.

"Gin?" she whispered.

The dog didn't even look at her. "Can't you see it, Miranda?"

She frowned. "What?"

Next to her, Slorn took a shuddering breath. "I thought...I mean, I always suspected, but I never imagined it would be so large. So...endless."

"*What?*" Miranda asked again, growing supremely annoyed.

"The world," a deep voice rumbled. "Or what it was."

Miranda jumped before she could stop herself. The voice came from under her feet, vibrating up through her legs from the stone below the fluttering illusion of flowers. Beside her, Gin lowered his head with a soft whine.

"Tell me your names." The words buzzed through Miranda's body, more vibration than sound, but they carried an authority she could feel in her bones.

"Teacher," Slorn said. "I am Heinricht Slorn."

"I know who you are," the mountain said, for Miranda knew it could be no other. "I remember all my children, even the ones who desert me. I am eager to hear what excuses you've thought up to convince me to take you back, but for now, tell me, who is this woman?"

Miranda stepped forward. "I am Miranda Lyonette, a Spiritualist of the Spirit Court. This is Gin, my—"

"I do not need the lesser spirits' names," the mountain rumbled dismissively. "They know their place. But I am curious as to how the core of a great water spirit came to live inside a human. Mellinor, can you still speak?"

"I can."

Miranda steeled herself as Mellinor's spirit surged forward, rising in a plume of deep blue water from her fingers, which she held out for him.

"I see you have escaped your prison," the mountain said.

The water dipped in a bow. "With Miranda's assistance, great mountain."

"A strange arrangement, to be sure," the mountain said. "But then, you water spirits always did flow down the easiest route."

"I did what I had to," Mellinor said.

The meadow flickered as the mountain laughed. "As do we all, inland sea, as do we all. I am satisfied. You may return to your human shore."

The water retreated, and Mellinor flowed back into Miranda, who lowered her arm cautiously. Something odd was going on, besides the obvious. Mellinor was being surprisingly deferential. Her sea spirit wasn't rude, but he was a Great Spirit and he didn't tend to let others forget that. This meekness was very out of character. Perhaps it was because the mountain was so much bigger than Mellinor's diminished form? But he'd shown no such deference to the West Wind.

"Now," the mountain said. "To business. Why have you come home, Heinricht? Or do I call you Heinricht anymore? You are as much bear as man, now."

"I am still myself," Slorn said. "And I came home because I had no more reason to run. Nivel is dead. Her seed has been taken by the League."

"I am sorry," the mountain said.

As the stone spoke, the flowering grass began to dance in an unfelt wind. All over the valley, the sunlight faded, and Miranda looked up to see dark clouds rolling in from the south. Within moments, the meadow was covered in a thin, misty rain. But though she could see the rain falling, hear it hitting her shoulders, she was not wet.

"What's happening?" she whispered.

"The Teacher is grieving," Slorn answered.

"Of course I grieve," the mountain said. "Nivel was my student before she was your wife."

"Then you should know she continued to abide by your teachings," Slorn said bitterly. "Even after you would have murdered her."

The soft rain became a downpour as Slorn finished, and the ground shook with the mountain's anger.

"It was the demon who murdered your wife," the mountain said. "Not I. Nivel died the moment the spirit eater took her. All you achieved by running was to delay the inevitable, putting all of us at risk in the process."

Slorn bared his sharp teeth. "The end might have been inevitable, but our work was not in vain. Nivel lived for ten years with that seed inside her, and even then it was not the demon who killed her. She was murdered by a rogue League member who took her seed for his own. Had he not appeared, she would still be alive, doing your work."

"And what work of mine could a demonseed do?" the mountain said. "Demon-panicked spirits cannot be Shaped."

"The first affirmation of all Shapers is the collection of knowledge," Slorn answered. "That's the pledge you have us make, and Nivel and I never forsook it. We spent those ten years researching demonseeds. Through our work, Nivel lived eight years longer than any seed on record." He reached into his coat, taking out a small, leather-bound book. "I have here detailed observations," he said, holding the book up in the phantom rain. "Mine and hers, from the day we left the mountain to the day I surrendered her seed to the League. I believe our research contains more information about the demon than any spirits have ever collected before, including the League, and I am prepared to give all of this knowledge to you. With the Shapers' help, we could save countless lives, maybe even one day reverse the demon infestation."

The rain began to slack as he spoke, and the clouds rolled away, leaving the mountain gleaming white in the freshly washed sunshine. Its stone slope had not changed, and yet, somehow, Miranda got the feeling the mountain was sneering at them.

"You would give me knowledge of how to prolong a demonseed's life?" the Teacher said.

"Yes," Slorn answered. "I can already make manacles that retard the seed's growth and cloth that hides the demon's presence, allowing it to walk among spirits without terrifying them. But these are only crutches, stopgaps. With your help, I hope to find a way to reverse the seed's conquest of the host, perhaps even remove the seed without—"

"Enough."

Slorn stiffened. "What do you—"

"You wasted your freedom studying the wrong thing," the mountain said. "Extending the seed's life? Hiding it? Why would we want to do that? If you'd found a way to pinpoint seeds before they wake, that I could perhaps condone, but demonseeds are a menace, Heinricht, not something to be coddled and hidden."

"Menace?" Slorn growled. "A feral dog is a *menace*. Demonseeds are the greatest disaster we've ever known waiting to happen. Each seed has the potential to become a demon every bit as dangerous as the one imprisoned under the Dead Mountain. I don't know if you were paying attention, but it nearly happened a few weeks ago not far from your own slopes. To ignore such a danger, to refuse to learn as much as we can about its nature, to remain willfully ignorant of the greatest threat to the spirits that form this world, *that* is the menace, Teacher. And that is why Nivel and my research is so important.

"Think what could happen if we could safely remove seeds from their hosts without killing them. Demonseeds would come forward willingly to be cured instead of running. The League would no longer have to hunt the seeds down or risk fighting them. Who knows? Each seed is an identical shard of the demon of the Dead Mountain itself. If we learn more about them, we might find a way to stop the Dead Mountain from sending them out, maybe even a way to get rid of the demon altogether. This knowledge, Nivel's knowledge, could be the beginning of the research that saves us from the demon forever."

The mountain rumbled as Slorn finished, a long, grinding slide of stone on stone that rattled Miranda's teeth. She barely noticed. This was it. This was why they'd come all this way. If the mountain got behind Slorn's plan, then this could well be the birth of an age of safety and freedom greater than anything the Spirit World had ever known. Not just freedom from the crippling fear she'd felt at Izo's and in the throne room at Mellinor, but also freedom for the seeds themselves. Unbidden, her mind flicked to Nico. Despite the company she kept and the wound she'd given Gin, Nico didn't deserve to be eaten by the demon. Neither had Slorn's wife. No spirit deserved it, and today she would make sure that, if the first steps toward ending the demon's infection of the world were not taken, it would not be because she did not try.

All around them, the scenery was changing. The flowering meadow withered and turned brown. Deep snow appeared on the mountain's slopes, and the sky grew dark as raw iron. Though the air had not changed, Miranda felt colder than ever. Still, she did not move until, at last, the mountain spoke.

"I am very sorry, Heinricht," it said, "but you have wasted your time. I don't know why you even thought to start this line of questioning, other than sentimentality. You should know better than any that demons are the sole realm of the Shepherdess and her League."

"But there's no reason we can't help." The words burst out of Miranda before she could stop them. "I've seen the League in action, and they are marvelous, but they would have lost at Izo's if not for Slorn and Mellinor's help."

"Who gave you leave to speak, human?" the mountain thundered, sending snow tumbling down its slopes. "Slorn is in disgrace, but he is still a Shaper. You are nothing to me. Why do you think you can raise your voice here?"

"Miranda!" Gin hissed, pressing his paw on her foot.

"No," Miranda said hotly, shaking her leg free of Gin's grip. "I've had enough of this. I may not be a Shaper, but I am a spirit. It's my world too. Why shouldn't I do whatever I can to help it?"

"It is not your place," the mountain rumbled.

"It is my place!" Miranda shouted back. "I am a Spiritualist! I am sworn on my life and my soul to protect the spirits from harm, and that's what I intend to do. You say this is League business, but I think it is reckless and ridiculous to leave the entirety of our well-being in the hands of a League we cannot call or control."

"The League is the only reason our world still exists, wizard," the mountain said.

"And I am grateful!" Miranda cried, shaking off Slorn's warning hand. "But if they, if *you* truly wanted to save the world rather than just preserve the status quo, you'd accept our help. If Slorn's knowledge truly can change the way we deal with demonseeds, if there's even a chance that this could prevent what happened in the mountains outside Izo's camp from happening again, then how can anyone say it is not worth trying?"

Miranda stopped, panting. She hadn't meant to say it that way, but the tirade had burst out of her. Gin was whimpering at her feet, his muscles tensed to grab her and run, even though there was nowhere to run to. Overhead, snow drifted silently from the gray sky, filling the valley in soft drifts until it was up to Miranda's knees. The snow hid the mountain like a veil, but nothing could dim the mountain's white, terrible presence. When the stone voice spoke again, its words were even colder than its icy slope.

"And what would you have me do, *Spiritualist*? Bring seeds here, into my stone, among my people, so that Heinricht can have his little experiments?" It gave a rumbling huff. "*You* are the one who is being ridiculous. Understand this, if you can: Letting a seed grow, even under controlled circumstances, is the most dangerous, reckless undertaking possible. Even if all of your postulations are correct, and some miraculous cure was found for the demonseeds, it would still not be worth the risk to my stone, my spirits, my people, or my standing with the Powers to pursue it. We have a system ordained by the Shepherdess for the protection of her flock. The Lord of Storms and his League have held back the demon since it was imprisoned. That is enough. Let it alone."

Miranda flushed and took a step forward, her mouth already open to challenge the mountain again, but Slorn's hand on her shoulder stopped her cold. She looked back to see the bear-headed Shaper staring up at the mountain, his yellow teeth bared.

"Were you just a Great Spirit, I would accept that logic," he growled. "But I am not the man I was ten years ago." He raised his hand and placed his longer fingers across his muzzle, the tips pointed at his large, brown, bear eyes. "I have seen many things since I merged with the bear. Learned many things that spirits have been taught never to speak of. But I am not a simple spirit. I am human. A human who *sees* as we were never meant to see, and I see you now, Durain, Lord of the Mountains."

"Stop," the mountain said.

But Slorn did not stop. "I thought the spirits deferred to you because of your great age and size. Now I see I was only half right. I see her mark on your soul. You are a star, a chosen spirit of the Shepherdess, elevated above all others. You are right. It would be intolerably risky for the Shapers to work on this problem alone, but we don't have to, do we? You can bring my knowledge to the Shepherdess herself—"

"*Enough!*" The mountain quaked, nearly knocking Miranda off her feet. Slorn stumbled too, but caught himself at the last moment. His eyes, however, never left the mountain.

"I begin to understand at last why the Shepherdess made your kind blind," the mountain said, its voice deep and annoyed. "Even though you see, you do not understand." The stone's shaking fell off to a slight vibration, almost like a sigh.

"What don't we understand?" Slorn said.

"Anything," the mountain grumbled, lowering its voice. "To start, you're right. I am a star of the Shepherdess, but the meaning of that title has changed over the long years." Its voice grew wistful. "We old souls were the greatest spirits left at the beginning. When the Shepherdess came into being and was given charge of the sphere, we worked together. She gave us her mark, her authority, which she herself had been given by the Creator, and made us her overseers. We were her hands in the world, keeping order among those spirits of our own kind. My twin brother and I were tasked with watching the mountains, and it took us both, for in those days all the mountains were awake. But then the world changed. The demon appeared."

The snow around the mountain began to swirl angrily. "Such a thing was supposed to be impossible. We gave up our freedom and entered the shell specifically to keep their kind out, and yet here was a demon, right among us. To this day, no one knows how it got in, but it destroyed half the world before the Shepherdess and her weapon, the Lord of Storms, cornered it. By that time the demon was so large the Shepherdess could not destroy it without breaking the world itself in the process. In the end, there was only one solution. It was my brother who made the sacrifice. He gave up his stone and his name to trap the demon so that we might live in peace. The Shepherdess took his body and buried the demon beneath it, fixing the prison in place with her seal. The moment the seal was in place, my brother's verdant slopes were abandoned, and his corpse became what we now call the Dead Mountain."

"Your twin brother," Miranda said, her face pale and her eyes wide. "You mean a mountain as large as you died to trap the demon?"

"Not died," the Shaper Mountain said. "Not entirely, though you would not recognize him if you saw him now."

The snow swirled, and Miranda shuddered as the weight of the mountain's full attention landed on them. "I tell you this, Heinricht, so that you may understand what those ill-gotten eyes of yours see. I may be her star, but it is the Shepherdess who rules this sphere, not us. Star or no, I am as much a slave to the Lady's will as any broken pebble."

"But you are no pebble," Slorn said. "You are the greatest spirit left in the world. And if you will do nothing—"

"You are a Shaper, Heinricht," the mountain said. "It is your nature to see a broken thing and wish to fix it. But this is our world, not a broken sword. We cannot simply reshape it into something better. We must live as the Shepherdess commands and hope things change before we all grow too sleepy and stupid to care."

Slorn frowned. "Too sleepy?"

"This world you know is a sad, diminished shadow," the mountain said. "Every year, more spirits fall asleep and do not wake. Of all my mountains, only a handful still answer when I call. The spirits grow small and stupid. They forget what lies beyond, what came before. But those of us who were Shaped by the Creator himself, we remember. We know the truth..."

As the mountain's voice faded, the landscape began to change. The snow slowed, and then stopped. The light shifted from slate gray to golden yellow as the icy clouds evaporated. Sunlight burst down onto the field, and the snowdrifts began to melt before Miranda's eyes. As they melted, flowers pushed their heads through the ice, opening in tiny bursts of color as the shrinking snowbanks gave way to bright green grass. But the flowers died almost as quickly as they had bloomed, their petals dropping to the grass, which was now fading to dead brown. The mountains vanished beneath a blanket of snow yet again as the meadow withered. But no sooner was the snow on the ground than it began to vanish, and the cycle began again.

Each time it was faster. The meadow and the mountains flashed between snow and life, blooming flowers, withered grass, and crusted snow trading places in breathless transition. Miranda shrank back against Gin, clutching his fur, but the ghosthound offered no comfort. His orange eyes were shut tight, and he was whining deep in his throat as the landscape around them melted, greened, bloomed, withered, and froze over and over again until Miranda was nearly sick from change.

Unlike Gin, Slorn's eyes were wide open. He was standing with his head tilted back, staring open-mouthed at the sky. Miranda swallowed and, against her better judgment, followed his gaze up. She was immediately sorry. The sky was changing just as fast as the world around them, flashing between day and night so rapidly it almost made her retch. But before she could look away, the cycle of dawn, day, dusk, and dark began to slow. At last, it stopped altogether, leaving her staring up at a night sky unlike anything she had ever seen.

She never knew how long they stared in silence. It felt like a lifetime. When she finally found her voice, the words came out more air than sound.

"What are they?"

"I don't know," Slorn answered just as quietly.

High overhead, cast around the crescent moon like scattered sand, points of light shone against the black velvet curve of the night sky. There were thousands of them, millions, more than Miranda could count if she spent the rest of her life doing nothing else. The twinkling lights seemed to gather at the middle of the sky, forming a road of light so beautiful and enormous, it brought tears to her eyes.

"This is my memory," the mountain said, its voice drifting on the gentle wind. "Here at my center, I am free of what the Shepherdess would have us forget. Here I remember the world as it was before, when time moved forward, when there were seasons and lights in the sky beside the sun and the moon. Back when there was no need for a Shepherdess. Back when every spirit woke and slept as it chose, when there were no humans, no wizards, and we hunted our own demons."

As the mountain spoke, the beautiful night sky full of lights faded. The valley faded, too, so did the mountains, and Miranda found herself standing beside Slorn and Gin in the plain white room.

"But that world is gone," the mountain said, his disembodied voice echoing through the empty chamber. "Broken, eaten, lost forever. We live in the Shepherdess's world now. If I question her methods, even to bring a new idea, even I could end up like Gredit."

"Gredit?" Slorn said, stepping forward. "You know what happened to the Great Bear?"

"We all know," the mountain said. "Before, stars were named so because they were the greatest, the only spirits large enough to watch over their own. But the Shepherdess picks her own stars now. Small spirits, creatures not even worthy of the name, elevated only because the Shepherdess found them beautiful. Even now she ignores the world to play her favorites against each other for no reason other than she likes to be fought over. Gredit, stubborn, noble old bear, thought he could make her see sense. To that end, he made the mistake of threatening her current favorite darling, and she killed him for it."

Slorn made a keening sound deep in his throat. Miranda flinched. It was the most animal sound she'd ever heard him make.

"With my twin dead, I am the last of the great mountains," the Teacher said. "I cannot leave my sleeping brothers without guidance. I cannot risk sharing Gredit's fate, no matter how noble the cause. I do not know if the Shepherdess is mad or simply foolish, but she has shown that she will kill an ancient spirit if the fancy strikes her, and we do not have so many stars that we can throw them away on your theories, Heinricht. Do you understand?"

"I understand, Teacher," Slorn said. "But I do not agree. I cannot accept that a Shepherdess who kills her flock when they question her is worthy of such worship."

"Then you should keep that opinion to yourself," the mountain rumbled. "I have heard your knowledge, Shaper. This hearing is adjourned. Go and make peace with your father. I cannot help you."

"Wait!" Miranda cried, but it was too late. The mountain's voice vanished without even an echo. A second later, the platform under their feet shook, and they began to descend. Miranda turned to Slorn, burning with questions, but one look at his face was enough to kill them on her tongue. She'd never seen him so angry. Behind her, Gin was still on the ground with his eyes closed, breathing the deep, measured breaths he used to keep himself calm when he was injured. Even Mellinor would not speak.

They emerged from the ceiling of the Hall of the Shapers to find the Guildmaster waiting for them with half a dozen Shapers spread out in a circle around the descending pillar.

"Heinricht Slorn," the Guildmaster said. "The Teacher has declared you a threat to the safety of the mountain. You will be taken back to your cell, there to live out the rest of your natural life."

"What?" Miranda said. "The mountain just said he couldn't do anything. How is Slorn a threat?"

"Do not speak!" one of the Shapers shouted, but he stopped when the Guildmaster raised his hand.

"Outsiders do not have a voice within the mountain," the Guildmaster said. Miranda glowered, but the old man wasn't talking to her. He was talking to Slorn. "The Teacher did not like your knowledge, it seems."

"Knowledge worth having is rarely pleasant," Slorn answered. "But I am not convinced the Teacher has truly made his decision."

The Guildmaster stiffened. "Was the Teacher not clear?"

"He was very clear," Slorn answered. "But he showed us much before throwing us out. The Mountain has and will always be our teacher, and a teacher does not show his students the truth if he does not wish them to learn. If he truly had no use for Nivel's and my work, or Miranda's presence, he would never have called us up in the first place."

"A wise observation," the Guildmaster said. "Though you may spend the rest of your life waiting to learn the Teacher's true intentions."

"I am prepared," Slorn said.

"But what about your companion?" the Guildmaster said, turning to face Miranda. "Is she ready? Or have you not told her yet?"

Slorn's jaw clenched, and a tremor of fear ran up Miranda's spine. "Told me what?"

"I'm afraid my son has done you a great disservice," the Guildmaster said. "You see, no outsider who has seen the secrets of the Shaper Mountain is ever allowed to leave."

"*What?*" Miranda shouted, turning to stare at Slorn. "What does he—"

The stone beneath their feet erupted, cutting her off. Great hands of white rock burst from the ground and clutched her body, crushing the air from her lungs. She fought the hold on instinct, but all she managed was to hurt her neck, the only part of her body she could still move. Slorn and Gin were caught as well, but when she snapped her head around to look at the Guildmaster, his old face was truly pitying.

"I am sorry," he said. "But Shaper secrets must be maintained. Out of respect for the great good your order has done for the world, I promise that your life with us will not be uncomfortable." He gave her a sad smile. "Good-bye, Spiritualist."

Miranda opened her mouth to tell him exactly what she thought of that, but the stone closed over her head before the words could form, yanking her down into the mountain.

CHAPTER

8

Dawn had barely broken when Eli woke to the feeling of something cold tracing a burning line across his cheek. He gasped before he could stop himself, his body going rigid. Slowly, deliberately, he forced himself to take deep, calm breaths. Only when he was sure his voice was neutral did he dare to speak.

"I asked you not to do that," he said, opening his eyes.

Beautiful, hated laughter floated through the glowing air as the too-white hand left his face and moved to linger on his chest. Eli swallowed against the bile that rose in his throat. Not now. He couldn't lose it now.

Benehime lay stretched out in the bed beside him, her white body pressed against his. Eli could feel every spirit in the room watching, their souls bowed in reverence to the White Lady, but the Shepherdess didn't seem to notice. Her attention was entirely on Eli as she buried her face in the hollow of his throat.

Remember when we used to spend every morning this way? she whispered, nipping at his windpipe with a little burst of the painless fire he'd learned to loathe. *You were so happy then.*

"I was very young then," Eli said, shifting away from her as much as he dared. "Why are you here, Benehime?"

Do I need a reason? she said, pushing up so that she was looking at him.

Eli said nothing, and Benehime relaxed against him with a long sigh. *If you must know, I've brought you some news. You always did love a bit of gossip.* She smiled, her hand tracing Karon's burn. Deep in his chest, Eli felt the lava spirit roll over in fear. Benehime felt it, too, and she laughed, leaning forward so her white hair fell across them both.

Nara's embraced her power again, she said, moving her hands up to play with his tousled hair. *She's putting together quite the little show. I have to say I'm impressed. She hasn't been this Empress-like in centuries. I'm beginning to remember why I loved her.*

She paused, watching his face for jealousy, but Eli flashed her a genuine smile.

"What a marvelous turn for everyone if she should manage it," he said. "The Empress always did adore you more than I ever could with my black heart."

Benehime's smile faded, and her fingers tangled painfully in his hair. *Don't be cold, Eliton,* she whispered, dragging his head back. *You need to remember that my love is something to be coveted, not taken for granted. I've played your game for many years now, watching you run free, chasing your ridiculous dream of that absurd bounty. It's been an adorable show, but the time for play is over, and I grow tired of waiting.*

"Why are you waiting for me?" Eli said. "Surely there's someone else who can keep you company. The whole world loves you."

What do I care about the world? Benehime said, her beautiful face falling into a sullen frown. *You're the only soul that matters to me, love. That's why I came to warn you.* She released her grip on his hair, pulling her hands down to cup his face instead. *Nara is coming to take me from you*, she whispered. *She's marshaled an army like none I've ever seen. There's no way you can beat her alone.*

Eli had to grit his teeth to keep from flinching as she stroked his cheeks. "With all due respect, Shepherdess, there have been a lot of things you've said I couldn't do, and I've done most of them."

Benehime stiffened, her hands tightening on his face, and for a moment Eli was afraid she was going to rip his head clean off. But then she smiled and leaned in, pressing a soft, burning kiss against his lips. *So arrogant,* she whispered, moving up to kiss the tip of his nose. *So self-assured. That's why I love you.* She kissed him one last time and pulled back. *Really, though, Eliton, you've never been an idiot. For all your puffed-up talk, you must know you'll lose in the end. Nara commands half the world, and now that she's got her spine back, she means to control the whole thing.*

Benehime began to laugh. *Poor thing still hasn't realized that ruling the world doesn't solve all its problems. I should know; I've tried.* She sighed against him, patting his cheeks with her fingers. *She's a lost cause, darling, but she's one you can't possibly hope to beat. Better come home now while things are easy. If you make me save you, I won't be so gentle.*

"But that's the game, isn't it?" Eli said, lying still as a board beneath her. "If I ask you for help, you win."

The Shepherdess's fingers froze against his skin. *You're not still on about that old thing, are you?*

"I most certainly am," Eli said. "And so are you, which is why you haven't just yanked me back yet. You want to win, but so do I, and I'm not one to just roll over." He broke into a wide grin. "You'll have to find something scarier than the Immortal Empress if you want me to come crying back to you, Benehime."

The Shepherdess's face closed like a slamming door. She sat back on top of him, suddenly cold and distant. *I was trying to let you keep your dignity,* she said with a sneer. *I should have known better. You always did enjoy throwing my kindness back in my face. But mark me, favorite, the*

Empress is coming and she has no love for you. I am your only hope. Try to keep that in mind the next time you decide to be rude.

Eli didn't answer. He just lay there, his body perfectly still against hers. The Shepherdess watched him a moment longer, and then she leaned down. *I'll be waiting,* she murmured against his mouth, kissing him one last time.

She kept her white eyes open the whole time, staring at him as her mouth crushed his. Eli stared back, not moving so much as a fraction as the burning feel of her lips grew from ticklish to nearly unbearable. Finally, with a slight smile, Benehime vanished. There was no white line, no change. She was just gone, leaving behind nothing, not even a warm spot on the bed. Eli didn't dare move a muscle. He lay perfectly still as the seconds ticked by with painful slowness, counting them one after another until he reached a full minute. Then, like a dam breaking, he collapsed into the bed, gasping as the lingering feel of her presence faded from his body.

Powers, he thought, rolling over as he curled into a ball, clutching his knees against his chest as he fought to get the burning feel of her off his skin. Powers, did he hate her.

"She's getting pushier," Karon whispered, his rumbling voice vibrating up from Eli's chest. "You better watch yourself. You might be the favorite, but it's unwise to push the Lady too far."

Eli squeezed his eyes tighter as he tried to find the words to tell his lava spirit that not pushing wasn't an option. Whatever she said, whatever she threatened, he couldn't go back. Not ever. Not to her. It wasn't just giving up his freedom, or the way she touched him whether he wanted to be touched or not. It wasn't even the fear, or the constant feeling of walking on eggshells whenever she was around for fear of sparking her terrible temper. No, what he hated most was the feeling of being owned.

The moment she'd decided he was her favorite, his life had stopped being his own, and from the time he'd been old enough to understand what that loss meant, what she really was, he'd been fighting to get away from her. He'd lied and conned and traded everything he had, his entire future, for the limited freedom he enjoyed now. But the slack she'd released into his leash depended on his continued ability to make it on his own. That was their wager; *that* was the game. The moment he admitted he couldn't make it on his own, the moment he reached out to her for help, Benehime won, and he went back to being her plaything forever.

"Do you think she's serious about the Empress?" Karon said. "Osera has no hope at all if Nara's coming this time, not unless you mean to take her yourself."

"I'm doing no such thing," Eli said, opening his eyes at last. "Nara won't come. The only thing that could get that woman to move is Benehime herself, and there's no way the Shepherdess would start a continental war just to squeeze me into asking for help. She's nuts, but not *that* nuts."

Karon rumbled deep in Eli's ribs. "I don't know what the Shepherdess is capable of anymore. She has changed very much from when I was young."

"And how long ago was that?" Eli asked.

"Not as long as it should be to account for so great a change," Karon said. "Be careful, Eli. Benehime was always a dangerous Power, but she seems to lose all sense when it comes to her love for you."

"No argument there," Eli muttered. There had been times when the Shepherdess was so angry that Eli had been sure she'd kill him. Sometimes, the dark times, he'd almost hoped she would. At least then he'd be free of her. But the older he got, the more he realized that even death wasn't an escape from Benehime. If he died, she would just catch his soul and put him back together. There was no escape from the Shepherdess's love.

"It has to be a bluff," Eli muttered. "The Empire has been planning to invade Osera for decades. Now that they are, Benehime is just using the timing to try and scare me. But I'm not a stupid kid anymore, and she's going to have to push a lot harder than that to break me." He forced himself to smile. "It's just another of her games, Karon. And I'm the best when it comes to playing games."

Karon grumbled, unconvinced, and Eli patted his chest with a confident thump, though he wasn't really sure whom he was trying hardest to convince with such bravado, the lava spirit or himself.

Outside, the sun was creeping over the castle walls, and Eli decided he'd better get up. He sat and stretched, running his fingers through his hair in a vain effort to remove the feeling of the Shepherdess's hands. He was just reaching for his blond wig when he heard the soft click of the door lock. Eli moved in a flash, grabbing the wig and tossing it on his head. He fell back into his bed just in time to see a young manservant carrying a shaving tray slip through the heavy door.

"Can I help you?" Eli said, his voice drawling in exaggerated sleepiness.

The servant, who obviously thought he was being stealthy, jumped a foot in the air. "Good morning, sir," he said when he'd recovered. "I am here to assist with your morning toilet."

"Splendid," Eli said, sitting up. "What's your name?"

The servant shuffled. "Stefan, sir."

Eli stood with a groan and walked across the room. He took the young man by the shoulder with a firm hand and turned him back toward the hall. "Stefan," he said. "Excellent. Now, when I need assistance with my morning toilet, I'll know exactly whom to call."

"But, Mr. Banage," the servant said, digging his heels into the rich carpet. "The queen ordered that we were to dress the prince and his guests for court."

"How lovely," Eli said, pushing harder. "Did she also order that we were to be starved to death?"

"No, sir!" the servant said, horrified.

Eli flashed him a winning smile. "Well, then, since I am perfectly capable of dressing myself, why don't you go above and beyond the call of duty and find me some breakfast before I eat one of your fancy end tables? Could you do that for me?"

The young man frowned. "I suppose I could, sir, but—"

"You are a prince among men, Stefan," Eli said, giving him a final push out the door. "Of course, considering the princes I've met, that might not be a compliment, but it was meant in good faith."

The servant stumbled into the hallway. "Are you sure you do not wish my help, sir?" he said one last time. "I could ask one of the others to fetch your breakfast."

"I trust no one but you," Eli said, slamming the door behind him. "Don't let me down!" he shouted through the wood.

If Stefan answered, Eli didn't hear. He was already across the room, digging through his bag. He pulled the wig off his head and brushed it out with his fingers before placing it on the washstand. Using hot water from the shaving tray, he washed his face and then wet his real hair, combing it back slick before pressing it dry with one of the hot towels. Next, he picked his shirt and breeches from last night up off the floor and, as they were far and away the nicest clothes he had, put them back on. When he was dressed and his hair was mostly dry, he pinned his wig back in place. He was adjusting the fall of the blond hair across his shoulders when he heard the lock turn again.

Eli glanced up, expecting the servant, or at least a breakfast tray. Instead, Josef marched into the room. The swordsman was also dressed in the same clothes from yesterday, but the fine shirt and trousers were wrinkled as though he'd slept in them. His knives, all of them, were belted on and the Heart was across his back, ready to go. For one soaring moment, Eli thought Josef had changed his mind about staying, but then he saw the pair of guards hot on Josef's heels and a servant hovering with lather bowl and razor in hand, and his spirits dropped.

"Have you seen Nico?" Josef said.

"Good morning to you, too," Eli said. "And no."

Josef grimaced. "I was sure she would come back, but she never did. I waited all night." He scrubbed his hands through his short blond hair. "Something's wrong, Eli. It's not like her to be gone this long without a reason."

Eli turned back to the mirror to contemplate his position. His swordsman could be unusually insightful about some things, but he was thick as a wagon of bricks about others. There was no easy way of explaining to him that, underneath the semisentient coat, monstrous strength, and shadowy past, Nico was a girl as well as a demonseed. Her relationship with Josef might be a nebulous, nameless sort of thing, but hearing that the man she trusted more than anything in the world, the man she followed with unquestioning loyalty, was *married*, had been married for a year, and never even thought to mention it...well, that had to sting, and Nico didn't exactly talk about her problems.

"I'm sure she's fine," Eli said, glancing at Josef and then pointedly flicking his eyes to the guards and the servant hovering behind him.

That, at least, Josef got. "Get out," he growled.

"But, my lord," said the guard at his left. "Your lady mother was very specific—"

"Where do you think I'm going to run?" Josef said. "This cell is the same as the one you just let me out of. I need to talk to my friend in private, so shove off. Now."

The guards backed off as one, bowing their way out the door. The servant, however, stayed, heated towel ready. Josef stared at him a moment, and then grabbed the man's shoulder. The servant made a sort of squeaking sound as Josef shoved him into the hall, closing the heavy door in his face.

"I can see why you had problems being a prince," Eli said, leaning on the washstand. "Not exactly the genteel epitome of magnanimity and tact, are you?"

"Shut up," Josef said, but there was no venom in it. He walked across the room and sat down on Eli's bed, putting his head in his hands with a deep breath. "I can't believe she'd leave without telling me."

"She didn't leave, Josef," Eli said with a long sigh. "She probably just needs some time to work things through. It's been a pretty dramatic week."

"But she's never done that before," Josef said. "Vanished like that, in front of everyone." He glanced up. "You're the wizard. You would have heard if something happened to her, right? With the demon?"

Eli watched the swordsman with new interest. This wasn't just bullheaded tactlessness. Josef was really worried. It was rather touching, actually.

"The whole castle would have heard if something had happened between Nico and her demon," he said gently. "The fact that we were able to sleep last night is proof that she's fine. She's probably hiding somewhere, waiting for us to follow the plan and get out. My biggest worry is how we're going to let her know the plan's toast. Assuming, of course, you haven't changed your mind since last night."

"No," Josef said, shaking his head. "I can't leave. I told you that."

"So you did," Eli said, exasperated. "But you couldn't have picked a worse place to have this fit of conscience. We're wanted criminals, remember? The longer we stay, the more likely it is that someone's going to put the pieces together and come after us, if they haven't already. Staying doesn't help anyone—not us, not Nico, and not your mother. You did your duty by showing up, so let's cut our losses, find Nico, and get out of here before things get worse."

Eli finished with a sinking feeling. Josef's head was down, his hands clasped behind his neck. When he spoke at last, his voice was very calm and very, very serious.

"Eli," he said. "I'm only going to say this once." He looked up, and his eyes were the eyes of a swordsman who has bet his life on his next stroke. "I may be in disgrace, but Queen Theresa is still my queen, and she's still my mother. I let her down before, and if staying here long enough to give her an heir is all she wants from me to make things right, then that's what I'm going to do. End of discussion."

Eli loomed over him, his mouth pressed in a tight, flat line. Josef glared right back, hands on his swords. Finally, Eli's shoulders slumped, and he flopped back against the washstand with an enormous huff.

"All right, all right," he said. "You win. When are you going to tell the queen your decision?"

"Right now," Josef said, standing up. "And you're coming with me."

"Wait," Eli said, holding up his hands. "Wait, wait, wait. Unless you're planning to steal that lovely set of antique tapestries she has above her fireplace, I don't have anything to do with this. For the next few weeks at least, you're the crown prince of Osera. I'm still the most wanted criminal in the Council. I don't care how forgiving your dear mother is, it's not exactly a winning match. Actually, it would probably be better for all involved if I lit out for a while. Go steal something and get my mind off things until you're done being a good husband."

Josef shook his head. "You have to be here."

"Why?" Eli said, truly mystified.

Josef looked away. Eli pursed his lips thoughtfully. If he didn't know better, he'd have said the swordsman looked sheepish.

"Being prince means I have to go to court," Josef said at last. "Court means politics and a lot of talking to people who can't be insulted. I'm not really—" He stopped and took a deep breath. "You're the one who's good with that kind of thing, all right? You have to stay."

"Josef," Eli said with a growing smile. "Could it be? Are you asking me for help?"

Josef glowered at him. "Not if you're going to say it like that."

"No, no, no," Eli said, placing his hands on his chest. "I'm flattered. I would be delighted to be your adviser."

"Good," Josef said, nodding. "That's settled, then."

"Of course," Eli added, raising one long finger. "You'd have to say what I told you to say, exactly as I told you to say it."

Josef grimaced, and Eli shook his head. "That's the only way it works. You can tell me to stay all you want, but if you're not going to listen to my advice, I'm not going to waste my breath giving it."

"Fine," Josef grumbled. "Just don't get carried away."

Eli flipped the edges of his golden wig. "When have I ever gotten carried away?"

Josef rolled his eyes and didn't answer.

"Now," Eli said. "Let's get started. Normally, I'd say we should put off seeing the queen. Let her sweat a bit. However, seeing as she's your mother, sweating would probably only make her more stubborn, so we're going to go see her immediately. When we arrive, you're going to tell her that you're staying and doing your part as a dutiful prince, but only if you get to keep your friends with you, and as soon as a pregnancy is confirmed, you're leaving. Also, you want full freedom of movement and all royal privileges for you and your entourage, meaning myself and Nico." He shot Josef a smile. "No reason we can't have a little fun while we're stuck here. Does that sound fair?"

Josef rubbed his chin. "I guess it does."

"Excellent," Eli said. "I'll need a full rundown on Osera's political situation before we do any more politicking than that, but hopefully we won't have to. If war's truly coming, Osera has bigger problems than us. All we need to do is keep our noses down, keep you in bed with your wife, and we'll be out of here in two months. Tops."

Josef winced. "I'm not a stud bull, you know."

"You are now," Eli said cheerfully, walking to the door. He opened it to find Josef's guards, his overzealous manservant, and Eli's own Stefan (now with a breakfast trolley instead of the shaving tray) standing in the hallway, whispering together. They all jumped when they saw Eli, but came when he beckoned, tiptoeing into the room as meekly as they could.

"So sorry about earlier," Eli said, clapping Josef's servant on the shoulders. "The prince had a bit of a bad night, but food will set everything to rights. Now," he said, pushing the man toward Josef, "if you would be so kind as to make your prince presentable, we'll see the queen as soon as she's ready."

Both servants cheered up immensely once they were free to do their jobs. Eli stepped aside to let Josef sit down at the washstand as both servants moved in and began cleaning him up. The swordsman sat glumly, letting them lather his chin and comb his hair. Meanwhile, Eli helped himself to a cup of tea, a plate of ham, and several scones from the breakfast tray before flopping down on the bed to watch the show. When Stefan asked if he would like a shave as well, Eli politely declined.

"It took me weeks to grow what I have," he said, rubbing his fingers over the sparse beard on his chin. "I'm not quite ready to sacrifice it yet. Besides," he nodded at Josef, who was gripping his swords as the manservant deftly ran the razor over his taut neck. "I wouldn't miss this for the world."

Josef shot Eli a murderous look. Eli answered with a wide smile as he shoved another slice of ham into his mouth.

When he was shaved and clean, Josef sent the servants running with a growl before joining Eli at the breakfast tray. He ate five slabs of ham in rapid succession and then stepped away.

"Let's go," he said, wiping his hands on the shaving towels.

"Not so fast," Eli said. "You can't go see the queen like that."

Josef looked down at his shirt. "Like what?"

Eli sighed and walked over to the mirror on the washstand, tilting it until Josef could see his whole body. Blades were strapped everywhere they could go. Hilts were visible at his sleeves, neck, waist, and boots. Bandoleers of throwing knives were crushing his dress shirt and his short swords were wearing a matched set of grooves into his new belt. Finally, there was the Heart of War itself, the wrapped hilt poking up high over his shoulder, just in case anyone wasn't intimidated enough by the rest of it.

Josef crossed his arms over his chest. "No."

"Josef," Eli pleaded. "You asked me to stay and help you be a prince. This is step one: not looking like a murderer."

"I'm not going unarmed," Josef said.

"No one's going to challenge you to a duel in the palace."

Josef snorted. "You obviously don't know Osera."

"Fine, fine," Eli said, throwing up his hands. "One sword, but you're leaving the rest."

Josef planted his feet, daring him. Eli glared right back, and then he started to push.

In the end, they compromised on one short sword, all the hidden knives, and the Heart, which Josef absolutely refused to leave behind. Eli would have kept going, but it was nearing midmorning and his plan of not making the queen wait was already an hour off schedule. He tapped his foot impatiently as Josef slowly divested himself of the knives he'd agreed to leave, and then he pushed the swordsman into the hall.

The soldiers were more than happy to escort the prince and his friend to the queen's chamber. The castle was bustling with morning activity. Servants, their arms full with trays, linens, and other vitals of a noble household, ran up and down the narrow halls, pressing themselves into the wall to make way when Josef and Eli passed. Eli watched the comings and goings with a keen eye. The queen ran a tight ship. Every servant was well groomed and well dressed in simple livery of good quality materials right down to their polished boots. It was little details like this, far more than any ostentation, that confirmed Osera's wealth in Eli's mind. He also noticed that everyone, even the servants, was armed with at least a dagger. He filed that tidbit away for questioning later. At the moment, though, he had more important blanks to fill in.

"Josef," he whispered, leaning toward the swordsman as they walked down the hall. "If I'm going to help you be a prince, there are a few things I need from you."

"Like what?" Josef said, visibly annoyed by the slow pace the guards set.

"Let's start with the princess," Eli said. "I'm guessing you two knew each other before all this?"

Josef nodded. "She's Lenette's girl."

"Lenette?" Eli said. "The queen's maid?"

"Lady-in-waiting," Josef corrected him. "Lenette is my mother's confidant and best friend. Has been for years. Adela's her daughter. We grew up together."

"I see," Eli said. "Your mother married you to your childhood sweetheart in the hopes you wouldn't complain as much."

"We weren't sweethearts," Josef snapped. "But otherwise you're right."

"Well, at least she tried to make you happy," Eli said, scratching his chin. "That's more than most royal mothers."

Josef didn't say anything to that, and they walked the rest of the way to the queen's chamber in silence. But when they got there, the queen was nowhere to be seen. Instead, her lady-in-waiting, the lovely woman in black from before, greeted them in the queen's entry chamber.

"Lenette," Josef said with a stiff nod as the soldiers left. "Where's the queen?"

"Your mother is unwell this morning, Prince Thereson," Lenette said, returning to the little table where she'd been sitting when they'd arrived.

"Let me see her," Josef said, crossing his arms.

Lenette took her time, focusing her attention on the leaves in the little stone grinder in front of her. "The queen's health is a delicate thing," she said at last, pushing the grinding wheel until the leaves were crushed into a fine powder. "Her rest is not to be disturbed."

"I'm sure she'll want to hear this," Eli said, cutting in before Josef could say anything he'd regret. "Can't you take us to see her?"

"No," Lenette said without looking up as she emptied the freshly ground leaves into the glass jar at her elbow. "Since you're here, I assume you mean to tell her that the prince has decided to stay in Osera and do his duty?"

Eli and Josef exchanged a look.

"More or less," Eli said.

"Good," Lenette said with a nod. "I'll tell her when she wakes up."

"Listen," Josef growled. "I don't care how far you've crawled into the queen's ear since I left—probably more than you should have, considering you convinced her to marry your daughter into the royal line of Osera. But you're not so important that you can keep me from seeing my own mother."

Josef's anger was usually enough to turn people into jelly, but Lenette remained calm and collected.

"I'm not the one keeping you from your mother," she said.

"These are her doctor's orders. If she is to be fit enough to appear at court today, she must be allowed to rest undisturbed. If you have an issue with that, the doctor keeps his office on the third floor. Take it up with him. Now, if you still feel the need to brag about your sudden decision to return to your duties, I suggest you find Adela. As your wife, it's her job to take an interest in whatever you have to say. She's at the guard keep, overseeing drill." Lenette gave him a slow smile. "My daughter is a fine guard captain and a dutiful child, which is more than I can say for some."

Josef's hand moved toward the blade at his hip in a way that would make anyone who knew him at all dive for cover, but Lenette just smiled and stood up, carrying her pot of ground herbs to the tea service against the far wall.

"I must take the queen her medicine," she said, tapping a spoonful of the ground leaves onto a silver mesh strainer before pouring a measure of hot water through the leaves into the cup below. "Is there anything else I can help you with, Prince Thereson?"

Josef turned on his heel and walked out of the room. Eli followed, glancing over his shoulder just in time to see the queen's lady-in-waiting smile as she blew on the steaming water. She was placing the cup on a serving tray when the door closed and Eli saw no more.

"Charming lady," he said, running to catch up with Josef as the guards fell in beside them. "Has she always been like that?"

"Long as I've known her," Josef answered with a growl.

"So, is she noble?" Eli said. "A cousin or something?"

"This is Osera, not Zarin," Josef sneered. "We don't marry our cousins. Lenette's not even Oseran. She married into money, turned that into a court invitation, and then wormed her way into the queen's favor. She's been glued to mother's side for as long as I can remember. People used to complain about a foreigner having so much power, but she's been here so long now, I don't think people even remember she's not from the island."

"Time changes many things," Eli said. "Are you going to see your wife, then?"

"And prove Lenette right?" Josef said with a snort. "Not a chance. We're going to use our time before court to look for Nico. I'd rather see her than Adela any day."

Eli smiled. "I'm sure Nico would be delighted to hear that."

"Why?"

"No reason," Eli said, rubbing his forehead with a long, deep sigh. "Lead on."

Josef shrugged and started walking faster. They ditched the guards on the next turn and went out on the rooftops to start their search.

After two hours of looking and nothing to show for it, Josef suddenly announced it was time to go to court. Tempting as it was, Eli resisted the urge to point out that they still had plenty of time before the ceremony began. For one, it might very well be time in Josef's mind. He was famously insistent about showing up early. Two, Eli had lived with the swordsman long enough to know that you didn't try reasoning with him when his face was set in that particular expression of cold rage.

As it turned out, it was good that they went down when they did. Despite being nearly an hour before court was scheduled to start, the throne room of Osera was already packed.

"I see you come by your predilection for early arrivals naturally," Eli said, poking his head through a side door to survey the scene. "I think we're the last ones here."

Josef didn't answer. He was standing by the door with his hands on his knives, looking suspiciously pale.

Eli poked him in the shoulder. "What's wrong?"

"Nothing's wrong," Josef said, taking a deep breath. "It's just been a while since I had to deal with this idiocy."

Eli gaped at him. "Josef, you're the wielder of the Heart of War. You've fought Berek Sted *and* the Lord of Storms. How can you be nervous about facing some nobles?"

"I'm not nervous," Josef snapped. "I just need a moment."

"It's a room full of rich, soft, old men!" Eli cried. "It's not an army."

"I'd prefer an army," Josef said. "You don't know what those people are like. If they would fight me openly, everything would be fine. But they don't. They just *talk*."

Eli smiled and held up a finger. "Just relax and remember the first rule of thievery: Shown weakness is your only weakness. Go in there with your head held high and leave the talking to me. That's why I'm here, remember?"

Josef released the death grip on his sword long enough to wipe the sweat from his brow with the back of his sleeve. "Just promise me you won't turn this into one of your overcomplicated Eli things," he muttered. "Please."

"I have no idea what you're talking about," Eli said, taking Josef by the arm and steering him toward the door. "Chin up. Try to look princely."

Josef nodded and set his features in the steely expression of a man bravely facing his own death. Eli grimaced, but didn't comment. Bad as it was, it was better than the cold rage from earlier. He gave Josef a firm push, and the two of them walked into the hall.

The Oseran throne room had what Eli thought of as a paranoid setup, usually found in kingdoms with a violent history. It was all one large room with a row of narrow support columns forming a corridor up the middle, but rather than placing the throne on a free-standing platform as in Mellinor or other, more peaceable kingdoms, Osera's throne was flush with the back wall, leaving no space for attack from the rear.

The throne room had no wings, but there was a gallery running around the upper level that was already full. Above the gallery, a line of thin windows carved the bright island sunlight into slices that struck the crowd at regular intervals, painting the hall in stripes of light. Down on the floor, the people were better dressed than in the gallery, but Eli saw none of the sort of ostentation normally found in the court of such a wealthy country. There was little jewelry to be seen, even on the older women. Dresses were muted colors, dark reds, greens, or navy. The men wore black almost exclusively, and everyone, even the women, was armed.

"I'm sorry I gave you a hard time about the knives, now," Eli whispered.

"What did you expect?" Josef said, pushing his way toward the throne. "This is Osera. They didn't call my grandfather Bloody Liechten because of his contributions to the arts."

Eli grimaced. Parts of Josef's personality were becoming more understandable by the second.

"I'm surprised no one's come up to you yet," he said, looking around. People were certainly staring but, oddly, no one had made a move to approach their long-lost prince. In Eli's experience, a prince, even an outcast runaway like Josef, was still someone who garnered favor currying by social climbers. These people seemed almost afraid.

Josef just shrugged. "They probably don't recognize me. I'm a lot bigger than I was when I left."

Eli kept his mouth shut about the likelihood of that explanation and focused on following the path Josef opened through the crowd.

As it happened, they made it all the way to the railing that separated the dais from the rest of the room without being approached.

This close, Eli could see the throne easily. Like everything in the castle, the throne of Osera radiated age and deep-rooted authority. It was enormous, a naked stone bench wide enough to seat two men of Josef's size with room to spare. The stone was the smooth, dove-gray rock of the mountain the castle sat on. It was carved with undulating patterns that mimicked the crashing sea so that whoever sat on the throne looked to be floating on a stone wave. A nice trick, all told, but the thing that really caught Eli's attention wasn't the throne itself, but the statues flanking it. Two enormous lions cast from midnight-black iron were anchored on either side of the throne. The lions stood rampant on their hind legs with their backs to the wall and their front paws reaching out to claw whoever defied Osera's ruler.

"Throne of iron lions, indeed," Eli whispered, leaning in to admire the delicate metalwork of their curling manes.

"What?" Josef said, looking up from his spot leaning against a support pillar.

Eli shook his head and set about studying the court instead. He scanned the people around them, trying to pick out Josef's relatives from the crush. It proved harder than he'd thought it would be. Tall, blond, and grumpy seemed to be the motif among Oseran nobility. He'd never seen a sourer-faced crowd in his life.

"Josef," Eli whispered. "Wasn't Osera founded on piracy?"

"Among other things," Josef said dryly.

Eli waved at the scowling crowd. "I thought pirates were supposed to be jolly."

Josef made a sound in the back of his throat that reminded Eli of a ghosthound's growl. "Maybe you haven't been paying attention, but Osera doesn't have a lot to be jolly about at the moment."

"I don't see that you were ever jolly," Eli said, glancing again at the lions.

Josef followed his gaze. "Not much room for it," he said quietly.

"Osera has always been ruled by the strong. Has to be. The sea eats the soft and the weak. The lions are there to remind people of that."

"Point taken," Eli said. He was about to ask another question when Josef suddenly pushed off the pillar.

"Eyes front," Josef said, pulling his jacket straight. "The queen's coming."

"But there's still half an hour before court!" Eli protested.

"Why do you think everyone gets here early?"

Eli's answer was drowned out by a peel of trumpets as a six squad of guards in full armor marched into the throne room. People scooted out of their way, clearing a wide swath down the middle. The guards walked the full length of the hall, peeling off in pairs to stand at attention before each pillar until they had formed an armed corridor from the door to the throne. When they were in position, the trumpets sounded again, and the room filled with the sweep of cloth and the creak of leather as everyone, nobles and servants, bowed in reverence as Queen Theresa herself entered the throne room.

The queen looked very different from the night before. Her white hair was pulled up beneath a plain, masculine crown of heavy gold. She was clothed in black, a widow's mourning dress of stiff, raw silk. Her lined face looked pale and pinched, but she stood straight, walking on her own with one hand resting on the arm of the tall, lovely woman in armor walking beside her—Princess Adela, Josef's wife.

The princess made an impressive sight. With her dark, glossy hair and bright silver armor, she shone like a beacon beside the queen's dour black, an effect that was not lost on the crowd. People glanced up from their bows as the princess passed. Their faces were a mix of envy and adoration. More adoration than Eli had expected. With great care, Adela helped the queen up the dais stairs to the wide throne. Beside him, Eli felt Josef stiffen, but the swordsman said nothing as his wife helped his mother down to the hard stone bench. When she was settled, Adela stepped aside, leaving Theresa to survey her court.

Eli swallowed. The queen of Osera on her throne was an impressive sight indeed. The black of her dress shone from the gray stone like a rock among the waves. Above her, the lions' extended paws framed her head like a second crown, a reminder of the power her position held, an ancient, bloody, visceral power that had nothing to do with the Council or Osera's newfound wealth. Theresa's pale eyes moved over the crowd, noting and dismissing each face until she found Josef's.

"You," she said, her voice echoing through the silent chamber. "Up here."

Josef and Eli exchanged a final look, and then Josef pushed off the pillar, stepped over the railing, and climbed the stone steps to stand beside his mother.

"My son," Theresa announced in a voice so harsh it made Eli wince. "Prince Josef Liechten Thereson Esinlowe, has returned from his travels to grace us with his presence one again."

A murmur rose up from the crowd, and Josef shifted uncomfortably. Eli bit his lip, half expecting Josef to walk out, but he stayed rooted to the step beside the throne, glaring at the crowded room like he was daring them to do something about it.

"Last year," the queen continued, "I declared the marriage of my son to Adela Theresa Reiniger, daughter of Lord Reiniger and his wife, the Lady Lenette, my dearest friend and lady of the chamber. Today, I reaffirm that bond."

She beckoned, and Adela stepped forward, her hard-soled boots clacking against the stone until she was standing directly at the queen's right. Theresa motioned again, and Josef reluctantly moved closer. Theresa took Adela's hand and pressed it to Josef, who took it hesitantly. The queen smiled as the connection was made and gave them both a push.

"People of Osera," she announced as Josef and Adela turned to face the room. "I give you your prince and princess. Through this union, the blood of the House of Eisenlowe shall flow to a new generation. May the strength of the Iron Lions breed true, and may the House of Eisenlowe never fall."

Applause erupted throughout the court, but the noise rang hollow in Eli's ears. No one looked particularly happy. Not the couple, and certainly not the party of large, blond gentlemen in rich suits standing across the aisle.

The room fell silent again as the queen raised a skeletal hand. "The royal couple will now perform the Proving," she announced. "Clear the hall."

"Clear the hall!" The cry went up as the guards began directing people to the edges of the room.

Eli glanced around in alarm. Up by the throne, the prince and princess separated without so much as a glance, Adela down the stairs toward the back of the room, Josef back toward Eli with a glum look.

"What's the Proving?" Eli hissed when Josef reached him. "You didn't say anything about any Proving." He looked sideways at the large, clear space that had formed at the center of the room. "Is this like the first dance, or something? Is her father going to give her away?"

"Adela's father is dead," Josef said, plucking knives out of his clothes and handing them to Eli. "And the Proving is an old Oseran tradition."

"Right," Eli said, taking the knives with trepidation. "So like a dance with quaint folk music?"

"It's not a dance," Josef said, lifting the Heart from his back and setting it gently against the pillar. "It's a duel."

"*A duel?*" Eli said, more loudly than he would have liked. The comment drew several nasty looks from the people around them. Eli gritted his teeth and dropped his voice. "I thought you just got married?"

"We did," Josef said, checking the short sword at his hip. "This is the next part of the ceremony. It's the duty of all members of the royal family to protect Osera. So whenever someone in the family gets married, both husband and wife have to fight a demonstration duel to prove they are capable of holding the throne."

"Holding the throne?" Eli said. "What century do you think this is? Are you going to drag her to the marriage chamber by her hair next?"

"Osera is an old country," Josef said. "My grandfather nearly killed the woman who was to be his first wife. Stabbed her twice before sending her away for being too weak."

"That's *horrible*," Eli cried.

Josef shrugged. "That's how things are here. But don't worry, I won't hurt Adela. I'm just going scare her into an honorable surrender." He grinned, patting the sword at his hip. "Shouldn't take long."

In anyone else, Eli would have called that remark arrogant, but this being Josef, Eli had to spot him that one. "Try not to embarrass her too badly," he said. "Remember, our getting out of here depends on your mother getting her grandchild, and that'll be a little difficult if your princess is making you sleep on the floor."

"I'll do what I can," Josef said, walking through the parted crowd.

Eli bit his lip and followed, clutching Josef's cast-off blades to his chest. Adela was waiting for Josef at the center of the makeshift dueling arena. She was flanked by two armored men, one young, one gray haired. Both looked unhappy, but the princess was smiling. She turned to her escorts and whispered something that made them smile as well before they stepped back, leaving her alone at her end of the cleared hall. The princess turned to face Josef as he moved to take his place opposite her, drawing her heavy short sword with a metal hiss as she took up her position. Josef drew his sword as well and stopped in a stance Eli recognized: first position, the root of swordsmanship.

The queen looked down on the combatants from her throne, her wrinkled face like a crumpled paper mask. Only her hands betrayed her true feelings. They were knotted in her lap, the heavy rings biting into the taut skin of her fingers as she lifted her chin.

"Begin."

The word was scarcely out of her mouth before Josef sprang forward. The crowd gasped, and even Eli stepped back. Josef charged like an avalanche, enormous and unstoppable with his sword flipped in his grip, the flat of the blade already whistling down to strike Adela's sword hand.

If Eli had not spent years watching Josef fight, he would have missed what happened next. As it was, he still wasn't sure how it came about. One second, Josef was perfectly on target, the next, Adela was behind him, her feet turning neatly as she slid around his blade.

Josef turned as the lunge carried him past where her hand had been, throwing his weight to bring his sword up in time to catch hers before it landed in his back. Their blades crashed in a shower of sparks, and Josef stumbled at the impact. Eli caught his breath. They were fighting with infantry short swords, so they were very close. That left little time to react to a strike and less to dodge. Adela had done both *and* come around with a counter. He could see the same thoughts on Josef's surprised face as he fell back, catching himself at the last moment with his free hand. The second his fingers touched the floor, he pushed up, forcing Adela back with his superior height and breaking their lock. The princess retreated neatly, letting her sword follow the force sideways and down for a blow at Josef's side. But surprise attacks work only once. This time, Josef was ready. He parried her blow with a dip of his blade and stepped in, slamming his shoulder into her chest. Adela grunted and fell, landing hard on her back with a clatter of metal. Josef followed her as she went down, planting his feet on either side of her body and placing his sword's point on her exposed neck.

Adela held up her hands immediately, and the crowd began to applaud. The duel was over. Josef had won. Josef stared at the downed princess a moment longer before swinging his sword away and offering his hand. Adela took it, and he pulled her up. The applause died down as they walked through the throne room and up the dais stairs to stand again before the queen.

"The proof has been made plain," Queen Theresa announced, smiling widely as prince and princess took their places at her side. "Both have shown before all they can wield a sword in Osera's name. The bond begun a year ago is now complete. Bow before your prince and princess."

The room filled with the rustle of silk as the crowd obeyed. Eli bowed as well, but he kept his eyes on Josef. The swordsman had that look on his face, the one he got when he was extremely angry and trying to hide it.

As people began to raise their heads, the queen said something to Adela that Eli couldn't hear. The princess nodded and motioned to someone down the steps. At once, Lenette appeared from the crowd and hurried to the queen's side. Theresa reached for Lenette, and the lady-in-waiting pulled her up, supporting the queen by her shoulders. The princess and Josef turned to help, but the queen shook her head and firmly pointed for them to turn back and face the people. They obeyed, Adela more swiftly than Josef, as Lenette helped the queen hobble slowly down the dais steps and out a side door.

With the queen gone, court was over, and people began coming up to the royal couple to offer their congratulations. Josef shot Eli a look that would have been panic on anyone else's face, and Eli, recognizing his cue, sprang into action, sliding deftly around the guards and up the dais stairs.

"Princess," he said, dropping another, shallower bow as he fell in beside Josef. "Congratulations on your nuptials. I don't think I've ever seen a more succinct royal wedding."

Adela gave him a skeptical look. "With war on the horizon, the queen saw no purpose in needless expense," she said. "Osera is a practical country, Mr. Banage."

Eli flinched in surprise before remembering the identity he'd chosen for this foray. Fortunately, the princess was too distracted to notice. She was already turning to greet the thin man with graying blond hair, a hawkish nose, and a stern expression very similar to Josef's, who was the first to climb the stairs.

"Duke Finley," Adela said, bobbing her head.

The man didn't even look at her. His eyes were on Josef, looking the prince up and down with his hands on his hips.

"The wayward prince, back at last," the duke said. "I suppose that means Osera is now mortgaged to whatever bounty hunter dragged you in?"

Josef stiffened. "There's no hunter involved. I came back on my own."

"Really?" the duke said. "Prince Thereson, doing his duty? That would be a first."

He said this last bit over his shoulder to the well-dressed group standing behind him, many of whom laughed out loud at the duke's daring. Josef clenched his fists and took a menacing step forward before Eli jabbed him hard in the small of the back.

"Do you think it is wise for you to speak so of the prince in the queen's hall, Finley?"

Josef and Eli both blinked. The words had come from Adela, who was glaring at the duke like he was a pebble she'd found in her boot.

The duke sneered back. "No wiser than addressing the next king of Osera without his title, *Adela*."

The princess's scowl deepened, but Duke Finley wasn't looking at her anymore. He leaned in to Josef, a smug smile on his face. "You've been gone awhile, cousin," he said in a low voice. "One man to another, let me give you a little advice. Theresa thinks she can cling to her father's throne even in death by marrying her failure of a son to the daughter of her favorite gold-digging maid, but you won't last a day past the queen's funeral. I am the named heir, but even if I weren't, the people of Osera would never stand to have a common murderer as their king. The only reason they tolerate one as their prince is because of your mother. In any case, I wouldn't get too comfortable, were I in your position."

Eli winced. Though the duke's voice was soft, the room around them had gone deathly still, and Eli had no illusions that the insult had somehow gone unheard. But before he could say anything to diffuse the situation, Josef opened his mouth and made it worse.

"I have no intention of being king," he said. "Never have. As for me being a murderer..." Josef lifted his chin, and his hands drifted to the sword at his side. "You're right. I've killed people. But I'm a swordsman, and so was every man I defeated. Death is something you learn to expect when you choose the life of the sword."

"You're quick to draw such a fine line," the duke said, leaning back. "Must help you sleep at night." He flashed the couple a final, thin smile and turned to walk back down the dais steps. "Congratulations on your marriage. I can't think of two people who deserve each other more."

Eli arched an eyebrow at the duke's retreating back. "What a lovely individual."

Josef grunted in reply, but Adela cast a cold eye at her husband. "Finley's not the only one who thinks that way," she said softly. "I wouldn't speak so freely of the men you've killed, Prince Thereson."

"I am not ashamed of what I am," Josef said hotly.

"But others are," Adela said. "You'd do well to remember that."

Josef stared at her, but Adela was the picture of serenity as she turned and took the hand of the elderly lady who was next in line to wish the royal couple well.

It took almost two hours to greet all the nobility. They were arranged by rank, but Josef glowered at everyone equally, so it was quite fortunate that Adela was there to give the proper greeting to each noble before any offense could be taken.

After all the Oseran noble families had their say, the royal couple was shuffled down to the front gate to be announced before the crowd that had gathered in the square. The people cheered when Adela appeared, and she smiled and waved at them like a perfect princess. Beside her vibrant happiness, Josef looked like a looming vulture, hunched and dour, glaring at everything.

Eli watched the whole thing from the back, blithely ignoring the servant who was trying to convince him that he would be more comfortable waiting in his room. He tried sending Josef cues to lighten up, but Josef was too far gone in his dudgeon to notice, and Eli soon gave up in favor of watching Adela.

It was quite the show. The princess was the perfect mix of sweet shyness and hard Oseran duty with her long, glossy hair, pretty smiles, and shining armor. The crowd was mad for her. They cheered wildly, pressing against the guards. Adela smiled and waved back, looking down with becoming modesty whenever the people grew too wild. This, of course, only made the crowd cheer louder. It was a perfectly played performance. So perfect that Eli was beginning to wonder how long she'd practiced.

Finally, the presentation ended, and the royal couple was escorted back to the throne room. Josef looked like a ten-year veteran returning from the front as he walked over to the pillar to retrieve the Heart of War and the rest of his weaponry. Adela, on the other hand, was prettier than ever, with her cheeks glowing from the warmth of the crowd. She stopped a moment to greet the knot of royal guardsmen who were waiting at the throne room entrance, and then she excused herself and walked over to her husband. Josef stopped strapping swords to himself long enough to give her a questioning look.

"The queen asked that I give you a tour of the barracks," she said, her voice almost shy. "In case you wanted to resume your duty as head of the Queen's Guard."

Josef wrinkled his nose. "Who's head now?"

"I am," Adela said.

"Impossible," Josef said, getting back to the business of reattaching his weapons. "That's a royal position, inherited by blood. Your father wasn't even titled. How'd you end up with it?"

"Because your mother was too sick to do it herself and she didn't trust Finley with her guards," Adela said, putting her hands on her hips. "It should be the prince's duty, but it's not like you were here, was it?"

Josef stopped midstrap. "I get it, all right? I wasn't here. I let people down. I'm a terrible prince. Message received, so you can all drop the guilt routine."

"You know, it doesn't have to be like this," Adela said, crossing her arms. "You could *try* being a prince, at least in public."

"I have tried," Josef said, buckling his second sword back onto his hip. "Didn't do me any good then, won't do me any good now. I just want to get this over with and get on with my life."

Adela gave him a scornful look. "Then I'll see you tonight," she said, turning on her heel. "And we can get on with getting this over with. Good afternoon, prince."

Josef sighed. "Adela..."

But the princess was already walking away. Josef watched her go and then he turned and grabbed the Heart of War, slinging it on his back with so much force that Eli winced.

"You know," Eli said as gently as he could, "she does have a point."

"Shut. Up," Josef said.

"It could be worse," Eli went on. "At least you're not stuck with some insipid court flower. I mean, despite the hobble of being married to you, she seems to be a popular princess. She's certainly not bad to look at, not stupid, and we've all seen she's a decent fighter."

"That's the thing," Josef said, dropping his voice. "I can't shake the feeling something was wrong with that duel."

"Josef." Eli *tsk*ed. "Calling foul just because she gave you a harder time than you expected isn't very princely."

"I'm not calling foul," he said softly. "Adela and I were kids together, remember? We had the same sword instructor, and we dueled a lot. I knew she would be good. I just didn't expect her to be that good."

"That fast, you mean," Eli said, lowering his voice to match Josef's.

"It's not even that," Josef said, shaking his head. "She could have dodged that blow to the chest. I saw her feet start to move, but then she stopped. She let me win."

Eli fought the urge to smile. "Maybe she didn't want to embarrass you?"

"She's not *that* good," Josef grumbled, marching toward the door. "Come on. I need a drink."

"But you don't drink," Eli said, running after him.

Josef started walking faster. "I do now."

Eli left it at that and focused on keeping up with his swordsman. This was going to be some wedding night.

Two hours later, Josef had almost finished his one drink when a servant entered and told him his room was ready.

"I have a room," Josef said, scowling up from where he sat on the floor with the Heart of War propped on his shoulder. "What do you think you just walked into?"

The servant flinched, and Eli gave him a sympathetic look from his spot on the bed, but he didn't do anything to save the poor boy. In the five years he'd known Josef, he'd never seen him in such a foul mood. He was happy to let someone else take the heat for a bit.

"Forgive me, my lord," the servant said at last, eying Josef's knives, all of which had found their way back to their places on Josef's body. "This secure chamber is for noble guests. I've been ordered to escort you to the rooms you will be sharing with your wife."

Josef set his glass on the floor with a bitter sigh and stood up. The servant stepped aside as Josef walked out the door, but when Eli tried to follow, the man cut him off.

"I am sorry, sir," he said. "The queen's orders were that the prince was to go alone. Respect for his wedding night, you must understand."

"Well, I would never disrespect a wedding night," Eli said, glancing over the man's shoulder. He caught Josef's eyes and gave him the look they'd shared a thousand times: *Do you want to get out?* Josef shook his head, and Eli stayed put, watching from the doorway as the servant escorted Josef down the hall. When they disappeared around the corner, Eli stepped back into the room.

He picked up Josef's half-empty glass from the floor and finished it in one long drink. He set the empty glass on the table and grabbed the bottle of spirits instead. He corked it tight and slid the bottle into his belt. When it was secure, he walked over to the window and hoisted himself up, sliding between the bars with practiced ease into the city night.

CHAPTER

9

Did you see his face?" Henry was laughing so hard he could barely get the words out. "You'd think he was standing for execution, not affirming his marriage."

Adela smiled and refilled Henry's cup from the fat bottle of dark wine. They were sitting in the officer's lounge of the castle guard, a little hallway of a room at the very top of the palace just below the tower where the Council wizards kept the queen's Relay point. There were three of them seated around the polished table: Adela; old Beechum, her sergeant; and Henry Finley, Duke Finley's eldest son and Adela's vice captain.

Henry took the refilled glass and downed its contents in one swallow. Adela leaned on the table, watching him with a wary eye. "Maybe you should stop, Henry," she said. "You're on duty tonight."

"Why?" he said, tossing his empty cup on the table. "If the prince of Osera is a murderer, why can't I be a drunk?" He lurched forward, bumping the table so hard he set the other glasses rocking. "It's a tragedy, that's what it is, you having to go to bed with that bloodthirsty—"

"Finley." Sergeant Beechum's voice was heavy with warning. "Like him or not, Thereson is our prince. You will be civil."

"Civil." Henry snorted. "There's a word that has no place in the same breath with Thereson. When my father's king, he'll turn that failure prince out on his glowering face. Just see if he doesn't. Then you'll be free, Dela."

"I'm sure your father will toss Josef into the sea the moment the crown's on his head," Adela said with a smile. "Just as I'm equally sure my mother and I will be tossed right behind him. The dear Duke Finley doesn't care much for us."

"My father doesn't like competition," Henry said bitterly, and then his face broke into a smile. "He doesn't know you like I do, princess. He's angry that the Queen's Guard loves and follows you with a devotion not seen since Theresa was young, or that the people cheer you louder than they cheer him. He doesn't understand that those things don't have to stand in his way. I keep trying to tell him that an alliance—"

"Is impossible now," Adela finished. "My husband's come home, Henry. I'm no longer a wife in name only. I'm afraid I now truly am the competition your father always accused me of being."

"More's the bad luck," Beechum said blackly. "Thereson is the shame of the Eisenlowe name. It's a disgrace for a prince of the Iron Lions to be a murderer and a thief and who knows what else. We'd have all been better off if he'd never come home."

"I don't doubt it," Adela said. "But he's here now, and we must make the best of it."

Henry sat back in his chair with a huff. "I still can't believe you let him beat you in the Proving. It would have done the country well to see that traitor get the beating he deserved."

"Who says I let him win?" Adela said, reaching for her own cup. "He *is* a renowned swordsman."

"Come off it, Dela," Henry said with a sly smile. "We all know you're the best fighter in the guard. There's no way that wastrel prince could beat you. What *I* want to know is how much the old battle-ax leaned on you to take the fall and make her brat of a son look good."

"Henry!" Beechum cried, eyes wide. "Mind your tongue!"

Henry shrugged and poured himself another drink. Adela sat back, swirling her own half-full cup thoughtfully. She was about to take a sip when a soft knock sounded at the door. A servant in royal livery poked his head in when she called, looking sheepishly at the princess. Adela took the hint with a sigh, setting her cup on the table.

"Excuse me, gentlemen," she said, standing. "It seems it's time for me to do my wifely duty."

"Good luck, Captain," Sergeant Beechum said, saluting her as she followed the servant out into the hall. Henry said nothing, just stared into his wine as Adela closed the door behind her.

She was scarcely down the stairs when she heard it open again. Adela stopped with a deep breath, catching the servant's sleeve.

"I know the way," she said. "Go on."

The servant looked at her, and she could see the conflicting orders warring in his mind, the queen's command that the royal couple be escorted to the chamber versus the princess's trusted word. But the princess was here and the queen was not, so the man excused himself, hurrying down the hall as Henry caught up with Adela.

"Don't go," he whispered, catching her hand.

"I don't have much choice, Henry," she said, deftly dodging as his face closed in for a wine-soaked kiss. "I'm married, remember?"

"Doesn't matter," Henry whispered. "The only reason anyone still cares about that runaway is because Theresa's still alive. When she's dead and my father's king, I'll be the prince, not him. But that doesn't mean you have to stop being a princess." His hands circled her waist, emphasizing his point. "Or don't you love me anymore, Dela?"

"Henry," Adela whispered, stopping him with a finger pressed against his lips. "Josef coming home changes nothing. You know that. But so long as he's here, we can't be seen like this. If the queen finds out, things could get very sticky."

"No, they wouldn't," Henry whispered, kissing her fingertip. "Theresa could never be mad at her perfect princess. Even if she was, your mother would smooth things over. Everyone knows the queen would never do anything to hurt her beloved Lenette."

"I'm glad you're so confident," Adela said, gently extricating herself from his arms. "But for the moment there are appearances to keep up."

Henry's face screwed into a pout, and Adela leaned in, lowering her voice to a purr. "Don't worry, love," she whispered. "This will all be over soon."

"I hope so," Henry said, crossing his arms with a scowl. "The thought of you with that highwayman they have the nerve to call a prince makes me ill. If I could, I'd call him out tonight and finish him. Then you'd be mine for good."

"That's sweet, Henry," Adela said, smiling. "But don't go challenging Josef. You're a decent swordsman, but I wasn't entirely faking today, and I prefer you whole."

Henry beamed at that, and Adela kissed him quickly on the cheek before turning away. "I'll see you tomorrow, Henry."

Henry stood in the hall, gazing after her. "Tomorrow, Dela," he whispered.

She waved one last time and vanished around the corner, leaving the young Finley alone with his longing.

Once she was away, she picked up the pace, walking briskly.

Servants bowed as she passed, smiling knowingly. Adela smiled back, but her mind was only half on the princess act. She'd taken the long way to the royal quarters without thinking, walking along the castle's eastern face, the face that looked out over the Unseen Sea. The sun was behind her now, and the ocean lay glittering beneath the light of the last sliver of the waning moon. She watched it as she walked, gazing at the long, flat line of the horizon. Somewhere out there, the Empress's fleet was preparing. Ever since the queen had declared that the Empress was on the move, Adela had been watching the sea day and night, waiting for the first glimpse of the ships that would change her life forever. Her hand sank unbidden to the heavy, ornate short sword at her hip. When the Empress came, she would be ready.

The servant led Josef to a suite in the oldest part of the palace. There were five rooms in total: a sitting room with a single, narrow window overlooking the castle's front courtyard, a dressing chamber, a washroom with a tiny fireplace and an iron tub, a small library, and, of course, the bedchamber with its massive bed cut from the wood of the last of Osera's oaks before the entire island had been deforested to make way for the growing city. The servant insisted on giving Josef the full tour, and Josef let him, despite the fact that he knew the suite with his eyes closed. After all, for the first half of his life, these had been his rooms.

Very little had changed. The rooms had been cleaned and divested of the clothes and toys he'd left behind the night he ran away to become a swordsman, but the suffocating feel of the place hadn't changed at all. If anything, the dark rooms seemed even smaller than before, though Josef supposed that was because he'd grown several inches since he was fifteen.

Josef let the servant finish his tour before ordering him to get out. When the man finally left, Josef sat down on the silk couch in the sitting room. The sky was dark outside the tiny slit window. Torches flickered down in the courtyard below, making it feel far later than it was. Sitting on the creaking couch, the same couch he'd sat on with his mother while she lectured him on being a prince, he felt strangely outside of time. He could still see his mother as she had been, tall and golden and unapproachable. A queen in every sense, not that bent, old woman sleeping in the room above him. Josef looked up, glaring at the wood-beam ceiling. Hot, childish anger welled up in his chest, surprising him with its vigor. The anger had been building since he'd set foot in Osera, since he'd first seen his increased bounty and realized what it meant. Being back here, in this palace, and now in these rooms, he felt like he was fifteen again—still trapped by duty he hadn't asked for and expectations he could never meet, still desperate to get out, to get away.

Josef frowned and took a breath, a swordsman's breath, as his old sword master had taught him, and let the anger drift away. The Heart's weight pressed on his back, reminding him of how far he'd come. He reached up with a reverent motion, drawing the black blade from its wrapping and laying it across his knees. He was not trapped, he told himself as his fingers traced the Heart's scarred surface. He was here by choice, a son doing a good turn for his mother, to whom he owed his life. When he was done, he would leave by choice. He would turn and walk away from the court and the crown and everything else that had no claim over him anymore.

Feeling slightly better, Josef leaned over and set the Heart against the stone fireplace. Realizing it could be a while before Adela arrived, Josef flicked a dagger out of his sleeve. He fetched his whetstone from his pocket and, sitting up on the pillows, began to sharpen his knives, killing the time with long, slow strokes as he waited for his wife.

He didn't have long to wait. He'd scarcely finished his daggers when the door creaked and Adela stepped into the room. Her armor was gone, replaced by a close-tailored jacket that showed off her figure and long leather trousers tucked into short boots. Her sword, however, was still at her side, and that comforted Josef. Princesses baffled him, but an opponent he could understand, and Adela had always been up for a fight when they were kids.

She stopped when she saw him, and he got the feeling she didn't expect him to just be sitting there, waiting. But, as always with Adela, she adapted, stepping into the room like this was how she ended every evening.

"Have you eaten?" she said, her voice bright and cheery.

Josef shook his head.

"I'll ring the bell, then," she said, stepping over the blades he'd laid out on the carpet.

Josef just nodded and began putting his knives back into their sheaths.

Dinner arrived a few moments later, a series of trays carried in by servants who gave Josef knowing smiles until he reached for his sword. After that, dinner was laid on the table with great efficiency and the servants vanished out the door as silently as they had come in.

Adela walked over to a cabinet and pulled out a bottle of dark wine, carefully pouring two glasses and setting them on the table.

"Sit," she said, sitting down.

Josef walked to the table. "Is that an order, captain?"

"No," she said. "You can starve if you like."

Josef arched an eyebrow, but he pulled out the chair and sat down. She pushed a plate of roast meat across the table at him. "Eat."

"Why the sudden concern for my well-being?" Josef said, taking the fork and helping himself.

"I want this over as much as you do," Adela said, spooning a pile of roasted vegetables onto her own plate. "And it's kind of hard to get a baby from a dead man."

Josef stabbed his fork down so hard the tines bent. "I can't believe you agreed to this," he muttered. "Marriage to an absent husband is one thing, but a baby?"

"You think too much of yourself, Josef," Adela said between neat bites of her food. "All you are at this point is an impediment to the progression of the bloodline, same as I'm little more than a useful vessel. The only thing anyone in this kingdom wants or expects from us is a child to carry on the line of Iron Lions. My life has always depended on being what was expected of me, and when you look at it that way, being a mother isn't so different from being guard captain."

Josef winced. "When you put it like that it kind of removes the nobility from the whole affair."

"There wasn't much to begin with," Adela said, drinking her wine. "We'll be done pretending one day. Until then, it doesn't have to be all bad, does it? I mean, we used to be friends."

"We did," Josef said quietly. "A lot can change in fifteen years, Dela."

"Nothing that matters, Josef," Adela said, putting down her cup and tossing her napkin on the table. "I'm going to bed," she announced, standing up and starting toward the bedroom. "Finish your damn wine and let's get this done."

Josef looked after her. "But I don't dri—"

The slam of the bedroom door cut him off. Josef sat at the table fuming for several minutes, and then he let the battle calm fall over him. He grabbed the small glass of wine and drained it in one gulp. When it was gone, he stood up, threw the empty glass on the table, and turned toward the bedroom. He marched across the room and opened the door with an angry tug, slamming it behind him as he vanished into the candle-lit bedchamber.

Nico crouched on the edge of the kitchen chimney, staring through the tiny strip of Josef's window at the closed bedroom door. She stared for a long time, digging her fingers into the sleeves of her coat until the fabric growled.

She was such an idiot. What had she been thinking, vanishing right in front of the queen? Hiding from Josef when he'd come looking for her? It was stupid, dangerous, and, worse, childish.

Nico put her head down, burying her burning face into the folds of her coat. Josef would be so disappointed in her. He'd always said she was a survivor, a fighter. He didn't know she was a coward, hiding away on the rooftop because she couldn't stand to see him with...with...

Nico sighed and jumped down, sprawling herself out on the steep slope of the palace roof to stare up at the long, snakelike creatures that were just barely visible against the flat black of the night sky. The worst part was she didn't even have a right to be this angry. After all, what was Josef to her? A partner in crime. A friend. A trusted companion. But all those things could be said about Eli, and she wouldn't be up here if Eli was the one who was married, would she?

Nico rolled over and punched the palace roof, breaking the tiles with a hard crunch. If she were honest with herself, she could trace her love for Josef back to the moment he picked her up off the shattered slope of that mountain. Maybe even earlier. She might have loved him from the moment she first saw his shadow, but whenever it had started, her love was her problem, not his. He hadn't asked her to love him, didn't return her love. And even if he miraculously did, she wouldn't let him. Though she was her own master now and the demon was sealed away, the seed was still inside her. She was still a demonseed, still a monster. If it wasn't for the coat, the world would turn on her the instant it recognized what she was.

And who could love a monster?

Nico closed her eyes. At once, the world faded away. She was standing in a dry, sun-drenched field, staring at the boulder that was sitting on the pit that held the demon. It was still secure, and Nico breathed a sigh of relief followed by a rush of profound self-pity. She might be her own master, but her control was still unstable. Even now she could feel the demon patiently pressing on the weight of the will that kept him trapped. He was always there, waiting for her guard to go down, for her determination to falter. Nothing she did could ever banish him for good. If she was ever weak, he would win, and she would become the monster the world thought she was. How could she ask Josef to love something so dangerous? She had no right.

She was still in her sunny field staring at the boulder when something cool, smooth, and hard touched her cheek. Nico jumped backward, returning to the dark rooftop with a jolt as she landed with her fists up to see Eli leaning against the chimney. It actually took her a few seconds to recognize him, on account of the light. Where everything else on the roof was dark and still, Eli was strangely bright, his skin almost luminous, like he was lit up from the inside. She'd never seen anything like it, and yet, almost as soon as she noticed it, the light vanished and Eli stood before her, same as always. He had a bottle in his hand, the cool thing she'd felt against her cheek. When he caught her eyes, he sat down and held out the bottle in obvious invitation.

Nico stayed back, suddenly embarrassed. She had almost certainly put him on the spot last night, vanishing like she had, but he didn't look angry. He just sat there, bottle out, his black hair standing up in all directions in celebration at being freed from the ridiculous blond wig.

Finally, she crept along the roof and sat next to him, taking the offered bottle gingerly, as though it might explode.

"It's brandy," he said before she could ask. "Drink."

She put the bottle to her lips and gagged almost instantly.

"It burns." She coughed, nearly throwing the bottle back at him.

"That it does," Eli said sagely, taking a sip himself before recorking the bottle. "But a little fire can be good at knocking people out of their self-pity."

She flinched and cursed herself for a fool. Of course Eli would know.

"I admit Josef's been an idiot about handling all this," Eli said, his smile fading. "But you can't hide up here forever, you know."

"I know," Nico said slowly.

Eli scowled. "Not that he doesn't deserve the cold shoulder after what he pulled. Honestly, married for months and didn't even—"

"No," Nico said, shaking her head. "It's not our business what he does with his private life. It wasn't like it was a problem until now."

"And now it's a very big problem," Eli said. "One that's going to get even worse if my instincts are right, and they usually are." He glanced at her. "I'm going to need you with me, Nico. Josef's in way over his head. He needs us, both of us. So, are we a team? Just like always?"

Nico sighed. "Yes," she said. And it felt good. It was time to stop sulking. But... "I reserve the right to get out if I need to, though." Just in case she couldn't take looking at his perfect, beautiful, demon-free princess.

"Fair enough," Eli said, grabbing her hand and shaking it before she could snatch it back. "Now that that's settled, there's something else I was meaning to ask you."

Nico froze. She'd been with Eli long enough to know that overly casual tone meant trouble, but he was just leaning back on the roof, completely relaxed. However, the moment their eyes met, the strange glow flashed again, brighter than before. Nico jerked back, covering her eyes. It did no good. The light shone through.

"Thought so."

Nico dropped her arms to find Eli was sitting up, looking at her like a cat who'd just cornered a mouse. "You can see, can't you?"

"See what?" Nico said, cringing.

"Spirits," Eli said. "You can see them, like Slorn."

Nico stared at him, dumbstruck. Of course. That's what they were.

"This is amazing!" Eli said, scooting so close he was practically sitting in her lap. "How long?"

Nico leaned away. "Since the valley," she said softly. "How did you know?"

Eli grinned. "I first suspected it on the boat. You were staring at the scenery a little too much, and that got me wondering. After all," he said, dropping his voice, "demons can see like spirits, and you're as close to demon as humans get. It makes sense that you should pick up a bit of sight along with your other gifts."

"They're not gifts," Nico said sharply.

Eli waved his hand dismissively. "But you *can* see, right?"

"I think so," Nico said. "I mean, it didn't exactly come with instructions. And I've never seen spirits, so it's not like I have something to compare it to." She left out the part where she'd thought it was another trick of the demon's. No reason to give Eli any more reasons to think she was unstable. But if she'd had any fears of Eli's rejecting her over this new development, they died right then. The thief was almost trembling with delight.

"Tell me about it!" he cried. "Slorn never tells me anything. He's so stingy. I think it's the bear in him. But you'll tell me, right?"

Nico frowned, confused. "Tell you what?"

"Everything!" Eli said. "Look, I've been wondering my whole life: What do spirits see that we don't? What does the world look like to them? What's hidden from us? I have so many questions, and you can see my answers."

Nico looked up at the long, weaving, transparent shapes that coursed across the night sky. Winds, she now realized. She was seeing the winds. "They're kind of hard to describe."

Eli rolled his eyes enormously. "Try me."

Nico bit her lip. At least he didn't think she was crazy. Honestly, the fact that the things she'd been seeing were spirits made her feel enormously better. Spirits she could deal with.

"Well," she said, pointing up. "There are hundreds of winds above us. Earlier, they were blowing in from the sea. In the daylight they looked like long, clear snakes, only without heads or tails. Just long, um, tubes."

"Tubes?" Eli said, arching an eyebrow.

"Shut up," she muttered. "I'm trying. So earlier they were all blowing in from the sea, but now they're turning around."

"Ah, the night wind from the land," Eli nodded. "Do they look different?"

"Yes," Nico said, squinting. "They're clearer. During the day they're kind of opaque, like frosted glass. But at night they're clear, and it's easier to see the stuff on the dome of the sky."

The catch in Eli's breath made her jump, and she turned to find him staring at her, pale as death. "Dome of the sky?"

Nico nodded. "It's hard to see because of the winds, but sometimes I can see movement in the sky. It looks almost like the dome of the sky is a cloth, and something's pressing on the other side. It's very faint most of the time, but if I look for it, I can always find it somewhere. Sometimes I see it on several parts of the sky at once." She looked up again. "They're always there somewhere. I can probably find you one if—"

A sharp pressure on her wrist cut her off, and she looked down to see Eli's hand gripping her arm. The thief was still smiling, his face still calm, but the look in his eyes was the closest to true fear she'd ever seen on him.

"Nico," he said, his voice quiet. "You can't look at the sky."

"Why not?" Nico said, tugging her hand away.

"It's the one of the rules all spirits must obey," he whispered. "The first rule the Shepherdess spoke."

"Rule?" Nico said. She didn't understand what he was talking about.

Eli nodded. "There are a lot of rules, actually. Humans don't know them because we're blind and we don't need to. But if you're going to keep looking, Nico, you have to stay away from the sky. If you keep staring at it, bad things will happen."

"What do you mean 'bad things'?" Nico said. "How do you know all this?"

Eli leaned back. "A long time ago I made a childish decision that led to a very strange period in my life," he said slowly. "I learned a lot of things that people aren't supposed to know."

"Are you talking about the other Monpress?" Nico said.

Eli smirked. "No, not that. Giuseppe might be an old fox, but this isn't exactly his area. This happened before my apprenticeship, and it has nothing to do with thievery." The smile fell off his face, and Eli suddenly grew very serious. "I don't actually know what you are now, Nico. You're a demonseed who beat the demon. I've never even heard of something like that, and so I don't know if the rules even apply to you. But, just in case, now that you can see, you should at least know the rules before something comes down on you hard for breaking them. Make sense?"

Nico nodded.

"Good," Eli said, raising one finger. "Rule one: Don't look at the sky. Even the winds don't look at the sky."

Nico scowled. "But why? What's wrong with—"

Eli put his hand over her mouth. Nico almost bit it, but she stopped and contented herself with glaring at him until he took it away.

"Rule two," he said. "Never ask about the sky. Ever. Ever, ever. Now, there are other rules, like don't tell humans about stars and obey Great Spirits and so forth, but those are the two really important ones. The ones you really can't break."

"Why not?" Nico whispered. "And what are stars?"

"Can't tell you," Eli said. "That's a rule. Weren't you listening?"

Nico crossed her arms with a scowl. "Who made these rules, anyway?"

The laughter vanished from Eli's eyes, and he looked back and forth, even though the roof was empty as ever. "The Shepherdess," he whispered at last, his voice so low she could barely hear him. "She makes the only rules that matter in this world. She's the power around here, and all spirits want to please her, which means any spirit who catches you looking at the sky or talking about it will try to stop you whether they know what you are or not, and if they peek under your coat, the jig is up. They could report you to the League, or worse, the Shepherdess herself." He took a deep breath. "Anyway, just don't do it. There's a rule against looking at the sky for a reason."

Nico tilted her head, still not fully convinced. "And do you know that reason?"

"I have a theory," Eli said. "But I'm going to leave it at that. Let's just say that's a mess even I won't touch. Now"—he clapped his hands together, making her jump—"let's move on to the good stuff. I have so many questions."

Nico stared at him, still trying to catch up with the subject change after all the puzzles he'd dumped on her, but Eli was already on his feet, reaching for her hands to pull her up as well.

"Come on, come on," he said. "Night is burning, and we have so much to look at."

She shook her head and let him pull her to her feet. He led her along the stone gutters all the way to his window. Eli swung in first. He was calling for the servants before he landed, demanding food and a whole list of other things that made no sense at all. Nico shook her head and jumped after him, closing the window firmly behind her against the evening chill.

High overhead, ignored and unseen, the outlines of the enormous claws scraped harder than ever on the black dome of the sky.

CHAPTER

10

Heinricht Slorn sat cross-legged on the floor of his cell, staring at the mountain. Looking with that sight that his human mind could still barely comprehend, even after so many years, he could see the pulsing core of the mountain's strength beneath the cell walls. The power of the spirit flowed like a glacier from its peak to its roots buried in the very foundation of the world. The Shaper Mountain surrounded him, cutting him off from the outside, and yet the more he looked, the closer he came to understanding the world he had seen in the mountain's memory.

But as he studied the spirit, a tiny sound drew his eyes away from the mountain to the much humbler shape of the vent above his door. Strong as it was, the Shaper Mountain had no dominion over the winds. This deep in the mountain, the Teacher had been forced to create ventilation shafts so his human followers would not suffocate. The vent in Slorn's chamber was far too small for a man of Slorn's size, but not all men were Slorn's size. His ears flicked as the tiny noise sounded again, the light, small sound of leather on stone. Slorn turned his head, bear eyes slowly moving back and forth across his tiny cell, but he saw nothing. In fact, he saw less than nothing, a blank emptiness that was itself telling. He smiled and focused his large brown eyes to see not as spirits saw, but the mundane shape of the physical world, and as he did, the man slowly appeared.

"Hello, Heinricht," Sparrow said, flashing a superior smile as he straightened up from where he'd landed below the air vent. "Been a while."

"Not long enough," Slorn said.

Sparrow shrugged and leaned against the door, his shape flickering. Slorn blinked in annoyance, struggling to keep his eyes focused only on the physical world, the only place where Sara's little weapon was visible.

Sparrow's smile widened at his frustration. "Aren't you going to ask what I want?"

"Why should I ask such an obvious question?" Slorn said. "You're here to offer me freedom in exchange for joining Sara's menagerie, correct?"

Sparrow shrugged. "Good guess."

"It was no guess," Slorn said. "You don't have to know Sara long to know she would never let a situation like this slip by without playing her hand."

"Way I see it, Sara has all the cards now," Sparrow said, looking around at the small cell. "You've gotten yourself into quite the mess, haven't you? Whatever you came to tell your former masters, they must not have liked it since you're in a cell rather than at the head of a workshop where you belong. Sara can change that."

"I'm sure she could," Slorn said. "But Sara's price is always too high."

"All she asks is that you share your knowledge," Sparrow said. "Is that so much?"

Slorn's calm expression turned into a snarl. "I've seen how she treats her people, Sparrow. I'm already a bear. I have no interest in becoming a dog. Besides"—Slorn looked down at the floor, toward the mountain's roots—"I have unfinished business here."

"What business can you finish here?" Sparrow said, laughing. "The Shapers are so bound in by law they've locked away their greatest asset for a minor transgression from a decade ago. Such people don't deserve access to talent like yours." He pushed off the wall, walking across the tiny cell until he was barely a foot from Slorn's muzzle. "Sara's different," he whispered. "She doesn't care about pasts or traditions, only results. Come with me to Zarin and nothing will ever stand in your way again."

Slorn looked him in the eyes. "And that is exactly why I'm not coming with you. I cannot work with someone who values only the ends and never the means."

Sparrow's face fell. "You're not exactly in a position to judge, bear man," he said in a low, sharp voice. "You were the one who led that poor, ignorant Spiritualist girl straight into the Shaper Mountain, knowing full well she'd never be allowed to leave. Tell me, Slorn, is that something a moral man would do?"

"No," Slorn said. "But I had no choice. I knew when I decided to return to the Shapers that I would never leave this mountain again. That's why I needed another wizard, someone I could trust, who could hear my argument and the mountain's reply and take that knowledge where I no longer could."

"And where was she supposed to take it?" Sparrow said. "Into her cell? Because that's where she is, you know. Alone, suffering, without even her puppy for comfort, and it's all because of you."

"I am fully aware of my fault in this," Slorn said. "But Miranda has a much bigger role in things to come than she knows. A role I forced her into by bringing her here, and a role I will force her to continue by hiring you to free her on my behalf."

Sparrow snorted. "I don't think you can afford me."

"Ah, but I won't be paying you," Slorn said, taking something from his jacket pocket. It was a fat, leather-bound notebook tied with a loop of string.

"What's that?" Sparrow said, leaning in for a better look. "Your diary?"

"My research notes," Slorn said, holding the book like a precious relic. "This book contains the complete record of Nivel's and my work for the last ten years. I may not be able to afford your services, but this book should be plenty to buy the services of the woman who owns you. Every answer to every question Sara has asked me about demons over the last decade is in his book. I'm giving it to her in exchange for Miranda's freedom, plus freedom for all her spirits."

A sly smile spread over Sparrow's face. "*All* her spirits?" he said, scratching his chin. "A clever touch, bear man." He eyed the book, and Slorn could almost see the scales weighing the danger of freeing Miranda versus the danger of angering Sara. Sara must have won out in the end, for a moment later, Sparrow's hand swooped in and snatched the book from Slorn's fingers.

"The Council accepts your offer," he said, hefting the book in his hands. "But I must say, you've become a very trusting bear in your old age, Heinricht. How do you know I won't just take this and leave poor little Miranda to the mess you made for her? I mean, it's not like you can go for a stroll to see if I kept my word."

Slorn smiled. "It was because I knew you were following us that I risked bringing Miranda to the Shaper Mountain in the first place. Sara's too good a judge of opportunity to abandon a spirit like Mellinor. My guess is that you have orders to take us both back to Zarin. However, breaking someone out of the Shaper Mountain is no easy feat, and since I'm not going, you might be tempted to cut your losses and just leave. With this in mind, think of that book as collateral. You'll find a letter to Sara on the inside cover explaining that Miranda is supposed to be with you."

Sparrow's smile faltered, and he flipped the book open, glaring at the note scrawled across the inside cover, impossible to rip out without ruining the first half of the notes.

"You can be a very conniving bear, Heinricht," he said, snapping the book shut with a deep sigh. "You know, of course, that this little payment is between you and Sara and won't spare the Spiritualist the enormous debt she'll owe the Council for her escape."

Slorn shrugged. "Miranda is a competent woman. I trust her to handle her own obligations."

"I'll be sure to tell her you said so," Sparrow said, tucking the notebook into his pocket as he walked back to the wall. "Lovely chatting with you, Heinricht."

"You take care of Miranda, Sparrow," Slorn said, his voice heavy with warning. "She knows things now that could save us all."

"What, haven't you heard?" Sparrow said, glancing over his shoulder. "The Empress is on the move. Nothing can save us now." He pressed himself against the wall and jumped, catching the edge of the vent with one hand. "Good-bye, old bear," he said, pulling himself expertly into the opening. "Maybe we'll meet again someday."

"Likely not," Slorn said.

Sparrow laughed and folded his thin body, slipping out of the cell like smoke. Slorn watched the place where he had been for several minutes, blinking his eyes every time his focus drifted from the physical world toward the spirit. Someday, he told himself, someday he would ask Sara where she'd found Sparrow and how his spirit invisibility actually worked. It was a lie, of course. In all likelihood he would never leave this cell again. Still...

Letting the spirit sight take over again, Slorn looked down through the heart of the mountain, down to its base, the enormous shelf of rock that supported all the mountains around the Shaper peak, and then down farther still to where its roots ended at the very bottom of world. There, the stone suddenly stopped in a smooth, curved base, as smooth as the arc of the sky, but upside down. Slorn swallowed. He'd never looked so deep underground before, and it was only because the mountain was one single spirit that he could do it now.

He almost wished he hadn't.

Slorn pressed his broad hands to the stone floor. Tiny tremors, too small for anyone who wasn't feeling for them to notice, ran through the Shaper Mountain. They came in long, jagged scrapes, as though something far away was rubbing against the stone. Every time the stone shook, he saw a flicker of movement far, far below, a flicker of movement in the horrible, familiar shape of an enormous, clawed hand.

Slorn lifted his hands from the stone and folded them in his lap. If the hands were above as well as below, then Gredit was right. There was something terribly wrong with the world, something the Shepherdess didn't want the spirits to see. The Shaper Mountain knew this, but it could not act because of the Shepherdess. However, Slorn was certain that, while the Teacher made all the motions of an obedient servant, not even the Shepherdess could cow such an old, stubborn spirit forever. All he had to do was wait.

With that, the problem of how to spend his imprisonment was decided. Slorn looked away from the bottom of the world and leaned back, settling against the cold stone of the mountain. When he was comfortable, he opened his mouth and, in a quiet voice, began to ask questions. He asked about the demonseeds, about the Dead Mountain, about the clawing hands. He asked about spirits, about humans, where they'd come from, why the Shepherdess had made them, why they were blind. Everything he wanted to know, he asked. No answers came, but Slorn did not stop. He would never stop until the stone replied. Nivel had told him once that he was as stubborn as a mountain. To honor her memory, to give meaning to her death, he was going to prove her right. And so he kept asking questions in the white silence until, far sooner than he expected, the cell door opened.

Miranda lay facedown on the stone floor, her eyes closed against the constant light of the mountain. It did no good. The light bled through her eyelids until even her dreams were suffused in white. She pushed herself up with a groan and stared glumly at the room that had become her world: a white box, ten feet by ten feet by ten feet, no door, no windows, nothing even to mark which wall was which. Twice a day, the wall opened and a Shaper appeared with food, but otherwise she had no outside contact, no company at all. After the stone swallowed her, she'd lost consciousness and woken up here, alone. She hadn't seen Slorn since the meeting, but worse than that, Gin was missing. His absence bothered her more than her own imprisonment, and since he wasn't a bound spirit, she couldn't even feel if he was alive or dead.

After she woke up, Miranda had spent the first dozen hours of her confinement trying to break out. Normally, this wouldn't be a problem. Again, the Shapers had left her rings, and though the walls of her cell were part of the mountain, they were still stone. Mellinor's water had broken down larger walls than these, so had Durn's boulders. But the problem wasn't the walls; it was her spirits. No matter how she harangued them, they refused to act against the mountain, and every time she asked why, every one of them gave the same answer: They could not raise their strength against a star.

Miranda pressed her cheek against the cold stone. A week ago, she wouldn't have bought that excuse for a second. Now, after her meeting with the mountain, she understood a little better. Stars were spirits even greater than Great Spirits, chosen and backed by the greatest spirit of them all, the one called the Shepherdess. Spiritualist oath or no, so long as the Shaper Mountain was her jailer, her spirits could do nothing to help her. Not unless she forced them. Revulsion flooded her mind at the thought. She would die here before she Enslaved any spirit, much less her own.

Of course, dying here was looking more and more like her fate. She didn't even know how long she'd been in her cell. Two days at least, but without a window she couldn't be sure, and the guard never answered her questions. All she had was the endless, unchanging light and the slow feeling of time crawling over her skin.

Abandoning sleep, Miranda pushed herself up with a frustrated sigh. She walked to the white wall across from where she'd been lying and began running her fingers over the smooth stone. It was a futile effort. She'd already checked the walls hundreds of times. There were no cracks, no weaknesses. Still, she kept looking. She had to keep looking, keep trying for an escape, or she would go mad.

She was standing on tiptoe, running her fingers along the corner where the ceiling met the wall, when she heard the familiar soft grinding of stone. Miranda fell back on her heels and turned just in time to see the stone of the far wall fold in on itself to create a small door. It happened instantly, the flawless stone she'd run her fingers over just a minute before curling away to reveal the stern face and tall, heavy frame of the Shaper who served as her jailer. He was glowering, as usual, and Miranda glowered right back.

She was about to make her traditional demand to be set free when she noticed something was wrong. The man's scowling face was off, somehow, his dark eyes unfocused and glossy. That was all she saw before he fell forward.

Miranda danced back with an undignified squeal. The Shaper landed face-first on the floor with a hollow thump, his arms flopping beside him in a way that made her stomach twist. She stared at him for several seconds before an infuriating, familiar voice brought her eyes back up.

"Well, well. Still alive?"

Sparrow was leaning on the door to her cell, a smug smile on his thin lips.

Miranda took a step back. "You!"

"Your gallant hero," he said, spreading his arms with a flourish.

Miranda took another step back, keeping her distance as Sparrow stepped into the cell. He was dressed in the same dull brown he'd worn to chase Eli, and though the color should have stood out like a stain against the pure white walls, she was having a hard time focusing on him. Slowly, subtly, she hid her hands in her pockets and began to wake her spirits, just in case.

"Why are you here?"

"To rescue you, of course," Sparrow said, his voice all sincerity.

Miranda didn't buy it for a moment. "If you think I believe that you snuck in here and killed a man to rescue me out of the goodness of your heart—"

"Perish the thought," Sparrow said. "I'm here because Sara wants you alive and useable, which means not locked up. And I didn't kill anyone, for your information." He kicked the downed man with his boot. "It's a paralytic poison. He'll wake up in an hour with pins and needles like he's never felt, but otherwise unharmed. Not to crush your ego, but Sara doesn't care enough about your rescue to risk angering the mountain by killing a Shaper."

"But freeing a prisoner is fine?"

Sparrow gave her a withering look. "My patience is very thin today, Spiritualist. If you would rather not be rescued, I can leave you here."

"No, no," Miranda said quickly, her shoulders slumping. "I'm in your debt, Sparrow."

"You don't know the half of it, dear," he said, walking farther into the cell. "Shall we be off?"

"No," Miranda said, shaking her head. "Gin and Slorn are still prisoners. I can't leave without them."

"Way ahead of you," Sparrow said. "I knew you wouldn't turn down an offer of escape, so I took the liberty of freeing the dog first. As for Slorn, he's decided to remain in the mountain, so we'll just have to make do without his sterling company."

Miranda gave an incredulous snort. "You actually think I believe that?"

"I don't much care what you believe," Sparrow said. "But understand that Slorn is worth a lot more to Sara than you are. I would gladly trade you for him if I could, but the bear man said he had unfinished business with the mountain."

"So you left him?" Miranda said, horrified. "Just like that?"

"Just. Like. That," Sparrow answered. "I have many jobs, Miss Lyonette. Bear wrestler isn't one of them. We came to an arrangement of mutual benefit to the reasonable satisfaction of both parties. Let's leave it at that. Now, we should be going before the Shapers miss our friend here." He tapped the prone man with his boot again. "Or before your overprotective dog gets nervous and decides to come find you himself."

Miranda paled. She wouldn't put it past Gin. "Fine," she said. "How are we getting out?"

Sparrow smiled and slipped his hand into his pocket. "The Shapers must not think too much of you," he said, pulling out something small, flat, and dark. "This cell is right up against the mountain's outer wall, so that's the way we're going to go."

"What?" Miranda said. "Through the wall?"

"A bit flashy, I'll grant you," Sparrow said, tossing the small, black object with one hand and catching it in the other. "But thanks to your overly inquisitive and suspicious nature, we don't exactly have the luxury of time."

Miranda's eyes darted to the thing he was tossing between his hands. It was shaped like a teardrop, smooth, dark, and slightly wrinkled, like a peach pit. "What's that?"

"One of Sara's experiments," Sparrow said, bending over and tucking the thing into the crook where the wall met the floor. "You may want to step back."

Miranda's eyes widened, but she obeyed, stepping back to the door to her cell while carefully avoiding the paralyzed guard. Sparrow followed a moment later. In the hall was the small cart that the guard had been pushing before Sparrow had interrupted him. It was loaded with plates of cold prison rations, which Miranda recognized far too well, and a stone pitcher of water, which Sparrow grabbed.

"This should do," he said, hefting the full pitcher with both hands.

Before Miranda could ask what he meant by that, Sparrow turned and threw the pitcher's contents across the room. The water flew in an arc, glittering in the mountain's white light for a moment before splashing down on the peach pit Sparrow had left against the wall.

The moment the water hit, the thing exploded. Miranda jumped back as a sound like a breaking tree cracked her eardrums. She slammed her hands over her ears, but it did no good. The sound was as much spiritual as physical, throwing her spirits into an uproar. Looking up, she saw why.

The peach pit was now a tangle of roots and branches. The wood seethed like a nest of snakes, coiling and shooting in all directions. Roots dug into the white stone of the mountain, crumbling the rock as they pushed their way down. The cell wall came apart in chunks as the growing limbs, now covered with the first growth of new leaves, shot out in search of sunlight. The cluster of wood doubled in seconds. Whole chunks of stone were breaking off the cell walls, falling away as the newborn tree fought to reach the open air. The mountain began to shake under Miranda's feet, but it was too late. With a final snapping crash, the tree broke through the last layer of stone and golden sunlight streamed into Miranda's prison.

She stood there gaping for a split second before Sparrow grabbed her hand and yanked her off her feet. They jumped over the paralyzed guard, now dangling from the branches like a caught kite, and ran up the trunk of the newborn tree. Branches were still exploding from the trunk under their feet as great clusters of green raced to catch the newly won sunlight. Sparrow dodged them deftly, pulling Miranda up through the hole in the mountain and into the sun.

"You've still got that sea in you, right?" he shouted over the roar of the growing wood.

"What did Sara do to this poor spirit?" Miranda shouted back, nearly slipping when a branch suddenly sprouted under her foot. "This violates—"

"Shut up and answer the question!" Sparrow snapped. "Sea, yes or no?"

"Yes," Miranda yelled. "Why?"

The tree bucked beneath them as the mountain wind tossed the branches. They were outside, but Miranda could see nothing but the backs of leaves. Sparrow grabbed her hand and pointed it down. "Make a chute of water here."

Miranda tried to rip her hand away. "What do you—"

A horrible sound of snapping wood cut her off, and she whirled around to see the white stone of the Shaper Mountain chomp down on the hole the tree had broken. The trunk squealed as the rock clamped down, shaking violently as the mountain began to chew through the wood. Miranda grabbed for a branch to steady herself, but Sparrow still had her hand. He yanked her forward until she looked at him. The minute he had her eyes, he made a good luck gesture with his free hand and pushed her off the tree.

For a breathless moment, Miranda felt almost weightless as her feet left the pitching trunk. Then gravity kicked in, and she began to fall. She plummeted through the branches, grabbing for them desperately as she passed, but every one broke in her hand, too new and thin to stop her fall. Sunlight blinded her as she burst through the canopy into the icy air. The mountain towered above her, enormous and blindingly white against the pale morning sky. The freezing wind tossed her as she plummeted in free fall, unable even to turn and see what waited below. It was at this point, hurtling through the air, that her mind finally caught up with her falling body and she began to scream.

The sound was scarcely made before Mellinor answered. Water poured out of her. It flowed through the air, catching her fall in a series of pools. She splashed through each one only to drop to the next, but every pool slowed her fall until, at last, she landed safely in the snow on the mountain's slope. Sparrow landed beside her and rolled just in time to dodge Mellinor's water as it hit the ground.

As soon as the water landed, Sparrow was on his feet. "Keep going!" he shouted, pushing her.

Miranda ignored him and looked up. High overhead the enormous tree still clung to the side of the Shaper Mountain. Its branches were still straining toward the sun, but its trunk was a gnawed mess of broken wood where the mountain was clamping down harder and harder as it fought to break through the tree and close the wound. The branches shook one last time before the mountain closed up entirely, cutting the core of the trunk with a final, echoing snap.

"Mellinor," Miranda said softly as the enormous tree began to fall, the wide green crown flying like a broad arrow straight at their heads. "Get us out of here."

Water exploded out of her, shooting down the mountain in a torrent. Sparrow jumped in first, and the water swept him away like a twig. Miranda went next, throwing herself into the fast-moving water just before the broken tree crashed into the ledge. The tree screamed as it hit, sending a wave of snow crashing down the mountain, but Miranda was already far away, racing down the icy slope on Mellinor's water.

It should have been a horrible ride. The mountain was almost vertical below the shelf where they had landed, and the slope was strewn with sharp outcroppings and sudden crags. But Mellinor was adept at keeping her afloat, and the inland sea's water buoyed her over the roughest bits. Ahead of her, Sparrow seemed to be having a much harder time of things, but she had no time to see why. Less than thirty seconds after picking them up, Mellinor washed them out onto the bridge spanning the ravine between the Shaper Mountain and Knife's Pass.

Miranda fell coughing and gasping on the cold stone, but before she'd pulled herself together enough to handle more than a simple breath, Mellinor's voice roared in her ears.

"Keep moving," he thundered as he drew his water back into her. "The mountain is furious."

As soon as he said it, Miranda heard it too. A deep roar vibrated through the air, and the whole world began to shake with fury.

"Sparrow!" she shouted, jumping to her feet.

Sparrow was lying on his stomach a dozen feet from her. He rolled over with a groan when she reached him, coughing and clutching his ribs. "Powers," he muttered. "How do you do that all the time?"

"We have to go," Miranda said, yanking him up. "The mountain's destroying the bridge."

Even as she said it, the stone beneath them started to rock violently back and forth. She pulled Sparrow to his feet and they began to run. The rumbling grew worse with every step, and a new sound began inside the mountain's furious scream, the sound of stone cracking.

"It's trying to cut us off," Sparrow wheezed.

"I know, I know," Miranda cried, dragging him faster up the arch of the bridge. Cracks spidered under their feet as they ran, spreading like lightning across the smooth stone. Miranda cursed and pushed them faster.

"Come on!" she shouted, dragging Sparrow until she was nearly ripping his arm out of its socket. "*Run!*"

They ran. They ran as fast as they could, but they could not escape the mountain's anger. Huge chunks of rock were breaking free all around them, plummeting into the ravine below with small, terrified screams. The cracks under their feet grew larger as the shaking grew more violent until, with a final, echoing crack, the bridge itself broke free.

They weren't going to make it. The realization hit Miranda like a blow to the face. Already the world was tilting crazily as the bridge, shaken free of its ancient supports, lurched sickeningly sideways. Even so, Miranda kept running. She didn't know what else to do.

Suddenly, something white landed on the falling bridge in front of them. At first, Miranda thought it was a pile of snow, but it was too gray for snow, almost silver, and moving in swirls. Then the pile stretched out and began to run. Miranda's eyes went wide, and she felt the scream leave her throat before she realized she'd made a sound.

"*Gin!*"

Gin tore down the falling bridge faster than the wind itself, barreling straight at them. Miranda held out her hand and jerked for Sparrow to do the same. Gin reached them a second later, and as he passed, she dug her fingers into his thick, coarse fur. The moment her fist clenched on his coat, she was ripped off her feet by the ghosthound's momentum. He turned on a pin, claws digging into the crumbling stone, and then he kicked off again, running even faster back toward the pass.

Miranda clung to his side, her legs tangled with Sparrow's as they fought to hold on. This close, she could feel Gin's lungs thundering, his legs pumping faster than ever before. But in the seconds since Gin had appeared, they'd already fallen a frightening distance. The wall of the ravine rose above them, sheer and white and impossibly tall, the edge completely out of reach. She felt Gin's muscles tense as his back legs folded beneath him, and then he sprung, kicking the broken bridge off behind them as he launched into the air.

For a breathless moment, they were flying, soaring up out of the ravine. The jagged edge of the bridge's broken end hung just above them, ten feet, five feet, nearly in reach. And then, just as quickly, it began to move away. Gin's legs kicked frantically, and Miranda realized they were falling. It was too far. Gin had missed.

From this point, everything happened both painfully slow and blindingly fast.

Miranda's hand shot out, Durn's cloudy emerald already flashing with light. The rock spirit tore himself from the ring, grabbing the bridge's broken edge with one enormous boulder of a fist. At the same time, his other hand swung down to grab Gin's middle. The stone wrapped around them in a vise and then released, flipping them up. Miranda's fingers were torn from Gin's coat as they tumbled through the air and landed sprawling on the smooth stone paving of Knife's Pass. She grabbed the ground and lay still, pressing herself into the stone to make sure it was real and, more important, not falling. When she was sure she really was grounded, Miranda lifted her head to check on the others. Gin, of course, had already rolled to his feet. Sparrow, on the other hand, was still flat on his stomach, staring at the ground like he'd never seen it before.

With a long, shaky breath, Miranda sat up and held out her hand for Durn. The stone spirit was still hanging from the remains of the broken bridge. When he saw her reaching, he pulled himself up and rolled to her.

"Thank you," Miranda said, patting the stone with a smile.

"My pleasure, mistress," Durn said, his gravelly voice smug with pride.

Miranda grinned. It wasn't often the stone got to play hero. Gin would never hear the end of it. She held her hand steady as Durn broke down and returned to her ring. When he was finished, Miranda let her eyes drift back across the ravine. The Shaper Mountain rose above her, as cold and enormous as ever. Its slopes were smooth and snowy with no trace of the hole Sparrow had punched or the tree he'd used to punch it. Two jagged edges at either side of the ravine, the remains of the broken bridge, were the only signs of the mountain's anger or their narrow escape from it. The ground, however, was still rumbling.

"Come on," she said, standing up. "Let's get out of here."

"What a wonderful idea," Sparrow said. "Little help, please?"

Miranda walked over and grabbed his hands, pulling him to his feet. He grimaced as he stood, bending slowly, like his ribs hurt him, but he didn't say anything when Miranda finally got him to his feet.

She left him to get his balance on his own and hurried to catch up with Gin, who was already making his way down the pass.

"Don't ask," the ghosthound growled, moving to walk so close Miranda couldn't take a step without bumping into him. "He'll hear."

Miranda nodded and kept her mouth shut.

"He showed up about two hours ago," Gin continued. "They had me chained in the front hall with the carriages. I would have eaten him, but I didn't know where you were. He kept saying he was going to get you next. I didn't believe him, but it's better to be out than in, so I let him spring me. If you hadn't shown by noon, I would have hunted him down."

"Thank you for the sentiment," Miranda said, glancing back at

Sparrow, who was limping to catch up with them. "How did he get you out?"

"Picked the lock," Gin said. "Impressive bit of work, actually. He's almost as good as Eli."

"That's saying something," Miranda grumbled, looking back again. Sparrow was falling behind. His face was set in a smug smile, but his body was moving in jerks, and Miranda realized that he must be really injured.

"Stop," she said, turning around. She caught Sparrow's eye before climbing onto Gin's back. "Get on. We'll be walking forever if we wait for you."

"How kind," Sparrow said, walking over to the ghosthound.

"Kind nothing," Miranda said. "Practical. We may owe you our freedom, but that doesn't mean I want to take a hiking holiday together. I just want to get to Sara and discharge my debt as soon as possible. And don't think I've forgotten about that horrible abuse of a tree spirit. I will be making a full report to the Court about that."

"I'm sure you will," Sparrow said, pulling himself slowly onto Gin's back.

Miranda glared, suspicious. "How did you get so injured, anyway?"

"Bit too much excitement for me," Sparrow answered, finally sliding into place behind her on Gin's back. "I don't usually get out this much."

Gin snorted. "Lies. He's a born sneak. I saw your crazy ride down the mountain. Mellinor cushioned you, but bird boy was bouncing all over, probably because Mellinor couldn't see him."

"See who?" Mellinor said, sloshing in Miranda's head.

Miranda tightened her grip on Gin's fur. "Don't do that," she whispered. "It makes me dizzy."

"Well, I don't know what you're talking about," the sea grumbled.

"Don't blame the water," Gin said. "I can't see him unless I look with my eyes. He doesn't even have much of a smell. You can't trust a man with no smell, but at least he's not flickering so much anymore."

"Would you care to explain any of that?" Miranda said, poking Gin in the back.

"I've already told you," Gin said. "Weren't you listening all those times I said he flickered?"

"You didn't explain then either!" Miranda cried.

"It's not something that can be explained to a human," Gin said, lashing his tail. "Right now, for instance, I can't see him at all unless I look with my actual eyes. Otherwise, he's like a nothing, a blank. I would say I've never seen anything like it, but I wouldn't know if I had, so forget it. You've thrown our lot in with his already. Just watch yourself."

"I still don't know what you're talking about," Mellinor said. "Who's a blank?"

Miranda shook her head with a frustrated sigh. Behind her, she felt Sparrow lean back. "Is everything all right? Your dog is growling more than usual, which I didn't think was possible."

For a moment, Miranda considered just asking Sparrow about the flickering, but quickly decided it would be a waste of time. Sparrow wasn't a wizard. He probably had even less of a clue than she did about whatever it was about him the spirits didn't like. Even if he did know, this was Sparrow. Getting a trustworthy answer out of his mouth was like a flood in the desert—not impossible, but very unlikely, and cause for alarm if it did actually happen. So Miranda dropped the subject and moved on to questions she might actually be able to get a straight answer for.

"Everything's fine," she said. "Where to?"

"Zarin, where else?" Sparrow said. "I've had all I care to see of mountains."

"There at least we agree," Miranda said. "Did you hear that, Gin?"

"No," Gin growled, more annoyed than ever. "I can't even hear him unless I concentrate. What is wrong with that man?"

"I don't know," Miranda said. "But I'm going to find out. Zarin, fast as you can."

"Got it," Gin said, laying his ears back. "Hold on tight."

Miranda didn't have time to relay the warning before Gin launched himself down the pass, nearly knocking Sparrow off. By the time Sparrow had regained his seat, they were well away from the Shaper Mountain. Miranda leaned forward over Gin's neck, getting as far away from Sparrow as she could, which wasn't very far. She had a lot to think about, but her mind kept drifting back to the mountain looming behind her and the man it still held prisoner somewhere deep beneath its stone. The image of the Shaper Mountain's memories still stood clear in her mind, and she gripped Gin's fur even tighter. Lock her up, would it? Well, she would tell everyone. She would tell Banage, she would tell Sara, she would tell anyone who would listen. That was her promise to Slorn, and she made it over and over again as they ran through the icy pass back toward civilization.

At the very, very top of the Shaper Mountain, perched on the crusted snow at the tip of the mountain's peak, a man stood with his arms crossed. Pure white hair covered his body like a coat except for the white hands stroking the long white beard that covered his front as he watched the three specks of the wizard girl, the ghosthound, and the man who looked like nothing flee down the path through the mountains.

You play a risky game, Durain.

"Nonsense," the mountain rumbled under his feet. "I am ever a loyal servant to the Shepherdess. And to you, Weaver."

The white man smiled. *I wouldn't say that too loudly. The Shepherdess doesn't like to share.*

"All the Powers are equal," the Shaper Mountain said. "Though she seems to have forgotten."

My sister forgets many things, the Weaver said bitterly. *And what she remembers, she ignores. But that is no call for you to risk our plans by openly defying her. Showing your memories to that group of children and then letting all but one free, what were you thinking?*

"They saw nothing that was not true," the mountain said. "I cannot help if I remember the truth. Anyway, I tried to keep her from escaping, but I am an old spirit. Too old to be looking after young idiots and too busy to spend my limited energy catching them when they run away."

Of course. The Weaver chuckled. *Very old. But do be careful, Durain. This is the Shepherdess's domain. I cannot protect you here. If she suspects, she will not hesitate to act, and we have lost too many irreplaceable spirits to risk another.*

"I have not forgotten Gredit," the mountain said, his great voice heavy with anger. "And I am not the only one. When the Hunter returns, we will be ready. I have already started the process. Heinricht is being briefed by his father as we speak."

The bear man? The Weaver frowned. *You put a great deal of faith in him.*

"I must," the mountain said. "He is the only one who can finish Fenzetti's work."

Is that so? The Weaver pursed his lips. *How fortuitous that he should appear now.*

"Fortune has nothing to do with it," the mountain rumbled. "The Creator is still with us. We will be free again."

You still believe that? the Weaver said.

"Yes," the mountain said. "You forget. We old ones, we were the first. I am older than you or your siblings, Shaped by the Creator's own hand. I remember the world as it was, as it was meant to be, and I know that world will return. It *must* return, or why are we still living?"

Why, indeed, the Weaver said, looking up at the sky. *I must go. I leave it to you.*

"We will not fail," the mountain said, but the Weaver was already gone, vanishing through a white cut in the thin air as though he had never been. The mountain rumbled at the Power's sudden absence and shifted its focus away from the outside world and the distant feel of the fleeing figures. Instead, it tilted its attention inward, down toward the long hall at the very heart of its roots. There, two humans, the current Guildmaster and the wizard who shared his spirit with a bear, walked the mountain's deepest path toward the vault where Durain, the Shaper Mountain, kept its greatest hope, the small, white kernel of a desperate plan many, many years in the making.

CHAPTER

11

Josef woke with a gasp. He froze, hands knotted in the sheets, body braced to kick or leap away, whichever was needed. That was when he realized he was in his old bedroom. He collapsed back into bed with a silent curse and took stock of his situation. He was naked, his knives stacked carefully on the bench against the wall beside him. But he had no memory of removing his knives or his clothes. He had no memory of going to bed.

Josef frowned. To wake that violently, he must have been sleeping very soundly. Even now, his head was still groggy, and that made him nervous. He'd shaken the sound-sleeping habit the first year he'd left home. Maybe being back in his old room had brought back old habits, but Josef didn't think so. He glanced at the bed. The space beside him was rumpled. Someone had slept there, but the sheets were cold when he slid his hand over them. His frown deepened. Whatever bad-sleep habits his old room could have lured him into, he'd *never* sleep that soundly next to a stranger, married or not. Something was going on, and he meant to find out what.

Josef slid silently out of bed and looked around for his clothes, but they were gone. He cursed under his breath and quietly took a knife from the pile. The door to the sitting room was closed, but he could hear movement on the other side of door that led to his dressing room. He put the knife in his teeth and pressed himself against the wall, easing his bare feet along the carpet until he was directly beside the dressing room door. Then, in one lightning-fast movement, he stepped in, opening the door with one hand while grabbing his knife with the other. He swung forward and grabbed the man on the other side, pressing the blade against his jugular.

The man screamed and began to thrash, nearly slitting his own throat in the process. Josef grabbed his shoulders and whirled him around, lowering the knife before slamming the man face-first against the wall.

"What are you doing here?" Josef growled, pressing the knife into the man's back.

"Please, my lord," the man whimpered. "I am here to help you dress."

Josef glanced down, noticing for the first time that the man was dressed in the well-cut, somber suit of Osera's high-ranking servants. With a horrible, sinking feeling, Josef released his grip and stepped back. The man fell to the floor, gasping and grabbing his throat.

The servant looked up with horrified eyes, and Josef felt his stomach sink even further. This wasn't going to help his reputation.

"Sorry," he muttered, reaching out to help. The man shied away from Josef's hands, using the shelves to pull himself up instead.

"Forgive me, your highness," he whispered, averting his eyes from Josef's nakedness. "I did not mean to startle you."

"Forget it," Josef said. "Where are my clothes?"

The man's eyes bulged like Josef had just asked for a carcass. "I gave them to the laundry, sir. I have fresh clothes for you, straight from the tailors." He nodded toward the chest against the wall where several starched shirts, jackets, and breeches lay neatly folded. "I can fetch your old clothes back, if you would like," he added cautiously.

"Those are fine," Josef said. He grabbed a shirt, jacket, drawers, and pants at random, pulling them on carelessly. He could still see the servant out of the corner of his eye, but the man made no move to help Josef dress. He seemed to be glued to the wall, eyes wide as a fish's. Josef grit his teeth and dressed faster, ticking the facts over in his head. It had been this man who'd taken his clothes, not Adela. Sleeping through Adela he could maybe understand; she was a fighter and knew how to move, but he would never sleep through this idiot entering his room, collecting his clothes, and leaving. There was simply no way two nights in Osera could have dulled his senses to the point where a servant could sneak past him.

By the time Josef had finished dressing, the man had collected himself enough to fetch Josef's boots, freshly polished and resoled, from the boot stand. He held them out with a shaking hand, keeping his eyes on the floor as Josef took them.

"Thanks," Josef said, sitting down to tug his boots on over his new socks. "Where's Adela?"

The man had already returned to his corner. "I'm not sure of the princess's whereabouts, sir," he said, wringing his hands. "I can send someone to find her, if you desire."

"No," Josef said, standing up. Best not to let Adela know he was looking for her before he knew what role she played in this. First, he had to find Eli. If the thief was good for anything, it was rooting out trouble.

He went back to the bedroom and grabbed the rest of his knives, slinging them into place as he walked into the sitting room. His frown tightened into a solid grimace at the bright, midday sunlight streaming through the narrow window. Not only had he slept soundly, he'd slept late.

"Worse and worse," he muttered, grabbing the Heart of War

from the fireplace where he'd left it the night before. He slid the enormous sword over his shoulders and onto its spot on his back. When the blade was secure, he stomped toward the door that led to the rest of the castle. He stopped when he reached it, looking over his shoulder at the servant who was still clutching the dressing room door, trembling like a kicked dog.

"Sorry, again," Josef said, struggling to think of the appropriate action for cases like this. "You can, um, have the rest of the day off."

The servant just stared at him blankly as Josef slipped out of the prince's chamber and started jogging through the halls toward Eli's room.

Eli's door was partially open when he reached it. Josef stopped, eyeing it suspiciously. He couldn't see any outward signs of trouble, but he checked his blades anyway, easing the knives down in his sleeves in case he needed them. When he was satisfied he could get any weapon he needed in a moment's notice, he stepped inside.

He stopped again almost immediately. The room was a disaster. There were piles of junk everywhere—furniture, produce, paper goods, candles, silverware, weapons, tapestries, building tools, a pile of locks, and the other things he couldn't see enough of to name. It was all piled around the room as though it had been thrown there, and sitting in the middle, perched on the rubbish like the king and queen of trash, were Eli and Nico. Judging by the dark circles under their eyes, they'd been up all night, but doing what he couldn't even begin to say. Neither of them seemed to have heard him enter. Instead, they were both staring at what looked to be the carved wooden end of the banister from the grand staircase in the castle's front hall.

"All right," Eli said, hefting the carved wooden hunk in his hands. "Closer to the door or the chess piece?"

"Neither," Nico said, scowling. "It looks almost fuzzy."

"Fuzzy," Eli muttered, scribbling on a piece of paper so covered with similar scribbles it was almost entirely black. "Interesting. Fuzzy like the fork or fuzzy like—"

"*What is going on?*" Josef roared.

They both jumped and looked at Josef, eyes wide with surprise.

"Good morning," Eli said.

"Don't 'good morning' me," Josef said, kicking the junk aside until he'd made enough space to close the door. "Did you rob a dump? What is all this garbage?"

"Not garbage," Eli said. "Experiments." When Josef gave him a skeptical look, he clarified. "Wizard stuff, as you would say."

"You know what?" Josef said. "I don't even want to know. All I care about is where you've been."

This last bit was leveled at Nico, and she flinched appropriately.

"Doesn't matter," she said quietly. "I'm here now."

"Doesn't matter?" Josef was surprised at his own anger. "*Doesn't matter?* Of course it matters! Do you even know how . . . how . . ."

"Worried?" Eli supplied.

"You keep out of this," Josef snapped. Eli held up his hands, and Josef locked his eyes back on Nico. "I didn't even know where you were! How can we be a team when you're not here?"

"I'm sorry," Nico said, fiddling with her coat. "It's done now, anyway. Won't happen again."

Josef clenched his fists. She wasn't giving him an answer, but he didn't know if he was ready to press for one. He was fighting battles on all fronts right now, and forcing Nico to tell him the truth would open up another. A close, dangerous fight that he wasn't sure he could win. Worse, he was still mad, furiously mad, though he couldn't say exactly what he was mad at. But he couldn't deal with this now. He needed his wits about him, so he took a deep swordsman's breath and made himself let it go.

"So long as we're all on the same front going forward, everything is well enough for now," he said. "We've got other problems. Something happened last night."

Eli leaned back with an infuriating smile. "Things tend to happen on wedding knights, Josef."

"Shut up and listen," Josef said, ignoring the murderous look that Nico shot at the thief. "I just woke up with no memory of the night before. I don't remember Adela getting up or the servant coming in. I don't even remember going to bed."

"Well," Eli said, standing up. "It isn't unheard of for humans to lose consciousness for six, sometimes eight hours a night. I know this may come as a surprise—"

"Can you stop being a smart-ass for five seconds and listen?" Josef snapped. "This is serious. I think I was drugged."

"Nonsense," Eli said. "Who would drug you?"

"I don't know," Josef said. "That's why I have you. Figure it out."

Eli scratched his chin. "Someone who doesn't want an heir for Osera?" he guessed.

"The duke," Josef said. "An heir by me would keep Finley's children from inheriting."

"Seems a little shortsighted," Eli said. "He can't expect to drug you every night. And how did he do it without drugging the princess as well? I can only assume that the drug was in your food, unless you were cut in the night?" He paused until Josef shook his head. "Food or drink then, for certain. But you ate with Adela, right? So unless you had something she didn't, she'd be down too. But she was up bright and early this morning. I saw her ride out myself."

"We ate from the same plates," Josef said. "Whatever I had, she had. Poison isn't the Oseran way, though. If the duke wanted me dead, he could challenge me to a duel at any time."

"Well, we still haven't established it was him," Eli said. "And you were drugged to sleep, not to death. Anyway, no one in their right mind is going to challenge you to a duel, especially not after your performance yesterday. You're the greatest swordsman in the world, remember?"

"Not yet," Josef said. "We need to find out what happened last night and why. We also need a who. Eli, I want you to go to my room and see what you can find. Nico, I'll need you to stake out the duke. I want to know what he's planning. Meanwhile, I'm going to go down to the kitchen and get the truth out of whoever cooked my food last night."

"Josef," Eli said cautiously, taking off his wig so he could look at the swordsman without hair getting in his eyes. "I know you don't generally listen to these, but the first rule of thievery is never jump without knowing where you're going to land. You're making a lot of assumptions here. We're not even sure you were poisoned."

"Of course I'm sure," Josef said. "I can tell when I've been poisoned."

"I don't doubt that," Eli said. "But try to consider this objectively. So far, all we have is that you slept until noon without waking and missed some people entering and leaving your room. Now, I can't remember you ever sleeping late, but it's not exactly enough proof to justify going down to the kitchens and scaring the daylights out of the servants. Especially considering the rumors going around."

Josef glowered. "What rumors?"

"That you're a killer, a bounty hunter gone bad, and a thief," Eli said with a shrug. "Of course, since all of that is true, they're less rumors and more facts-in-a-bad-light."

"How did they get to you?" Josef said.

"You hear things when you spend all night bribing servants to fill your room with junk," Eli said, flashing him a grin. "Seriously, though, is it really so unexpected that people think poorly of you? You haven't exactly been the storybook icon of the long-lost prince."

"Good thing I gave up being a prince, then."

"But you *are*," Eli said, rubbing his temples. "So long as you insist on staying here and playing along, you are a prince, like it or not, and people are going to judge you as one."

"Then they'll just have to get over it," Josef said, crossing his arms. "I'm here only to help my mother."

"Well," Eli said, crossing his arms as well. "You're not helping her by acting like a thug. You can't have it both ways, Josef. I'm not asking you to embroil yourself in politics. I'm not even saying we shouldn't investigate what happened last night, but if we're going to stay here, you're going to have to learn some *tact*."

Josef tilted his head back, bumping it soundly against the door. Leave it to the thief to make everything more complicated. "Fine," he said at last. "What do you suggest I do?"

"Leave it to me," Eli said, standing up. "We'll go to your room and see what we can find. Since no one knew in advance that you were coming back, whoever poisoned you had to set things up fairly quickly. Haste leaves clues." He paused. "I don't actually think that's a rule of thievery. I should make it one."

"Whatever," Josef said, pushing himself off the door. "Let's get this done. It's nearly noon already, and I want to be able to go to sleep tonight knowing I'll wake up."

"Fair enough," Eli said, setting the wig on his head again. "After you, Prince Thereson."

Josef rolled his eyes and tugged the door open, stepping into the hall with Nico right behind him and Eli on her heels.

His room was empty when they reached it. Josef let them in before entering himself. He closed the ancient door carefully, and then took the Heart of War from his back and leaned it against the door. The blade leaned heavy against the wood, blocking it from opening inward.

Eli's eyes widened in horror. "You're using the greatest awakened blade in existence as a door stop?"

"Why not?" Josef said. "I don't want servants disturbing your work, and it's not like anyone besides me can move it."

Eli sighed loudly and turned back to the task at hand. "I suggest you get comfortable. This may take a while."

Nico and Josef exchanged a look and sat down together on the couch. As soon as they were settled, Eli got down on his knees and started waking up the room.

"There," Eli said, straightening up. "That should do it."

Josef folded his arms and gave the thief a skeptical look. So far as he could tell, Eli had just spent the last hour crawling around on his hands and knees and muttering to himself. The thief had always been a little odd when he was doing his wizard nonsense, but this had been downright strange and a little embarrassing. He was doubly glad he'd thought to put the Heart in front of the door now. Forget keeping their investigation secret, he was more concerned that no one would barge in and see Eli acting like a lunatic.

"All right," Eli said, clapping his hands together as he looked around the room like a mayor about to give a speech. "Listen up! There's a lot at stake here. Someone has been poisoning the prince." He pointed at Josef. "We need to know how."

Eli looked over his shoulder and motioned for Josef to stand. After a moment of hesitation, Josef got off the couch and stood beside Eli, feeling uncomfortably stupid. But, as soon as he was in place, the room began to rattle like it was the epicenter of a tiny earthquake.

"One at a time," Eli said, holding up his hands.

The rattling stopped except for the fireplace. Eli turned and knelt down, nodding as the stone mantel began to creak. Occasionally, another piece of furniture would rattle. When that happened, the stone mantel would rock violently until every other sound stopped. Eli listened patiently, nodding the whole time. Back on the couch, Nico kept very still, her eyes as wide as saucers.

When the mantel's movements finally stilled, Eli stood up with a long sigh. "How many wizards have been in your family?"

"Are you talking to me?" Josef said.

Eli rolled his eyes. "Who else?"

Josef gestured at the rattling room. Eli just gave him a sharp look.

"I don't think we've ever had a wizard," Josef said. "Maybe a cousin or something, but no one I can think of."

Eli frowned. "And how long has this room been like this? With this furniture?"

"Like this?" Josef said. "Forever. This has always been the prince's room, or princess's, in mother's case. Everything in here's a family heirloom."

"Well," Eli said. "At least that explains it."

"Explains what?" Josef said.

"Them." Eli pointed at the room. "They seem to have you confused with another prince. Several other princes, actually. Which one started a fire?"

"That would be my great-grandfather," Josef said. "Knocked over a lamp twice when he was ten, starting fires both times. Earned him the name Wallace the Clumsy for a while, until he became Wallace the Black Scourge."

Eli winced. "That hardly sounds like an improvement."

"It was fitting," Josef said. "He sank a lot of ships. Don't forget, Osera was a nation of pirates before the war made us part of the Council."

"How fascinating," Eli said. "But if we can leave the history lesson aside for a moment, I'm afraid we're in a bit of a bind. I don't think a wizard other than myself has entered this room in a century. The whole place was dead asleep before I came in, which was why this took so long. If they had been awake, it would still have been tricky since you, Adela, and the servants all seem to be spirit deaf, but I could have found out *something*. As it stands, they just want to tell me stories of grievous abuse at the hands of your violent ancestry."

"So," Josef said. "No wizard solution?"

"No wizard solution," Eli said, shaking his head. "But while I was waking things up, I did find this."

He held up a plain porcelain medicine bowl filled with a dull yellow powder that smelled vaguely bitter, like walnut shells. Josef looked at Eli skeptically. "Is that poison?"

"No," Eli said, pulling his hand back. "It's called orobin, and it's a perfectly normal stimulant. I've taken it myself on long jobs where I couldn't afford to be dozing off."

"If it's perfectly normal, why are you showing it to me?"

"Because this is a very large amount of orobin," Eli said, hefting the bowl pointedly. "A pinch dissolved in tea is plenty for any normal person. This is enough to stock a reasonably sized shop."

"So?" Josef said, crossing his arms.

"*So,*" Eli said. "I found it tucked away in a cabinet full of lady's supplies, which means, unless you've taken to washing your hair with essence of rose water, that this bowl belongs to your lovely wife. Who, I might add, eats and drinks the same as you, but does not seem to suffer from involuntary deep sleep."

"Wait," Josef said. "You think Adela's behind this? That she's drugging both of us but is taking the stimulant to counteract the effect?"

"That would be where I'm going," Eli said, placing the bowl on the table.

"But why would she drug me?" Josef said. "That doesn't make any sense."

"Maybe your pillow talk needs some work," Eli said with a smug smile.

"Shut up and listen," Josef growled. "I'm not saying I trust Adela, but she owes the queen everything. Even if she didn't, why would she knock me out? She needs this baby to secure her position or Finley's going to send her and her mother packing the second the crown is on his head."

"I don't know the whats and whys," Eli said. "I'm not even saying for sure that she's the one drugging you, but I think we can safely assume she knows what's happening and how to counteract it. That alone is proof enough that thing's aren't what they seem. If Adela was pregnant, this would be more damning. But with you being, well, you, and totally uninterested in the throne, a baby's her only shot at keeping her position. That leaves us with circumstantial evidence but no motive, which isn't much better than where we started."

"Well, I intend to find out," Josef said, crossing his arms. "Next time I see Adela, she's not leaving until I have an answer."

Eli frowned. "I'm not sure direct threats are going to—"

He was interrupted by the soft clatter of someone trying to open the door. Nico, Eli, and Josef froze as the door's handle turned down. But the person on the other side didn't get much farther. The moment the door hit the Heart of War, it stopped cold. The person cursed and tried again, harder this time. The sword didn't even wobble.

Silence fell again as the person stepped back, and then there was a soft, almost embarrassed knock.

Josef walked over and pulled the Heart out of the way, opening the door to reveal an elderly man in a somber suit. He looked shocked and a little bewildered by the sudden opening, but his face quickly arranged itself into an expression of bored politeness the second he recognized Josef.

"My lord prince," he said with a perfunctory bow. "I was sent to find you."

"So I gathered," Josef said, sliding the Heart back into place on his back. "Get on with it."

The man's eyes widened, but he gathered himself again. "My master, the excellent Duke Finley, requests your presence this afternoon."

"Oh yeah?" Josef said. "What's Finley want?"

"Only your company, my lord," the man said.

Josef looked back at Eli, who shrugged. "Company, huh? When?"

"At your earliest convenience, sire," the servant said. "Though I have been led to believe it is a matter of some urgency."

Josef glared at the servant, who just smiled politely. Shaking his head, Josef looked over his shoulder. "I'm going to see what this is about," he said. "You two stay here and keep working on what we were working on."

"Sure thing, boss," Eli said with a salute. But Nico met Josef's eyes as she nodded. Josef smiled. She at least could be trusted to stay on target. That would be enough. He checked his blades one last time before he followed the servant into the hall, closing the door solidly behind him.

CHAPTER

12

As many times as she'd seen the white walls of Zarin rising in the distance, Miranda had never been so glad to be home. Gin's time chained in the mountain seemed to have left him ready to run. Even with two passengers, he'd raced down the mountains in record time, though Miranda wasn't sure if that was because of the urgency of the situation or if he just wanted Sparrow off his back. For his part, Sparrow hadn't changed a bit. He still took up every bit of breathable air.

"Finally," he cried as Zarin came into view. "Civilization. Powers, it's been too long. I can't wait to eat something that hasn't had dog slobber all over it."

Miranda sniffed indignantly. "You're free to catch your own food, you know."

"Hardly matters now," Sparrow said. "We'll be at the gates in an hour if your little puppy keeps up the pace."

Miranda winced and glanced down at Gin. He'd threatened to eat Sparrow if the man called him a puppy one more time, but the ghosthound kept running as though nothing had happened. She sighed. Sparrow had no idea how lucky he was that spirits had a hard time hearing him. Of course, Miranda could hear him just fine, and that was enough to make her consider letting Gin eat him anyway.

As their road joined the main highway connecting Zarin to the northern Council Kingdoms, Miranda was astonished by the volume of traffic. Loaded carts filled the paved highway, forcing people on foot and horseback to spill over onto the fields beside the road. Since a ghosthound isn't the sort of thing you want in the middle of a crowd of horses and ox-drawn carts, Gin had to turn out farther still, beyond the hard-beaten grass that lined the road and into the mud of the freshly plowed fields.

"Lovely," Sparrow said, lifting his boots as high as he could.

Miranda ignored him. "What's all this?" she said, nodding at the packed roar. "It's months too early for the new year's market, unless I am drastically wrong about how long we were under that mountain."

"Those aren't farm carts, either," Gin added. "I smell steel."

"You're right," Miranda said, straightening her knees so that she was almost standing on his back. "And they're marked, look."

Every cart was marked with a flag or seal. The traffic went on farther than she could see in both directions. Hundreds of carts from more countries than she could name hauling what had to be thousands of tons' worth of goods into Zarin. But for what?

"They're supply wagons," Sparrow said, yawning. "You know, for the war."

Miranda stopped Gin right there, nearly throwing Sparrow off. "*War?*" she yelled, whirling around. "*What war?*"

"The upcoming war with the Immortal Empress," Sparrow said, resettling himself.

Miranda was staring at him like he'd just grown a second head. "The Immortal Empress?"

"Yes," Sparrow said. "You know, terrible lady? Comes from

across the sea with thousands of ships to kill us all? Don't they teach you any history in that little social club of yours?"

"*I know who the Immortal Empress is!*" Miranda shouted. "What I want to know is what is she doing *back*? I thought she was defeated at Osera two decades ago?"

"Defeated?" Sparrow snorted. "She lost a few ships and a little pride, but women who own half the world don't roll over just because you beat up their forward fleet. She retreated is all. Your real question should be, what took her so long to come back and finish the job?"

Miranda stared at him. "Well?"

"Well what?" Sparrow said, leaning back tiredly.

"What took her so long?" Miranda said, gritting her teeth on each word.

"How in the world should I know?" Sparrow said. "But she's back now, and word is she's got a fleet large enough to crush us flat five times over. Of course, that's probably an exaggeration, but there must be some truth to it if Whitefall's worked up enough to squeeze the Council Kingdoms this hard. There must be carts from here to Gaol."

"I can see that," Miranda snapped. "What I want to know is, if you knew all this, why you didn't see fit to *tell me*."

Sparrow arched his thin shoulders in a nonchalant shrug. "What good would it have done you to know? You were already running your darling dog into the ground to get to Zarin, so it's not like the knowledge would have spurred you any faster."

Miranda's jaw clenched. "And did it never occur to you that a continent-scale war is something I should be informed of?"

"It did," Sparrow said. "But quite frankly, Miranda dear, you have a bad habit of getting bent out of shape over things that have nothing to do with you. Remember who sprung you out of your charming little cold cellar under the mountain. You're working for

Sara now. She, not I, decides what you need to know and when, and she said nothing about telling you anything about the war."

Miranda's eyes went wide. "*Said?*" she hissed. "When did you—"

Before she could finish, Sparrow flicked his hand and a blue ball the size of a marble attached to a leather cord rolled out into his palm. Miranda snapped her mouth shut. Of course. She'd forgotten he had a Relay point. How stupid could she be?

"You still should have told me," she grumbled.

"Think that all you like," Sparrow said, rolling the Relay point in his hand. "I'm not sticking my neck out for your desperate need to meddle." He flicked his hand again, and the blue orb disappeared. "Remember, little Spiritualist," he said, smiling at her startled jerk. "Sara owns you now. I suggest you do as I do and do just what she says, no more and no less. In the meanwhile, get moving. You're wasting our time."

Gin snarled and craned his head back, enormous teeth bared, but Miranda shook her head.

"Ride," she said.

Gin snapped his teeth. "Let me teach this—"

She dug her fingers into his fur. "Go."

Gin snarled one last time, but then he turned and dashed toward the northern gate as fast as he could go, his fur bristling in wild gray swirls. Miranda hunkered down on his back, grateful that the rushing wind made further conversation impossible.

Zarin's gates were thrown wide open to accommodate the massive influx of people. The northern gate was staffed with a squad in Whitefall's white and silver directing traffic. They waved Gin forward without question, and Miranda immediately turned them down a side street, dodging the crowds as best she could. When they were clear of the gate's confusion, Miranda nudged Gin west, toward Whitefall Citadel. It felt strange to enter Zarin and not go directly to the Spirit Court, but she had the feeling that if she didn't see Sara first, things would get ugly. Still, she couldn't help craning her neck as they rode, watching for any flash of the Spirit Court's white walls between the buildings as Gin began the run up the hill to the citadel.

The approach to the Council's stronghold was even more crowded than the road into Zarin. The city was packed to bursting. Troops in a rainbow of country colors clogged the streets and side alleys in noisy, suspicious packs. Everyone made room for Gin, even bravado-filled soldiers weren't stupid enough to stand in a ghosthound's way, but it was still infuriatingly slow going. Finally, after almost an hour of climbing, they made it to the citadel gate.

The guards stepped aside the moment they saw Sparrow, and Gin trotted into the citadel's paved yard. Even here, the traffic was heavy. Ornate, official carriages clogged every inch of the Council's entry, and servants, footmen, and guards stood in every available space, waiting for their masters with sullen, suspicious looks. Gin turned immediately, sticking to the fence until he found a space under the ornamental trees wide enough for his passengers to dismount.

"Wait here," Miranda said, eyeing the other carriages nervously. "And try not to startle the horses. I'm going to see what's going on."

Gin nodded and sat down with a huff, growling deep in his throat. He was still biting mad, but he'd been with Miranda long enough to know that acting out wouldn't get him anywhere but into her bad graces. Still, swallowing anger graciously was not a ghosthound virtue, and so Miranda had to content herself with leaving him growling in the shady corner of the packed citadel yard. This should have made her nervous, but today she was too angry herself to care. And so, filthy, bedraggled, and furious, Miranda marched past the carriages and up the stairs of the Council of Thrones. Sparrow drifted along behind her, thoroughly amused by the whole affair.

A page separated himself from the flock in the entry hall the moment they entered to inform Miranda and Sparrow that Sara was expecting them.

"Of course she is," Miranda muttered, waving for the page to lead the way.

But rather than leading them down to the dark cavernous room where Miranda had met Sara before, the boy led them up a grand staircase and into a series of richly appointed halls. The outside commotion was here as well. Servants in a rainbow of liveries were constantly running by with papers tucked under their arms. Here and there, doors were guarded by solemn-faced soldiers who watched them suspiciously as they passed. These crowded hallways lasted only two floors, however. After climbing another set of stairs, they entered a quieter hall of elegant offices with important-looking brass nameplates on the doors, all of which were closed. After climbing yet another set of stairs, they entered an elegant waiting room full of serious-faced men in excessively expensive jackets talking in hushed, urgent voices. The men fell silent the moment Miranda stepped into view, and she paused at the top of the stairs, watching to see where the page wanted her. But the page walked right past the waiting men to the closed door at the far end of the room, which, unlike all the others, bore no nameplate at all.

The page stopped at the door and motioned for Miranda to step forward. The waiting men were openly glaring at her now, and Miranda glanced back at Sparrow only to find that she was alone. She turned in a full circle, eyes wide, but Sparrow was nowhere to be seen. Miranda cursed under her breath. She was less annoyed at Sparrow for vanishing than at herself for being surprised. For a moment, she considered turning around and walking out, obligation or no, but even as she thought about it, she knew she couldn't. Sparrow and, through him, Sara had saved her from the mountain. The least she could do was show up and see what Sara wanted. After that, she would go straight to Master Banage and tell him everything.

Decision made, Miranda lifted her head and smoothed her dirty hair and travel-stained clothes with quick fingers. When she was as presentable as she could make herself, she walked past the glaring men and through the heavy wooden door the page opened for her.

A roomful of people turned to look at her. A few she recognized at once. Sara stood beside the large wooden desk at one end of the lavish office, a pencil in her mouth and a stack of papers dangling from her hands. Opposite her was Tower Keeper Blint, one of Hern's old cronies. He was leaning over the desk as well, tapping the map that covered its surface with his jeweled fingers and looking just as displeased to see Miranda as she was to see him. Seated at the desk between them was a man Miranda had never seen personally, but whose face she knew by heart. Though he'd gone a little grayer since the parade days of her youth, no Zarin native could fail to recognize the current head of the family who had ruled Zarin since there was a Zarin: Alber Whitefall, the Merchant Prince himself.

Left alone, Miranda might have stood gawking in the doorway forever. Fortunately, Sara didn't have that kind of patience.

"Finally," she said, snapping her fingers and motioning for Miranda to come stand beside her. "What took you? I was beginning to think Sparrow was lying."

Miranda started to answer, but Blint cut her off.

"What's this, Sara?" the Tower Keeper said, his voice dripping with insult. "The Lyonette girl? This is your plan? She's cut from the same cloth as Banage. What good do you hope to accomplish, bringing in another traitor?"

"More than I can accomplish waiting on you to do more than complain," Sara said, crossing her arms with what felt like a long-standing huff.

"Enough," Prince Whitefall said, glaring at both of them. "If you must bicker like children, you can do it outside. I've got representatives from every kingdom in the Council waiting for audiences today, and that's enough childishness for any man. Now," he said, glancing at Miranda, "who are you, young lady?"

Miranda straightened up, self-consciously hiding the worst of her stained clothes by clutching her arms in front of her. "Miranda Lyonette, your majesty," she said with a deep bow. "Spiritualist of the Court and former apprentice of the Rector Spiritualis Etmon Banage."

She said this last bit with a pointed scowl at Blint, but it was the Merchant Prince who spoke next.

"Ah yes," he said with a wry smile. "The one who keeps losing Eli Monpress."

Miranda felt her face go red.

"You see?" Blint snorted. "Incompetent as well as treacherous, just like her master."

"Now see here!" Miranda said, her voice quivering with rising anger. "Master Banage has never betrayed anyone. If anyone is a traitor here, it's you, Blint. How dare a Tower Keeper speak ill of the Rector Spiritualis to outsiders?"

Blint arched a gray eyebrow at her. "Incompetent, treacherous, and ignorant," he said, glancing at Sara. "You certainly can pick your champions."

Sara's jaw clenched, pressing her lips into a thin line.

"What is he talking about?" Miranda demanded.

Merchant Prince Whitefall looked pointedly at Sara. She tossed down her papers with a sigh and walked over to Miranda, grabbing her arm and steering her toward the large bay window that took up most of the office's right wall.

Miranda tried to yank her arm away. "What are you—"

"Just look," Sara said, pushing her toward the window.

Miranda stumbled forward and landed on her knees on the

padded window seat, her face inches from the clear glass that separated her from all of Zarin. The city lay spread out before her, every street alive with activity and packed to bursting. But that much she had already seen, and her eyes moved up, following the city east, down the slope of the river, and then up again to the other colossal building that dominated Zarin's skyline, the Spirit Court's white tower.

Even from this distance, Miranda knew something was wrong. The Tower looked strange. Its sides were stripped of the usual red banners and the great red doors had vanished. The spiraling windows were gone as well, leaving the Tower smooth and solemn, an impenetrable spire of cold, white stone.

"The Tower is sealed?" she said at last, her voice shaking as the truth dawned on her. Every apprentice in the Court knew the Tower could be sealed, though Miranda had never seen it happen. But...she looked over her shoulder at Merchant Prince Whitefall. "Why?"

"As you no doubt know, our lands are soon to be under siege by a foreign power," Whitefall said calmly as Sara returned to his side. "Any hope of survival rests on our ability to stand together. To that end, I asked Banage for his help in the fight against the Empress. He refused. The rest you can see."

So that was it. Miranda swallowed.

"With all due respect, Merchant Prince," she said, turning away from the window, "the Spirit Court exists to protect spirits from human abuse. We do not go to war."

Whitefall's eyes narrowed. "And whose land do you dig your heels into to make that statement? When the Council falls and the Empress makes slaves out of every man, woman, and child, do you think she will spare the Spiritualists?"

Miranda stiffened. "Every Spiritualist swears an oath to protect their spirits, to use them only in self-defense. They are not weapons."

Whitefall sighed. "So that's a 'no' for you as well, then?"

"I am a Spiritualist of the Spirit Court," Miranda said. "I follow the will of my Rector."

Whitefall leaned back in his chair. "And I suppose that appealing to your sense of duty to your country would be a waste of time? No point in reminding you how many of your countrymen will die when the Empress rolls us over because we cannot stand up to her wizards."

"Or how she owes the Council her life, at the moment," Sara added, resting her hands on her narrow hips.

Miranda swallowed against her suddenly dry throat. "I owe you my life and my freedom," she said, picking her words carefully. "But you should know by now, Sara, I choose my oaths over my life every time. But even if helping you didn't violate my pledge to guard my spirits, I would still say no. I am sworn to follow the will of the Rector. If Master Banage has already refused as you said, then his refusal is the Court's refusal. Though," she glared accusingly at Tower Keeper Blint, "apparently some Spiritualists understand their obligations differently."

Blint rolled his eyes in disgust. "Spare me," he said. "I've followed Banage longer than you've worn your rings, little girl. Long enough to see the cliff his absolute refusal to compromise is leading us toward. This is the real world, Miss Lyonette, not some morality play. Standing firm on the letter of our oaths may sound noble, but the reality is that the Empress is coming, and her wizards have no qualms over using spirits in the fight. We will all perish if we do not meet her in kind."

"So because our enemy abuses her spirits, we must abuse ours?" Miranda cried. "Is that what you're saying?"

"I'm merely stating fact," Blint said. "The army with spirits defeats the army without. The Spirit Court represents nearly all of the wizards within the Council Kingdoms. If we all follow Banage and bury our heads in the sand, the Council will be defenseless.

The Empress will conquer everything, and if you think she will let an organization like the Spirit Court remain when these lands are hers, then you are delusional."

Miranda clenched her fists, her rings glowing like torches on her fingers. "I will not abandon my oaths," she said fiercely. "And I will not abandon Master Banage."

Sara and Blint both started to speak, but the Merchant Prince cut them off with a wave of his hand. He turned in his chair to look at Miranda directly, and when he spoke, his voice was kind and genteel. "I understand you've been through a lot lately, and this may all be a bit much. Please know that I admire your loyalty. I wish I had someone on my staff half as willing to stand up for me as you do for Banage, but a lot has changed since you last left Zarin."

He stood up and walked around his desk, taking Miranda gently by the arm as he turned her back to the window. "Look there," he said softly, pointing down, toward the streets. "Do you see those soldiers?"

Miranda nodded. She could hardly miss them. The streets of Zarin were full.

"Three days ago I called in the pledges for the first time in Council history," Whitefall said. "Three days, Spiritualist, and already we have so many men ready to defend their homes. Every country in the Council is sending its army to help defend the whole against the Empress. Several of those men down there are conscripts, boys taken from their mothers' skirts. Most have never even seen the coast they are going to defend." He looked down at her, his eyes sad. "Banage told me he would not force the spirits to fight a war that has nothing to do with them, but those young men are here to fight a war that ostensibly has nothing to do with them either. Even so, here they are. They have come to fight because their countries have spent the last two and a half decades benefiting from the Council, and the time has come to pay."

Miranda stiffened. "The Spirit Court is not part of the Council of Thrones."

"No," Whitefall said. "But the Rector has had a place at our meetings since the beginning. The Court has benefited from the peace and prosperity of the Council as much as any country. Maybe more. But even if the Court was as fully aloof as you claim, you and Banage and every Spiritualist who serves the Court were born on what is now Council land. Spiritualists you may be, but that membership doesn't change the fact that you are all citizens of the Council, and you are beholden to the same rules that govern everyone else."

Miranda stepped away. Though the Merchant Prince had not said it, she could read his meaning plainly. "You mean to conscript us too?" she said softly.

"Not 'mean to,'" Whitefall said. "I have. I delivered the order to Banage himself, and then he tore it up, threw it in my face, and sealed his Tower. Do you know what we call that, Spiritualist Lyonette?"

Miranda began to tremble. "Treason?"

"Treason." Whitefall nodded. "It is a mistake to think that your duty to the Court outweighs all others, my dear. Tower Keeper Blint here understands that. So do the other Spiritualists who have chosen to fight for their homes and way of life. They understand that if we continue to divide ourselves, the only person who will triumph is the Empress."

"Merchant Prince," Miranda said. "I understand what you're saying, but if Master Banage refused, I'm sure he had good reason."

"Really?" Whitefall said, his voice low. "How sure?"

"Absolutely," Miranda said, drawing herself up. "You may call it treason, but we must follow our oaths to the Court and our spirits above all other obligations. Master Banage understands this better than any Spiritualist I've ever known."

"I'm sure he does," Whitefall said. "That's why I'm sending you back to him with a compromise."

Miranda blinked. "What?"

"A compromise," Whitefall said, his stern face breaking into a smile. "I realize you Spiritualists don't have much knowledge of the concept, but they can be very useful."

"But you just said Master Banage was a traitor," Miranda said, staring at him.

"He is," Whitefall said. "But he doesn't have to remain one. Listen, child, no one wanted things this way less than myself. Banage is a hard man. I thought if I laid things out in hard terms he would see reason, but all I managed was to divide the Court, which was the last thing I wanted." He tightened his hand on her arm. "I don't want Spiritualist defectors. I want the Spirit Court—the *whole* Court—fighting with us against a common enemy."

He turned Miranda around to face him, looking down at her with a sad, serious expression. "I am not a proud man," he said quietly. "I am not afraid to eat my own words if that's what's best for the Council. If the Spirit Court will agree to help us in this war, I swear that they will be kept in a purely supportive roll—no fighting, no risk to your spirits, no danger to your oaths. In addition, I am prepared to give Banage something he's been angling at for a long time: a Council law making Enslavement illegal."

"Illegal?" Miranda said.

Whitefall nodded. "Think of the possibilities. The Court will no longer have to deal with rogue wizards alone. You'll be able to call on Council law to demand backup from local officials. The Court will have authority like it's never had before. Plus, you will save your Spiritualists from a division that could doom your entire organization without compromising your ideals, *and* you'll help me keep our necks out from under the Empress's boot. Now"—he smiled—"is that a compromise that could interest you?"

Miranda bit her lip. It was a good offer, a potentially fantastic offer, but... "I'm not the person who can make that decision."

"I know," Whitefall said. "Sara says you owe us a debt. I'm calling it in. Take my compromise to Banage. I've tried sending him messages, but he won't open his Tower for anything. That said, I'm betting he'll open it for you. Make my case to your master and I'll wipe your obligation to Sara and the Council clean. There is no downside for you in this, Spiritualist Lyonette. Even if Banage refuses, you'll still be with him, and your debt to us will still be forgiven. What do you say?"

Miranda thought the words through carefully. "Just support?"

"Just support," Whitefall said, nodding.

"All right," Miranda said at last. "But I want everything in writing first."

Whitefall smiled. "Very shrewd, but I expected no less." He walked back over to his desk and drew out a thick stack of papers. "I had the clerks draw it up the moment Sara told me you were on your way."

Miranda took the papers. The offer was all there, just as he'd said. Copied in triplicate, she noticed with a sigh, but what else could you expect from the Council?

"I'll take this to Banage at once," she said, tucking the papers under her arm. "But I wouldn't get your hopes up."

"With Etmon, I never do," Whitefall said, sitting down at his desk. "Nice meeting you, Spiritualist."

Miranda bowed from the waist, turned on her heel, and left. The men in the waiting room sneered at her as she pushed past them, but Miranda didn't even notice. Her head was reeling with everything that had happened. This morning she'd been preparing for the potential pitfalls of telling the story of the Shaper Mountain to Sara, now she was bringing the Council's compromise to Master Banage with war looming over them, and there was still the issue of the demons, the stars, and the Shepherdess. She didn't even know what crisis to focus on anymore but, pressing the papers hard against her chest, she knew where to begin. First she had to find Master Banage and explain everything. Once all the cards were on the table, he would know what to do.

That thought alone was enough to calm her mind as she marched down the stairs toward the citadel yard where Gin was waiting to take her home to the Tower.

Tower Keeper Blint turned to face the Merchant Prince, brandishing his rings as he did. "You do realize you just gave Banage back his greatest weapon?"

"A calculated risk," Whitefall said, leaning back in his chair. "And the best choice, given our options. She certainly wasn't going to turn against Banage, and you can't force a Spiritualist to work. That left locking her up, which I don't have the resources for at the moment, or sending her running home to sulk with her master. At least this way I can get an offer through that stone wall of his, and who knows, the old zealot just might take it."

"He won't," Blint said. "Banage would die before he compromised his integrity."

"We also thought he would die before he split his precious Court," Sara said. "But he laid down the line and shed you Tower Keepers without so much as a look back, didn't he? But you saw the girl's eyes light up when Alber offered to outlaw Enslavement. The Court's been after that apple for *years*. It might just be enough to convince Miranda that the Council's position is in the right, and she can be very persuasive when she thinks she's on the moral side of things."

"It will take more than an apple and an earnest girl to talk Banage out of that Tower," Blint said, his voice dripping with superiority. "The Rector Spiritualis is a slave to his pride. I don't even know why you want him along. He'll just get in our way."

"With all due respect to you and your Tower Keepers, Blint," Whitefall said in a tired voice, "you'd better hope Sara's right. It's no secret that Lyonette and Banage are the two strongest wizards in the Court. They are weapons we cannot afford to lay by, however much trouble they may be. If sending the girl doesn't work, we'll just have to try something else. Now, if you'll excuse me, I have other people to mollify today."

Blint opened his mouth, but he closed it again as Sara swept by to open the door. Duly dismissed, Blint stomped out. Sara followed right behind him, stepping out of the way as the pages showed in the royal ambassador from some country she couldn't be bothered to remember.

As ordered, Sparrow was waiting in the hall for her. He was freshly washed and dressed, and his hair was pulled back in a long, blond snake of a braid over the shoulder of his impressively garish orange coat. He stood aside for Blint with a flourish as the Tower Keeper stomped down the stairs and then turned to Sara, smiling as he handed her a lit pipe.

"Thank the Powers," she muttered, snatching the pipe from his hand and putting it to her mouth with a deep draw that she held for nearly half a minute. "At least something's going right," she said, letting the breath go at last. "Do you have it?"

"Of course." Sparrow pulled a worn leather book from his sleeve. "Just as I told you."

Sara snatched the book with greedy fingers, her eyes widening with delight as she flipped through the pages. "Not as good as the man himself," she said. "But I'll take what I can get."

"You're welcome," Sparrow said pointedly as they started down the stairs.

Sara blew a line of smoke at him. "Did you manage to plant the point?"

"Not an hour ago," Sparrow said. "Just before we entered the city."

"And she didn't notice?" Sara asked, taking in a fresh lungful of smoke.

Sparrow looked affronted. "Who do you think you're dealing with?"

"Just checking," Sara said. "I've been far too much in the company of idiots lately."

"That's the risk you take working with the Council," Sparrow said cheerfully. "Are you sure about this Miranda thing? I mean, I went through all that trouble to get her in debt to us, I'd hate to think we let her off the hook too easily."

"I'm sure," Sara said, flipping through Slorn's book. "I got back from the desert this morning, but Alber's weapon isn't ready yet, and at this rate I don't know when it will be. I need more wizards, and fast. Myron's already drawn up plans for more spirit defense points than I can man, even with Blint's deserters. That militaristic idiot doesn't seem to understand that wizards are not interchangeable. There's a huge power difference between a man like Blint and our Miranda. I'd hoped that by making Banage a traitor we could squeeze the Court enough to get what we needed, but it looks like all the true talent has stayed loyal so far." She blew an angry line of smoke. "They're worse than burned sugar, the way they stick together."

"If you're holding out for Miranda to turn, it'll be a long wait," Sparrow said. "Banage could say the sky was green and she would still back him."

"It's her loyalty I'm counting on," Sara said with a sad sigh. "Blint was right, you know. Banage will never back down now that Whitefall's forced him to make his stand. He won't budge an inch from that tower until I roll over. We've been playing this game for twenty years now, he and I, but not for much longer. I didn't want it to be like this, but the Empress is the trump that forces all hands, even mine."

"Well, that's the problem with games," Sparrow said. "Sooner or later, someone has to lose."

Sara sighed again and tapped out her pipe. Sparrow just smiled and held the door for her as they started down the dark stairs toward her office in the Relay chamber.

Outside, at the edges of Zarin, another hundred soldiers arrived at the gates.

CHAPTER

13

Josef stomped after Duke Finley's servant as they wound down through the ancient warren of Osera's royal offices. But rather than stopping at one of the venerable old doors, the servant led Josef out past the stables to the little paved yard at the rear of the palace. A black carriage was waiting there for them, and the servant hurried forward to open the door.

Josef paused. This was all getting a little too suspicious—the sudden invitation, the backdoor exit, the unmarked carriage. Though, Josef reminded himself, suspicious as it was, he wasn't exactly a soft target. If Finley wanted to try something, let him. At least it would be a straightforward fight. Grinning at the thought, Josef climbed into the carriage. It rocked under his weight as he pulled himself inside. The servant followed, shutting the door behind them. The moment the door closed, the carriage shot forward, clattering through the yard and out the iron gate.

The back gate of the palace faced east, toward the Unseen Sea. Here, on the side of the island farthest from the Council and the wealth it brought, the scars of the war with the Empress were still evident. The houses were still built in the old way, stone shacks never more than a single story tall, most without windows, only a chimney and a door covered with oil cloth to keep the weather out. The houses clustered together, leaning on each other for comfort, but between the clusters, breaking up the flow of buildings like rocks in a stream, were the craters.

Josef wasn't born when the Empress's fleet first attacked, but he knew those craters same as any Oseran. They were the legacy of the Empress's war spirits, great monsters of stone and fire that came from the sky, striking the ground in enormous eruptions of burning rock. Even now, decades later, the ground was still black at the crater's base, the bedrock itself scorched and broken where the Empress's wizards had struck.

As they drove down the island's eastern slope, the houses grew smaller and the craters more numerous. The road they followed was narrow and winding, changing from smoothly paved stone to gravel and finally to rutted, sandy dirt as it snaked down the mountain. Ahead of them, Josef could see the glitter of the Unseen Sea. He knew where they were headed now. Osera, steep and rocky as it was, was not without beaches. This road led to the only sheltered bay on the island's eastern side, a protected curve of sand called the Rebuke, for it was here that the Council forces, led by his mother, had finally turned the Empress away.

The carriage bounced down the rutted road and came at last to a halt. Josef was out before the wheels stopped moving. Finley's servant hurried after him only to find Josef standing at the bottom step of the carriage, staring at the water with a strange look on his face.

The Rebuke was a curving oval bay ringed in by steep cliffs to form a narrow mouth leading out to sea. This much at least was still as Josef remembered it, but everything else had changed. When he'd come here as a boy to swim, the Rebuke had been little more than a grassy hill leading down to a narrow strip of rocky sand wedged between a cleft in the sea cliffs. Now that scrubby hill was gone, replaced by a smoothly paved walkway wide enough to march ten men abreast circling the inside of the bay all the way to the cliffs. Squinting against the salty wind, Josef ignored the servant's insistent tugging and walked out onto the stone. The paved area wasn't just a flattening of the old hill; it wasn't even just a walkway. It was a rampart, the flat top of a great wall that ran all the way along the bay's inner curve, forming a third, manmade cliff to join the natural barriers on the bay's north and south. Below the flat walkway he stood on was a steep, unclimbable slope of enormous, sharp, piled stone held together with sandy cement.

Josef looked over his shoulder. "When did they build this?"

The servant, not at all pleased by this delay, answered in a clipped voice. "Construction on the storm wall was finished five years ago, sir. It is the duke's greatest project."

Josef looked down at the solid stone beneath his feet. Not bad. Considering the gentle hill that had been here before, the wall of sharp rock and the wide rampart running along its top were certainly defensive improvements. Leaning into the wind, he looked over the wall's edge. Down below, the narrow beach had been widened as well, the sand combed and relayed to create a wide space between the surf and the wall. A tiny stair, steep as a ladder and barely wide enough for one man, cut down between the sharp rocks at the wall's midway mark, the only access Josef could see to the wide wooden docks that crowded the new beach. The docks themselves were large and freshly built, the tar still gleaming on the jutting joints that pushed out into the bay's blue water, but they were nothing compared to the ships.

Oseran runners filled the blue bay in long, precise lines, the fresh-cut wood of their narrow, high-running hulls gleaming white in the afternoon sun. Josef whistled appreciatively. Runners were the pride of Oseran shipbuilding and notoriously hard to make. It was no easy task getting hardwood long and straight enough to bear the carving needed to make a runner's long, curving keel, but that difficult shape was what let a runner weave through shallows and move faster on open water than any other ship on the sea. Back when Oserans had been pirates, the runners had been the reason they were feared. There had to be near a hundred of them bobbing in the water below, more than Josef had ever seen in one place, and every one of them new.

"Finley had this built?" he said, trying not to sound as impressed as he felt.

"Yes, your majesty," the servant said with barely disguised disgust. "*Some* members of the royal family cherish their position and strive to serve Osera's interests."

"I bet," Josef said. "All right, take me to him."

The servant bowed and turned toward the large tower that dominated the storm wall's northern half. Josef followed him, squinting up against the bright sunlight. The tower was square and solid, four stories tall with foot-thick walls and made of imported granite twice as strong as Osera's native stone. The door was solid iron, as were the stairs that wound up the tower's core. They passed an armory filled with racks of crossbows and crates of bolts, a small but well-equipped mess and sleeping barracks, and a nicely appointed officer's lounge. There were soldiers everywhere, navy officers mostly in their distinctive tight coats, but there were palace guards as well, standing watch in their chain and quilted surcoats with their short swords ready on their hips.

The top floor of the tower was separated from the others by a heavy door. Finley's servant stopped and knocked, a rapid double tap. The response was instant.

"Enter!" The heavy door did little to muffle Duke Finley's booming voice.

The servant opened the door and stepped aside with a sweep of his arm. Josef looked back down the winding stair, checking for emergency exits, just in case. There was only one, the way they'd come, but he was certain he could overpower the soldiers if it came to that, so he set his face in a scowl and marched into the room.

The top of the tower was unlike the other floors. Instead of smaller partitions, it was one open room, a great loft with a high ceiling going all the way up to the tower's pointed peak. There were tables here, including a large desk at the tower's center, all done in the same style as the rest of the tower's furnishings. But where the other floors were dark and sheltered by the tower's thick walls, this room was bright with sunlight streaming in through enormous, panoramic windows that ringed the room on all sides. The windows were set with thick glass, high-quality stuff, showing the view without so much as a single distorting wobble. And what a view it was. Josef could see the entire sweep of the bay below, the wide ocean spread out in front of him, the tops of the high cliffs to his right and left, and the eastern slums behind him running almost all the way to the weathered walls of the palace at the peak of the mountain.

Finley was standing beside the window that looked due east, talking into his palm while an older man in somber civilian clothes stood beside him, watching intently. He glanced at Josef as the prince entered, and then turned away, continuing his low speech into his palm where Josef couldn't see him. Josef glowered at that, but before he could say anything, Finley finished speaking and held out his hand to the man beside him. The older man moved forward, taking what looked like a small, blue marble from Finley and placing it carefully into a padded box.

The man bowed slightly to the duke and, holding the box in both hands, walked to the door. He did not bow to Josef, just slid by him and started down the stairs. Josef ignored the insult, focusing instead on his cousin and, so far as Josef could tell, greatest enemy in Osera.

"Ah," Finley said, turning at last to Josef. "The prince graces me with his presence."

Josef hooked his thumbs into his sword belt. "What do you want?"

Finley blithely ignored him. "I was just reporting our latest bit of bad luck to the Whitefall running the Council's forces, Lord Myron." He crossed the room as he spoke, stopping in front of a small wooden cabinet set between the windows. He unlocked the door with a key from his pocket. Inside was a cut-glass bottle filled with amber liquid. Finley took it out with loving hands, smiling at Josef over the glass stopper. "Would you like a drink?"

"No," Josef said. "What are you doing out here with the Relay point? It's supposed to be kept in the palace for the queen's use only."

"The first one is," Finley said, reaching back into the cabinet for a crystal tumbler. "That was our second point, provided for this watchtower."

"Osera has two Relay points?" Josef scoffed. "Since when? I thought they were incredibly rare."

"They are," Finley said, filling his glass halfway. "But considering how this tower will be the first to spot the Empress's fleet, I convinced the Council to give us another."

Josef narrowed his eyes. "So what were you relaying just now?"

"That," the duke said, tipping his glass toward the southern window.

Josef turned skeptically. He couldn't see much because of the cliffs, but he could see what looked like a plume of black smoke billowing up from somewhere down the coast.

Josef glanced back at the duke. "What's that?"

"Our clingfire depot," the duke said. "Or, rather, it *was*."

Josef swallowed. Clingfire was an old Oseran secret, a blend of pitch and sticky oil that clung to wood and burned even when wet.

It had been invented so that Oseran pirates on their fast, narrow ships could take down larger freighters. It was also the only way the Oseran navy had been able to fight the Empress's palace ships.

"What happened?"

"We're not sure," Finley said, his voice grave. "The whole depot went up sometime early this morning. It's been burning for nearly twelve hours already, and since we had almost five tons of clingfire ready for the Empress's assault, it will likely burn another twelve."

"Five tons?" Josef took a step back. He'd never heard of so much clingfire in one place.

"At least," Finley said. "Osera's not the little fishing village you left, Thereson. My factories have been producing clingfire day and night on the queen's order since word came that the Empress was on the move. I'd ordered it stored on one of the uninhabited southern islands for safety purposes, and good thing too. If we'd kept it in the city, the whole island would be burning by now."

Josef glanced again at the column of smoke. "You think it was arson?"

"Arson or carelessness," the duke said, sipping his drink. "Your wife's investigating as we speak, so I suppose we'll know soon enough. I may not like Adela, but even I can admit she's good at what she does." He left the words hanging, watching Josef over the rim of his glass.

Josef got the point well enough. "Better than me," he finished.

"Well," the duke said. "You ran away, so I guess we'll never know what could have been."

Josef barely stopped himself from rolling his eyes. "I've got better things to do today than listen to you gripe, Finley," he said. "If you've got something to say, say it. Otherwise, I'll be on my way."

"You haven't changed a bit, have you, Josef Liechten?" Finley said, setting his drink down on the window ledge with a clink. "Still unable to even play at manners."

"I don't play at anything," Josef said. "Get on with it."

The corner of the duke's mouth twitched. "Very well," he said. "I called you out here because I would like to propose an arrangement. These last two days have been very hard on you, haven't they, prince? You've never bothered to hide how much you hate being in your own country. Frankly, I'm surprised you're still around."

Josef's glower deepened, and the duke began to grin. "I can see I'm taxing your miniscule patience, so I'll get straight to the point. I want you to leave."

"I know that," Josef growled.

"No," the duke said. "I mean I want you to vanish. Go. Crawl back to whatever miserable, violent life you enjoyed before Theresa got this fool idea of grandchildren."

Josef bared his teeth. "If this is about the damn succession—"

"The succession does not concern me," the duke said. "Whatever hopes your mother holds, the truth is that my line will inherit the Throne of Iron Lions. Ancient as the blood of the Eisenlowe is, Osera is a land ruled by the strong, not by unborn children."

"And you would be that strength?"

"Of course," the duke answered. "I've been leading Osera since your mother first fell ill years ago. It was my money and my sway that fortified this bay. My pull with the Council that got us two Relay points, my shipyards that built a fleet of runners, and my factories that produced the five tons of clingfire it's going to take to sink an armada of palace ships."

Josef cocked his head toward the plume of smoke. "You mean the five tons that's burning right now?"

"A minor setback," the duke snapped. "The Empress won't be here for another month and a half. That's more than enough time to rebuild our supplies and secure my rule."

"*Your* rule?" Josef said, scowling. "I hate to disappoint you, Finley, but last I checked, my mother was still alive."

"Not for much longer," the duke said, smiling. "For all your faults, Thereson, you're a loving son, but you're kidding yourself if you actually believe our dear queen will be alive to lead Osera to another victory over the Empress."

"Shut your mouth, Finley," Josef said, taking a menacing step forward. "Or I will shut it for you."

Finley rolled his eyes. "Spare me the bravado. Believe it or not, my boy, I'm actually on your side. You don't want to be here, and I don't want you here either, so why shouldn't we work together to get you out?"

"Because I'm not going," Josef said. "I made a promise to my mother, and I mean to keep it."

"How novel of you," Duke Finley said, grabbing his drink again. He downed the rest of the glass in one swallow, keeping his eyes on Josef the whole time. "Tell me, Thereson," he said when he'd finished. "Are you trying to be as difficult as possible, or it is your natural state?"

"What do you care, anyway?" Josef yelled. "You just said you're not worried about the succession. Shouldn't you be off giving orders and being kingly? Why are you wasting time with me?"

"Because *you* are in my way," Finley yelled back, slamming his glass on the stone so hard it cracked. "You are a millstone around this country's neck, Josef Liechten. You always were, what with your moods and your stubbornness. But just when the people were learning to love you for your mother's sake, you run away to become a traveling swordsman and a thief." The duke let go of his cracked glass with a scowl. "We all breathed a sigh of relief when you left. The selfish boy was gone, and good riddance. But your selfishness knows no end, does it? For here you are again, back to weigh down your country one last time at the hour of her greatest need."

Josef took a deep, shaking breath. "You think I don't know that I let this country down?" he said. "No one was more aware of how great a failure I was than myself."

"Good," the duke said. "So prove it. *Leave.* Your presence in Osera is a disruption. The people are confused. They fear that this wandering swordsman, this no-account murderer who abandoned them has returned to be king. This fear causes division and distraction at the time when we must be the most focused and united. If you love your mother, Thereson, if you want to preserve the country she fought so hard for all her life, then do us all a favor and remove yourself from it. I swear I will take good care of our people. I will defeat the Empress and lead Osera into an even brighter age of wealth and prosperity. I will be the king you never could be, and I will even make sure your legacy of failure is forgotten. All you have to do is go."

Finley reached into his pocket and pulled out a heavy bag. He swung his arm, tossing the bag on the floor between them. It landed with a bright, metal *chink*, spilling open in a shower of gold coins.

"That's a hundred gold standards," the duke said. "There's also a pledge that can be used in Zarin for five hundred more. If you ever loved Osera, take it and leave before you do irreparable harm."

Josef stared at the bag of coins, and then, without a word, he swung his boot back and kicked it as hard as he could. The kick sent the gold flying, the coins tinkling like golden bells as they scattered across the heavy wooden planks.

The duke stepped back in surprise as coins bounced across his boots. When he raised his head, his face was pale with rage. "That was very foolish."

"Then you should have expected it," Josef said. "Given your opinion of me."

Finley began to shake, but before he could open his mouth, Josef moved in. He closed the distance between them in one long step, pointing his finger right in the duke's face.

"There's only one understanding we need between us, cousin," he whispered, his voice sharp as his blades. "Whether my mother is alive to see it or not, I will honor her wish and continue the blood of our house. That wish is the only thing keeping me in this country, and the moment it is fulfilled, I will vanish so quickly not even you will be able to find fault. But until that time, nothing, not gold, not threats, not even poison in the night, *nothing* is going to make me abandon the one duty my mother has ever asked of me that I could actually deliver. Everything else, the throne, the people, I gladly leave to you, but I will not betray my promise now that I've made it, and I'm not going anywhere."

With a final glare, Josef turned on his heel and walked toward the door. Behind him, he heard the duke's boots scrape as the old man recovered.

"Thereson!"

Josef stopped and looked over his shoulder. The duke had pulled himself up to his full height, his face scarlet with barely leashed fury. "I have given you every chance to do right by your country, but if you will not leave on your own, I will not hesitate to do what is best for Osera."

Josef's hands went back to rest on the swords at his hip. "You're welcome to try, old man." With that, he flashed the duke a long, bloodthirsty smile and walked out the door.

The servant was waiting just outside. Josef pushed past him, sweeping down the stairs. When he reached the bottom of the tower, he kept going, walking past the waiting carriage to the rutted road leading back to the city. The moment he hit the dirt, he started jogging, his legs eating the distance in long steps as he pushed up the slope into the poor, crater-pocked neighborhoods covering Osera's eastern side. People came out to gawk at him as he passed, the tall man with his fine clothes hidden under blades. Josef ignored the stares and kept running, his hands clenched in white-knuckled fists.

The sun was going down by the time he reached the palace at the top of mountain. Servants threw themselves out of his way as he stomped through the rear gate. He heard them whispering his name as he crossed the yard, as well as other things—thief, deserter, murderer, disappointment, failure—before he shut his ears and set himself on a single-minded path back to his room.

When he arrived, he opened his door to find Nico and Eli sitting at his table eating his dinner.

"Welcome back," Eli said around an enormous mouthful of food, glancing over his shoulder just long enough to give Josef a stuff-cheeked smile. "How was the meeting?"

Josef ignored the question. "What are you doing?" he said, shutting the door.

"Dinner," Eli said, turning back to the table. "We started without you. Hope you don't mind."

"Wouldn't matter if I did," Josef said, looking at the decimated plates. "There's not enough left to get mad over."

"You should be grateful," Eli said, shoving another forkful of potatoes in his mouth. "A man came by about a half hour ago with a message from your wife. Something about a fire? Anyway, he said that she said to tell you that she's going to be late tonight and you should eat without her, so *I* took the liberty of telling him to go ahead and bring up your dinner. After all"—Eli swallowed loudly—"we'll never get a better chance to test it for poison without having to worry about the sweet princess."

Josef's eyebrows shot up. "So you decided to test the food for poison by eating it all? That's the stupidest idea I've ever heard."

"You have no vision," Eli said. "I'll have you know I have a very sophisticated pallet for this sort of thing. The old Monpress fed me every poison under the sun during my thief training days. Ah," he said, licking his fingers. "Memories."

Josef shook his head. "So what have you found?"

"Nothing," Eli said, snatching the last delicately folded roll from the basket at the center of the table. "Your food seems perfectly safe, so either your poisoner decided to take the night off, or it's not coming through the food."

"Or it's something you don't recognize," Josef added.

"Impossible," Eli said. "If it's used in the Council Kingdoms, I've tasted it. Poisoning's a subtle art, but it's very set in its ways."

"I'll keep that in mind," Josef muttered. He walked over to the table and picked up a plate of beef scraps, all that was left of what must have been a lovely roast. "Meanwhile, you can get out. I'm going to wait up for Adela. I have some questions to ask her."

Eli shrugged and stood, taking his wineglass with him. "I'm going to poke my nose down around the castle," he said, refilling his glass to the rim from the bottle on the mantel. "Do a little good-will work with the spirits, just in case we have to make a quick getaway."

Josef ignored the stab of bitterness that came with that. "What makes you think we'll be leaving?"

"First rule of thievery: Never be without a quick exit," Eli said, sipping the top of his now very full glass. "Of course, there's also the fact that you just walked in from a meeting with a powerful man who doesn't like you very much looking like you're ready to kill something. Even without the rules, that's reason enough for me."

Josef couldn't argue that point, so he let Eli go. But when Nico got up to follow, he reached out.

"Stay," he said, grabbing her shoulder gently. "Please. I want you to help keep an eye on things, in case I fall asleep again."

"You want me to stay here," she said, slowly. "With you and your wife?"

"Yes," Josef said. "In case I—"

"Fall asleep again," she finished, turning away. "I heard you the first time."

She vanished into the long shadows of the dressing room before he could add anything else, and Josef bit back a curse. He was trying to think of something to say when the door creaked, and he snapped his head around to see Eli hovering.

"Josef," he said, very quietly. "Do you want to talk about—"

"No," Josef said.

Eli bit his lip and, for a long, tense moment, Josef worried that the thief would push. But then Eli nodded and vanished into the hall, closing the door silently behind him. Once he was sure Eli was gone, Josef sat down on the couch and stared at the destroyed remains of his dinner, mechanically shoving the last scraps of the roast into his mouth as he waited for his wife to appear.

CHAPTER

14

The Empress stood on the balcony at the top of her war palace, looking over her fleet. It was an impressive sight. Even Nara, who had fielded countless armies in her conquest of the continent that was now her Empire, had never seen its like.

Palace ships filled the bay, packed so close that the sailors could step from one ship to the next without stretching their legs. Overhead, wind spirits kept a smooth inland wind blowing at her command, filling the enormous sails and keeping the ships together against the ocean's tide. Each palace ship was large enough to fill three blocks in one of her well-ordered cities and as tall as the war palace at Istalirin would be were it perched on the sea instead of a mountain. Square sails as large as wheat fields hung from the tower masts, and each enormous, tar-black, iron-girded wood hull was packed to capacity with men ready to die at her command.

For the first time in many centuries, Nara felt a quickening of the excitement that came before a conquest. She had emptied her garrisons for this day, marched her troops to the bay at Istalirin from all corners of her Empire. Before her lay the largest fleet ever assembled, carrying the largest army she'd ever fielded, the largest army the world had ever seen.

"It's beautiful," said a deep voice beside her.

Nara caught herself seconds before she jumped. Excitement turned to cold rage as she turned to face the man who had impertinently joined her on her balcony.

Den wasn't even looking at her. His eyes were locked on the fleet, his face pulled into a wide, white-toothed grin that was more snarl than smile. "I think that's the most beautiful thing I've ever see."

"I'm glad you're pleased," Nara said sharply. "But I didn't build it for you."

"Pity," Den said with a sigh. "It would be a real challenge to take that army."

Nara sighed. "That's an absurd joke, Warlord."

"I don't make jokes," Den said, reaching in his pocket. "Look here, I made you something."

He pulled out a folded paper and jabbed it at her like a spear. Nara took it gingerly, eyebrows going up in surprise as she shook the paper open. It was a map. A hand-drawn, surprisingly detailed map of lands she did not recognize.

"The western continent," Den said. "Your maps were a bit sketchy. I filled in the details."

"My maps were taken from description given by the winds," Nara said crossly.

"What do winds know of war?" Den said, shrugging. "War is a human enterprise, woman. See here." He snatched the map back and laid a calloused finger on the long chain of islands just off the continent's eastern seaboard.

"Osera," Den said. "We have to take them first or you'll have their runners on your back the whole campaign. Now, your maps showed only the coastline, but look here." He moved his finger to the cross-hatching that surrounded the islands. "These are the shallows, the rocks and reefs that guard Osera's eastern shore. Your big ships run deep. They'll ground themselves if they get too close."

"I am well aware of that," Nara snapped. "You presume too much. Remember, my generals have fought at Osera before."

"And they let Whitefall and his cronies lure them into the handful of deepwater approaches like idiots," Den countered. "That one act of stupidity narrowed their fleet, lowered the effectiveness of superior numbers, and lost them the war. If I hadn't switched sides and taken out Whitefall's army on the cliffs, your ships would never have made it back here to report their own defeat."

Nara glared at Den's weathered finger on the cross-hatched shading marking the dangerous water. "You never did tell me why you turned that day. You were the greatest threat to our soldiers, greater than the wizards or the ships with their clingfire." She glanced up at his dark eyes. "Tell me, why did you do it?"

Den looked genuinely puzzled. "Why do you ask?"

"As your new master, I think it is wise to know what triggers your betrayal."

Den threw back his head and laughed. He laughed long and loudly, frightening the servants who hovered just out of sight. Nara stayed still, growing angrier with every passing second. Finally, Den's laughter died away, leaving him grinning at her like a wolf.

"You don't get it, do you?" he said. "That war was the happiest time of my life. For the first time ever, I could fight as much as I wanted. Strong men literally jumped out of the sea at me. No more wandering looking for a challenge, no more wasting my time. Truly, I'd found paradise. So when your fleet started to lose, it was the natural choice to switch sides and keep my paradise going. It worked for a bit, but then your coward of a general ran home. I considered slaughtering him and what was left of his crew, but I wanted to meet the woman who could start a war without even going to the front herself. I thought if you could start one war, maybe there were others." His grin widened. "But you should know, Nara, it wasn't betrayal. Betrayal requires loyalty. I had no loyalty to Whitefall, and I have no loyalty to you. You can call yourself my Empress all you like, but I have no king by myself."

With that, he started to laugh again, and for a moment, Nara seriously considered killing him. She turned the idea over, toying with how to do it. She could order the air around him to stop moving and suffocate him where he stood. She could open the floor below him and let the fall break him on the rocks. But she did none of these things. Instead, she turned back to her fleet.

"You know I could kill you before you lifted a hand."

"But you won't," Den said. "A woman who's spent ten lifetimes conquering knows better than to throw away her best weapon."

Nara stiffened. "And if we start to lose now, will you kill five thousand of my men and join the other side?"

"Five thousand of your men wouldn't even be a dent," Den said, grinning down at the endless ships. "But what a fight that would be, eh?"

The Empress shook her head. "Go and take your place, Bloody Den. Take your map to the fleet head and tell him I said to put you on the first-wave flagship."

Den took his map back, folding it neatly. "Just so long as you promise I won't die of old age waiting for you to get moving. We're not all immortal here, Nara."

"I'll throw you into war soon enough," the Empress said. "When this is done, even you might have had your fill of fighting."

"Impossible," Den said, laughing as he vanished through the curtained door.

Nara did not watch him go. She watched her fleet, standing still as a gold-plated statue on her balcony until, hours later, the last of her army had finally marched up the plank from the dock to the waiting ships. As the captain called for the plank to be raised, a shiver went through her. Almost, she breathed to herself. Soon, sooner than Den could dream, her fleet would be landing on the far-western shore. Soon she would carve a swath across the world large enough that even Benehime would notice. She would force the Lady to look up from her spoiled boy, and when she did, she would see Nara standing triumphant with the world in her hands, ready at last to shape it to the perfection she'd dreamed of that night in the swamp so many years ago.

Will you, darling girl?

The voice broke over her like a shower of ice water. Nara froze, unable to breathe, unable to think as the thrill of that beloved, beloved tore through her. When she could move again, she turned and fell to her knees before the pure white light.

Benehime sat on the balcony railing like a great white bird, a smile on her perfect, white face. She was glorious, beautiful, and so beloved Nara could barely look at her. Instead, the Empress kept her face down, biting her lip against the overwhelming tide of emotion threatening to capsize her.

Are you crying? Benehime's voice was cool and soft as her white fingers lay their burning touch against the crown of Nara's head. *Did you think I had forgotten you, Nara?*

"No, Lady," Nara lied, raising her tear-streaked face to kiss the Lady's fingers.

I could never forget my dashing Empress. Benehime's voice floated over her mind. *Just because you are no longer first in my heart does not mean I do not care for you.*

Nara shook with rage. Second. Second. How could she be *second*? Above her, the Shepherdess put on a hurt face.

Why are you mad, darling?

"How can I not be?" Nara cried. "You love that boy more than me!"

The Shepherdess smiled, stroking Nara's face with her finger-tips. *Jealousy becomes you. You were so dull while you were sulking.*

Nara flinched, cheeks coloring with shame. "I am through with that," she said bitterly. "I love you, Lady. More than he ever could."

Do you? Benehime's voice was close to laughter.

Nara looked away. Her words sounded so needy, so desperate, even to her. But she could not stop. The Lady's presence was intoxicating after so long without.

Benehime's sigh floated over her, and when Nara looked up, the Lady was gone. Panic shot through her, but before she could move, white arms encircled her from behind. Relief so strong it was almost painful hammered her chest, and Nara fell back, letting Benehime's white beauty engulf her.

There, there, my love, Benehime whispered, pulling Nara into her lap. She kissed the Empress's forehead, cradling her armored body to her breast. Nara gave herself over, burying her face in the impossibly soft cascade of Benehime's white hair as she began to weep in earnest, surrendering completely to the burning, beloved feel of her Lady's touch.

"You forgot me." Her words were broken to pieces by sobs.

Benehime made a soothing noise. *I did not forget you. I simply had others more worthy of my attention. How could I visit you when you had cast yourself into that stinking cave?*

"What else was there for me?" Nara whispered. "I was lost without you." She raised her head, looking into the Lady's white eyes. "I love you," she whispered. "I live for you, Lady. I always have, ever since that first night. I will never hide again. I swear it, so please, please come back to me."

Come back? Benehime's voice was soft as new snow. *How could I come back to you now? What have you done to deserve me?*

"I'll do anything," Nara whispered, digging her fingers into the white flesh of Benehime's lovely shoulders.

Benehime bent down, cupping Nara's chin in her burning fingers as she laid a kiss on Nara's lips. Nara shuddered, her eyes slamming closed to shut out everything but the feel of the Shepherdess. It was a brief touch, barely more than a flash of heat, but it was enough to bring centuries of memories flooding back. Nara reached out desperately, clinging to the lost time when Benehime loved her best of all. But no matter how tightly she held them, the memories were flat. That time was gone, leaving her alone and forgotten, empty but for one burning desire.

When Nara opened her eyes again, she was no longer crying.

"Lady," she promised. "I will be your favorite again, or I will die trying."

Such talk, Nara, Benehime said, stroking her hair. *Second in my heart is still beloved. Is that not enough?*

"No," Nara said, sitting up straight. "I know now, life without your attention is no better than death." She reached out, seizing the Lady's hand between her own. "Tell me what to do," she whispered. "How can I make you love me best again?"

Benehime smiled and stood, taking Nara with her as though the Empress weighed nothing. She turned slightly, facing them toward the fleet that spread out across the sea. *I always loved you best as a conqueror,* she said. *Do you remember when I first found you? The wish you made?*

"To bring all the world under righteous rule," Nara said.

Benehime smiled. *It was those words that made me love you then. So audacious, so determined. If you want me to love you now as I did then, use the power I gave you to fulfill that wish. Give me the world, Nara. Be the conqueror, the righteous, perfect Empress I saw in you so long ago. Crush all who stand in your way, and maybe I will have reason to love you best again.*

Nara leaned back, her hand going to the beautiful sword at her hip. "Watch me, Shepherdess," she said, her voice firm as stone.

"You will see your conqueror in all her glory and terror. I will give you a world made perfect, a world without unfairness or disobedience. A world deserving of you."

Benehime laughed, a beautiful chime, and leaned in to drop a kiss on the Empress's forehead.

I'll be watching. Her whisper thrilled against Nara's skin. *Do not disappoint me, darling star.*

And then she was gone, her beautiful whiteness vanishing into the air, leaving only the blinding afterimage of a white line. Nara fell to her knees as the overwhelming feel of the Lady's presence vanished. She knelt for several moments, clutching herself and trying not to sob at the loss. When she was sure of herself again, she stood and walked to the balcony's edge, reaching out with her spirit as she did. The war palace answered at once.

"Hail, Empress," the stones rattled.

"Are the ships loaded?"

"Yes, Empress," the stone said. "The docks report that the last of your legions and the man called Den are boarded."

Nara nodded. "Time to go."

The stone gave a final, sobbing shudder before bowing to her will. "Yes, Empress. As you command."

As the words faded, the war palace began to shake. The bay rocked as the tremors shot through the ground. She could dimly hear the cries of her men on the ships, but Nara brushed them aside, focusing her attention on the palace around her. She stretched out her spirit, wrapping it through the stone and down to the very roots of the mountain she'd used to form the fortress hundreds of years ago, and then, one by one, she ripped those roots out. The stone screamed every time she pulled one free, yammering in pain as she severed its connection to the world's foundations.

Nara scowled. *Quiet.*

The command left her with a stab of her will, and the screaming stopped. After that, the mountain bore the pain in silence as she tore the last of its roots free.

Move, she said, pouring her will into the command.

The stone obeyed. With a great crash, the war palace Istalirin, and the mountain it was attached to, fell into the sea. The stone docks crumbled with a cut-off cry as the mountain fell on top of them, and the ocean rose up in a great wave from the impact, tossing her palace ships like toy boats. Her winds moved the moment she brushed them, tearing down from the sky and forcing themselves between the ships to cushion them as they bumped against each other. Other winds pressed on the water itself, flattening the bay until the sea was as smooth as glass and the war palace floated among the fleet, a true palace ship riding atop a great stone island.

"Empress," the mountain's voice was pleading. "I cannot hold, Empress. I will sink."

"You will not," the Empress said. She flung out her will, reaching over the bay, over her ships, and out into the ocean. The moment she hit open water, her spirit dove. She plunged into the water, ignoring the mad rush of the water spirits and sinking deep into the black abyss until she found what she wanted. At the bottom of the trench that ran along her continent was a current, one of the great highways of the sea. This current was not a spirit in itself, but a union of the tattered remains of shredded water spirits torn apart by the ocean's pull. These spirits, no longer large enough to have minds of their own, banded together to flow as one in one direction, operating with a herd mind that had only one purpose: to flow. And that was the purpose Nara took.

She grabbed the current with her will. The water screamed and fought as she pulled it up, too mindless to care that she was a star. But Nara fought harder, crushing the spirits until the water cried out in surrender. When it was pliant in her grip, Nara pulled the current up from the seafloor and into her bay. The deep, cold water flooded into the warm shallows with a scream, lifting her fleet in a great swell before slamming into the gap between her war palace and the seafloor. The palace shook in relief as the current lifted the uprooted mountain, floating it like a cork under Nara's iron command.

Nara smiled as her palace bobbed and shifted her focus westward. Screaming, the current had no choice but to follow. The blast of water caught the palace ships at once, and her fleet shot out, riding the great wave of water westward toward the unconquered half of the world.

Panting, Nara fell to her knees, clutching the balcony rails to keep herself upright. Even as a star, moving such enormous spirits was exhausting. But it was done. Her fleet and her war palace were racing out of the bay, carried into the sea by the great current that flowed at her command. There was nothing that could stop her now.

Slowly, she stood and drew her sword, raising its gleaming blade to the fading sunlight. "Are you watching, lady?" she cried, holding her sword to the sky. "With this, I begin your war."

As she spoke, words appeared on the sword's blade, a single sentence etched in gleaming steel.

Sleepers wake, I am coming.

Nara held her breath. The rushing wind filled her ears, but if she strained, she could hear the Shepherdess's beautiful laugh at the very edge of her hearing. That was enough. Smiling, Nara sheathed her sword and walked into her palace.

High overhead, those winds who were not yet loyal turned and rushed west to bring word to their master of the star's coming.

Duke Finley arrived at his town house shortly after sunset. His servants ran out to greet him as the coach pulled to a stop. Finley stepped down, letting the valets take his overcoat while his footmen ran to close the elegant iron gate that separated the mansion from the street. Henry was waiting for him at the door, a glass of wine ready in his hand.

"Welcome home, father," he said. "How was your day?"

"What you doing here?" Finley said, snatching the glass with enough force to spill half its contents on the marble entry. "You're supposed to be heading the palace watch tonight."

"The captain gave me the night off," Henry said. "She heard about your meeting with our beloved prince and thought you could use the company."

"Did she?" Finley downed the wine in one gulp and tossed the glass at his manservant, who caught it expertly. "How thoughtful of our dear princess."

Henry's smile wavered as he followed his father into the house. Like all high-ranking Oseran nobility, Duke Finley's mansion was located in the tangle of fine houses just down the mountain from the palace. But though his house was less than a block from the castle, it was worlds away in style. Where the royal palace was a stalwart relic of a lost era, the duke's home was impeccably modern. The smooth, austere facade presented a clean face to the street while delicate flourishes of carved waves lapped tastefully at the cornerstones. Inside, wide halls paneled with carved slats of imported wood led to rooms filled with windows. Elegant lamps enhanced with crystals hung from the ceilings, and fine rugs covered the floor with rich colors. The furniture was ornate, painted gold and upholstered in silk in the Zarin style.

But for all this modernity, Finley was still the heir to the throne, and was he guarded accordingly. Because of this, the delicate ambiance of his brightly lit stone foyer was marred by a pair of guards in full armor standing at attention. A second pair of guards, scarred veterans, stood at the top of the grand stair where they perpetually got in the way of the servants. A third pair of guards watched the door to the duke's small garden, their great armored shapes ridiculous against the outline of the delicate fruit trees. Each post saluted the duke as he passed, and the duke saluted back, muttering to himself the whole way up to his study.

"Honestly," he growled as Henry closed the leather padded study door. "You'd think we were still an island of savage barbarians murdering each other in our beds."

"The queen cares deeply for your safety, father," Henry said. "As do we all."

"Nonsense," the duke said, sinking into his cushioned chair by the fire. "Theresa may set the guard, but I'm the one who has to pay for it. And you can stop trying to butter me up with that 'as do we all' rot, Henry. You're not going to be king."

The dutiful look fell off Henry's face. "What?" he cried.

"He didn't take the bait," the duke said, shrugging. "Josef Liechten is determined to stay and get his mother her grandchild whether she's alive to enjoy the brat or not. You'd think after abandoning every other shred of duty, this would be easy, but *no*."

"What are we going to do?" Henry said, sinking into the chair beside his father's.

"Nothing," the duke said and snorted, staring into the fire. "We're going to sit and we're going to wait. Even if he got her with child last night, the queen won't live long enough to confirm the pregnancy. Once the old cow is dead and I'm on the throne, no one will care what's in the princess's belly."

"Father," Henry said delicately, sitting on the edge of his chair. "Aren't you dismissing Adela too quickly? She's very popular with the people. We could use that. I—"

"I am well aware of your shameless infatuation with the princess, Henry," the duke said dryly. "Now, and I'm not going to tell you this again, forget her. She's nothing but trash who knows how to play a crowd, just like her mother. If you speak of her again, I'll pull you off the guard and put you on a deepwater patrol boat for the rest of the year. Do you understand?"

Henry bit his lip. "Yes, father."

"Good," the duke said, sitting back. "Powers, the way my luck's been going, you'll be the one to get the princess pregnant and lose your throne to your own son."

"Father!" Henry cried.

"You can't hide things from me, boy," Finley said, glaring. "Not that you've tried. Honestly, I don't know why I'm working so hard to secure your place in the succession when you seem intent on ruining your reputation, cornering the princess in hallways in sight of anyone who walks by."

Henry looked away, cheeks scarlet. "Doesn't matter, anyway," he grumbled. "Everyone's saying we're done for now that the cling-fire's up in flames."

Finley sat up. "Who's saying that?"

"All the guards, for one," Henry said. "It's common talk on the docks, and why not? You could see the smoke from the mainland. Everyone knows that we can't down the palace ships without cling-fire, and if the palace ships don't go down, the Empress wins."

"A minor setback," the duke said dismissively. "I'll have the crown make a statement tomorrow that we have a backup clingfire stock hidden."

"But we *don't*," Henry said.

"Well, no one needs to know that, do they?" Finley said. "The last thing we need is a panic. If we are to stand before the Empress, we must be united, and we can't do that if people are scared."

"You can't just lie about things like that," Henry said.

"I can and I have," Finley said. "How do you think this island's been functioning for the last month? We've been plagued by set-backs since we heard the Empress was on the move. First there was the queen's dramatic turn for the worse that put everything in uproar and brought back the idiot prince, and then we had that horrid mess with the tar eating through the wood in the new ships. We had to scrap half a fleet of runners thanks to that one. And there was the dry rot in the corn vault." The duke shook his head. "Trust me, Henry, this fire was nothing. Just another headache in a long line of bad, bad luck."

Henry stared at his father. "I didn't hear about any of that."

"Of course you didn't," Finley said. "That's what it means to keep things *secret*. Fortunately, we've still got time to make up the shortfalls before the Empress arrives. Assuming, of course, nothing else goes wrong."

Henry paled. "What else *can* go wrong?"

"Never ask, my boy," Finley said quietly. "Never ask."

They sat in silence for several minutes, both lost in their own dark thoughts as they watched the fire burn lower and lower. And then suddenly and without warning, Henry sat bolt upright.

"What was that?" he said. "Did you hear that?"

"No," the duke grumbled, sinking lower in his chair. "Probably our idiot porter getting into the—"

The sound cut him off before he could finish. It was a soft, rolling thump, followed by a clatter. Finley looked at his son, all tiredness gone, and they stood up together. The duke's hand dropped down to the old sword at his side as he crept toward the library door.

Just before his hand touched the handle, the door flew open, and a white-faced servant burst into the room.

"My lord!" he whispered, his voice cracking with panic. "You have to get out!"

"Why?" the duke said. "What's happened?"

The servant looked over his shoulder at the dark hall. "An intruder, sir."

"Intruder?" the duke said. "Nonsense, let the guards have him. That's what I pay them for."

The servant shook his head, grabbing the duke's arms. "The back, quick—"

The word ended in a tight gasp. The servant's mouth was still moving, but no sound came out. His eyes were wide as he crumpled, the back of his neck cut wide open. He was dead before he hit the ground.

The duke jumped back before he realized what was happening, drawing his sword on instinct alone. Now that the servant was out of the way, he could see the guards at the end of the hall. Both men were down, lying in dark pools with the back of their necks cut, spines severed cleanly, just like the servant's.

Finley grew very still, eyes searching the shadows while his fingers tightened on his sword. But the house was still, silent except for his own ragged breaths and those of his son behind him.

Without taking his eyes from the door, he motioned Henry back to the fireplace. Other than the windows, the room had only one entrance. Finley kept his sword up, watching the shadows for any trace of movement. On the floor, the servant's blood was seeping into the thick carpet. It was so quiet the duke could hear the liquid spreading through the fibers. Panic began to rise in his stomach, but Finley fought it down. He took a deep breath, ignoring the taste of blood in the air and forcing himself to be calm, to look.

That was when he saw the killer.

The man stood at the corner where the stairs met the hall, less than five steps from the fallen guards. He was so still that the duke's eyes had a hard time picking his dark clothes out of the shadows. Finley blinked several times, still not sure if his eyes were telling the truth. If the man was standing at the other end of house, there was no way he could have killed the servant, not from that distance. Perhaps there were two intruders? As Finley's mind scrambled to reconcile the facts, the man began to move. He rushed forward, racing down the hall in a handful of seconds, his padded feet completely silent on the hardwood floor.

Finley gritted his teeth and cursed himself for a fool. He'd just wasted his only chance to escape. Now the man stood in the study door, blocking the only exit with his body.

"What do you want?" Finley said, surprised at how stern and clear his voice was.

The man didn't answer. Now that he was standing in the well-lit library, the duke could see the intruder was slender and tall. He was wrapped head to toe in dark cloth, and even his eyes were hidden beneath black netting. He had a sword at his hip, the sheath wrapped in black as well, but Finley could tell it was a short blade. The duke hefted his own sword. There was still a chance. He had reach on the assassin, so did Henry. The killer had lost his chance at surprise by running forward, and it was two on one now.

At once, Finley felt his confidence returning. He inched his feet forward, stepping into position. Behind him, he heard Henry follow his lead. Finley licked his lips, getting ready to shout for Henry to begin the attack. But the words died on his lips, for at that moment, the assassin drew his sword.

The sword appeared with a flash of silver. Its blade was heavy, short, and gleaming with its own silver light. Finley sucked in a breath. A man in Osera didn't go through a lifetime of sword training without learning to recognize an awakened blade. The duke was no wizard, but even he could see the sword's surface trembling in anticipation as the assassin stepped over the servant's body.

The blow came before the duke could think to raise his sword. One moment the assassin was facing them, short sword in hand, the next the sword was *through* him. Finley gasped more in surprise than pain, looking down at the blade through his chest, and then up again at the man still standing in the doorway holding a sword that was no longer short, but long as a spear with its point jutting out Finley's back.

On the other side of the room, the assassin flicked his hand. The sword flashed like a wave, the steel sliding out of Finley's body, and Henry began to scream. The duke jerked in surprise and turned to help his son, but his body wasn't moving anymore. He toppled, falling to the carpet. He turned as he fell, looking back just in time to see the glowing blade snap like a whip as it finished slitting his son's throat.

The duke could only stare as Henry fell, hitting the carpet with that now-familiar soft thump. Behind him, he heard the hiss of steel on steel, and he rolled his eyes to see the swordsman's blade shrinking back to its original size, the glowing metal folding into itself until the assassin held a short sword once again. The killer lifted his gleaming weapon and walked to the window, using the duke's velvet curtains to wipe Henry's blood from the blade. Finley's breath was growing scarce now, but he hardly noticed. Rage filled his body in a way life no longer could, and he lunged across the carpet, grabbing the man by the ankle.

"You dare!" he hissed. "Who are you?"

The swordsman turned to face him and slowly raised his hand to the cloth over his face. He unhooked something behind his ear, and the covering fell away. The duke's hand went limp with surprise, and he collapsed back to the carpet.

"You," he whispered in disbelief. And then, with his last breath: "Why?"

The question was barely past his lips when the sword swept down, giving Duke Finley the last and only answer he would ever receive.

CHAPTER

15

It was full dark when Gin pushed through the last crowd of soldiers and under the gate that separated the Spirit Court's district from the rest of Zarin. Miranda clung to his back, staring bleakly at the wide, suddenly empty streets. The colored lamps were lit and swinging gently in the night air, but no one was around to enjoy the light. From the moment they entered the Spirit Court's district until Miranda slid off Gin at the foot of the Tower, they didn't see a single soul.

Stomach sinking, Miranda started up the stairs. She'd always known that the Rector Spiritualis controlled the Tower, but it was an academic, abstract sort of knowledge. She'd seen it in action only once, at her trial. Even so, she never would have imagined something like this.

The Tower was completely sealed. Its enormous red doors lay abandoned on the ground, shed like outgrown scales. In their place, a wall of white stone rose smooth as river rock from the ground. It was as though the entire Tower had become a solid stone pillar, and though she walked all the way around the base, Miranda could find no way in.

"Try knocking?" Gin suggested.

Feeling more than a little foolish, Miranda reached out and rapped her knuckles on the stone. Nothing happened. She pulled her hand back, frowning, and then she reached out again, with her left hand this time, knocking with the heavy gold band on her ring finger, the one set with the Spirit Court's perfect circle. The gold made a lovely ringing sound when it touched the Tower, and the stone began to twist. The Tower wall rumbled softly, opening like a flower to reveal a tunnel just large enough for Gin to squeeze through.

With one final glance at the empty street, Miranda stepped inside. Gin followed on her heels. The moment his tail was clear, the Tower closed behind them.

They came out in the Spirit Court's grand entry hall, which looked exactly as it always had except that the grand doors were now grown over with stone and the center of the room was full of huddled people. Spiritualists sat in circles on furniture pilfered from other parts of the Tower. Several had their fire spirits out, and the warm, flickering light filled the void left by the missing windows, giving the room a primal, cave-like feel.

She was scarcely inside when someone shouted, "Miranda!"

She looked up to see a young man break away from the main group and run toward her, waving.

"Jason!" she cried, recognizing him at once.

He stopped in front of her, grinning wide in the light of the will-o'-the-wisp that floated in his wake. Miranda smiled back. She and Jason had been in the academy together and taken their oaths on the same day. He'd gone on to apprentice for some distant Tower Keeper after that, and they saw each other only rarely. Still, they'd always been friends.

"I'm happy to see you," she said.

"Not as happy as we are to see you," he said. "Hello, Gin."

Gin blinked slowly, which was as nice a greeting as one could expect from a ghosthound.

"The Rector said you'd entered the city this morning," Jason said. "I have to admit, when you didn't show up at once, some people worried you'd gone over to the Council. I knew better, though. That bunch of traitors are as bad as Hern."

"No one's as bad as Hern," Miranda said. "Where's Master Banage?"

"Upstairs," Jason said, nodding toward the grand staircase. "Powers, I'm glad you're here. The Rector has been looking grimmer than usual." Jason lowered his voice. "I don't think he expected quite so many of the old guard to turn on him."

Miranda frowned. "How many are here?"

"A little over a hundred," Jason said. "We're mostly Journeymen Spiritualists down here. The Tower Keepers are upstairs in the private rooms for the most part, or the library." His hands moved as he talked, and the will-o'-the-wisp followed his fingers like an eerie, blue-green firefly. "We've got close to eight hundred Spiritualists still unaccounted for, though I don't know what's taking so long. It's been three days since the Rector called us in. That's enough time for a determined Spiritualist to get to Zarin from anywhere on the continent." Jason bit his lip. "You don't think they've all gone over to the Council?"

"No," Miranda said, shaking her head. "I just came from there. Blint's in charge, and he had only three hundred a few hours ago. Hern's old cronies, mostly, but that's no surprise. They always did prefer politics to spirits."

"Three hundred," Jason said with a dismayed sigh. "Still, where's everyone else?"

Miranda shrugged. "Probably waiting to see how things play out before they cast their lot."

"Cowards," Jason said, sneering.

"Maybe," Miranda said. "But they're still Spiritualists." She turned and started toward the stairs. "Speaking of which, I'm going to see Master Banage."

"Of course," Jason said. "Good to have you back!"

She waved as he jogged back to the main group to share the good news. Miranda started up the shadowy staircase, Gin slinking behind her.

The climb to Banage's office was surprisingly short. It was the Tower's doing, Miranda was sure. Things had always been a little strange inside the stone pillar the Spiritualists called home, but what else could one expect from a tower raised in a day by Shapers? After her unwilling stint in the Shaper Mountain, Miranda was surprised the Tower didn't move more. Even so, despite the shorter-than-expected climb, she was still out of breath when she reached the landing outside of Banage's office where Spiritualist Krigel, Assistant to the Rector Spiritualis, was waiting.

"Took you long enough," he said.

"Sorry," Miranda panted. "I didn't even know there was a war until this morning. Where's Master Banage?"

Krigel jerked his head toward the closed door.

Gin sat down without being asked, stretching out down the long staircase. Krigel gave the dog a nasty look, and Miranda took the opportunity to slip past the old Spiritualist, pushing open the door to Banage's office as quietly as she could.

The office of the Rector Spiritualis had changed dramatically. The first thing she noticed were the windows. The large panes of clear glass were still there, but they looked out into a wall of solid white stone. Still, the office was not dark. White light radiated from a small, unflickering flame burning at the bottom of a large, metal bowl on the floor. Miranda recognized the fire immediately. It was Krinok, a rare type of chemical fire spirit Master Banage had rescued from a rogue Tower Keeper turned Enslaver back when she was still his apprentice. Krinok's harsh, white light threw everything into sharp, monochrome relief, but even that couldn't drown out the light coming from Banage himself.

The Rector Spiritualis was sitting on his desk, which was uncharacteristically empty. For the first time Miranda could remember in many years, he was dressed not in the formal red robes of the Rector's office, but in a plain, somber suit. Over that, around his neck, the regalia of the Rector Spiritualis shone like a collar of light. The heavy necklace with its golden chain of jewels glowed in a rainbow of colors, humming with power. Even standing at the door twenty feet away, Miranda could feel the enormous pressure of the Rector's connection to the Tower and, woven into and through that, the power of Banage himself. She took a deep breath, her own spirits waking to the familiar weight of Banage's soul, and for the first time in a long time, she felt like she was home.

"Miranda," Banage said, opening his eyes. "It is good to see you. I wish the circumstances were better."

"Whatever the circumstances," Miranda said, walking across the room to stand before him, "it is good to be back."

Banage smiled, a slight turn of his thin mouth. "Sit," he said softly, "and tell me what you have seen."

With a deep breath, Miranda sat cross-legged on the stone floor and told him.

She started from the moment she left Zarin, chasing Sara's tip about Eli north with Tesset and Sparrow. She told him about entering Izo's camp and the Council's deal with the Bandit King. She told him about catching Eli and losing him again. She told him about Slorn and the wondrous things the bear-headed Shaper could do. After that, things got harder. She told him about Sted, about the demon and the League. She told him what she had seen in the arena after Josef beat Sted and about working with Alric to defeat the creature Sted became. Then, after a couple of deep breaths, she told him as best she could about the thing she'd seen in the woods beyond Izo's camp, the creature made of shadows and hunger, eating the world. Even as she told him, the afterimage of the hideous shape flickered across her vision, forcing her to turn away. When she had control of herself again, she looked her master in the eye and told him how that vision had cemented her decision to go with Slorn to the Shapers. She told him about their arrival at the mountain, her imprisonment, and what she'd seen in the mountain's memory. She told him about stars, the spirits lifted above all other. She told him all the mountain had told her about the Shepherdess, the sleeping spirits, everything. The world the mountain had shown her was still clear in her mind, the great valley changing between life and death and the endless night sky filled with strange, sparkling lights, but describing it was harder than she imagined. Still, in fits and halts, she told him the whole naked, disjointed truth Slorn had asked her to spread.

She finished in a great rush, panting as the weight of the secrets lifted from her chest. She paused, waiting for the questions that were sure to come, but Banage just sat back and motioned for her to continue.

Miranda nodded and moved on to her cell. She told him about her solo imprisonment, Sparrow's offer and their escape from the Shapers, the journey home, and learning about the war. Finally, she told him about the meeting with Sara, Blint, and Whitefall. She handed him Whitefall's written promise as she told him the details of the Merchant Prince's compromise. Banage took the paper with a strangely closed look on his face, reading it over as Miranda's long story finally came to an end.

When it was done, she leaned back, exhausted. Though in all her years with the Court, all the missions she'd done in its name, none had taken so long or so much to tell. With the windows blocked, it was impossible to tell how long she'd been speaking. It felt like hours. However long it was, Banage had not moved at all. He was still sitting on his desk, his stern face warped into a mask of itself by the strange light of the mantel and the bright white fire on the floor.

"I'm not surprised Slorn stayed," he said at last. "How very like him to pit his stubbornness against a mountain."

Miranda looked up. "You know him?"

"Some," Banage said. "He's hard to avoid when you involve yourself in the politics of spirits to any depth. He's a good wizard, though, and a good man. You made the right choice to go with him."

Miranda let out the breath she didn't realize she'd been holding. "Thank you, Master Banage."

Banage nodded. "So," he said. "The mysterious Shepherdess who commands all spirits. I'd heard snippets, hints, but you can never get a spirit to talk plainly about such things. To hear it from the Shaper Mountain is something indeed, though I suppose demons large enough to make Alric panic can get even Great Spirits talking about things they'd rather not." He started chuckling, like this was some kind of joke, and looked over at Miranda. "You never bring good news, do you?"

"You never send me anywhere easy," Miranda protested.

Banage smiled. "You would be wasted on easy things."

"It seems nothing is easy anymore," Miranda said with a deep sigh. "It feels like the world is falling apart. Enormous demons, the League in panic, spirits growing sleepier, the Shaper Mountain talking about the Shepherdess with her stars and favorites and how this world isn't as it was. Two weeks ago, I didn't even know for sure if the Shepherdess existed. Now I'm terrified that she's not doing whatever it is she's supposed to do. How can we do our job and protect the spirit world when we know so little?"

Banage shook his head. "As my spirits love to remind me, humans are creatures of blindness and ignorance. We must always remember that although we tend to see this world as ours, we are only tiny pieces of the larger whole and there is only so much we can change. The demons, for instance, we must leave to the League. We certainly cannot fight them, not without risking our spirits. Even if we were willing to face them, we would only be defeated. As for the rest, we can only do what we have always done. The Court will stand by its oaths and do what it can to protect the spirit world from whatever threatens it—wizard, star, or Shepherdess."

"Master Banage," Miranda said, her throat going dry. "With all these threats, I have to wonder, perhaps we should take the Merchant Prince's compromise."

The Rector's head snapped to look at her.

"He promised it would only be defense," Miranda said quickly, before she lost her courage. "Look around, we are alone. The Spirit Court is splitting in two. How can we stand firm when we are so divided?"

"We are not divided." Banage's voice cut the heavy air like a bitter, burning knife. "The true Court is here. Those who choose political ambition over their oaths are not Spiritualists."

"But this is the Immortal Empress!" Miranda cried, her voice pleading. "If this were just a war between countries, I would not question your decision, but the Empress is different. Her first attack was terrifying enough to make the warring kingdoms forget their bickering and unite as a Council to face a common foe. But even united, it took everything we had to turn the Empress away. Now she's coming to finish the kill, and everything we have might no longer be enough. I don't like Blint, but I understand where he and every Spiritualist who went to the Council stands. They are fighting to defend their lives as they know them."

"And there they betray their oaths," Banage said. "Spiritualists do not fight for their own comfort, but for what is good and right for the spirit world."

"How do we know the two aren't the same?" Miranda countered. "Every child in the Council learns about the Empress's invasion, and the terror trotted out more than any other are the stories of the Empress's wizards. There are tales of them working together to control enormous spirits of fire and iron, monsters built only for war that fight until they're torn apart. Those spirits *died* fighting for the Empress, and though I don't know for sure what the empire wizards did to whip those poor spirits into such a frenzy, I'd wager Eli's bounty that it wasn't nice. Enslavement, or close to it. That is the enemy we face, and you're saying we should just sit back and let her come? That it is politics to side with the Council and fight her? If anything of that sort went on here, we would mobilize the Court to stop it at once. Is it any different when it comes from across the sea?"

Miranda stopped, terrified she'd said too much. Master Banage's expression was unreadable in the harsh light, but he didn't look angry. When he spoke, his voice sounded tired.

"Your reasoning is sound as always, Miranda," he said. "But no matter what, I can never allow this Court to go to war again beside the Council of Thrones."

"Why not?" Miranda demanded, frustration rising.

Banage looked up, his dark eyes catching hers with a look that killed her anger in one shot.

"May I tell you a story?"

Caught off guard, Miranda nodded.

Banage got up from his desk and walked over to the window, looking out at the lid of solid stone that covered it.

"I fought in the first war against the Empress," he said. "I've told you about it before."

Miranda nodded again, though, since Banage had his back to her, it scarcely mattered.

"I fought with the fledgling Council," Banage said, his voice soft. "With Sara." He looked over his shoulder. "We were younger than you are now, a year out of our apprenticeships, and newly married."

"Married?" Miranda could scarcely form the word. She could scarcely believe what she was hearing. "You were *married*? To *Sara*?"

"Are married," Banage corrected her, turning back to the window. "We never formalized our separation. I think we each believe we'll eventually bring the other around to our way of thinking."

"But...Sara?" Miranda shook her head. "How? *Why*?"

"I was young," Banage said. "Sara is a genius and very charismatic in her own way. I'd like to say she's changed over the years, but she's always been high-handed, single-minded, and cruel. However, she was also ambitious in a way I'd never seen. She wanted to do things with magic I'd never even imagined. When the Empress attacked, the lands we now call the Council were in chaos. No one had ever seen anything like the fleet that was pounding Osera's shore. In her desperation, the young Oseran queen threw away centuries of isolationism and begged for help. Zarin was the first to respond, and Sara went with them."

He took a deep breath. "I'd known for some time that Sara was drifting away from the Spirit Court, doing her own work with money from the Whitefall family. When she said she was following Whitefall to war without even asking permission from the Rector, the Tower Keepers, who did not yet understand the threat of the Empress and had no interest in risking themselves for Oseran pirates, threatened to strip her of her rings and kick her out of the Court. And they would have, but I volunteered to go with her as the

Court's eyes on the front. That was how I ended up at her side when the Empress's forces made their second, largest attack on Osera."

"The project she was working on for Whitefall," Miranda said, wide-eyed. "Was that the Relay?"

"It was," Banage said, his voice strangely strained. "The Relay was the only way we kept ahead of the Empress's forces. By this time, rumors of the Empress's army were beginning to catch up with its actual size. More and more countries, seeing that this could well spread to their lands if left unchecked, began sending their armies to the coast. But they were a rabble, a hodgepodge of men who'd spent centuries fighting each other. Only the Relay could coordinate them into a force capable of meeting the Empress's fleet, and Alber Whitefall knew it.

"But that came later," Banage said, waving his hand. "Before the other countries joined in, Queen Theresa's ships with their ever-burning fire were all that held the Empire at bay. The event I want to tell you about happened late at night the second day of the attack. I'd left Sara with Whitefall and gone to help the Oserans repel a charge. The Oseran clingfire were simple spirits, easy to direct. I had made a cliff out over the bay and was using my fire spirit to guide the clingfire throwers and sink the incoming ships. But then my stone spirit was hit by one of the Empress's war spirits, and I fell."

"You fought a war spirit?" Miranda said, breathless.

"Not at first." Banage's voice grew raw. "I fell nearly fifty feet into the sea. My stone spirit shattered beyond repair trying to break my fall. I would have died there, if not for him. As it was, my fire spirit went out when I hit the water. I managed to swim to shore, but I was disoriented. I'd never lost a spirit before, and now I'd just lost two. I did not know what to do with the enormous emptiness that is left when the connection vanishes."

He stopped for a moment and sat very still. Miranda held her breath, afraid to make a sound. At last, Banage continued.

"When I made it to the beach, the Oseran guard was fighting the siege spirit, or trying to. Swords did nothing. The spirit killed a dozen men as I watched, and then it turned to me."

Banage lowered his head. "I was terrified and enraged. I knew I was about to die. That I would be crushed, and all my remaining spirits crushed with me. So I did the only thing I could think of. I opened my soul and took control of the siege spirit."

Miranda's breath caught in her throat. "You Enslaved it?"

"I tried to," Banage said, his voice very low. "Desperation is no excuse. I tried to take control of the spirit to save my life in violation of all my oaths. Tried, and failed."

Miranda looked away, scrambling to get her feelings under control. The thought of Master Banage Enslaving anything nearly made her sick. He was the Spirit Court, the embodiment of everything it stood for, and yet.

"Failed?" she said. "How could you fail? You are the strongest wizard I've ever met."

"Strength has nothing to do with it," Banage said, shaking his head. "The problem was with the spirit itself. No matter how hard I pushed, it would not bend to my will. It did stop, however. I think it was confused. But then it looked at me. Not looked, exactly, for it had no head to speak of, but I knew it was studying me. And then it spoke."

Miranda swallowed. "What did it say?"

"'Loyalty to the Empress,'" Banage quoted, tilting his head back. "'Always and forever, I will be loyal.' And then it turned and walked into the ocean, back toward the ships where the Empire wizards waited."

"It left?" Miranda said. "Why?"

"I don't know," Banage admitted. "I have asked myself the same question over and over. But one thing was certain. That spirit was not Enslaved. There was no fear in it, no panic. It was bound through a loyalty so deep, so intense, so *primal* that even with my panicked strength I could not break its will to be faithful to its mistress. A mistress who wasn't even there."

Banage ran his hand through his graying hair. "After that, I knew no peace. I kept wondering what kind of person this Empress was to command such loyalty. As Whitefall's forces grew and the war began to turn around, I saw several of the Empress's war spirits go down. Every one of them fell fighting to the last inch, and every time I saw it happen, I wondered why? But the war was over before I could find out. The Empress's ships retreated as quickly as they'd come, and Whitefall, ever the opportunist, used fear of her return to found the Council of Thrones with himself at the head and Sara's Relay holding it all together."

Banage looked down at his glowing spirits. "It was around that time that Sara quit the Spirit Court of her own volition," he said. "I was furious, of course, but she was within her rights. She'd freed her spirits and received the Rector's approval, done everything properly. I was promoted to Tower Keeper after the war, but Sara was still my wife, and I stayed in Zarin to be with her. But as she spent more and more time in the caverns she'd built beneath the Council Citadel, I began to wonder. Sara gave me Relay points several times during the war, and afterward I went down to the Relay tank rooms often to see her. Even so, she would never let me near the heart of the Relay that lay at the bottom of the large tank she still uses as an office, nor would she ever agree to tell me exactly how the Relay worked. Every time I asked we would fight, and eventually I became suspicious."

Miranda bit her lip. "What did you do?"

"There was nothing I could do," Banage said. "Sara wasn't a Spiritualist, and the Spirit Court had no jurisdiction within Whitefall's rapidly growing Council. I also had no proof she was doing anything wrong, but I knew. Why else would she refuse to show me?"

"There could have been a reason," Miranda said softly.

"Do you honestly believe that?" Banage said, turning to face her. "You've worked with her, you've seen how ruthless she can be. If you were in my position then, would you have come to a different conclusion?"

Miranda shook her head. "What did she say when you confronted her?"

"Nothing," Banage said bitterly. "She said nothing. The Spirit Court would not listen to me and call for an investigation. They were too busy courting the Council. Everyone was then. So I went to her one last time and told her that if she didn't show me how the Relay worked, I was leaving. Again, she refused, so I went. I took our son and went as far away as I could."

"Wait," Miranda said. "Son?"

It might have been her imagination, but Miranda thought she saw Banage wince. "Yes, I have a son."

"But where is he?" she cried. "Why have I never heard of him?"

Banage turned back to the stone-blocked window. "He left. Many years ago."

Miranda cringed at the edge in his voice and dutifully dropped the subject.

Banage continued as though nothing had happened. "I came back to Zarin only when they told me I'd been chosen to be the new Rector Spiritualis, and the first thing I did was try to use the Court's sway to finally break open whatever Sara was hiding. But by that time the Council was the greatest power on the continent, and I could make no headway. To this day I don't know what she's got beneath the Council citadel, Relay or otherwise, but I understand Sara well enough now to know it can't be good." Banage shook his head. "As Rector, I have danced to the Council's tune along with everyone else, waiting for my chance to force Sara to open up and accept the Court's standards. When Whitefall asked for my help in the war, I thought I'd finally found it, but I was wrong." He looked up. "Whitefall doesn't want change. He wants warriors. I've been to war, Miranda, and I am poorer for it. I cannot, will not, order my Spiritualists into that suffering, especially not as ally to an organization that may well be worse than the enemy we're fighting."

"How can you say that?" Miranda said, horrified. "I'll grant Sara's pretty suspicious, and I'm positive she's up to no good, but worse than the Empress?"

"Yes," Banage said. "Weren't you listening? I told you. I met one of the Empress's war spirits. I saw firsthand the deep loyalty she commands. It's not so different from the loyalty our spirits give us as Spiritualists. You can't fake loyalty like that. Think about it, Miranda. On the one hand we the Council of Thrones, an organization of profit and power built by a merchant prince and a ruthless woman on a work of wizardry so suspect Spiritualists aren't allowed near it. On the other, we have an Empress who commands the abject love and loyalty of the spirits. Put that way, it's not a hard choice."

Banage began to pace. "I gave Sara and Whitefall every chance to make good. I flat out told them I would fight if they would only open the Council to Spirit Court inspection, and I was met with nothing but excuses. Sara does not share our respect for the spirits, nor our duty toward them, and I am tired of playing her game. The more I see, the more I'm convinced that the future she and Whitefall are building isn't one I want to live in. It may well be that the Empress's coming is the dawn of a new age for the Spirit Court and the spirits."

Miranda stared at her master, horrified. "What you're saying is treason."

"Is it?" Banage said. "I've sworn no oaths to Zarin. My only oaths are here, with the Court and the spirits, and I see no reason to take either to war for a government that cares nothing for them."

Miranda licked her lips. She knew that calm tone in Master Banage's voice. He'd already made up his mind. Made it up long ago, it seemed. She wasn't happy at all with the idea of sitting back and letting the Empress conquer her homeland, but she wasn't about to go against her master, not after everything he'd done for her and the spirits. Still...

"We must do *something.*"

"We will," Banage said. "We'll keep doing what we have done for the last four hundred years—protect the spirits and obey our oaths. Do I make myself clear, Spiritualist Lyonette?"

Miranda swallowed. "Yes, Master Banage."

"Good," he said, standing up. "For now, I want you to write up your experience inside the Shaper Mountain. When you're finished, you have my permission to go through the archives for any information on this Shepherdess and the Great Spirits called stars."

Miranda perked up considerably. "All the archives?"

"Yes," Banage said. "The Shaper Mountain did not show you that vision by accident. Far more important than this war is what is happening at the top levels of the spirit world. I want you to find out whatever you can. The Court will not sit idle."

Miranda couldn't help grinning. The Spiritualist archives were the repository for the collective knowledge of the Spirit Court. Every Spiritualist report ever written was stored there. Previously she'd had access to only the lowest level of common reports. Now she'd get to read the recollections of the secret missions as well. Bad as everything else seemed, that, at least, was something to look forward to.

"Go on," Banage said, waving her off. "But get some sleep and food first. You look dreadful."

Miranda blushed and glanced down at her filthy clothes. "Yes, Master Banage," she mumbled, dropping a deep bow before retreating. Her mind might still be racing with everything that had happened, but her body was more than glad to put it all off in favor of food, a bath, and a bed. Smiling at the prospect, she closed Banage's door softly behind her and went to wake up Gin, who was sleeping on the stairs where she'd left him.

Sara leaned back in the tall armchair, heavy smoke trailing from the corner of her mouth. Alber Whitefall sat across from her, his chin resting on his hands. They were both staring at the blue ball on the table between them as the soft, watery light began to fade.

"Well," Sara said. "I think that should be proof enough."

Whitefall dropped his head into his hands. "Sara," he said, grinding his palms into his eyes. "I'm not going to ask how you got a Relay point into Banage's office. I'm not sure I want to know. The only thing I'm going to ask is *why.*"

"I thought that would be clear," Sara said. "You heard it from his own lips, in his own impossibly long-winded style. Etmon Banage is a traitor. He's sided with the Empress against his own people."

Whitefall sighed. "We need him."

"We need the Court," Sara countered. "Banage is the one standing in our way. It's loyalty to him that keeps those idiots in the Tower. Break Banage and the Court will come to us. Well," she said, putting her pipe stem back in her mouth. "Most of them. Some attrition is unavoidable."

"We'll never get this to stick," Whitefall said, moving his hands down to his mouth as he considered his options. "An overheard confession's not enough on its own, and he's not going to repeat it."

"Of course he will," Sara said. "This is Etmon Banage. The man can't lie to save his life, or anyone else's. Pull him out and ask him openly whom he supports, the Council or the Empress, and then sit back while he digs his own grave."

Whitefall gave her a long-suffering look. "Isn't this a little much, Sara? The man is still your husband."

Sara sniffed. "I loved Banage when I was young and stupid enough to get caught up in his idealism. But that world never existed, Alber. There's no place for men like Banage who refuse to admit that there is no absolute right or wrong, that everything is relative, even morality. Never was. I won't see my life's work stomped under just to keep his hands clean."

She reached out and snatched the Relay point off the table, sliding the blue marble into her pocket as she stood. "We need those wizards if we're going to survive, Alber. I've given you your linchpin. All you have to do is pull it."

Whitefall turned and stared unhappily into the cold, empty fireplace. "Fine," he said quietly. "Send word to Myron."

Sara nodded and marched out of the room. Sparrow fell in silently beside her, giving Whitefall a sickening smile as he closed the door behind his mistress. As their footsteps faded down the long hall, Whitefall stood and walked to the window, opening the glass pane to let the night wind clear out the stinking pipe smoke. As he stared down at his brightly lit city, the streets packed and humming with life, he wondered, not for the first time, who really ran the Council of Thrones.

"That was impressively ruthless," Sparrow said as they walked through the dark, empty halls of the Citadel. "Even for you. Good to know the enormous risk I took planting that Relay point paid out."

Sara arched an eyebrow. "Enormous risk?"

"Have you *seen* the dog she rides?" Sparrow shuddered. "I could have lost a hand. Or more."

"Your sacrifice wouldn't have been in vain," Sara said as they started down the stairs to her underground workshop. "I couldn't have asked for a better confession. I always knew something changed in him the night he lost his spirits, but I didn't know he'd gone that far."

"Well," Sparrow said, smiling slyly. "He certainly had enough to say about *you*."

Sara shrugged. "No worse than he's said to my face."

"I never could understand what you saw in him."

"He was uncompromising," Sara said. "I felt like a better person when I was around him, like I was one of the good guys. But he had no vision, no reach. He never understood that some of us can't be happy just maintaining the status quo. It didn't matter what miracles I showed him, he always found some fault." She shook her head. "Uncompromising men are easy to admire, but they're impossible to live with."

"I can imagine," Sparrow said as they reached the foot of the stairs. "Still, congratulations. You won!"

"Hardly a glorious victory," Sara said, walking between the suspended Relay tanks toward the brightly lit platform at the center of the enormous cavern. "I'd always hoped that Etmon would see things my way someday, understand the great work I'm doing." She heaved an enormous, smoky sigh. "Considering our history, I suppose it's only fitting that I be the one to deal the breaking blow."

"How *do* you mean to do that, by the way?" Sparrow said. "He's locked himself up quite nicely, and I don't think he's going to come out to talk to you."

"The Spirit Court's Tower is still only stone," Sara said with a smile. "And I've been needing something to test our new weapon on."

"It's done, then?" Sparrow said.

"Done enough," Sara said, sticking her pipe into her mouth. "Words won't do it justice, though. You'll just have to wait for tomorrow."

Sparrow smiled a wide, toothy smile. "And see the haughty Spiritualists brought low? I can't wait."

"I'm sure," Sara said distractedly. "Come on, we've got work to do."

Sparrow fell in behind her as she marched out onto the platform around the enormous tank that served as her headquarters and began shouting for her assistants.

CHAPTER

16

Josef woke with a snort, hands going instantly to his blades. He looked around a moment in groggy confusion, grinding his teeth as the world came together. It had happened again. He was still on the couch where he'd sat down to wait for Adela, only now it was morning. But the sunlight streaming through the window was still more white than yellow. Early morning, then. That was better than yesterday.

He looked around for Nico and found her sitting behind the couch, wrapped in her coat with her back resting against his through the wooden frame, sound asleep. Josef smiled. Catching Nico asleep was rare. Then his smile fell. Rare, and a sign of something very wrong.

A knock sounded at the door, and Nico's eyes popped open. She saw him at once and rolled to her feet, a confused and slightly alarmed look on her pale face. Josef put up his hand, motioning her to keep out of sight. She nodded and shrank back behind the couch. The knock sounded again, soft but urgent. Josef pulled his shirt straight and started for the door, but whoever was knocking must have grown impatient. Before Josef had gone two steps, the lock rattled. The door opened with a click and Eli stepped in, palming his lock pick with a hurried glance over his shoulder.

"Good," he said, closing the door behind him. "You're up. We have a problem."

"We have several," Josef said as Nico stood up from behind the couch. "What's going on?"

"I'm not sure," Eli said. "But word is the queen's up and on the warpath. I'm surprised she hasn't—"

A banging on the door cut him off, and the three of them froze. Josef was the first to recover. He caught Nico's eyes and glanced at the corner. She nodded and slid sideways, fading into the small shadow behind the fireplace. When she was gone, Josef walked to the door. He motioned for Eli to get behind him before lifting the latch.

A page stood in the hallway, his hand raised to knock again. He was flanked on both sides by stern, armored guardsmen and looking decidedly unhappy about it.

"My lord prince," the page said, recovering from his aborted knock with impressive speed. "Your royal mother requests your presence."

Josef frowned. "Now?"

"Now would be good," the man said.

Josef shook his head and turned back to the room, leaving the door open. He walked to the corner and grabbed the Heart. When it was securely on his back, he walked back to the door. Eli stepped into place beside him, ready to go.

The servant glanced nervously from Josef to Eli. "My lord," he started. "Your mother specifically asked—"

"My adviser comes with me," Josef said, stalking into the hall.

Eli gave the servant a winning smile as he followed Josef out the door. The guards fell in around them, setting the pace as they walked up the stairs toward the royal suite.

A larger than usual squad of guards lined the gallery leading up to his mother's door, all of them at full attention. Josef pushed his way through, opening his mother's door with a rough jerk.

The queen was waiting for them. She was dressed and sitting on her chair at the center of the raised platform at the far end of the room, Lenette at her side, as always. There were several nobles in the room as well, all of whom Josef knew he should probably recognize. But he'd never been good with remembering court officials, even back when he was actually trying, so he dismissed them and focused on his mother. Queen Theresa looked more tired than ever. Her papery skin was almost gray against the harsh black of her dress and veil, but her eyes were as sharp as knives, and they pinned Josef to the floor.

"Where were you last night?" she asked the second the door closed behind Eli.

"Asleep," Josef said.

The queen arched her eyebrow. "Asleep? All night?"

Josef crossed his arms. "All night. Why?"

For a split second the queen looked relieved, and then the scowl was back. "Finley is dead."

"Dead?" Josef said. "How?"

"Stabbed," the queen answered. "Someone, or several someones, broke into his mansion last night. His honor guard is dead, as are most of his servants, his son, and, of course, the duke himself."

Josef frowned. "Was there a fight?"

"Adela is investigating as we speak," the queen said. "In the meantime, why don't you tell me."

The room filled with whispers as the nobles began to talk. Josef ignored them.

"How should I know?" he said.

"You were with the duke a few hours before he died," the queen said. "You had an argument, a loud one, after which you left. What did you talk about?"

"Nothing of consequence," Josef said. "He told me he was going to be king, and I said go ahead."

The queen's eyes narrowed. "Really? That's all?"

"That's all," Josef repeated firmly. "I didn't kill him, if that's what you're implying."

The queen's fingers tightened on the arms of her chair. "The report said the guards died with swords in scabbard, killed by a blow to the back of the neck from a long blade. Finley was heir to the throne of Osera, guarded by the best the country can offer. So either his guards were killed treacherously by someone with enough rank to avoid a challenge, or they were taken out by a master swordsman before they could draw. You are both, so you can see how suspicions could rise."

Josef rolled his eyes and reached over his shoulder. He drew the Heart with a flourish, slamming the point into the wooden floor at his feet. All around the room, people began to shout. The guards drew their swords and encircled the queen. Even Lenette shrank back against her mistress, but Queen Theresa just watched, her eyes hard as iron as she glared at the large chunk that was now missing from her floor.

"Blow to the back of the neck?" Josef said, turning the Heart so everyone could see the size of the blade. "This is the only blade I keep that could be considered long. If I struck someone across the back of the neck with this, I would take their head off."

The queen sniffed. "Are you saying you're not clever enough to hide a murder weapon?"

"I'm saying I had no reason to kill Finley other than he's an ass," Josef answered. "And if I was going to kill him for that, I would have challenged him openly and had the pleasure of thrashing him in front of everyone."

"That, at least, I agree with," the queen said with a long sigh. "You can put away your iron bat, Thereson. I don't think you killed

Finley, but the fact remains that the heir to the throne of Osera is murdered, and I have to determine how, by whom, and why."

Josef slid the Heart back into place on his back. "Easy enough," he said. "We'll go investigate."

"You will do no such thing," the queen snapped. "I said I don't think you did it, but that does not remove you from these matters. You are still under suspicion, and until my people get to the bottom of this, you will remain in your rooms where I can keep an eye on you."

"What?" Josef shouted.

"I don't see why you're surprised," the queen said, her voice rasping. "You were the one who chose to pursue a life of violence. You cannot now turn and condemn us for judging you by it. Our country is on the brink of war, and the people have just lost the man they thought would be their king. Now more than ever, Osera must be united. Lawful. Its throne without reproach."

"But I didn't do anything!" Josef cried.

"I believe you," the queen said earnestly. "And I have no doubt our inquiry will absolve you of all guilt, but I cannot shield a known murderer from investigation just because he is my son."

"I never murdered anyone," Josef said hotly. "I killed swordsmen in battle. There's a difference."

"A subtle one," the queen said. "Countries on the brink of war that've just seen their duke murdered don't appreciate subtlety."

"I don't care what they appreciate," Josef sneered. "I'm not going to let you lock me up for something I didn't do."

"You don't have a choice," Theresa said. She turned to her guard. "Take his swords. The prince is under arrest."

"Are you out of your mind?" Josef roared. "You're not taking my swords!"

"I am queen!" Theresa roared back. "I take whatever I—"

The queen's words dissolved into a coughing fit as she doubled over, heaving into her handkerchief. Several of the nobles started to run forward, but Lenette was there first, waving the rest away.

"The queen's medicine!" she yelled. "Hurry!"

A servant grabbed a kettle, a cup, and a folded paper sachet from the tray in the corner and ran to Lenette, pouring the steaming water into the cup as she went. Lenette grabbed the sachet and the cup. She shook the folded paper open, dumping green powder into the hot water. She stirred it once with the spoon the servant offered and then, grabbing the queen's convulsing shoulders, pushed the cup to her lips.

The queen drank, choked, and drank again with Lenette's help. Her coughing subsided, and she slumped back into the chair. For several minutes she did nothing but sit with her eyes closed, breathing as though taking in air were the hardest task she'd ever attempted. When she did finally open her eyes, they looked immediately at Josef.

"My order is final," she said in a strained, husky whisper.

Josef stared at her, helpless, and then looked plaintively at Eli, but the thief was already a step ahead of him.

"My lady," Eli said gently, stepping forward. "Think a moment. Someone out there is knocking off members of the royal family. Do you really think disarming the prince at such a time is a wise—"

"I will not be disobeyed," Theresa said, closing her eyes again. "This meeting is over. Take the prince to his chambers and make sure he stays there."

The guards bowed and moved to Josef's side. With a final glare at his mother, Josef raised his hands and let the guards guide him toward the door. Eli followed with his own escort. Looking back, Josef caught a final glimpse of his mother slumped between Lenette and the serving girl, and then the door closed and he saw no more.

The palace seemed empty as the guards marched Josef and Eli back to the prince's suite. The usual bustle of nobles and servants rushing on Osera's business had been replaced by grim-faced guards standing in knots wherever corridors connected.

When they reached Josef's rooms, the entire squad circled round as Josef disarmed to make sure he surrendered every blade. It took a good thirty minutes, partially because Josef was taking his time about it, but mostly because he wore a lot of weapons. It took two men to hold Josef's arsenal of daggers, throwing knives, and short swords, and Josef spent the entire time making it very clear what would happen if every one of those blades didn't return to him.

When he finally announced he'd handed everything over, the guards stepped in to pat him down, just in case. This uncovered another two blades, one at the small of his back below his belt and one tucked into the heel of his shoe, both of which Josef claimed he'd forgotten. The guards gave him a sour look and added the blades to the pile. Then they came to the main bone of contention.

"The sword on your back," the soldier said. "Hand it over."

"This?" Josef lay his hand on the wrapped hilt of the Heart of War. "I don't think so."

The soldier crossed his arms. "The queen said every blade, Prince Thereson."

Josef smiled at him. "Fine," he said. "You want my sword?" He reached up to his shoulder and undid the strap that held the Heart on his back. "Take it."

The Heart fell to the floor with a crash that rattled the windows. The soldier jumped back in surprise, and Josef, still grinning, stepped aside so the guard could retrieve the Heart. The soldier glowered and reached down, grabbing the Heart by the hilt to lift it onto his own back.

Nothing happened.

The soldier's anger turned to confusion. He added another hand to the Heart's hilt and pulled again, harder. The Heart didn't budge. The soldier braced his legs against the wall. His face turned pink, then red. Sweat poured off his brow as he pulled with all his might, and nothing happened.

He let go at last, panting as he stared at Josef. "What is that thing?" he said, too out of sorts to remember the proper address for a prince. "It weighs more than a bloody mountain."

"It's my sword," Josef said. "Everything else you can take. This one stays with me."

The soldier shook his head. "Queen's orders," he panted. "I can't leave you with a weapon."

"Forget it," Josef said. "I didn't kill the duke. The queen knows that. Now, you cannot lift this sword. No one can, except me. You've done your job disarming me as best you could. Let it alone."

The soldier glanced at his companions, rubbing his strained shoulders. The other guards eyed the Heart with trepidation and, one by one, shook their heads.

"Right," the guard said at last. "Move out. You," he said, looking Eli up and down. "Coming?"

"I'll stay here, if it's all the same to you," Eli said, flopping into a chair by the hearth.

"Suit yourself," the guard said. "But no one gets out of this room until the queen gives the order."

"That's fine," Eli said. "I think our poor, maligned prince could use the company during his wrongful incarceration. But thank you for your diligence, officer."

The soldier gave Eli a sideways look, like he wasn't sure if that was sincerity or an insult, maybe both. In the end, he let it go, walking out with a shallow bow and locking the door behind him. As the lock clicked, Josef grabbed the Heart and returned it to his back.

"This is a fine mess," he grumbled, walking over to the tiny window.

"Mmm," Eli said, staring absently into the fireplace. "Josef, is your mother-in-law a card player?"

Josef blinked in confusion. "What?"

"Lenette," Eli said. "Is it possible she used to be a cardsharp?"

"No," Josef said, appalled. "Why in the world would you even ask that?"

"Because she pulled the best snake-in-the-sleeve I've ever seen," Eli said. "And I've seen a lot."

If possible, Josef grew even more confused. "Snake-in-the-where?"

"Snake-in-the-sleeve," Eli said slowly. "It's a gambling move. Watch." He held out his empty hand, and then, very subtly, flicked his wrist. Out of nowhere, a Daggerback card appeared between his fingers. "See?" he said, turning the card over. "Looks easy, but it takes years of practice."

"Wait a second," Josef said. "That's a Shepherdess." His eyes widened. "How long have you had a trump up your sleeve?"

"A long time," Eli said, grinning wide.

Josef crossed his arms over his chest. "I want my money back."

"Josef," Eli said, looking hurt as the card disappeared back up his sleeve. "I would never cheat you."

Josef rolled his eyes.

"Anyway," Eli said. "That's hardly the point. What matters is that I saw Lenette do that exact move when the servant handed her the cup."

Suddenly, Josef was paying very close attention. "Are you sure?"

"I wasn't at first," Eli said. "I caught it only by chance. But then I saw her do it a second time, while she was stirring. That time there was no mistaking it."

"Right," Josef said, rubbing his neck. "And what did she take out?"

"I don't know," Eli confessed. "As I said, she was really good. I couldn't even see if she was taking something out of her sleeve or putting something in. But I saw her wrist move, and I've been in enough card games to know that when you see someone flick their hand that way, you either call your bets or start cheating better."

Josef scowled. "What would Lenette be putting in the queen's cup? She owes my mother everything. Her position, her wealth, her daughter's place as princess, everything. The second the queen dies, Lenette goes right out the door. She knows that better than anyone. So why would she take the risk of doing something that could possibly be seen as treasonous?"

"I have no idea," Eli said, standing up. "But the royal family's luck is getting a little too bad for me to buy."

Josef winced. He knew that look on Eli's face. "What are you going to do about it?"

"First," Eli said, walking over to the table beside the door, "I'm going to find out who's been drugging you at night, and how. I'm guessing it happened again?"

"Yes," Josef said. "And it got Nico too."

"Really?" Eli said. "How curious."

Josef frowned. "Why curious?"

"Because it didn't get me," Eli said. "Which rules out the food."

"And you think the sleeping thing is related to the duke's death?"

"I don't know," Eli said, running his hands along the wall. "But as I said, this is too much bad luck, even for you. Now keep your voice down." He glanced pointedly at the door. "Bored soldiers have surprisingly sharp ears."

Josef looked skeptically at the door, but he nodded and moved over to the couch, sitting down with the Heart between his legs.

"Where is Nico, anyway?" he said, trying to keep the annoyance out of his voice.

Eli ducked his head to examine the bookshelf. "Probably making herself useful. She's not locked up, after all. No point in sticking around here."

Josef had to give him that one. Still, it annoyed him that he didn't know where Nico was. But complaining wasn't going to get him anywhere, so he sat and stared at his sword, letting his mind go blank as he traced the Heart's scarred surface. He could feel the battle coming, like a storm on the horizon. Good. Let it come. He would be ready.

Josef took a deep breath, letting the anger and frustration flow out of his mind. Then, in one smooth motion, he stood up and stepped into first position. Mindful of the small space, he raised the Heart and began to practice his swings. Eli shot him an annoyed look and stepped out of the way, continuing his investigation around Josef's sword work.

Outside, dawn turned to morning as the sun peeked over the mountain.

Josef had just passed his one hundredth swing when Eli shouted, "Got it!"

Josef lowered his sword. Eli was standing in the corner looking unbearably smug and holding a candelabra.

"It's the candles," Eli said, wrenching a candlestick out of its holder. "Here, smell the wax."

"No," Josef said. "You just said it's poison."

"Only if you burn it," Eli said, shoving the candlestick in his face. "Smell."

Josef sniffed, wrinkling his nose. "Smells like bitter greens."

Eli nodded. "That's incenteth. Doctors use it to knock patients out for amputation, usually by making them smoke it. I never even thought of putting it in candles." He sounded deeply impressed.

"Kind of brilliant, actually. The candles burn down, slowly filling the room with the drug. Servants and others can enter and leave with no ill effects except a little drowsiness, but anyone staying in the room would get the full dose and fall into a deep sleep until the candles burned out and the drug stopped."

"Well, I'm glad you're impressed," Josef grumbled. "But unless someone signed their name on those candles, we still don't know who did it."

"Up to this point, I'd have said the duke," Eli said, putting the candle back with a long sigh. "I still think it could be, but that's a moot point now, isn't it?"

Josef scowled at that comment, but before he could answer, he heard a familiar step on the carpet behind him. He turned just in time to see Nico step out of the deep shadows by the window.

He smiled, but his smile dropped when he saw the expression on her face. "What?"

"Something's going on down at the storm wall watchtower," she said. "Two guard squads have already been sent in."

Josef caught his breath. That was where he'd had his argument with the duke the day before. "What have they got against me now?"

Nico shook her head. "I don't think that's it," she said, her voice low. "They called in medics as well."

Josef frowned. "How close did you get?"

"Close enough to smell the blood," Nico answered.

Josef nodded and turned toward the door.

"Josef," Eli said. "Hold on just a—"

Josef didn't wait to hear the rest. He grabbed the door handle and turned it sharply, snapping the lock. He pushed the door open in time to see the two door guards turn and scramble to block his way.

Josef glowered. "Move."

"I'm sorry, my lord," the left guard said, shaking his head. "We can't let you—"

Josef reached out with both hands and grabbed each guard by the helmet. Bracing his feet, he slammed their heads together as hard as he could. The helmets hit with a metal crash, and the two guards dropped.

Josef nodded and stepped over their prone bodies.

Eli poked his head out, his mouth forming an O when he saw the moaning guards. "Aren't you Prince Charming?"

"Their fault," Josef said, starting down the hall. "They didn't move."

The palace was surprisingly empty. The guard posts were abandoned, probably in answer to the new threat at the bay. That suited Josef just fine. He jogged through the empty halls, following the twist of the castle toward the kitchens. He trundled down the narrow servant's stair and burst out into the paved yard where he'd met Finley's carriage the day before, scaring the daylights out of a serving boy in the process.

"You," he barked before the boy could bolt. "Two fast horses. Now."

The boy stared at him wide-eyed. "This is the back stable, sire. We only got—"

"I don't care about the quality," Josef said. "If it's fast, bring it. *Now.*"

The boy ran off, returning moments later with two long-legged bays already saddled and bearing the queen's colors.

"Aren't these reserved for messengers?" Eli said, scrambling onto the smaller of the two.

"Royal privilege," Josef said, pulling himself onto the other. He held out his hand for Nico, but she stepped away.

"I'll meet you there," she said, wrinkling her nose. "Horses and I don't get along."

Josef nodded, but she was already gone, her body dissolving into shadows. Behind them, forgotten, the serving boy shrieked.

"He'll get over it," Josef said. "Come on."

He kicked his horse and thundered out through the open gate. Eli shook his head and followed, bouncing in his saddle behind Josef as the prince forged a path through the crowded streets to the sea.

The queen supplied her messengers well. The horses made the trip down the mountain to the Rebuke in record time. Ahead of them, the flat walk of the storm wall was crawling with soldiers.

Eli stood up in his saddle, squinting at the horizon. "I don't see any ships. No invasion yet, at least."

Josef hopped off his horse and started pushing his way through the crowd. The soldiers looked at him sideways and whispered among themselves, but no one tried to stop him as he made his way to the heavy watchtower. Once they were inside, Nico was suddenly there.

"They're at the top," she said. "The light's too good for me to get in and the only door is guarded. Sneaking's not an option."

"Good thing we're not sneaking," Josef said, starting up the stairs. "Come on."

They climbed the four flights of stairs without challenge, but the door to the watch room at the top of the tower was blocked by a man in the polished chain of the royal guard. The soldier gripped his short sword when he saw Josef's face and pulled himself as tall as he could.

"Prince Thereson," he said in a voice that failed to be as authoritative as he probably wanted it to be. "You're supposed to be under arrest."

"Change of plans," Josef said. "Step aside."

The guard tightened his grip and held his ground.

Josef reached for the Heart, but Eli's hand on his shoulder

stopped him. The thief leaned forward, fixing the guard with his sweetest smile.

"Listen, young man," he said. "The prince has had a really bad morning. So either you step aside and let us take responsibility for what's about to happen, or Thereson here lives up to his murderous reputation. We clear?"

The soldier looked from Josef to Eli and back again before he let go his sword and stepped aside in one shaky motion.

"Good choice," Eli said as Josef slammed the door open and stepped inside. He stopped again almost immediately, eyes going wide. He felt Eli stop as well and then hastily turn away. Josef didn't blame him. The sight was enough to turn even his stomach.

The watch room where he'd met with Finley was now slick with blood. Six dead guards lay on the floor below the windows, their necks slit at the back. Blood pooled on the wooden floor, reflecting the morning sunlight, and the smell of it was thick in the air. Around this gruesome scene stood a ring of royal guards, their faces pale and tight beneath their helmets. Medics waited at the edges, but there was very little for them to do when the patients were already dead. At the center of the room, two men stood over a wide table where a seventh dead man sat slumped over a blood-splattered pile of maps, his fine-tailored gray suit now a sickly reddish black thanks to the gaping wound at the back of his neck. Josef frowned and flicked his eyes to the men standing over the table. The one on the left in the fancy coat he recognized as his mother's admiral, though he couldn't remember the old man's name. The other man also looked familiar, but Josef couldn't place him either.

Eli, however, had a better memory. "Josef!" the thief hissed, grabbing his wrist. "That's Tesset!"

"Who?" Josef said.

"*Tesset!*" Eli whispered again. "Council man from Izo's, works for Sara. Powers, he'll ruin everything."

Josef stared at the man in question. He vaguely remembered that swarthy face and large figure standing outside the hut with Sted, the one who'd gone after Nico. He could already feel Nico fading into the shadows behind him. Eli was still tugging his arm, trying to pull Josef back down the stairs, but Josef shook his head and yanked his arm free. If this Tesset was good enough to subdue Nico, then he'd already seen them, and running would do no good. Besides, Josef had questions to answer.

The admiral looked up when he heard Josef enter, and his face went scarlet.

"Prince Thereson!" he shouted. "You are confined to quarters!"

Josef ignored him, focusing on Tesset as the Council man looked up with a knowing smile.

"Good morning, Josef Liechten," he said. "Or Prince Thereson, I should say. I trust you're well."

"Well enough," Josef growled. "What are you doing here? When did you arrive?"

"Last night," Tesset said. "And I'm here as the Council's forward agent to help Osera prepare for the war. Your mother welcomed me herself just before all this unpleasantness. Condolences, by the way, on the death of your cousin."

"Keep 'em," Josef grumbled, making his way over to the closest body. The guardsman was on his stomach with his arms splayed out in an instinctive attempt to catch himself from a fall he'd never get up from.

"Back of the neck, just like the duke's men," Josef said, kneeling to get a better look at the gash that severed the man's spine. "Quick too. Poor bastard couldn't even get his sword out." He nodded down toward the guard's belt where the short sword was still snugly in its scabbard.

"Prince Thereson," the admiral said again. "Stop this at once!

This tower is controlled by her majesty's navy. Prince or not, I won't hesitate to lock you up if you do not return to the palace at once."

"What?" Josef said, straightening up. "You can't blame this one on me. Eli and I were stuck in my rooms since this morning, just like the queen ordered. Look at the blood. These men haven't been dead more than half an hour. I was probably still being disarmed when it happened. And since it's clear that whoever did the duke's house did this as well, I'd say I've been exonerated. Isn't that right, Eli?"

"Beyond a doubt," Eli said.

The admiral stiffened. "When your mother hears—"

"So go tell her," Josef said. "Later. Now, what was security like in this room?"

The old man clenched his teeth, his brow furrowing into a knot as he weighed his outrage against the presence of a prince, even a despicable one. Royalty must have won out, for the admiral's shoulders slumped and he began his report.

"Security is as you see," he said. "Six guards watching, two at the door, four in the room, and the Council's wizard for the Relay so that we could notify Zarin the moment enemy ships were sighted."

"Yet all are dead inside," Eli said, silently counting the bodies. "Including the ones who were supposed to be in the hall. And they all died with their swords in their sheaths, correct?"

"Yes," the admiral said, looking cautiously at Josef. "Sir."

Eli grinned manically at his newfound authority. "I can see from the lack of blood trails that the bodies haven't been moved. Combine that with the sheathed swords and we can safely assume that all the soldiers walked in here of their own volition. That means whoever did this was someone the guards knew, else they would have barred the entrance and died outside. Someone respected, for they escorted this person in and were subsequently too shocked to draw their swords when this known, respected person turned on them."

"Impossible," the admiral said. "Only officers and members of the royal family can enter this room without challenge." He said this last bit with a pointed look at Josef, which Josef ignored.

Eli scratched his chin thoughtfully. "My real question is, why the watchtower? The duke I could understand, but why here?"

"I believe I can answer that one for you," Tesset said.

They all turned to look. Tesset had been standing quietly beside the table. Now, though Josef had not seen or heard him move, he was several feet away, kneeling on the floor. The boards there were scuffed and dusty like any well-used surface, but one spot was darker than the rest. Josef frowned and walked over, kneeling for a closer look. It wasn't blood, though there was certainly enough of that around. It almost looked as though someone had spilled a tiny bit of water and then tried to wipe it up.

"What's that?" Josef said.

Tesset leaned down and pressed his finger delicately against the floor. When he lifted it, something was stuck there, glinting in the light. A tiny, curving splinter of glass.

"Question still stands," Josef said, glancing at Tesset.

"It's the Relay point," Tesset said. "Or what's left of it."

"Powers," the admiral whispered, staring at the wet sliver of glass. "I never knew they could be broken."

"They're quite delicate, actually," Tesset said, standing up and placing the sliver of glass on the table. "Sara will be extremely distraught. Relay points are difficult to make, and we are very short at present."

"I don't understand," Josef said. "Why would someone break a Relay point?"

"To cut Osera off from the Council," Tesset said.

"But, why?" Josef asked again. "Osera has ships going to the mainland all the time. Any disruption in communication wouldn't last past low tide. Six hours at most."

"Six hours is plenty of time for many things," Tesset said, pointedly not looking at Eli. "For example, if a thief were going to pull a heist, six hours would be amply sufficient to grab the goods and get away."

"Nonsense." Eli's voice was equally disinterested. "No thief worth the name would break something as rare and valuable as a Relay point. Not when he can steal it, anyway. Honestly, what kind of idiot thieves do you chase?"

The admiral looked from Eli to Tesset, utterly confused. "Thieves? What are you talking about?"

"Nothing," Tesset said. "An idle comment. Anyway, if the criminal's objective was to isolate us, he failed."

"How's that?" Eli said. "Point looks pretty broken to me."

"That it is," Tesset said. "But Osera has two Relay points. This tower's point was a first alert supplied by the Council specifically for this emergency. Osera's official point is kept in the palace for the queen's use."

Josef set his jaw, glancing from the dead solders to the dead wizard and back again. "Admiral," he said quietly. "Who reported this?"

The admiral blinked. "Excuse me?"

"Who found these men dead?" Josef said, his voice annoyed. "You? A guard?"

"Oh." The admiral wiped his sweating brow. He looked as though this was all getting to be a bit much for him. "It was Princess Adela."

Josef stopped. "Adela?"

"Yes," the admiral said. "She had me take over here so she could go secure the Relay point at the palace."

"Adela went to the palace?" Josef shouted.

"Yes, your highness," the admiral said, baffled by his sudden outburst. "She thought that would be the criminal's next target. But don't worry, sire, I've yet to meet a swordsman who could get the better of your—"

Josef didn't have time to listen, he was already headed for the door. A hundred things were clicking together in his mind: the precision of the sword strokes, the speed with which they must have been laid down, Adela circling him in the throne room, holding back. The deep sleep that he felt and she didn't, the drugged candles and the bowl of stimulant. He glanced out the window at the castle high above them on the mountain. Even with the horse, it would take him five minutes at least to get to the back gate and another three to run to the Relay room at the top. Josef shook his head. He had no time. He had to get there now.

He hit the door to the stairs with his shoulder, slamming the poor guard on the other side into the wall. Josef didn't even notice. He stared into the dark and shouted.

"Nico!"

She appeared before he'd finished saying her name, and Josef took a relieved breath. For a moment he'd been afraid she wouldn't come. "I need your help."

Nico's pale face broke into a thin smile. That was all the answer Josef needed.

"I have to get to the palace," he said. "Can you take me?"

Her eyes widened. "Through the shadows?"

Josef nodded.

Nico bit her lip. "I can try."

"Try is all I need," Josef said. "Take me to the top, if you can. The queen's point will be in the palace watchtower."

Nico nodded and Josef stepped forward, snatching his hand away a second before Eli's fingers grabbed his wrist.

"I'm going," he said before the thief could speak.

"I realize that," Eli whispered. "But think a second, Josef. Just because she's been drugging you to sleep doesn't mean she's guilty of everything else. This could all be a setup."

Josef moved to stand beside Nico. "We'll see soon enough, won't we?" He looked down. "Ready?"

Nico nodded and hesitantly slipped her arms around his waist. She didn't look at him while she did this, keeping her face tilted down so that she was hidden in the deep folds of her hood. That was the last thing he saw before the world twisted and everything went black.

Eli jumped back with a curse as Josef vanished, tripping over the top stair and right into the point of the door guard's sword. He raised his arms on instinct, letting the guard walk him back into the watch room. The admiral was still staring at the space where Josef had been, his wrinkled face as pale as chalk.

"Before you do anything rash," Eli said, arching away from the sword in his back, "I'll have you know that there's a perfectly reasonable explanation for this."

"Hang it all," the admiral muttered. "I don't care anymore. You're all going in irons until we get this mess straightened out."

"All is a bit much, don't you think?" Eli said. "It's just me at the moment."

"Then we'll start with you," the admiral growled. "Tie him."

Eli heaved an enormous sigh as two guards stepped forward to secure him. They were fastening the rope around his hands when the admiral turned to Tesset.

"I am so sorry you had to see this, Councilman Tesset," he said. "Prince Thereson has always—"

His voice trailed off. Tesset wasn't listening. He was standing at the window, staring out at the smooth sea. The admiral blinked and looked as well, squinting against the morning sun, and then what little blood was left in his face drained away.

"Powers help us," he whispered.

No one answered. Everyone, even Eli, was staring at the line of tiny dots on the eastern horizon. Far below, the water on the beach began to churn against the rocky face of the storm wall. Out in the bay, the lines of docked Oseran runners rocked against their moorings as the sea swelled beneath them, the bay's water pushed aside by the new, enormous current flowing from the east in a perfectly straight line.

CHAPTER
17

Josef gasped as the dark washed over him. This was true dark, not just lightless, but light consuming, and so cold he felt it like a punch all over his body. He couldn't hear anything, but he could *feel* the darkness screaming, vibrating against his skin. Panic like he'd never felt began to close over him like a sheet of ice, and he began to sink. The darkness sucked him down like a hungry mouth, screaming and laughing at the same time. Josef couldn't even move to defend himself, all he could do was sink and wait as the darkness poured down his throat, eating everything it touched.

Just before he was consumed, Nico's arms tightened on his chest, pulling him back. All at once, the sinking stopped, and his limbs were free. The feeling of motion was so beautiful, Josef almost laughed with joy. Instead, he clung to the familiar realness of Nico's wiry body with everything he had.

In less than three heartbeats, the light returned.

Josef fell to the ground, clutching his chest. He felt heavy and weak, like he'd been laid up with fever for weeks, and cold like he would never be warm again. He could feel Nico's hands on him. Her voice was in his ear, asking if he was all right. Josef nodded and reached for the hilt of his sword. The Heart leaped into his hand, and the weakness began to fade. When he was sure he could stand, Josef pushed himself up and looked around.

He recognized the place at once. They were in the hall that ran through the center of the royal guard's headquarters at the top of the palace. They'd come out next to the barracks door, but the barracks were empty. So was the hall. Josef's stomach began to sink. This was the heart of the guard. Given the current crisis, it should be crawling with soldiers as the reserves reported in, but the floor was silent. His face set in a grim line, Josef drew the Heart. He turned the sword in his hand, testing the grip in his palm. An echo of power flowed back like a greeting. Josef held the sword close as he tugged open the door to the stairs leading up to the watchtower. Nico fell in behind him, skipping from shadow to shadow.

The stair was a narrow spiral ending at a heavy door that was usually guarded and locked. But there were no guards now, and the heavy door hung open a crack, as though someone had just stepped inside and forgotten to close it. Pressing his body flat against the wall, Josef reached out with his sword, opening the door with the Heart's blade.

Even though he knew it was coming, the sight of the watchtower stopped him in his tracks. Men lay sprawled on the floor, their white faces still wide with shock above their severed necks. Josef took a quick count. Fifteen bodies, all guardsmen, far too many for the small tower. Josef set his jaw and raised his eyes to the only figure still standing.

Adela stood beside the table where the Council wizard lay slumped in his chair. Her helmet was off, and the dark braid of her hair hung free down her back, which was turned to Josef. For a moment, Josef thought maybe they'd snuck up on her, but before the thought could even finish, Adela turned to face him with a warm smile.

"I told you one day we'd be done pretending."

Josef cursed. No point in hiding now. "Adela," he said, stepping fully into the doorway. "Stand down."

"Little late for that, husband," Adela said. Her hand moved, and Josef raised his sword, but she wasn't drawing a weapon. Instead, she held up something small, round, and blue between her fingers.

"What's that?" Josef said with a sinking feeling.

Adela's smile widened, and she clenched her hand in a fist. There was a sharp crunch, like an eggshell breaking, and then she opened her hand again, letting broken glass and a tiny amount of water fall to the floor.

"It *was* a Relay point," she said, shaking the last drops of water from her fingers. "The last Relay point in Osera."

Josef stared at her, trying to put words to everything that was going through his mind. But he wasn't Eli. Words didn't come easily. In the end, he managed only one.

"Why?"

"Because it is my duty," Adela said calmly. "And because I have waited my entire life for the day when I could leave this miserable dirt scratch of a kingdom."

"*Duty?*" Josef roared. "The queen raised you up from nothing! Defended you and your mother when everyone else wanted you cast out. She made you an Eisenlowe, captain of her guard, and this is how you repay her?" He swung his sword over the dead soldiers. "You have a twisted sense of duty, *princess.*"

"And what of that matters to me?" Adela sneered. "I serve a higher power than you could ever imagine." Her voice grew deep and resonant as she spoke, and her eyes lit with a fire Josef had never seen there before. "There is no loyalty except loyalty to the true queen of the world," she said. "No duty except in her service."

Josef was beginning to wonder if she might be truly mad. "What are you talking about?"

Adela reached down and drew her short sword with a metallic hiss. Josef braced himself, but she didn't point the blade at him. Instead, she held the sword in front of her with the flat side facing him. Josef was so busy trying to guess her ploy, he didn't see the words etched into the metal for several seconds.

Sleepers wake. I am coming.

Josef's eyes darted from sword to swordswoman. "Who is coming?"

"Who do you think?" Adela laughed, swinging her sword until the point was leveled at the eastern window.

Josef kept his eyes on her, but she made no other moves. Finally, he risked a glance. He had to glance twice before he realized what he was looking at. There, miles out on the line where the Unseen Sea met the sky, the horizon was peppered with tiny dots running north and south as far as he could see.

"Oh yes," Adela said as the realization broke over his face. "The Immortal Empress is here at last to finish what she started two and a half decades ago." She brought her sword back around, aiming the point at Josef's heart. "We are the sleepers," she said, her voice trembling with emotion. "For years we've worked to weaken this island in her name. Now, your country, divided and hollowed by our hands, shall break like rotten fruit when her boats strike the shore."

"That's impossible," Josef said, forcing himself to ignore the rapturous smile on her face and keep his eyes on her sword. "You weren't even *born* when the Empress invaded."

Adela lifted her chin with a haughty sneer. "Loyalty to the Immortal Empress is not constrained by time. Our duty is passed down from mother to child, for generations if need be. We who sleep are called the ever faithful, all of us waiting generation to generation for the day she calls our blade."

"*Loyalty?*" Josef shouted. "*Faithfulness?* You betrayed your country and your queen! You killed your own men, and for what? Loyalty to an Empress you've never met?"

"Yes," Adela said, holding her short sword steady. "And I will be rewarded in ways you cannot comprehend."

"Not if I can help it," Josef growled. "Nico, go tell the admiral I have our traitor."

Nico didn't even get a chance to respond before Adela started to laugh.

"Go ahead, little girl, it doesn't matter now. Your kingdom is broken, your queen dying and alone. Her duke, the only man who could have rallied Osera, is dead. Your army is terrified and without leadership, your clingfire, the only weapon against the palace ships, destroyed. And since both Relay points are gone, you can't even use what little time remains to warn your allies. Now do you understand, prince? Send your girl, it will do no good. Osera has already fallen."

Josef glowered. "I never picked you for a fool, Adela," he said. "But I guess I was wrong about that too. Only a fool counts a battle won while the defenders are still standing."

Adela smirked at him. "Not for long."

Behind him, Josef felt Nico tense, ready to jump through the shadows and land on Adela's back. He stopped her with one word.

"Go."

Nico snarled at Adela one last time and vanished into the dark. If Adela was surprised by this, her face didn't show it.

"Quite the little monster you've got there, Thereson," she said. "Are you sure it was wise to send her away?"

"Yes," he said. "I'm the prince of Osera. It's my duty to finish you myself."

"Duty? You?" Adela laughed with delight. "The murderer prince who ran away?" She paused. "Actually, you were the only variable. When Theresa gambled the treasury to bring you home, we never thought you'd actually come home. But I'm glad you did, husband. Having the marriage bed for an alibi gave me more freedom to move than I could have hoped for, and your presence made my mother's job easier. The queen gets herself very excited when you're around. Such exertion makes it so much easier to explain her worsening fits."

Josef's eyes widened. "My mother's not sick at all, is she?" he said in a low, dangerous voice. "You've been poisoning her."

Adela shrugged. "Hard to say, at this point. After close to ten years of drinking my mother's tea, Theresa's condition has become quite real. I doubt she'll last out the week, especially once she hears that her son, her last, ridiculous hope, finally gave in to his violent nature and had to be put down like a mad dog."

"If that's how you see this playing out, you haven't been paying attention," Josef said, raising the Heart as he stepped into position. "I may not be much of a prince, but I am the best and, unless you surrender now, the last swordsman you will ever meet."

"We'll see about that," Adela said, stepping into first position.

Josef looked her over. His instincts during the proving had been right. The stance Adela took now had none of the stiffness from before, and her fingers gripped her sword with a master's assurance. But even so, even if she somehow was a master duelist, there was no way she could hope to beat the Heart of War with an infantry short sword.

He glanced down at the Heart. It was a pity to use it for a fight like this, but he didn't have the luxury of a handicap. He needed to end this quickly and warn his mother. If he moved fast enough, he might even be able to save her. Josef gripped the Heart with both hands, sliding his feet forward across the stone. Finish it fast, he thought. Finish it now.

The Heart hummed in agreement, and they moved as one, bearing down on Adela like an iron wave. The princess's eyes widened at his speed, but she didn't try to dodge or spin away as she had in the Proving. Instead, she lifted her short, stocky blade and braced for the Heart's impact. The short sword looked so pathetic before the Heart's monstrous weight, Josef almost laughed. But Adela didn't break her guard, even as the Heart struck her sword with the force of a mountain.

The two blades met with a scream of metal, and Josef watched in satisfaction as the short sword crumpled. He could feel the impact moving through her blade like the Heart was an extension of his own arm, but as he stepped in for the follow-through that would shatter Adela's ribs, he realized something was wrong.

The short sword was still breaking. The metal was still folding in on itself, still crumpling like ash as it absorbed the Heart's strike. Josef's eyes widened. He could feel the blow spoiling even as he carried it, feel himself slowing as Adela slid backward, letting her sword break and break and break, drinking in the blow. Before the force could fade completely, Josef abandoned the strike. He swung the Heart back and turned midstep, using the last of his spoiled momentum to step out of her range, coming to a stop a few feet away with the Heart between him and Adela as he tried to figure out what had just happened.

Adela straightened with a smile and raised her sword, holding up the crumpled blade for Josef to see. Josef didn't see how there had been enough metal in the sword to crumple as much as it had, let alone enough to absorb the enormous power of the Heart. He was still trying to make sense of it when Adela's sword began to change. The etched words on the blade flashed with blinding light, and the crumpled blade began to straighten. The metal moved like a living thing as it pushed out of the stocky, confined shape of the short sword, growing longer, sharper, and slightly curved. The whole process took no more than a handful of seconds, and then Adela was holding a sword that looked nothing like the one she'd held a moment ago. The new blade glowed with a light of its own. It was delicate and straight now, without a single mark from the crumpled mess it had been moments before. Even the handle had changed, pushing out of the squat single hilt to a two-handed hold with a thick guard chased all around with stylized waves that seemed to dance across the glowing steel.

Josef kept his face neutral, refusing to let her see his surprise. "An awakened blade," he said. "Are you a wizard as well as a traitor and a spy?"

"I could scarcely be a sleeper if I was a wizard," Adela answered, swinging her newly changed sword in a whistling arc. "Wizards attract attention. To serve the Empress, we must be invisible. But this blade is not the crude, half-alert spirit you people call 'awakened.' Like me, it is a servant of the Empress." She held the sword out for him. "What you see before you is one of the Hundred Conquerors, a treasure of the Empire given only to those who serve behind enemy lines."

"Really?" Josef played along. "What's it made of that it crumples like trash when struck? Tin?"

"Steel," Adela said. "A mile of steel compressed into a blade by the Empress's own hand."

This time, Josef couldn't hide his surprise. "A *mile* of steel?" he cried. "How can a mile of steel become a blade?"

"All things bow before the Empress," Adela said. "Metal is no different. It followed her command as everything does, becoming her soldier, just as I am. The Hundred Conquerors have served thousands of soldiers in countless battles, passing from sleeper to sleeper as the Empress conquers the world. Each sword has been trained over hundreds of years to follow pressure commands so that even the spirit deaf can use it to its full potential. This blade cannot be defeated, it cannot be escaped, and, as you just saw, it cannot be broken." Her eyes flashed with a cruel light. "Not even by the Heart of War."

Josef's mouth twitched. After all her revelations, he shouldn't be surprised she knew his sword. But... "If you think a mile of steel will be enough to save you from the Heart, you've got another thing coming."

Adela sneered, but whatever she meant to say, she never got the chance. Josef was already flying toward her. This time, he kept both hands on the Heart's hilt, letting the blade guide him. He could feel the Heart's spirit moving through him, filling him until he could see the mountain behind his eyes, the great peak cutting the clouds, the deep roots holding up the world. An awakened blade was nothing. A mile of steel was nothing. The Heart of War moved with a mountain's rage, and Josef gave himself to it, letting its strength take him over with a furious cry.

Again, Adela raised her blade to parry, but her smug look faded as the blades collided. As before, her glowing sword crumpled, the metal folding over on itself so fast it sparked, but this time, it wasn't enough. Josef's cry became a roar as the Heart's power thundered through him, forcing Adela and her collapsing sword backward. They crashed together into the wall of the watchtower with an explosion that carried them through the stone and out into the air. As the blow finally left him, so did the overwhelming will of the Heart, and Josef realized he was falling. In front of him, almost lost in the enormous cloud of dust and broken stone, Adela was falling as well, her face a mask of shock and horror as the last of the Heart's force ran through her crumpled blade to finally hit her body. As he felt the strike connect at last, Josef got one final glimpse of her face screwing up in pain before the blow sent her flying out of the dust cloud like an arrow.

Josef was still trying to see where she'd gone when he crashed into something hard and brittle. He grunted as he hit and rolled on instinct. The landing hurt far less than it should have. The echo of the Heart's power was still crashing through him, drowning out every other sensation. He'd joined with his sword before, but never like that. The black blade had moved not with him, but *through* him. Its power was his power, its will, his will, and as it began to drain away, Josef felt emptier than ever. But as he lay still and fought to steady himself, the Heart's hilt pressed against his hands, warning him that the fight was not over.

Like a man waking from a deep sleep, Josef shot up and the world returned. He was in a crater on the roof of the palace's western wing. The watchtower, what was left of it, loomed above him. Its entire north face was gone, the stone sundered by the force of the Heart's blow. There were great holes in the tile roofs of the stylish buildings around the castle where the blown-out chunks of the broken tower had landed, but Josef's eyes skipped over them, looking for his target.

Adela lay in the ruins of what had been the top floor of the most prestigious bank in Osera, her body cradled by a great wave of shining steel. The metal moved as he watched, throwing off the rubble, and Josef cursed as it lifted Adela to her feet. When she was steady, the metal retreated, flowing back into the shape of the long, curved sword.

She shook her head, as though trying to clear it, and Josef started to grin. Challenge the Heart, would she? But the weakness lasted less than a second. At once, her head snapped up, her eyes finding him instantly among the wreckage. Josef got to his feet, watching to see what she would do. Even after cutting through a mile of steel and the wall of the watchtower, the Heart's blow had been enough to throw her far. It was a long jump from the wrecked bank where she stood to the palace roof. He planted his feet, easing the Heart in his hands as he waited to see how she would handle it, but Adela made no move to close the distance. Instead, she raised her sword, pointing the tip at Josef's chest in challenge.

Smirking, Josef held up the Heart in answer, his mouth opening to taunt her into a wild charge.

He never got a chance. The moment he moved the Heart, the tip of Adela's silver blade shot out. It flew like an arrow, cutting through the air with a screaming whistle. By the time Josef realized what was happening, it was nearly too late. With no time to duck, he defended the only way he could. He raised his sword and flipped it, holding the Heart's broadside like a shield over his chest. For a split second, it looked like this would work, but then the tip of Adela's blade flickered, and the sliver shot forked left in midair. There was no time to adjust, no time for Josef to do anything but brace himself as the sword point slipped around the Heart's defense and stabbed through his left shoulder.

It happened so quickly, there wasn't even any pain. One moment he was braced, the next a length of shining steel pierced his shoulder like a spit through a roast. He could feel the metal in his muscle, slick and burning hot from the expansion. He was still staring dumbly at it when the blade began to lift. Across the expanse, Adela was raising her sword, lifting Josef up until his feet were dangling.

Now it hurt. Every centimeter she raised him sent a new bolt of pain sharp enough to make his vision go dark radiating from his shoulder. He struggled because he felt he should, but it was a futile effort. Her sword had skewered him like a speared boar. He couldn't even slide himself off the blade. All he could do was grip the Heart as Adela lifted him farther and farther into the air like he weighed nothing.

Just when Josef was sure his arm was going to rip off, Adela flicked her wrist. The sword snapped in a mirror of the motion, slinging Josef off the end. He was dimly aware of tumbling through the air, but his real attention was on the blinding pain of the sword as it slid out of his body. The agony made him sluggish, too sluggish to do more than tuck his head as Adela's throw sent him through one of the palace chimneys. The bricks crumbled when he hit, falling on him in a rain of broken stone as he tumbled down the slope of the palace roof until, at last, he hit one of the stone gutters and stopped.

For several moments, all he could do was lie still and try to breathe. His body was seizing up around him, his blood grinding to a halt in his veins. His right arm was a bar of pain, but even though he couldn't feel his right hand, or form a coherent thought, Josef clung to the Heart instinctively, knowing without knowing that it was his best chance of survival.

As his mind slowly came back to the present, the first thing he heard was the soft hiss of steel as Adela's sword shrank back to its usual shape. Groaning at the effort, Josef turned his head to see her walk to the edge of the bank's broken roof and hold out her sword again. He sucked in a breath, bracing for another blow, but her sword was pointed down. The blade extended again with a metallic whine, and he heard the stone shatter as the tip hit the street below. Then, using her sword as a pole, Adela stepped out into the open gulf of air between the bank's ruined roof and the palace. The sword began to fall at once, carrying her across the gap until she landed neatly on the edge of the palace roof. Her sword retracted the moment her feet were firm, returning to the long, gently curved blade as Adela advanced on Josef.

He sank to the ground, bringing the Heart up as high as he could. The wound in his shoulder burned like a hot poker, but the Heart's strength was already washing the pain away. He probably could have stood if he'd really tried, but Josef stayed put, watching Adela as she stopped by his feet. Her braid was skewed from the impact earlier, and the wind whipped her long hair across her face as she stood over him, surveying her kill. Her sword shone with harsh light, steam rising off the blade in long tendrils as she planted the point between the tiles and leaned on it like a walking stick.

"Still alive?" she cooed.

That was when Josef struck. He pushed up with his uninjured shoulder, the Heart of War moving in a black flash as he swung straight for Adela's neck. For a split second, he saw true panic in her eyes, and then her fingers tightened on the hilt of her sword.

The blade responded instantly. It flew out like a silver rope, loping up and back with a scream of steel to hook the Heart's blade. Josef grunted as the Heart of War jerked in his hands. Had he been standing, he could have held the blow on course, but striking up from the ground and on one injured shoulder, he simply didn't have the strength. Adela's sword pulled the Heart's trajectory off at the last second, flipping the black blade and Josef with it.

Josef cried out as he slammed into the tiled roof for the third time, rolling as he hit in a desperate effort to save his injured shoulder. He ended up on his stomach, but just as he kicked his legs under to get up, Adela's boot landed on his neck and slammed him down again.

Adela leaned over him, panting wildly as she ground her boot down with all her weight. Josef gritted his teeth and shifted, turning his head so he could see her face. She was glaring down at him with pure, righteous fury. One hand held her sword, its flexible blade still wrapped around the Heart, but her other hand was pressed against her neck, staunching a shallow wound half an inch from her windpipe. Despite the boot grinding into his neck, Josef grinned. She wasn't quite as fast as she liked to think.

"How are you still alive?" Adela whispered, her voice shaking with rage. "You should be bleeding to death." Her dark eyes darted to his hands, still gripping the Heart of War with all their might. "I wonder."

She jerked her fingers along her sword's hilt. The flexible blade followed the motion, slinging down in a flashing arc. Josef's eyes widened, and he dropped the Heart a second before the whipped blade would have sliced off his fingers. Adela laughed above him, but Josef had both hands free now. He reached up with his free arm, fingers closing around her boot before he threw her as hard as he could. Adela's laughter cut off with a strangled cry as she fell, but Josef had already put her out of his mind. Every sense he had was focused on the black blade lying crooked on the tiles. He'd been separated from his sword for only a few seconds, but already the pain was threatening to knock him out. The Heart was all that mattered. If he couldn't reach it, he was down for good. But as his fingers brushed the hilt, a flash of silver cut him off.

Adela's sword whistled over his head, landing on the Heart with a whine of cutting metal. Josef snatched his fingers back with a curse as the flexible blade wrapped itself around the Heart like thread around a spindle, and as it wrapped, the blade began to spin, surrounding the Heart in an impenetrable cocoon of whirling steel. The moment the sword was completely covered, Adela flicked her hand like she was cracking a whip and the blade of her sword snapped off, freeing her from the tangle of whirling metal she'd woven around the Heart.

"There," she said, smiling as the broken length of sword in her hand folded and re-formed until it was a slender, curved blade once again. "Let's see how well you fight now, Thereson."

Josef's eyes flicked back to the Heart. Despite Adela seemingly snapping her blade in two, the cocoon of spinning steel around the Heart was going strong, grinding into the tile below with a whining scream. He crouched on his knees, considering his options. It didn't take long, since there was only one. Blood soaked his arm, back, and chest, and he was starting to feel light-headed even through the pain. If he was going to do anything other than sit here and bleed to death, he needed the Heart, but there was no way through the spinning coil of Adela's blade. Not without losing a hand, or worse.

Josef gritted his teeth with a growl of frustration. "That's a very annoying weapon you have there, Dela. Does your Empress fight all her battles so cheaply, or am I the exception?"

"The Empress fights for victory," Adela said. "Anything else is merely the conceit of prideful swordsmen." She tapped his shoulder with her blade, forcing him to turn and face her. "You are defeated, Prince Thereson," she crowed, beaming down at him. "Your wound is bleeding as it should now that I've separated you from that hunk of iron you call a sword. Give up. As it stands, I can still save your life, but you will be dead for certain if you persist in fighting."

"Why should I give up?" Josef said, sitting back on his heels as he pressed both palms against the hole in his shoulder in a futile attempt to hold in the blood. "You think I believe you'll let me live? After everything you've admitted to me?"

"Of course," Adela said. "With the duke dead and your mother soon to follow, you are next in line for the throne. If you die here, the succession will be broken completely."

"What do you care about the succession?" Josef wheezed. It was getting hard to sit straight now. "I'm not about to make you queen, if that's what you're after."

Adela's lips peeled up in a sneer. "Why would I want to be queen of this pit? Osera is a savage place, even by the standards of this savage, backward continent. To be honest, I don't think this island is worthy of the Empress's conquest, but my lady is more forgiving than I am."

Adela lowered her sword and leaned down, bringing her head to Josef's level. "The people of Osera are stubborn brutes," she whispered. "Even without a king, they will throw themselves at the Empress's soldiers, breaking like waves on the wall of her palace ships until the sea is red with Oseran blood. But there's no reason the Empress's coming has to be a massacre. Think, Thereson. If you live, you will become king of Osera with the power to make your people surrender. Since you came home when your mother raised the bounty, I can't believe you're as indifferent to your homeland as you pretend. It's true that nothing you do can save Osera now, but there's still a chance you can save your people. Pledge your loyalty to the Empress, and she may be merciful."

Josef stared at her for a moment, and then he started to laugh. Each seize of his chest sent a wave of pain that nearly knocked him out, but he couldn't stop. "You actually think..." He gasped. "You actually believe Osera would listen to *me*?"

Adela scowled. "If you don't like the terms, I can always stand here and watch you die." She straightened up again, flicking her sword until the point was level with Josef's throat. "What will it be, Josef Liechten Thereson Eisenlowe? Life for you and your people at my Empress's mercy, or certain death for every soul on this island? Choose quickly, we're drawing a crowd."

Josef glanced down. Sure enough, the square in front of the castle was packed with people. Some were pointing up at the prince and princess; others were simply staring dumbstruck at the cratered roof and shattered buildings. The crowd was entirely citizens, no guards or military, and Josef turned away to focus on the more important matters of Adela's sword and his bleeding shoulder. But, just before his eyes left the crowd, he caught a pair of familiar faces.

A second later, a cool breeze ruffled Josef's hair.

"Can't we go faster?" Nico said, leaning out the carriage window.

Eli clung to his seat for dear life. He'd been making the most of his first nonthieving-related arrest when Nico had come charging out of the shadows by the door and told everyone Adela was their traitor, that she'd killed her own guards and broken the queen's

Relay point, and that Josef was fighting her as they spoke. That was five minutes ago. Now, thanks to a few well-placed scares from Nico and Eli's quick hand with knots, they were in a requisitioned military cart hurtling over the rutted streets of east Osera toward the palace.

"Any faster and we'd end up flat against a building," Tesset answered from his perch on the driver's seat, holding the horses straight as the road veered and dipped. Tesset had come along without being asked, but Eli hadn't complained, as the Council man had offered to drive. He was starting to regret that decision. Tesset made him nervous. Despite the plunging horses, the man's expression never changed from interestedly neutral, as though this was all nothing more than a play he hadn't quite decided he liked yet.

Of course, if this was a play, Eli didn't like the way the plot was going one bit. Clinging to the vibrating carriage, he glanced up at the rapidly approaching palace. It looked fine from this angle, but they'd heard the enormous crash a few minutes ago. From here, Eli couldn't see what had caused it, but whatever it was, it couldn't be good. Nothing good ever came of noises that loud.

"We're turning," Tesset said. "Hold on."

The carriage careened sideways, nearly sending Eli and Nico tumbling into the street. Nico was back in her seat a second later. Eli took significantly longer to pull himself upright.

"What was that about?" Eli groaned, clutching his bruised shoulders as he watched the palace fly by on his left. "Stop! The palace is right there."

"The fight's on the western wing," Tesset said. "We're on the wrong side. If we stop here we'd have to walk through the palace. Better to drive around."

Eli grimaced. "Just don't take us into the front square. That's where every—"

He cut off as Tesset careened the cart again. "Would you stop that?" Eli shouted, holding on for dear life.

If Tesset heard him, he gave no sign. They were darting through the rich neighborhood just below the palace now, weaving in and out of the growing traffic. But as they turned down a street that led to the palace square, Tesset reined the horse to a skidding halt, forcing Nico and Eli to hold on or be thrown.

"Didn't I tell you?" Eli cried. "Not the square!"

Tesset ignored him and hopped down. Shaking and cursing, Eli followed, leaving the cart and the panting horses standing in the middle of the street. As Eli had predicted, the entrance to the palace square was blocked by a mass of people crawling over each other to see what was happening.

"I told you," Eli said again, pointing disgustedly at the wall of backs. "We'll never get through now."

"What's the matter, thief?" Tesset said. "Afraid of a little crowd?"

Eli started to tell him exactly what was wrong with that question, but before he could get a word in, Nico and Tesset stepped up to the edge of the crowd and began pushing people out of the way. Fortunately for all involved, the crowd in the square was too preoccupied to care about a little pushing. They were all staring up at the palace roof. Some were pushing toward it, but more were trying to get away. Eli didn't blame them. The western side of the palace was a wreck. The palace watchtower was half gone, its northern side blown out completely, which explained the *boom* from earlier. Fallen hunks of stone littered the square and the buildings around it, especially the elegant building at the castle's northwest corner, which seemed to have lost a large chunk of its roof. Eli was still wondering what could have caused such massive destruction when Nico grabbed his arm and pointed up at the palace roof.

Of course, Eli sighed. Who else?

Josef was on his back on one of the castle gutters with Adela standing over him. Even at this distance, Eli could see it was bad. The stone beneath Josef was dark with blood, and the Heart was nowhere to be seen. Adela's mouth was moving, but this far away her words were lost in the noise of the crowd and the endless wind.

"It's a bad position."

Eli glanced at Tesset, who had stopped pushing the crowd and was now eyeing the battle with professional interest.

"Liechten should be able to take a girl like that," he continued. "She must have a gimmick, and he must have fallen for it hard if he's on his back, especially considering how he took Sted. Still, won't be long if he keeps bleeding like that."

"Josef will win," Nico hissed.

"I'm with Nico," Eli said. "I would be an old man by now if I let myself panic every time I saw Josef at death's door. He'll win, I'm sure. Our problem is what comes after."

Nico shot Eli a furious look. "What do you mean?"

"Listen," Eli said, dropping his voice.

Nico and Tesset obeyed, falling silent as the noise of the crowd rolled over them.

"Go on, princess!" an old man shouted. "Kill the traitor!"

"Thereson is a murderer!" someone else shouted behind them. "He killed the duke! Avenge Finley!"

"He's no prince of ours!" a woman cried. "Kill him! Kill the traitor!"

And on and on and on.

"I see what you mean," Tesset said at last.

"They're all idiots," Nico said at the same time. "How dare they—"

"Nico," Eli's voice held a sharp warning. Nico glared at him, but shut her mouth. Eli smiled apologetically at Tesset and grabbed Nico's shoulder, turning her around and leaning down so that their heads were together.

"Listen," he whispered. "Josef's going to win this fight, but it's our duty to make it count."

Nico nodded. "What have you got in mind?"

"We're going to clear his name," Eli said. "But first, I need you to find me a wind."

Nico gave him a skeptical look, but she didn't question him. Instead, she looked up, her eyes darting across the sky. "There," she said, pointing up.

Eli followed her finger with his eyes. "You!" he cried, layering just a hint of power into his voice as his finger shot out, pointing at the same spot in the sky as Nico. "Can I ask a favor?"

He felt immensely stupid yelling at the empty air, but he hid it with a confident smile. Thankfully, a few seconds later, a strong breeze ruffled his hair.

"Good guess," the wind whispered in his ear. "I'm impressed enough to hear you out, wizard."

"You're too kind," Eli said. "I have a bit of an odd task for you, but I promise I'll make it worth your while."

His shirt fluttered as the wind turned in a circle. "I'm listening."

Eli glanced at Nico with a wry smile and launched into his plan. Beside him, Tesset listened with growing interest. By the time the wind agreed and blew away, he was grinning as wide as any of them.

"Never boring with you, is it, Monpress?"

Eli flinched at the mention of his name, but he hid it flawlessly, turning on Tesset with a winning smile.

"I should hope not, Mr. Tesset."

He would have said more, but Nico smacked his arm and put her finger to her lips. Eli nodded and turned back to Josef, who was still lying on his back looking at Adela, who wasn't talking anymore. The seconds crawled by, and then, without warning, a great wind picked up around them.

That was his cue. Eli cleared his throat and cupped his hands over his mouth. A small, thin flow of air whistled through his curled fingers. Eli licked his lips as the wind brushed over them and very softly began to speak.

High above the crowd on the palace roof, Josef held Adela's gaze, his lips pursed in exaggerated consideration as he made a show of thinking her offer over. But his attention was on the wind in his ears and the familiar voice it carried.

"Josef," Eli's disembodied voice whispered. "If you can hear me, give a sign."

Josef shifted his knee, nudging a chunk of broken stone so that it clattered down the roof.

"Good enough," Eli said. "I'm guessing Adela has come clean as a traitor by now?"

Josef nodded without thinking, and then froze when Adela's eyes narrowed suspiciously.

"*Powers*, don't do that," Eli hissed in his ear. "Listen, before you roll out whatever you're planning, I need you to follow my instructions to the letter."

It took all his willpower not to roll his eyes, but Josef stayed still, listening to Eli's plan. Adela tilted her head at his silence, obviously growing impatient, but by the time she got mad enough to show it, Josef knew exactly what to do.

"I grow weary of this," Adela said, edging her sword a little closer to Josef's neck. "Which will it be, Thereson? Die here and doom your island, or surrender and spare yourself and your people?"

Josef leaned back. "You tell me."

Adela paused. "What do you mean?"

"This is the day you've been preparing for all your life, right?" He jerked his head to the east. "Your Immortal Empress is finally coming, and you've dutifully done everything you could to pave the way for her. You killed Duke Finley and his son, poisoned the queen, probably burned the clingfire stock too, now that I think about it. Doesn't really matter anymore, I guess."

Adela's hand tightened on her sword. "What are you playing at?"

"I never play, princess," Josef said, his voice deadly serious. "It's no secret I'm a terrible prince to Osera. I don't even know what's going on half the time. Now you're standing there asking me to make decisions about the country's future?" He shrugged as far as he could with his wound. "How should I know? Traitor or spy or whatever your true colors, the sad truth is you've done more as Osera's princess than I ever did as her prince. This is your moment, Dela, not mine. So you tell me, what should Osera do?"

Adela lowered her sword with an exasperated look. "Leaving his country's fate to her betrayer? You truly are a terrible prince, Thereson."

She stabbed her blade point down into the roof and leaned on it, the loose strands of her dark hair blowing wildly in the strong wind. "You want to know the fate I would choose for Osera?" she said, smiling down at him the way she used to when they were kids. "Fine. I want it to burn. All of it. Do you know what it was like, growing up here? You people are barbarians, with your insistence on blood lines and noble houses. My mother grew up in the bosom of the Empire. She told me stories of a perfect land where everyone is judged on merit and loyalty. Where disobedient idiots like you are cast away while people like me become leaders because of our skill, not our birth. People still die of hunger here. Can you believe it? In the Empire there is no war, no famine, no natural disasters. Spirit or a human, everything there is clean, ordered, and perfect, and all the Empress asks in exchange for this perfection is obedience."

She flung out her arm, pointing at the city below. "You can't know what it's like!" she cried in disgust. "To *know* that paradise exists while you are trapped in this pigsty. But my exile is over." She grabbed her sword and swung it back toward him with a mad, enraptured smile. "My mother and I have fulfilled our purpose. We have cleared every obstacle that stands in the Empress's path and offered up this pathetic excuse of a kingdom to her like a peeled grape on a platter. When the Empress arrives, we shall be rewarded beyond anything you can imagine, and when I'm standing at her side, I will look down on the burning shell of Osera, and I will laugh. I will laugh and sing my Empress's praises while her soldiers slaughter every last one of you ignorant, barbaric savages."

"Then you're not sorry," Josef said, leaning away from the quivering point of her sword. "Not about killing the duke and his son? Or about the years you've spent poisoning my mother?"

"Of course not." Adela laughed, her voice echoing in the wind. "I'd kill Finley again if I could, the pompous bore. And Henry. I can't tell you how happy I am that the Empress came quickly and I don't have to waste my life being his queen and bearing his dull-witted children. As for Theresa, she deserves what she got for being so trusting. The only thing I regret is that I had to pretend to lose to you at the Proving, but I intend to remedy that now." Adela smiled, her sword inching forward to press against the naked skin of his throat. "You should have been smarter, Prince Thereson, than to let your enemy choose your fate."

"I don't think so," Josef said, tilting his head into the wind. "Is that enough?"

"More than enough," Eli's voice drifted on the breeze. "We heard the whole thing."

Adela's eyes went wide, and she swung around, searching for the source of the voice, but the roof was empty.

"Who's there?" she shouted. "Show yourself!"

Her only answer was the wind's low moaning as it swept past her, blowing her voice down over the now completely silent crowd.

"Well," Josef said, pushing himself up. "If you've got all you need, we'll finish it from here."

Adela spun back around, bringing her sword right up to the skin beneath Josef's chin. "What do you mean 'we'? You are alone! No one can save you!"

Josef didn't move, not even to flinch away from the blade at his throat. "Wrong, princess. You were the only one who was fighting alone."

Adela bared her teeth with a snarl and flicked her wrist, sending a wave of steel down her sword that would slice Josef's neck in two. But before the wave was halfway down the blade, the Heart of War's spirit exploded open, and the weight of a mountain fell on the palace.

CHAPTER

18

Eli watched in amazement from his place in the equally amazed crowd as the corner of the palace where Josef and Adela's drama had been playing out suddenly fell straight down. There was no warning, no crumbling, no falling stone. One moment Adela was standing with her sword at Josef's throat, unknowingly incriminating herself to all of Osera, and the next the entire western side of the palace had flattened as though stepped on by an enormous, invisible foot.

For three heartbeats, the people simply stared, and then the crowd turned as one and began to stampede out of the square. Tesset calmly retreated to the recessed entry of a nearby building as the tide of people surged past. Eli dove behind him far less calmly, pressing himself flat against the painted door as far from the panic as he could get. He was thinking about picking the lock when a wind's voice giggled in his ear.

"Helping you was more fun than expected," the wind said. "Now, you said you'd make it worth my while?"

"Of course," Eli said, recovering instantly now that there were deals to make. "How about a favor of your choosing from the prince of Osera?"

"A favor from a human?" the wind puffed, considering. "That's a fine turnaround. I'll take it. I'll call him when I think of something."

"Do, please," Eli said.

But the wind was already blowing up into the sky to tell the others about how a *human* owed *him* a favor.

Tesset patted down his collar where the wind had blown it up. "You do realize that when the wind comes to claim that favor, the spirit-deaf Prince Josef won't be able to hear him."

"Winds like having favors more than claiming them, in my experience," Eli said. "But if it does ever come to that, I'm sure the wind will find a way. They're very resourceful."

"I'm sure," Tesset said, eyes darting pointedly to the square. "You should look to your young lady."

Eli followed Tesset's look and saw, without surprise, that Nico was no longer beside them but across the square and pushing her way toward the palace wreckage. With a long-suffering sigh, Eli started after her. Tesset went with him, gently pushing the panicked people out of their way with his long arms.

They caught up with Nico at the edge of the crushed palace. Eli was about to ask why she'd stopped when he felt it. The Heart's spirit was still open, sitting on the wreckage of the palace's western corner like an invisible mountain. Another step and Nico would have been on the ground like everything else.

The Heart had done a very neat job, crushing only the area around Josef and Adela but leaving the rest of the palace intact. It looked like someone had dropped a brick on this corner of the building, ripping away the walls and the roof but leaving everything else mostly intact. Servants were already peering over the ragged edge from the now-open rooms, their eyes as wide as dinner plates.

Where the Heart's spirit was open, however, nothing moved.

Even the dust was pressed indelibly into the ground. The stone wall had been crushed into the palace's foundations by the Heart's weight, bringing the roof down to eye level from the ground, and there, lying on her back and half buried under a cascade of cracked tiles not a foot away, was Adela. She lay completely still. So still that, for a moment, Eli thought she was dead. Then he saw her chest rise in a tight, tiny gasp, and he realized the truth. She was crushed, like everything else. In fact, the only thing not crushed beneath the Heart's enormous weight was Josef.

He sat at Adela's feet, watching her with a disgusted look. When he saw the three of them waiting at the edge of the destruction, Josef stood, walked over to what looked like a tangled ball of steel, and held out his hand. With a squeal of ripping metal, the Heart cut up through the twisted steel like a knife through ribbon and leaped into Josef's grip, its hilt pressing firmly into its swordsman's palm. The second Josef's fingers closed on his sword, the monstrous weight lifted.

There was a whoosh of air as the winds rushed to fill the void. Josef let it blow over him, breathing deeply as the bleeding from his shoulder eased, then stopped altogether. When the wound was staunched, he turned and walked back to Adela. Now that the weight had lifted, the princess was coughing and struggling to roll over. She'd made it to her side by the time Josef reached her, and Eli saw her eyes widen in fear as she brought her hand up with a silver flash.

The Heart was there before she finished, the black blade slamming down just above her fingers. A spirit screamed, and Adela looked down in horror.

Just above the guard that protected her fingers, Adela's sword was now little more than a ripped metal edge. On the ground in front of her, the rest of the bright steel blade twisted like a trapped snake beneath the Heart of War. The metal screamed as it thrashed, but every scream was fainter than the one before it. Finally, the sword fell still, its light fading like a dying ember, leaving the blade motionless, dark, and dead in the rubble.

"No," Adela whispered, her fingers trembling on the hilt of her broken sword. "*No.* It's *impossible.*"

Josef looked away in disgust. "Nico?"

Nico was behind Adela before Josef finished speaking her name, her hand coming down on the back of the princess's neck. The blow hit with a solid *thwack*, and Adela slumped forward, her eyes fluttering closed.

"That should keep her for a bit," Josef said, leaning on the Heart.

Nico stepped over Adela's body to stand beside him, her eyes locked on his blood-soaked shoulder.

Josef began to fidget under her scrutiny. "I've had worse," he muttered.

Nico's eyes widened, but she let it lie.

"Well," Eli said, stepping onto the rubble as well. "Now that that's over, what next?"

"Get to the queen," Josef said. "Before Lenette hears her daughter failed."

"What about..." Eli tapped Adela's body with his boot.

"They can handle it," Josef said, nodding over Eli's shoulder.

Eli turned to see the admiral and several guards marching toward them across the now-empty square. When he turned back, Josef was already off, trotting into the palace through the sundered wall with Nico hot on his heels. Muttering the usual curses about bullheaded swordsmen, Eli ran after them. Tesset followed a step behind, swift and silent as a shadow.

The wall the Heart had collapsed at this level turned out to be the outer wall of the pantry. Josef ran through the stocks of grain and flour, bursting through the door to the kitchen with a swift kick. The kitchen staff screamed and scrambled to get out of the prince's path. Eli called out apologies as he ran past, but he stayed right on Josef's heels as they cleared the kitchens and started up the servant's stair toward the queen's chambers.

They'd reached the third floor and were rushing toward the royal wing when Josef skidded to a stop, causing Nico and then Eli to run into him.

Eli poked his head around Josef's broad back. "What is it n—"

The question died in his throat. Queen Theresa was at the other end of the hall. She was in a dressing gown, her face sweat soaked and pale as death. Long white hair tumbled loose from her head, the wispy ends nearly brushing her bare feet. Lenette was at her side, and the queen clung to her with skeletal hands. A small knot of worried guards trailed behind them, following the queen and her lady as they made their way slowly down the hall.

It was Lenette who saw Josef first. Adela's mother stopped in her tracks, her face suddenly stricken, as though she'd seen a ghost. Theresa stumbled at the sudden stop and raised her head, her eyes lighting up as she saw her son.

"Josef," she said, her voice relieved. "They said you were fighting Adela."

Josef didn't seem to hear the queen. His eyes were locked on Lenette. "You," he hissed, marching forward. "Get away from my mother."

Nico started to follow, but Eli grabbed her shoulder. Lenette, on the other hand, stepped forward, putting herself between the queen and Josef.

"My queen!" she cried. "This man is a murderer. He killed his cousins and now he comes for you. Look at the blood on him." She clutched her chest with a sob. "Where is my daughter, killer?"

"Step away, Lenette!" Josef shouted, walking faster. "It's over. Adela confessed. We know everything. You're an agent of the Empress left here to destabilize Osera after the war, and you trained your daughter to follow in your footsteps. You've been poisoning the queen for years, but your treachery ends now. *Step away!*"

Theresa looked at her lady-in-waiting. "Lenette?"

But Lenette's face had changed. She glared at Josef with open hatred, and that was when Eli saw her hand flash.

"Josef!" he shouted.

He was too late. Lenette's hand flew from her skirts, the knife flashing silver before it plunged into the queen's chest. Josef and the guards rushed forward, dragging Lenette off the queen, but Lenette twisted free with surprising strength. She staggered, the knife dripping red in her hands.

"Long live the Empress," she said, raising the knife to her own throat.

Eli winced and turned away, but it didn't save him from the unmistakable *thump* as Lenette's body hit the floor. When he looked back, she was lying crumpled on the carpet at the center of a spreading, dark stain. Josef didn't even look at her. He dropped the Heart and ran to his mother, falling to his knees as he dragged the queen into his lap. Theresa's dressing gown was more crimson than white now, and her breath came in ragged little gasps. Her face, however, was calm.

"Josef," she whispered. "Listen."

"Stop talking," he said, pressing one hand against her wound as he slid his free arm under her. "We're going to get you to the surgeon."

"No," she ordered, grabbing his hand with surprising strength. "For once in your life, mind me."

Josef froze, letting his mother guide his hand up to her face.

"Listen," she said again. "You've never made a secret of how much you hated being a prince, and for that I've tried my best to spare you, but now I'm afraid we no longer have a choice." She took a shuddering breath. "The throne of Osera has endured for centuries. Through our history we have lived as outcasts and pirates, shunned by all. I spent my life pulling us out of that pit, turning Osera into a land of prosperity and peace. Now the Empress comes again, and now more than ever we *cannot* fall. Promise me, Josef. Promise, no matter what happens after, no matter your feelings, you will take the crown and lead our people through this crisis."

Josef gripped her hand. "Mother, this isn't—"

"*Promise me,*" the queen gasped, pulling herself up until her face was inches from her son's. "One last battle," she whispered, clutching his fingers. "Swear to me you will not let Osera perish."

Josef pressed his lips to her pale forehead. "I swear, mother," he whispered. "I swear it."

The queen fell back with a pained sigh. "You are all witnesses," she said, glancing at her guard. When they nodded, she turned back to Josef, reaching up to touch his cheek with her thin, bloody hand.

"Hail the House of Iron Lions," she whispered, her voice little more than a breath.

"Hail the House of Iron Lions," Josef repeated. "I will not fail you, mother."

For a moment, Eli thought he saw the queen smile. Then her body shuddered one last time, and she lay still.

The guards began to creep forward, but Josef didn't move. He sat on his knees, cradling his mother's skeletal body. He made no sound, no noise at all, but when the light shifted, Eli saw his cheeks were wet, and he realized Josef was crying. He looked away at once, painfully aware that he was seeing something he shouldn't. But the moment was just that, a moment, and by the time he'd turned away, it was over.

"You there," Josef said to the closest guard.

The guard stepped forward with a salute, and Josef stood up, bringing his mother's body with him. "Take the queen," he said, gently passing Theresa's body to the guard. "See that she is laid in state."

"Yes, majesty," the guard said softy, taking the queen as gently as he could.

Josef stepped back, his hands lingering on the dark stain that covered the front of his shirt, though whether it was his blood or his mother's, Eli couldn't tell.

"You." Josef looked at the next guard. "Bring someone to clean that up." He nodded at Lenette's body. "The rest of you, I want whoever's in charge of the military to report to the watchtower at once. Every man who can hold a sword is to report for duty immediately."

"Everyone, sir?" the guard said.

"Yes," Josef answered, scooping up the Heart as he marched down the hall. "The Empress is here. We're going to avenge our queen."

The guards looked at each other, their faces pale with disbelief. Then, in unison, they saluted and began to divide the prince's orders between them.

Eli watched them work for a second, and then he jogged after Josef.

"You're serious about this?"

"I made a promise," Josef said, walking faster. "I intend to see it through."

"All right," Eli said softly. "But if it's war we're talking about, I should point out that we have a problem."

Josef sighed. "What?"

"The Relay," Eli said. "Adela destroyed both of Osera's points. I don't know if you had a chance during all that to actually look at the ocean, but the Empress's fleet fills the horizon. There's no way Osera can stop all that on its own. If we're going to survive, we have to get word to the Council immediately for reinforcements."

"That's not a problem," Nico said.

Eli glanced at her. "Pardon?"

"We've got a Council representative following us."

Everyone stopped and looked at Tesset.

"What a remarkably good point, Nico," Eli said, all smiles.

"Don't get your hopes up," Tesset said. "I don't have a Relay point on me."

Eli blinked. "That's a bad joke, sir. You want me to believe that Sara let you loose without an ear in your pocket?"

"Relay points are short these days," Tesset said with a shrug. "And I *was* going to a country that had two points of its own."

"Well, that's just perfect," Josef grumbled, resuming his previous pace. "A Council watchdog with none of the benefits."

"You should be counting your luck," Tesset said, falling into step beside him. "I did just watch a known conspirator of the world's most notorious thief become king of Osera without comment, after all."

"Flattery will get you everywhere," Eli said. "But outing us would have hurt your cause too, so don't pretend you're doing us a favor. If you actually want to be useful, you could think of a way for us to get word to the mainland."

Tesset scratched his chin. "What about the Spirit Court? Osera has a Tower just like anywhere, and Spiritualists are always talking among themselves."

Eli looked at him, genuinely impressed. "That is a surprisingly good suggestion," he said. "To think, the Spirit Court, useful at last!"

By this time they'd reached the back door of the palace. A crowd of guards was waiting in the kitchen yard, whispering nervously as they stared down the mountain at the fleet stretching across the horizon.

"You," Eli said, grabbing the closest solider. "Would you be so kind as to fetch us Osera's Spiritualist?"

The guard stared at him in confusion. "Sir?"

"Do it," Josef snapped.

The guard, obviously not sure if the traitor prince's orders should be obeyed, took one look at Josef's bloody front and enormous sword and decided to save his doubts for later. He bowed and ran down the hall as fast as his legs could carry him, pausing only to salute the admiral as the old man appeared from another door flanked by the queen's guards who'd witnessed her death.

"Prince Thereson," the admiral said, falling to his knees at Josef's feet. "My king, I just heard. Forgive me for insulting you with my suspicions."

"Get up," Josef sighed. "We don't have time for this."

"Yes, my lord," the admiral said, standing.

"What's our situation?"

"Not good," the admiral said. "I've sent fast ships to all the villages and the bells should be ringing any moment now to summon the sailors to their posts. With any luck, the runners will be ready to sail within the hour, but without clingfire, I don't know—"

A great jangling racket of bells drowned out the rest of his report. More bells followed, until the entire city shook with the clanging sound.

"We'll cross that bridge when we get there," Josef shouted as a military carriage pulled up through the palace's eastern gate. "What about the guard?"

The admiral's face paled. "When the princess turned traitor, she killed out the barracks. The sergeant..."

"Beechum, sir," the closest guard put in.

"Beechum," the admiral said. "He's taking the body count as we speak, but it may be a while before we know how many guardsmen are still in service."

"Why so long?" Josef said as he climbed into the carriage.

"If I may, sir," the guard said, holding the carriage door as Eli, Nico, and the admiral climbed in after Josef. "The princess was our captain like Theresa was our queen. She raised most of us up from the city guard, and we were loyal to her like none other. Some of the men still don't believe she betrayed us. If I hadn't seen the queen's death with my own eyes..."

"She was certainly thorough in her treachery," Josef muttered, leaning out the tiny window. "Just tell the sergeant to send whatever guards he can down to the storm wall. Meanwhile, I want the city watch to start moving people toward the western docks. Get them as far from the east coast as you can. I want Osera empty if war spirits start falling. "

"Yes, sire," the guard said, saluting.

Josef saluted back, and the carriage pulled away with a lurch, leaving the guard to deliver the king's orders.

"I can't see how she could have put us in a worse position," the admiral said, rubbing a handkerchief across his ashy face as the carriage rattled out into the street. "The queen, the clingfire, and now the guard in shambles. She certainly knew where to hit us."

"Adela always was good at her job," Josef said quietly.

The admiral went paler still and kept any other opinions to himself.

The storm wall was crawling with sailors by the time they arrived. The man made way for the carriage, and the driver pulled them right up to the tower door. The admiral led Josef and his companions up the stairs, calling for his captains as they went. When they reached the top of the watchtower, Eli was pleased to see that the bodies from earlier had been removed. The stains on the wood floor remained, however. A grisly reminder.

"Right," Eli said, surveying the room and the commanding view of the sea. "This will be our headquarters. Can we get a map of the coastline?"

The admiral jerked. "I don't take orders from—"

"Eli's with me," Josef said firmly.

The admiral dropped his eyes. "Yes, majesty."

Eli smiled as the admiral turned and started toward the steps. "And don't forget my Spiritualist!"

The old admiral's shoulders twitched, but he nodded as he disappeared down the stairs.

"I could get used to this," Eli said, but Josef wasn't listening. He was standing at the window, his face pale as he stared at the now clearly visible line of ships on the horizon.

"Surely the master of the Heart of War is not afraid of death," Tesset said, stepping up beside him.

"Not mine," Josef whispered as the admiral returned with soldiers bearing tables and maps, which they set up under Eli's direction.

Thirty minutes later, news of the queen's death had spread throughout the city. Surprisingly, this seemed to calm the panic spurred by Josef's fight with Adela. Whatever his faults, Josef was an Eisenlowe, and with news of the princess's betrayal and the Empress's arrival spreading fast, having a murderer as a king suddenly didn't seem so bad. Riders moved constantly back and forth between the bay and the palace, bringing Josef reports. The royal guard had recovered faster than the admiral had estimated. Adela's betrayal had caught them hardest of all. Of the two hundred men once under the princess's command, half were now dead by her hand. This had galvanized the hundred that remained, however, and they marched to the coast to put themselves under Josef's command.

Men from the city were pouring down the mountain as well, answering the call of the bells to defend their homeland. They gathered on the storm wall, accepting their orders from the captains with stern-faced determination. Eli watched from the tower, impressed. He'd expected a riot, or at least more panic, but the people of Osera seemed to be handling the wave of change that had crashed into their kingdom by focusing on the one thing that was still the same—defending their home against the Empress.

The captains were dividing the crowd into crews when a carriage pulled onto the storm wall. A few minutes later, a guard poked his head into the watchtower and announced that Eli's Spiritualist had arrived.

"Excellent," Eli said. "Show him in."

The guard opened the door for an elderly man whose elegant jacket was cut short at the sleeves to show off his four large, jeweled rings. He stepped into the tower and stopped, casting disdainful looks at the soldiers huddled around the maps, particularly Josef.

"Spiritualist," Eli said, shaking his hand. "How nice to meet you."

"It's Tower Keeper," the old man said with a sniff, snatching his hand back. "Who are you? I was told the king wanted me."

"The king doesn't deal with 'wizard things,'" Eli said with a smile. "He leaves those to me."

He glanced pointedly down at Eli's empty fingers. "And again I say, who are you?"

"We have a bit of a crisis on our hands here," Eli said, ignoring the question. "I need you to send a message to Zarin."

"Why?" the Tower Keeper said suspiciously. "What's wrong with the Relay?"

"I've heard that Spiritualists have their own way of communicating with Zarin," Eli said. "*Outside* the Relay."

"Yes," the old man said testily. "They're called letters."

"I'm not talking about *letters*," Eli said. "I'm talking about emergency messages." He stopped and looked around pointedly, lowering his voice to a conspiratorial whisper. "Look, chum, the Relay's down and the Empress is about to fall on us like a hammer. We need to call for reinforcements immediately."

"The Relay, down..." The Tower Keeper's lined face turned ashy. "Powers, man, why didn't you call the Council earlier?"

"If we could have, we would have," Eli said. "If you Spiritualists have something up your sleeves, now's the time to show it."

"And I'm telling you we use letters!" the Tower Keeper cried. "An express courier switching horses can get a letter to Zarin in a day."

Eli stared at him. "You're kidding. The great and mighty Spirit Court uses *couriers*? That's *it*? What about wind spirits?"

"Wind spirits?" the Tower Keeper said, aghast. "Do you know anything about wizardry? There aren't five Spiritualists in the Court who've bound wind spirits. It's not like I'm just keeping one in my pocket."

Eli leaned back with a groan. "Please don't tell me I had it good with Miranda."

"Miranda?" The Tower Keeper jerked as though he'd stepped in something. "Lyonette? How do you know Banage's favorite?"

"I can hardly seem to avoid her," Eli said, ears perking up. "But why so bitter, Mr. Tower Keeper?"

"Bitter?" The man drew himself up to his full height. "Hardly, sir. Say what you like about our letters, but you're the one out of touch if you haven't heard that Banage's turned traitor. He refused to help the Council fight the Empress and shut himself up in the Tower. I imagine Lyonette is in there with him, along with all the other traitors."

Eli paused for a moment. "That is actually very interesting," he said finally. "And not entirely surprising." He sighed loudly. "Well, Mr. Tower Keeper, I'm afraid I've wasted your time. Thank you very much for coming. I'm sure someone will show you out."

The Tower Keeper looked at Eli with utter confusion, but Eli just turned him around by the shoulder and pushed him toward the soldiers. "See he gets home safely!"

The soldiers saluted and began to escort the Tower Keeper down the stairs. The old man recovered his wits about three steps in and began protesting loudly that the prince had sent for him personally. That was all Eli heard before the door slammed shut.

He caught Josef's eye and motioned him over.

Josef nodded to the admiral and stepped away from the map, joining Eli by the window. "Well?"

"No dice," Eli said. "I keep forgetting what a gulf in power there can be between Spiritualists."

"What about a broker?" Josef said. "They talk to each other, right?"

"Actually, that's a phenomenal idea," Eli said. "I never thought of using a broker to *send* information instead of finding it." He thought for a few seconds and then shook his head. "If we had more time I'd try it, but brokers go to ground when trouble comes, and I'm not about to waste the few hours we have trying to root one out now."

"What about Nico?" Josef said. "She can jump there."

"Who'd believe the Daughter of the Dead Mountain?" Eli said, biting his lip. "There's nothing for it. I'm just going to have to send a message myself."

"You?" Josef snorted. "If people won't believe Nico, they'll never believe you."

Eli held up his hands. "I admit, aside from you and Nico, there are very few people who know me well enough to know when I'm being sincere, and of those people, only one has the power to bring the kind of help we need. Fortunately, thanks to our guest, I have a pretty good idea where she is."

Josef gave him a horrified look. "You can't be serious."

"Normally I'd agree," Eli said. "But today is a serious sort of day. You worry about all that king nonsense. I'll take care of this."

Josef shook his head. "Just don't mess it up."

"Do I ever?" Eli said, but Josef was already walking back to his map.

Eli arched an eyebrow at the king's back and went to look for Nico. He found her deep in conversation with Tesset, of all people. He approached silently, hoping to catch a snatch of whatever it was they were talking about, but his efforts were fruitless. Both of them fell silent before he was close enough to hear anything.

She walked over when he beckoned. "Spiritualist didn't work?"

"Not at all," Eli said, glancing over her shoulder at Tesset, who was watching them. "What were you and the Council man talking about?"

"I was thanking him," Nico said. "His advice was very useful."

"Advice?" Eli said curiously. "What kind of advice?"

"Good advice," Nico said in a tone that signaled the end of that part of the conversation.

For once, Eli took the hint. "Glad to hear it. Now, I was hoping you could do a little repeat of our exercise earlier today. I need another wind."

"That's easy," Nico said. "They've been swarming ever since you talked to the first one. I think they want a wizard indebted to them as well."

"Really?" Eli grimaced. He hated owing favors, and winds were impossible to escape, but he had little choice at the moment. "Can you pick me out a fast one?"

Nico stared up at the afternoon sky for a moment before her hand shot out, pointing at something just above the horizon. "There."

Eli popped the latch on the window, opening it just enough to stick his hand out. He opened his spirit a crack as well, sending out a beckoning tendril of power. A few seconds later, a strong breeze rushed over his face.

"My," the wind whispered. "Aren't you a bright one? Are you the wizard making deals?"

"I am," Eli said. "And do I have a deal for you. How fast can you fly to Zarin?"

"Where?" the wind said.

"Large city," Eli said. "West of here on the mainland, white buildings, river through the middle?"

"Oh, there." The wind circled around them. "Fast enough, if I have reason to hurry. Why?"

"I need you to take a message to the Spirit Court."

"That'll cost you," the wind huffed. "Spiritualists can be pompous."

"That they can," Eli said. "But a powerful, clever wind can make them listen, I'm sure."

"Of course," the wind said. "If the price is right."

"Friend," Eli said, leaning into the breeze. "Today's your lucky day."

The wind rushed away from the watchtower feeling extremely pleased with itself. For being a gullible sap, the bright wizard certainly knew how to sweeten a deal. The promise of a personal debt from the human who'd freed Mellinor was a prize indeed, and all for passing on a few words. Plus, he'd been so nice looking, so bright. The wind spun in a circle. It wasn't every day you met a wizard like that.

By this point, the wind had cleared the strip of ocean between the island and the mainland. It dipped on the warm air, readying itself for the straight push overland to the white city with the tall towers. But as the wind turned west, it jerked to a stop, frozen in the air. For five long seconds the wind hovered, completely unable to move, and then it curled in a deep bow.

"All hail the lord of the west."

The air flickered as the West Wind suddenly filled the sky, his breezes reaching as far as the wind could see. "Where are you off to in such a hurry, little wind?"

"Zarin," the wind answered, trembling against the West Wind's hold. "I promised a wizard I would bring a message to Spiritualist Miranda Lyonette."

"I see," Illir said. "And the wizard who gave you this message, he was a bright wizard, was he not?"

"The brightest I have ever seen, my lord," the wind whispered.

"Thought so," Illir said. "Very well, give me the message. I will deliver it."

The wind hesitated. "But," it whispered. "My deal—"

"Nothing *that* wizard promises ever comes out as you would like," Illir said. "I'm taking the message. Give it to me and you will have my high regard."

"Yes, Lord Illir," the wind whispered, trembling as it repeated the bright wizard's words.

"Thank you," Illir said, freeing the little wind with a toss of his gale. "You may go."

"Yes, my lord," the wind whispered, bowing. "Thank you, my lord."

But Illir was already gone, flying across the sky with the impossible speed only the greatest winds could dream of. With a great sigh, the little wind sped away to brag to its brothers about how Illir himself had stopped just for it, the wizard's deal already forgotten.

CHAPTER

19

After ten hours of sleep, a bath, and an enormous breakfast, Miranda was a new woman, and the first thing she'd done with her newfound energy was attack the restricted shelves of the Spirit Court archives. She'd spent all morning reading spectacular stories of Spiritualists doing the impossible—talking down erupting volcanoes, brokering peace between warring rivers, even ending a five-year drought by freeing a wind spirit whose capture by an Enslaver had so angered the wind courts that they'd held off the rain in retaliation. There was even a description of the meeting four hundred years ago between the first Rector of the Spirit Court and the Shaper Mountain that had led to the raising of the Spirit Court's Tower in a single day. The actual deed the Tower was in thanks for had been carefully omitted, but Miranda's frustration was soothed by the dozens of secrets that hadn't been crossed out.

For someone who'd given her life to the Court, it was breathtaking reading. It was also infuriating. All of the restricted reports dealt in one way or another with a star. Of course, they were never *called* stars, but now that Miranda knew what she was looking for, it was easy enough to read through the sometimes excruciatingly vague language and find the truth. The Spirit Court had encountered stars numerous times over centuries of enforcing the good treatment of spirits, but every time the real nature of these greater than Great Spirits had been hushed up and locked away in the archives. It was enough to make Miranda grind her teeth to stubs.

"I don't understand," she said, yet again. "What's the point of hiding this? If we were only taught about stars, told these stories… Look here, the great river Ell that runs through the southern kingdoms is a star. All that time we spent two years ago badgering the Felltris River to flood the fields and not the houses? Wasted. We could have solved the whole thing with one trip down to the southern delta to chat with the river all the others have to listen to."

Gin flattened his ears against his head with a whine. "Can you *please* stop talking about stars? You're going to get us all in trouble."

"*In trouble with whom?*" Miranda said, slamming down the report and spinning around in her chair.

Gin looked away.

"You mean the Shep—"

"Stop," Gin growled, lashing his tail. "Don't say her name. It attracts her attention."

"Fine with me," Miranda said, crossing her arms. "There are several things I want to ask her."

"Get in line," Mellinor rumbled bitterly. "But if the Shepherdess could be appealed to, I wouldn't have spent four centuries locked in a pillar of salt."

"Mellinor," Gin said in a warning tone.

"No," Mellinor said. "I don't care if it's forbidden to speak of the Shepherdess's business with humans. The Shaper Mountain already broke the edicts. Why should we bother keeping them?"

"The Shaper Mountain is one of the oldest spirits in the world," Gin said. "He's also the biggest. He can afford to take risks."

"So can we," Miranda said firmly. "Slorn said the Shaper Mountain showed us the truth for a reason."

Gin snorted. "Yes, because the mountain knows you're ignorant. The old rock pile wants you to take the fall for asking questions spirits shouldn't ask."

"What do you mean?"

The ghosthound sighed. "There are things that it's better not to know, Miranda. And just because some great mountain and his pet bear man are fed up with the Shepherdess's antics doesn't mean you should go putting yourself in danger."

"If the Shepherdess isn't doing what she should, then I have to take action, danger or no," Miranda snapped. "I'm sworn to protect the spirits."

"Good," Gin snapped back. "So do that. Kill Enslavers, stop abusive wizards, but don't go poking your nose where it'll get bitten off."

Miranda turned away with a huff. Gin crouched low, his swirling fur moving in quick little patterns, and Mellinor began to rumble.

"Listen," she said, calmly now. "Whatever happens from here out, I'm always going to choose the path that leads to a better, fairer world for all of us. That's my job. That's why I became a Spiritualist. And if that path leads me off a cliff, then so be it, but I will not turn back. If you don't like it, you don't have to follow."

Gin bared his teeth. "Don't even try," he growled. "I go where you go, no matter how reckless or stupid. But that doesn't mean I have to keep my mouth shut about it."

Miranda couldn't help grinning at that. "Nothing could make you keep your mouth shut, mutt."

Gin snorted and put his head on his paws. "Better put away your reading. Someone's coming."

Miranda glanced at the door a split second before the knock sounded. Gin gave her a superior look, and Miranda rolled her eyes. She stood up, carefully marking her place before closing the record book, and walked to the reading room door. A young man in apprentice robes was standing on the other side. His face lit up when he saw her.

"Spiritualist Lyonette? Master Banage wants to see you at the top of the Tower. He says it's urgent."

"The top of the Tower?" Miranda said, wrinkling her nose. "You mean his office?"

"No, ma'am," the apprentice said, shaking his head. "He said the top."

"The top?" Gin said, suddenly behind her. He grinned, showing a wall of teeth. "I've never been to the top."

"Neither have I," Miranda said, elbowing her dog. The apprentice was staring at Gin's teeth like he might faint. "Take us there."

"Yes, Spiritualist," the boy said, starting down the hall sideways so he wouldn't have to put his back to Gin. "This way."

Miranda shook her head and followed. Behind her, Gin crawled through the door, slipping his long body through the small opening with practiced ease. They climbed up and up, past floors of meeting rooms, guest rooms, and storerooms, until they reached the landing outside the Rector's office. This was where the stairs usually ended, but now there was a new opening in the wall beside the Rector's office door, a set of stairs Miranda had never seen before, leading up.

"We can make it from here," she said, smiling at the apprentice. "Thank you for your service."

"It is an honor to serve, Spiritualist," the boy said with a half-hearted bow. After a final, terrified glance at Gin, he vanished down the stairs like a frightened rabbit.

"That one knows his place," Gin said, flipping his tail smugly.

"Stop it," Miranda muttered, starting up the new stairwell. "You'd better stay here."

Gin growled and sat, ears turned forward so he wouldn't miss anything.

The new stairs wound up for a dozen feet before stopping at a little stone door barely larger than she was. It opened when Miranda touched it, and a blast of wind nearly blew her back down the stairs. The door let out on the very top of the Tower's spire. Below, she could see all of Zarin and the plains beyond. The white buildings were almost blinding in the afternoon sun, and the Whitefall River was little more than a glittering thread between the dark shapes of the bridges and barges. The wind roared around her, and for a moment Miranda was afraid it would blow her off altogether. Thankfully, the door was set back in the Tower's spire, and the tiny alcove provided just enough shelter to keep the wind from ripping her off the Tower. Master Banage was already here, standing with his back pressed against the stone and his head tilted up toward the sky.

"Miranda," he said in a voice that carried over the wind. "Glad you could join us."

The moment he said it, Miranda felt the truth. The wind howling around them wasn't the usual gusts found this high up. There was a familiar heaviness to it, a great spiritual pressure that made her ears pop, and she didn't need Eril's frantic clamor to know who, or what, she was facing.

"Lord Illir," she said, clutching her wind spirit's shaking pendant against her chest. "It is a pleasure to meet you again."

"Pleasure tainted with crisis, I'm afraid," the wind hummed around her. "Let the little one pay his respects before he bursts."

Miranda let Eril fly at once. The smaller wind tore out of his necklace, spinning in a reverent circle before returning to Miranda's side.

She exchanged a brief look with Master Banage, and then the Rector Spiritualis stepped out a fraction and addressed the wind. "Lord of the West, Miranda Lyonette is here, as you asked. Now, how may we help you?"

"I bring a message," the great wind said. "From Osera."

That threw Miranda. Who in Osera could use one of the four great winds as a messenger?

"The Immortal Empress has arrived," the wind continued. "Her ships will reach Osera by evening, if not sooner. War is here."

Miranda and Banage exchanged a wide-eyed look, and then Miranda looked toward the Council's citadel. It looked the same as ever—no panic, no surge of troops.

"They don't know," the wind said, answering her question before she could ask it. "And they won't, unless you tell them. Osera's Relay points were destroyed by a traitor on the inside. That is why I've come." There was a shift in air pressure as the wind turned to focus on Banage. "I know you have declared that your Court will not enter the human's war, but I am here to ask you, on behalf of all spirits on this continent, not to let the Empress land on this shore."

For the first time in all their years together, Miranda saw Master Banage look completely bewildered.

"How do you know..." he said, and then shook his head. "Never mind. Why do you care what human rules this land? The Court will always look after you no matter who calls themselves Merchant Prince or Empress."

"You don't understand," the wind rumbled. "If the Immortal Empress were only human, I would agree with you. But she is more, far more."

Banage scowled. "What do you mean 'more'?"

"I cannot tell you," the wind said. "It is forbidden, even for me."

Miranda frowned. Forbidden? Even for a spirit as great as the West Wind? But as she tried to puzzle out what Illir meant by that, the wind shifted and grew colder. Suddenly, she could smell cold stone, snow, and thin high air. The smell of the mountain filled her lungs, and everything came together.

"The Empress is a star."

"What?" Banage turned to her. "Impossible. The Empress is human."

"Humans are spirits as well," the wind said. "And the Empress is not called Immortal for show."

The blood drained from the Rector's face. "Then the obedience I saw?" he whispered. "The war spirit's devotion?"

"Any devotion you saw is the result of the obedience stars command," the wind said. "She is no Enslaver, so I doubt you would feel anything wrong, but the truth of her control is almost worse. Enslavers are human. They can be defeated. They can die. But the Empress is immortal, her life held sacred by the White Lady. Her control over the spirit world is complete, eternal, and inescapable. To disobey a star is to disobey the Shepherdess herself."

The West Wind grew cold enough to make Miranda shiver. "The Empress comes here to bring the whole world under her control, but I am the West Wind. I am freedom itself. The winds have no star; we have no need of one. It is not our nature to serve, but if the Empress comes here, we won't have a choice. Nothing will. So I am asking you as a spirit, as the voice of all spirits on this continent who as yet have no idea of what they are about to lose, fight the Empress."

"How?" Miranda said. "My spirits couldn't go against the Shaper Mountain even to set me free. What can we do against the Empress?"

"Your spirits could not," the wind said. "But you are different. Even a star cannot change the laws of magic. Immortal though she may be, the Empress is still human, and no human spirit can force another. That's why she needs an army to beat her human opponents the old-fashioned way, and that's why you humans are the only ones who can stop her and save us."

Miranda looked at Banage, but he was gripping the Tower wall, his face deathly pale. "How could I have been so mistaken?" he whispered. "All this time I thought spirits obeyed the Empress out of love and respect, as our spirits obey us."

"That is our own fault," the wind said. "We are forbidden from speaking of the stars to humans. It is the Shepherdess's will that you stay ignorant. Really, I shouldn't even be talking to you, but the secret's already out, told by a star, no less."

"Wait," Miranda said. "The Shaper Mountain told you about us?"

"No," the wind said coyly. "But I always find out. The wind is everywhere, Miranda. You should know that by now."

"Our path is clear," Banage said, straightening up. "We must fight. Star or not, the Empress is human. Though she's not technically an Enslaver, I think we can all agree that controlling spirits by force is an abuse the Court cannot tolerate."

"We must warn the Council and get down there as soon as we can," Miranda said, looking up at Illir. "You said she was landing in Osera?"

"Yes," the wind said. "And precious little stands in her way."

"Then we will ride at once," Banage said.

"Hurry," the wind whispered.

"Wait!" Miranda cried as the wind turned. "Why did you not ask our help earlier?"

"I could not," the wind sighed. "All spirits are forbidden from interfering in a star's affairs by order of the Shepherdess. The Shaper Mountain might have told you about stars, but talking about them and asking for help in fending one off are entirely different matters. Were it not for this message, or, more correctly, for the wizard who sent it, I couldn't have asked your help in this at all."

Banage scowled. "What wizard is powerful enough to command you to break the Shepherdess's law?"

The wind turned, and Miranda got the feeling it was smiling. "I believe you call him Eli Monpress."

The tower fell utterly silent. Miranda and Banage stood stunned, unable to speak, and the wind used this gap to make his exit. As the pressure of the Great Spirit faded, Miranda clenched her hands into angry fists.

"Always," she muttered. "I swear, he's always at the center of everything that goes wrong in the world."

"It doesn't matter," Banage said quietly, running his hands over his face. "We have to get to Osera."

"At least the Council will be with us now," Miranda said. "If we're going to fight the Empress, then we have no more quarrel with Whitefall."

"I fear it's too late for that," Banage said. "Look down."

Confused, Miranda grabbed the wall and leaned out, peeking over the Tower's edge. It was a terrifying view. She'd never really appreciated how tall the Tower was until she was looking straight down it with nothing but her own grip for an anchor. Still, it wasn't the height that made her flinch back.

Directly below, the Spirit Court's district was no longer empty. Soldiers in Council white circled the Tower on every side. There had to be a quarter legion of infantry down there with another squad of archers on the rooftops to back them up. But worse than the soldiers was the line of wagons set up across the main boulevard and watched over by a small figure standing beside a man wearing a pink coat so vivid Miranda could see it from the Tower's peak.

"Sara," she hissed, leaning back.

Banage nodded. "They've been setting up since shortly after

dawn. Apparently, Whitefall has decided he cannot afford to harbor traitors."

"But we haven't done anything except sit here!" Miranda cried.

"We," Banage stopped. "*I* refused to help. Whitefall's played the game of nations long enough to know that those who won't be allies will eventually be enemies. He's taking us out early rather than risk us at his back while he's fighting the Empress."

"What are we going to do?" Miranda said. "We have to get to Osera. *They* have to get to Osera, while there's still an Osera to get to."

"Then we'll have to hope they'll listen to reason," Banage said.

Miranda bit her lip. "I hate to say this, master, but they're never going to believe you've changed your mind."

"They'd also never believe I'd tell a lie to save my skin," Banage said. "Being intractable has its advantages as well as its pitfalls."

Miranda gaped at him in disbelief. "Master Banage," she whispered. "Was that a joke?"

Banage looked almost affronted. "I have been known to tell them on occasion," he said, starting down the stairs. "Come, we don't have time to stand around with our mouths open."

Shaking her head in wonder, Miranda hurried down the stairs after her master as the Rector Spiritualis called for the Tower to spread the word. The Spirit Court was going to war.

"How much longer does Myron mean to make us wait?" Sara grumbled, trailing smoke as she stalked back and forth in front of her wagon. "He has an entire city full of soldiers. How long can it take to surround one tower?"

"I think the good general is dragging his feet on purpose," Sparrow said, buttoning his garish pink coat against the wind. "He doesn't care much for wizard business, after all."

"And I don't care for standing around," Sara snarled. "We were supposed to crack the Tower at ten. It's nearly noon."

"Well, here's your chance to tell him yourself," Sparrow said, nodding at the knot of armored men riding toward them.

Sara turned and marched toward the riders, biting her pipe as the leader, Myron Whitefall, the Council's general, dismounted.

"Are you done wasting my time?" she cried over the clatter of the horses.

"Only if you're done wasting mine," Myron answered. "I have a war to prepare for, Sara. The Empress could arrive as early as next month. I don't have men to waste on your marital spats."

Sara lifted her chin. "Try fighting the Empress without the wizards that I'm going to get by cracking this Tower and then say that again, Myron."

Myron's reply was predictably nasty, but Sara wasn't listening anymore. Sparrow had touched her arm. She turned, and her eyes widened. "I don't believe it."

"What?" Myron snapped. "That you're a waste of Council resources and—"

His voice sputtered out as Sara hurried away. She ran to the front of her wagons and stopped, watching in amazement as the blank face of the Tower peeled open like a curl of shaved wood and Banage himself stepped out into the sunlight. He was dressed in a dark suit with the great gold and jeweled mantle of the Tower on his shoulders. Bow strings creaked as the Council archers trained their arrows at his chest, but Banage paid them no mind. He just stood there, glaring defiantly at Sara with his arms crossed over his chest.

"I'd never believe it if I wasn't seeing it myself," Sara said, grinning around her pipe. "Have you come to your senses at last, Etmon?"

"I never took leave of them, Sara," Banage answered, glancing at the gathered troops in disdain. "Unlike some."

"That's enough, traitor!" Myron shouted, recovering at last. "You have exactly three seconds to surrender before—"

Sara rolled right over him. "What brings you out of your little spire? I can't believe you're giving up."

Banage straightened. "You can't 'give up' being right, Sara. But the situation is no longer what it was." He reached out his arm, pointing east with one ring-covered finger. "The Empress has arrived. She is about to attack Osera, if she hasn't already."

"Are you mad?" Sara laughed. "We've heard nothing of the sort."

"You wouldn't," Banage said. "Both of Osera's Relay points were broken this morning, just before the ships appeared."

Never taking her eyes off Banage, Sara reached down, sorting through her pouch for the two orbs that controlled Osera's Relays. She brushed each of them with her spirit, probing the connection. But her prod faded off into nothing. There was no echo, no reply.

Her mouth pressed into a thin line against the narrow stem of her pipe. "It seems the Rector is right," she said slowly.

"That's impossible!" Myron shouted, stomping up to stand beside her at last. "We heard the Empress shipyards were reactivated only a week ago. Even if she'd sailed that day, there's no way the Empress could have a fleet here so quickly. It's a bluff!"

"He doesn't bluff," Sara said with a sigh. "But even if you're right, and the Empress *is* about to attack, it doesn't explain what you're doing out, Etmon. The whole reason I'm standing here is because you swore up and down that your Court would never go to war."

Banage stiffened. "We have our reasons, Sara. Unfortunately, I am not at liberty to share them. You will remove your troops and let us pass. There is no time to waste."

"Enough," Myron said. "Do you think just because you've decided to fight that you can do as you please? The Merchant Prince's order is still in effect. The Spirit Court is under the control of the Council. You'll do as we tell you."

"The Spirit Court obeys no laws but its own," Banage said, his voice deepening as the mantle on his shoulders began to glow. "Step aside, General."

As he spoke, the ground began to rumble. All across Zarin, buildings began to shake. Windows rattled against their panes and awnings rippled like water above the merchant stands. Down on the river, barges rocked and bumped together. Even the Whitefall Citadel was shaking, its golden-roofed towers trembling in the sunlight.

Back at the Spirit Court's tower, the Council soldiers gripped their swords, bracing their feet against the shaking ground. Myron grabbed Sara's wagon, his face as pale as cheese. Sara smacked his hand away, blowing out a huff of smoke.

"Enough dramatics, Etmon," she said. "Myron, move your troops and let them through."

Myron gaped at her. "What? You can't be—"

"Do it," Sara said.

The general's face went from pale to scarlet, but Sara cut off his tirade before it could start. "*Now*, Myron. That mantle of his is tied to the great bedrock spirit that runs below Zarin. He can destroy this city in a heartbeat if he wants to. I'm not about to risk that to keep him from doing what we were trying to make him do in the first place."

"But, Sara," Myron's voice was almost pleading. "He could be lying."

"He's not lying," Sara said.

Myron snarled. "How do you know that?"

"Because the world's not ending," Sara said with a sigh. "Move your men, Myron. That's an order."

She smacked her closest wagon, and it began to trundle out of the way. The other wagons followed, each wheeling itself over to the side of the road. Myron sputtered a moment before turning on

his heel, waving for his men to follow. As the Council soldiers reluctantly cleared a path, the shaking stopped. Banage stepped back
into the Tower, and Sara peered through the hole to see him removing his heavy gold mantle. She arched an eyebrow as he handed the
gem-studded chain of his office to old Krigel before stepping out of
sight.

When the road was clear, Banage came out again. With a final
glare at Sara, he held out his hand. The heavy ring on his middle
finger flashed dark green, and his enormous jade horse erupted out
of the ground beside him. It knelt so Banage could climb onto its
back. The moment he was seated, the Spirit Court rode out. They
flashed down the street, Banage first on his jade horse followed by
Miranda on her ghosthound. The dog snapped at Sparrow as they
passed, but Sparrow looked more amused than frightened as he
leaned out of the way. They were gone in an instant, replaced by
more Spiritualists, apprentices, Tower Keepers, journeymen, everyone in the stone spire who'd ever sworn an oath. Sara sucked on her
pipe, more interested than ever. Whatever caused this change of
heart, it was deathly serious if Banage was emptying the Tower.

The Spiritualists thundered down the street and vanished into
the city at full speed, riding east as fast as they could. The soldiers
watched in awe as the wizards rode by, keeping well out of the way
of the sand tigers, stone snakes, and, of course, the ghosthound.
When the last Spiritualist was out of sight, Myron turned to Sara.

"What do we do now?" he asked, his voice uncharacteristically
bewildered.

"Well," Sara said, tapping out her pipe. "*You* had better get on
those Relay points I've been giving you and start ordering the
Council fleet to Osera. You should probably also warn Alber that
the Empress is running ahead of schedule."

"And what are you going to do?" Myron said, his face pale.

Sara just smiled and walked away. She snapped her fingers as she went, and with each snap, a wagon rolled out. Sparrow jumped onto the driver's seat of the largest and lowered his hand to Sara. She took it, and he pulled her up. The moment her feet left the ground, the wagons tore off down the road, following the trail of dust left by the Spiritualists until they too vanished into the city.

Myron Whitefall stood staring for several moments. Finally, he turned and began shouting for his Relays. Within the hour, the news had spread across the continent. The Empress had arrived. The Council was going to war.

CHAPTER

20

Josef Liechten, king of Osera for nearly two hours, stood at the watchtower window. Eli stood beside him, watching the sea with an uncharacteristically serious expression on his face. He'd finally ditched the ridiculous blond wig, and even his hair looked subdued after so many days of being pinned down.

"Not you too," Josef grumbled, glancing at his friend. "If you're looking gloomy I might start thinking we really are doomed."

"Well," Eli said softly. "That *is* a lot of ships."

Josef looked back at the sea. "That it is."

The Empress's armada stretched from horizon to horizon. Black ships, each the size of a small city, rode deep and heavy in the water. Their sides were like cliffs, rising a hundred feet above the ocean's surface. Their masts were great towers, and their decks swarmed with countless men in black armor. Josef swallowed. He'd seen paintings of the Empress's ships before, but nothing could have prepared him for their true size. For the first time in his life, he understood why they were called palace ships.

"Majesty?"

Josef looked to see the admiral standing in the door. "The fleet is ready, sir."

"Good," Josef said. He turned to go, but stopped again as Eli's hand closed on his wrist.

"Are you sure about this?" Eli whispered.

"Doesn't matter," Josef said. "If even one of those ships makes landfall, we'll be overrun. Our only hope is to sink them before they reach the shore. The real question is, are you sure you can hold up your end of the plan?"

"Not in the least," Eli said with a broad smile. "But we're going to try." As he said this, he laid his hand on his chest, just above the burn that held his lava spirit.

Josef nodded and started for the door. "Tell Nico to meet me on the ships when she gets back. And Eli," he said, glancing over his shoulder. "Good luck."

"You too," Eli said.

Josef waved and stomped down the stairs. When he reached the landing, he saw Eli turn back toward the window, his face strangely determined, almost angry. The light around him seemed wrong, too white for this time of the afternoon. And then, as the door swung, Josef caught a glimpse of what looked like a woman's white arm slide around Eli's chest. Josef froze as the door clicked shut, and then he shook his head. It was way too early in the fight for him to be seeing things. He took a deep breath to clear his mind and hurried down the stairs.

Eli stood perfectly still as the Shepherdess wrapped herself around him from behind.

Why so dour, darling? she whispered in his ear. *I told you this was coming, didn't I?*

Eli closed his eyes. "I was wondering when you'd show up."

Benehime laughed in delight and spun him around. *You were waiting for me?*

"Don't get the wrong idea," Eli said, pulling away. He reached out, pointing to the endless line of ships. "Did you do this?"

Benehime tilted her head. *Do what?*

Eli had to fight to keep the shaking rage out of his voice. "You said that the Empress was coming to kill me in revenge for taking you away. Did she think of that herself, or did you plant the idea in her head?"

What a thing to say. Benehime pulled her arms back with a pained expression. *I'm the Shepherdess. I don't start wars.* She paused, waiting for Eli's expression to soften. When it didn't, she walked to the window with a sigh. *I don't see how this is so difficult for you to grasp, love. Nara is a warrior; war is her nature. What other retaliation can she have but to come and kill the one who stole me from her?*

"She could be mad at you," Eli snapped. "You were the one who left. I was eleven and unconscious when you made me your favorite. That hardly counts as stealing."

She can't be angry with me, Benehime said, her voice ringing with musical laughter. *Nara loves me. Everything does. You said it yourself.*

Eli could feel the anger boiling up his body, and he forced himself to bite his tongue before he said something he'd regret. Beside him, the floor creaked in reverence as Benehime leaned over and laced her arms around him.

Don't be stubborn, darling, she whispered, pulling him close. *I don't want this war any more than you do, but I can't help you unless you ask. Your rule, remember? Not mine. Even so, I tried to warn you. I told you to come home, but you never listen.*

Eli jerked out of her grip. "The moment you say something that isn't self-serving, I will."

Benehime's eyes narrowed, and her fingers tightened, digging into his shoulders like claws. *Must you always be so stubborn?* she hissed, pulling him against her with terrifying strength. *How can you stand there and play that you're still capable of getting by on your own? Give up, darling! It's over. You and I both know your swordsman's pathetic little country has no hope of beating the Empress. All those men down there are going to die if you don't ask for my help, maybe your Josef along with them. Can you bear that much blood on your hands?*

"Blood on *my* hands?"

The words ripped out of him before he could stop them. This was too far.

"What of that is my fault?" he cried. "*You* were the one who abandoned the Empress. *You* were the one who made me your favorite. I had no say in any of it! I was a child. All I wanted was to live my own life. Now the Immortal Empress is here to destroy a kingdom in order to kill me because you don't care for her anymore, and you're saying the blood is on *my* hands?"

Dress it up however you like to make yourself feel better, Benehime said, her white face cold and haughty. *Nothing changes the fact that you could stop this war right now. All you have to do is draw on my power, your rightful power as my star, and you could set everything right, but you won't. People and spirits are going to die today, and it's all because you're a prideful, hateful boy who's too stubborn to know his place and come back home where he belongs.*

"You think I don't want to go back because of *pride*?" Eli shouted. "Do you have any idea what it was like to live with you?"

Benehime's voice grew frigid. *Yes,* she hissed. *It was paradise, but you were too spoiled to know it.*

Eli squeezed his eyes shut. He was going too far. The Shepherdess was very dangerous when she got cold, but he was so sick of this. So sick of walking the line of her favor. So sick of pretending.

"I'm not going to ask for your help, Benehime," he said, his voice as cold as hers when he opened his eyes again. "I'm not going to use any power you gave me. And I'm *never* coming back to you."

The temperature in the room dropped as the Shepherdess studied him. *You shouldn't tell lies, Eliton.*

Eli balled his hands to fists at his sides. "I'm not lying."

The Shepherdess looked at him a moment longer with that cold, terrible expression, and then she turned away. *We'll see how you hold on to that arrogance once the dying starts,* she said, her voice tight. *I will see you soon, beloved, and when I do, it will be on your knees.* She looked over her shoulder one last time. *That I can promise you.*

She pursed her lips in a silent kiss, and then she was gone, vanishing through a white hole in the air.

Eli stood with his fists clenched and his chest straining, holding in all the foul names he desperately wanted to fling after her. Some risks were too great even in his anger, but he didn't hide the look of disgust as he turned away from the empty air where she had vanished and began marching toward the door.

"Eli?" Karon whispered cautiously. "What are you doing?"

"What do you think?" Eli snapped, nearly pulling the door off its hinges. "We're going downstairs, and we're going to help Josef win this bloody war." And he was never going back to her. Never. *Never.*

Karon didn't say another word as Eli took the stairs three at a time down to the storm wall.

Josef's admiral was waiting for him on the vertical stair leading down the storm wall to the bay. Tesset was standing beside him. They both stepped aside to make room as Josef joined them.

"You coming out on the water with us?" Josef said, studying the Council man.

Tesset smiled politely. "Absolutely not. I don't care for boats, and I have a feeling I'll be more useful here."

"Have it your way," Josef said. "But it'll be a boring post. Nothing's getting to the shore."

"Consider me as insurance," Tesset said. "On the off chance anything should slip by your blockade."

Josef shook his head and pushed by, slapping Tesset on the shoulder as he passed. Tesset didn't even wobble under the blow. He just stood there, smiling as he watched Josef and the admiral head down to the beach.

"Are the boats supplied like we talked about?" Josef asked, taking the steep, treacherous steps two at a time.

"Yes, majesty," the admiral said. "All our remaining clingfire has been loaded, though I don't know what good it'll do."

"We only need a little," Josef said. He jumped the last stair and hit the sand running. All the boats but one were already out in the water. The last and largest, the Oseran flagship, was waiting for him at the end of the dock. It was a beautiful runner, twenty feet long and narrow as a barrel with a crew of fifteen strong oarsmen as well as a high, narrow sail. The men saluted as Josef ran up the plank, jumping onto the deck with a force that rocked the ship.

"I've put archers on the cliffs to cover your retreat, my lord," the admiral said from the dock. "Remember, there's only two hours left until the tide. I'll set the signal fire thirty minutes before. You'll have that much time to get in."

"More than enough," said the flagship captain, an enormous sailor who looked like he'd spent his life on the sea. He turned to Josef, and the swordsman saw a flicker of disgust on the sailor's face. Josef tensed. King he might be, but most of Osera still thought he was dirt. But whatever the captain's private feelings, he hid them with the discipline that made the Oseran navy famous.

"On your word, sire," he said with a sharp salute.

"Go," Josef said, moving up to the prow of the ship.

The moment the word was given, the deck jerked under his feet as the oars hit the water, and the narrow ship darted into the bay. The other ships rocked to life as well, falling in behind the king's flagship as the fleet shot out of the sheltered Rebuke and into the blue water of the open sea.

Josef stood on the prow, letting his body adjust to the wind and the pitch of the boat. He'd almost got it when the boat suddenly dipped. Josef turned as the sailors cried in alarm, and his face broke into a smile as he saw Nico stepping out of the shadows beneath the mast.

"We're fine," Josef said. "She's with me."

This didn't seem to reassure the sailors, but they kept rowing, glancing sideways at Nico as she squinted at Josef from beneath her dark hood.

"How'd it go?" Josef said.

"Pretty well," Nico answered. "I went to every one of the outer villages just like you said. They didn't believe me at first, but once I pointed out the Empress's ships, they went along just fine. The catapults are being set up right now. If a palace ship gets within two hundred feet of the outer island shores, it'll be bombarded."

"Good," Josef said. "Won't be enough to sink a palace ship, but a barrage will make landing troops hairy. That'll have to be enough to protect our flank for now." He squeezed Nico's arm and stepped past her, climbing back up on the prow so he could look the rowers in the eye. "Listen up!" he shouted. "The admiral and I explained this earlier, but since we're the flagship and everyone's following our lead, I'm going to say it again. We're not out here to fight the Empress's fleet. Our only objective is to stop her advance long enough for reinforcements to arrive from the mainland."

He threw out his arm and pointed down at the water. This far out, it was beautifully clear. Down below, the shadow of their boat shot across the bright, rocky reef that waited thirty feet below the waves, the natural barrier between their island and the sea. "See that?" Josef said, stabbing his finger at the reef. "That's our weapon. All we have to do is hold them over the shallows and let the tide do our work for us."

The captain gritted his teeth. "Begging your pardon, majesty, but how are we going to hold ships that big with no clingfire? The admiral said you had some kind of secret weapon, but, and I ain't intending to be speaking above my station, I don't see nothing on you but a big metal bar."

Josef grinned wide and reached over his shoulder, drawing the Heart in a smooth arc. "This big metal bar is all we need. Just row where I tell you to go. I'll do the rest."

"Aye, sire," the captain said, though he couldn't hide the tremble in his voice. "Full ahead."

The flagship shot forward, cutting through the water like a knife toward the front line of the palace ships.

The Empress's fleet slowed to meet them, the palace ships halting their unnatural speed as they reached the edge of the reef. Josef fell to a crouch. The other runners had fanned themselves out around the flagship and were keeping pace, just as they were supposed to. Josef was just starting to feel good about this whole crazy operation when he felt Nico tense beside him.

"What?" he said, glancing at her.

Nico was staring straight ahead, eyes wide. "Was there always an island there?"

"What are you talking about?"

Nico pointed at the sky behind the palace ships. Josef squinted against the bright sun, and then his eyes went wide as he saw it too. There, rising like a specter over the enemy fleet, was the shadowy shape of a large, rocky island. But that was impossible. Osera was the last land in these waters. Yet there it was, sturdy and large as any of the Oseran mountain islands. Even this far away, Josef could make out the shape of buildings clinging to the island's rocky slope. Buildings in a style he'd never seen before.

His blood began to run cold, but even as the fear rose, Josef made himself let it go. "Forget it," he said, raising his voice. "Nothing has changed! Full ahead!"

"Aye, sire," the captain said. "Steady!"

The sailors obeyed, and the Oseran fleet flew at the line of palace ships like a tiny bird flying at a wall that spans the world.

Nara stood on the balcony of her war palace, watching the tiny specs of the Oseran fleet approaching her front line. Her ornate sword was out and naked in her hand, a rare sight, and one that made her general extremely uncomfortable.

"Hail, Empress," he said after waiting a solid minute for her to notice he was there.

"One of the Hundred Conquerors has fallen," the Empress said, raising her sword for him to see. "I still don't believe it. I haven't had a sleeper fall since I took the high mountains. What was that, two hundred years ago?"

"Two hundred and fifty-three," the general said. "If my Empress is referring to her war with the Ascetics of the Great Glacier."

"Oh, yes," the Empress said. "That pack of ice builders. A good war, if I remember. I think I ended up commanding their glacier to provide the water that turned the northern plains green."

"For which your people will forever sing your praises, Empress."

The Empress nodded and sheathed her sword. "So long as the sleeper accomplished its task, it matters little, I suppose. I'll just have to make a new Conqueror when this is finished. We have more with us, don't we?"

The general bowed. "Seventy-three of the Hundred ride with your fleet, Empress. They await your command."

"That should be more than enough," the Empress said. "Report."

The general stood at attention. "A hundred ships approaching from the island, all light attack craft, just as in the last war. None have shot the clinging fire yet, but your wizards are standing by to squelch the flames if needed."

The Empress nodded. "And the shallows Den warned us about?"

"At our present speed, our front line should cross them in plenty of time to avoid the tide," the general said.

The Empress frowned. "The front line is fifty palace ships?"

"Fifty-five, Empress," the general corrected gently. "More than enough to take such a small island. We'll begin bombardment as soon as the first ships are in range. The land will be yours before nightfall."

"See that it is," the Empress said.

The general bowed and backed into the palace, closing the curtain behind him. The moment he was gone, Nara felt the hair on the back of her neck prickle in a familiar way. A smile of pure joy spread over her face as she turned to find the Shepherdess lounging on her imperial couch.

"My Lady," the Empress whispered, falling into a deep bow.

How goes the invasion?

Nara stiffened. The Lady did not sound happy.

"We're about to crush the Oseran fleet," she said quickly. "Do not worry, Lady. I told you I would give you the world, and I will, starting with this island."

It is a dour little island, the Lady said, twisting her snowy hair between her fingers. *Promise me you'll burn it to the ground.*

"I will crush it into the sea," Nara swore. "Anything to make you smile."

And to her great joy, the Shepherdess did. She held open her arms, and Nara ran to her, falling into the Lady's lap like a lost child.

Darling, loyal Nara, the Shepherdess said, stroking her dark hair. *Would you die for me?*

"In an instant, Lady," Nara said, tears rolling down her cheeks as she pressed her fingers against Benehime's bare, white skin. "I am loyal to you body and soul, life or death. Every breath I take is yours, as it always has been." *Unlike the boy*, she wanted to say, but she did not dare. She would not bring that thief into this precious moment when she had her Shepherdess to herself at last.

The Lady pet Nara's head like a cat's. *Remember*, she said. *Crush this island and its defenders. Break them utterly. I want them desperate.*

"It will be done, Lady," Nara said, clinging tighter than ever. "I swear it."

The Lady smiled one last time and vanished, her body slipping through a white line in the air. Nara fell forward, collapsing on the couch where the Lady had been. As always, her absence left Nara reeling, and she lay gasping on the silk cushions, her eyes shut tight against the hateful darkness that remained when Benehime was gone.

When the weakness finally passed, Nara pulled herself onto the couch and opened her soul a fraction. A wind answered at once.

"Tell the front line commanders to fire as soon as they're in range," the Empress said. "I mean to make an example of this island. Tell the wizards to use every war spirit we've got. I want Osera burned to ash."

"Yes, Empress," the wind whispered, spinning away.

Nara smiled. She wasn't sure what the island had done to deserve the Lady's displeasure, but it was a boon to her. An absolute victory here could be enough to make the Lady remember at last who her true servant was. That thought made her sigh in happiness, and Nara sank into the pillows to watch the show as the first of her palace ships hit the Oseran fleet.

The Oseran runners darted between the palace ships, the flagship shooting ahead as arrows rained down on them from the enemy decks.

"Hold steady!" Josef cried, cutting an arrow out of the air just before it landed in the rower behind him. "Are the others in position?"

"Right behind us!" the captain shouted.

Josef looked over his shoulder. Sure enough, the other runners were coasting right on their tail with their clingfire already lit in the throwers. Josef grinned and pointed the Heart at the palace ship on their left. "Bring us up right next to the hull."

The flagship surged forward, cutting through the breakwater until they were an arm's length from the palace ship's cliff-like side. Josef set his feet on the bucking deck and held the Heart in front of him, closing both hands on the wrapped hilt. He closed his eyes with a deep breath and let his thoughts go. His mind cleared like the sky after a storm, leaving only the sword in his hands. He could feel the Heart's presence resonating with his own, and the image of a mountain appeared behind his eyes. An enormous, sharp peak, cutting the clouds. A sword cutting a ship.

The cut would have to be perfect, a niggling voice whispered. Any amount of drag and he would crash his own ship before the enemy's. Josef snarled and pushed the doubt away. He gripped the Heart until his hands ached, letting the sword's weight anchor him as the rest of the world fell away, leaving only the feel of the wind and a profound stillness. As the quiet settled, he could almost feel Milo Burch standing in front of him, his old face smug as ever as he spoke the first truth of swordsmanship.

A sword cuts whatever its swordsman wants it to cut.

Josef gripped the Heart tight, relaxing his body until the Heart was part of it. Part of him.

A sword cuts whatever its swordsman wants it to cut? Josef smiled. Time to test the limits.

Giving himself fully to the weight of the mountain, Josef opened his eyes, and the world rushed in.

The palace ship's hull was right beside him. He could smell the tar on the wood, feel the iron strength of the enormous black beams. His body moved with the buck of the sea as he braced the Heart in his hands and lifted the blade, its scarred face a black hole in the afternoon sunlight. And then, in the emptiness between one wave and the next, between the breath let out and the breath inhaled, he struck.

The Heart flew in his hands, moving like an extension of himself. He did not feel the wood as it passed. Did not feel the nails as he cut them. All he felt was the *will* to cut swelling through his body and into his sword. The Heart sang as it struck, a great iron *gong* vibrating through the sea.

Josef's knees buckled as the blow left him. He fell into the boat as the runner turned midstroke and began to race away from the palace ship. The sailors were rowing with all their might, arms straining as they pushed the runner faster and faster. For a moment, Josef couldn't understand why they were running, and then he looked back at the palace ship, and he saw.

The palace ship was carved open, its great side split just above the water, starting at the ship's middle and running all the way to the stern. The cut was perfectly clean, slicing through the wood without so much as a splinter, and wherever the wood was cut, the ship was bowing. A great creaking sound drowned out the waves as the palace ship's side began to slide, pushed sideways by the ship's own enormous weight. The ship groaned as the sundered boards ground together, and then, with an earsplitting crack, the wooden supports snapped, and ship's side began to fall open.

Suddenly, Josef could see the inner decks and the sailors running through them, scrambling for cover as the metal skeleton that held the ship together folded under the pressure of the unsupported hull. Already the water was flooding through the crack to fill the lower decks, soaking the sailors who scrambled for the pumps as the entire ship began to tip. But then, just before the hull cracked completely and began to crumble into the sea, the falling wood stopped. For a breathless second, the ship hung frozen, the collapsing side poised in midair. And then, with an ear-splitting crack, the wood shuddered and began to pull itself back together.

"Now, you idiots!" Josef screamed. "Do it now!"

His voice shot across the water, and the crews in the assist ships stopped gawking and began to scramble. The air was filled with the sound of snapping rope as crews hit their clingfire launchers and a rain of ever-burning fire shot out from the Oseran fleet into the palace ship's closing breach. The clingfire exploded when it hit, sending sticky, burning pitch flying in all directions. Everything it touched caught fire, no matter how wet. If it could burn, it did.

The moment they'd launched their fire, the runners peeled away, darting across the water as arrows from the other palace ships chased them. The blobs of clingfire had been small, and only half the runners had shot on this attack, but the damage was done. As the fire spread through its belly, the broken palace ship began to groan. Even Josef heard the agony in the sound as the hole that had been pulling itself together began to slip once again, the great beams falling into the water as the hungry sea rushed in to fill the void.

The palace ship was leaning at a thirty-degree angle now. Sailors slid overboard as the enormous deck tilted, their bodies vanishing into the churning waves as the sea surged through the broken hull. Through the ship's cracked side, Josef could see sailors flinging water at the clingfire, but it did no good. Clingfire could burn for three days underwater so long as it had fuel. The ship would keep burning even after it sank.

When they were safely over the shallows again, the flagship slowed, and the oarsmen turned to survey the destruction.

"It's a miracle. That's what it is," the captain muttered as the palace ship began to sink in earnest. "A bleeding miracle."

"No," Josef said, pointing out to sea. "That's the miracle."

The sailors' eyes followed his gesture. A few hundred feet away, the Empress's fleet had ground to a halt. Several of the palace ships were dropping lifeboats as men jumped from the sinking ship, and the whole fleet seemed to be turning in on itself. In toward its own, and away from Osera.

"And that's how one runner fleet stops the Empress," Josef said, leaning on the Heart as Nico helped him to his feet. "And the longer they stay like that, the closer we get to low tide and the *real* miracle. Now, bring us around. Those ships may be stopped, but they've still got their bows, and we've more palaces to sink."

The captain blinked, eyes wide. "Aye, my king."

Josef just nodded and pushed off Nico to resume his position on the prow as the runner turned to join the others already darting between the stopped fleet.

Den the Warlord hung over the railing of the palace ship, watching with an enormous grin as the ship ahead of his begin to sink. Beside him, the captain was throwing a full-on fit.

"We cannot lose a palace ship before we've even reached land!" the man was screaming. "Get the wizards on deck and take out those blasted fishing boats!"

There was more, but Den ignored it. He was watching the man standing on the prow of the fastest boat, the man who had just sliced open a palace ship. Den breathed deep, savoring the anticipation. Now there was the kind of opponent he'd been waiting for, but how best to go about it? A duel on boats would be no fun. No real footing, not for the kind of power he'd be throwing around. Maybe he could spoil the man's ship and send him running to shore?

Den was still thinking over his options when he felt something brush against his spirit. He froze, taking in the feel of it. It was a wizard's will, a familiar one. He focused on the pressure, trying to place it, and found himself facing the shore. Den leaned out over the railing. A man was standing on the beach. This far, his face wasn't clear, but Den didn't need to see his face. That stance was unmistakable.

Pure joy flooded through him. He'd thought he was lucky to find the swordsman, but here was a fight Den had been waiting on for decades. He glanced back at the Oseran boats. They were coming around again, the swordsman riding the prow of the flagship with his sword out. Shaking his head, Den turned away. The swordsman could wait. If he was good enough to split a palace ship, then these idiots wouldn't be able to touch him. He'd still be around later. Meanwhile, he was going to deal with some unfinished business.

Den turned to the panicking captain and grabbed him by the shoulder, lifting him clear off the deck and holding him there until he was sure he had the man's undivided attention.

"I need a boat."

The captain's face went pale with terror. "The Empress said—"

"The Empress and I have a deal." Den tightened his grip. "I get to kill whomever I want. Now give me a boat."

"Fine!" the captain cried. "Just put me down!"

Den dropped him, and the captain collapsed in a heap. His officers rushed forward, but the captain waved them away. "Give the Empress's champion a boat," he gasped, clutching his shoulder. "Let him do as he likes."

The officers looked at Den, and then one ran off toward the lifeboats. Den nodded to the captain and turned to follow. He stepped into the boat and sat down, waiting impatiently as a crew lowered him down the long drop from the deck to the sea. The moment he hit the water, Den opened his spirit.

"Take me to the shore," he said, stomping on the boards.

The boat gave a terrified creak and obeyed, shooting across the water as fast as it could go.

"Sire!" one of Josef's rowers shouted. "There's a boat headed for the shore!"

Josef looked over his shoulder. They were circling to avoid the arrows, waiting for their chance to strike the next palace ship. Now was the perfect moment for the enemy to counter.

"I'd hoped we'd have a bit longer," he said. "How big a boat?"

The captain grabbed the glass from his neck and peered through it. "Looks like a lifeboat, sire. I see one man."

Josef held out his hand and the captain handed the glass over. Sure enough, a rowboat with one occupant was rushing toward the shore faster than their runners. Josef scowled. The sailor looked normal enough. Huge, certainly, and a fighter, but he didn't seem to have a weapon. The man's face was in profile, but he looked familiar, somehow. Josef was trying to place him when he heard Nico suck in a breath.

"That's Den the Warlord."

"The traitor?" the captain said, squinting at the tiny boat. "Impossible. He'd be an old man by now if he's still alive at all."

"It has to be Den," Nico said with absolute certainty. "He's the only person whose soul could look like that."

Josef had no idea what she meant, but he was too preoccupied to care. "Captain, turn us around. Den the Warlord killed five thousand men in one night when he defected. We can't let him land."

"No," Nico said.

Josef looked at her in surprise, but Nico just clenched her fists.

"You're the only one who can sink the palace ships," she said. "And that's the only thing keeping the fleet at bay. If you leave now, the fleet will cross the shallows before the tide and this whole mission is for nothing."

"It won't matter if Den's already finished the job," Josef growled. "Turn us around."

"*No,*" Nico said again.

Josef jerked at the determination in her voice. "Nico..."

"You're king now," Nico went on. "Your duty is here." She looked back at the shore. "I'll stop Den."

"Nico, no," Josef said. "Den's the highest bounty in Council history and maybe the best fighter in the world. I have to—"

"You can't make it there fast enough," Nico said, her voice firm. "I can. Or don't you think I can win?"

Josef set his mouth in a stubborn line. "It's not that I think you can't win," he said. "It's what I think you'll have to do to get there."

"I already won my hardest fight," she said, lifting her chin. "Stay and be king, Josef. It's what you promised. Besides, it's my turn to do something for you."

Josef clenched the Heart's hilt. "This isn't some damn give-and-take, Nico. You don't owe me this."

"You're right," Nico said. "I don't. It's my choice to fight for you, and that's what I'm going to do."

Josef turned with a curse. "Fine," he growled, running his free hand through his wet hair. "Just promise me you won't do anything stupid."

"I'll do what I have to," Nico said, sliding into the mast's shadow. "Same as you."

"Nico!" Josef's arm shot out, but his fingers caught nothing but air. He was too late. She was gone.

The boat rocked as he lurched toward the shore, but he couldn't see anything from this angle. He cursed again, louder this time, slamming the Heart's pommel against the boat so hard they nearly tipped.

"Sire?" the captain said nervously when the worst of the boat's rocking had passed. "Are we going back?"

Josef closed his eyes and took a deep breath. Nico was a survivor. If she decided to win, she would win. She would survive and come back to him, no matter what. Josef held that truth in his mind as tight as he held the Heart and he forced himself to let the anger, and the fear at its root, go. Slowly, the battle calm settled over his mind again. When he was sure he could trust himself, Josef straightened up and turned to face the captain.

"Our job hasn't changed," he said. "But we're fighting on two fronts now. Nico will hold the beach, so it's up to us to hold the water. Now bring us around, and let's hit another ship."

"Aye, sire," the captain said. "Full speed!"

The men shouted to the other boats as the Oseran fleet shot forward. Josef stepped back onto the prow, Heart in his hand, but when he tried to clear his mind in preparation for the next strike, all he could see was Nico vanishing into the dark.

The Heart jerked angrily in his hands, and Josef pushed the vision away, pouring himself into the present as the runners raced toward their next target.

CHAPTER
21

Nico stepped out of the shadows and onto the small crescent of sand beneath the storm wall. Tesset was already there, standing with his boots in the surf as he watched the lone boat that was just now entering the bay's mouth.

"You should not have come," he said without looking. "This man is mine."

"And this island is Josef's," Nico said, moving to stand beside him. "I have no interest in interrupting your fight, but I cannot let Den past this beach."

Tesset laughed softly. "What did the swordsman do to deserve such devotion? Save your life?"

"Countless times," Nico said. "But that's not why." She raised her arms, pushing back her hood. "He believed in me, even when there was nothing to believe in."

"You are a strange creature, daughter of the demon," he said, shaking his head. "I am glad I met you."

"And I you," Nico said, walking back up the beach. "Fight well, Tesset."

Tesset nodded, but his eyes never left the man standing in the boat that cut across the bay on its own power.

Nico sat down on the narrow stair that led up the storm wall, keeping herself well out of the way as Den's boat hit the surf and beached itself with a terrified squeal. Twenty-six years later, his face still looked exactly like his wanted poster. Den the Warlord, traitor to the Council, the most wanted man on the continent. He was bigger than Nico had expected, taller than Josef by several inches with shoulders to match. He was dressed in the Empress's black, but he wore no armor, just a long-sleeved sailor's shirt, heavy woven breeches, and tall boots. His dark hair was cut ragged around his face without a trace of gray. He had no weapons, not even a knife. Instead, his hands were open, hovering ready at his sides. Even so, the sight of him was enough to make Nico cower against the rocks.

Unarmed and alone, Den radiated a killing instinct like nothing she'd ever felt, and worse, nothing she'd ever seen. The glimpse she'd caught on the boat with Josef was nothing compared to seeing him up close. She'd always thought of Tesset as a man who'd made himself iron, but Den was a man who had made himself a fortress. Now that she saw them side by side, she couldn't help shaking. She had seen many monsters, and been many more, but not even the demon's predatory hunger matched this man's pure, undefiled will to kill.

Den stepped onto the surf and stopped, surveying the beach. He dismissed Nico at once, focusing on Tesset with a grin that made her chest close up.

"Tesset, wasn't it?" Den said, looking the Council man up and down. "I thought I'd find you alive someday. Finally conquered yourself, did you?"

"Yes." Nico was impressed by the calm determination in Tesset's voice. "To meet you again, master. And to defeat you."

"A worthy goal," Den said. "I can think of none better for a bloody day like this one." He threw out his arms, fists clenched as he grinned wide. "Come then. I let you live in the hope that one day you could give me a fight worthy of my full attention. Let's hope you don't disappoint me."

Tesset smiled back, a tight, controlled turn of the mouth, and then, without warning, he charged.

Tesset flew at Den faster than wind, faster than sound, focusing all his speed, all his strength into the fist that was already inside the Warlord's guard. Before Nico's mind could catch up with what was happening, Tesset's fist landed on Den's unguarded jaw. Sand exploded as the force of Tesset's charge and the blow at the end of it reverberated through the beach.

Nico threw her arms up, her coat swirling over her face just before the sand hit it, but behind the barrier, she was grinning. She'd felt the force of Tesset's blow in her stomach. Famous as he was, if Den hadn't even been able to block such a straightforward strike, maybe they weren't in as much trouble as she'd thought. She knew Tesset's strength firsthand. He was far stronger than he looked. Strong enough to stop her demonseed barehanded. A clean punch with that kind of strength behind it might be enough to end this fight before it started.

The wave of sand passed, and she lowered her arms, looking down the beach to see where Den had landed. But he wasn't there. She looked around, confused, and then she saw it. Den was still standing exactly where he had been, leering at Tesset with a horrible, wolfish grin.

Tesset himself was frozen in place. He was still inside Den's guard, his fist still resting where it had landed on Den's jaw, but his face had changed from quiet determination to open horror. The moment Nico saw it, she knew why. She could read the thoughts in his wide eyes as clearly as print on a page. Tesset had just hit Den with his best blow. He'd hit him with his full strength, unhampered by tiredness and unspoiled by the need to dodge a defense, and nothing had happened. Den was still standing exactly as he had been before the hit. He hadn't fallen, hadn't stumbled, hadn't been pushed back. He hadn't even turned his head. He'd simply taken the blow as though it were nothing, a child's play punch, and that realization had hit Tesset harder than any retaliation.

The seconds dragged on as the men stood there like players in a pantomime fight. Even Nico was frozen. She couldn't help it. The idea that Tesset's strength, the strength that had overpowered her so easily, meant *nothing* to Den had stopped her mind cold. All she could do was watch dumbly until, at last, Tesset stumbled back.

He fell to the sand, panting, staring up at Den with wide, unbelieving eyes. For his part, Den raised a hand to his cheek, rubbing the uninjured skin with a disappointed sneer.

"Is that it?"

It was, and they all knew it. But no one who could master his own spirit was one to give up when faced with the impossible, and Tesset was no exception. Hands clenching in the cold sand, Tesset stood up. He set his stance, his feet solid on the wet beach. His breathing steadied, calm returned, and he raised his fists to face Den again.

Den's eyes lit with a mad gleam as he looked down on his former student. With a joyous shout, Den attacked.

Nico had never seen anything like Den's charge. The enormous man moved like water, each step flowing into the next with the kind of speed she'd seen only in Josef when he was moving with the Heart. His feet hit the beach with such force, such precision, that the sand did not shift beneath his boots. But even as his fists came up to strike, Tesset was already moving. As Den's foot landed to brace the blow, Tesset's landed right beside it. He moved with Den, matching his body to the Warlord's as he stepped inside Den's guard. His arm moved with a speed Nico couldn't follow to catch

Den's punch at its farthest, weakest point while his other hand landed in Den's side, right over his liver.

Or it would have.

In the split second before Tesset's hit connected, Den stepped back. Tesset, still holding Den's fist, was pulled forward. He teetered a moment trying to find his balance, and in that moment, Den's knee shot up to knock him in the jaw.

Tesset flew backward and landed sprawling on the sand. Nico held her breath, waiting for him to roll over, to cough out the blood and stand up. His jaw was almost certainly broken, but that shouldn't have been a fight-ender, not for a man like Tesset. And yet he didn't move. He just laid there, glassy eyes staring at the sky, his chest rising in tight little gasps, and she realized he was stunned.

Den walked across the sand, his smile fading. He bent over, grabbing the fallen man by the shoulder and lifting him with one hand until Tesset dangled in front of him. The motion must have snapped him out of his stunned state, for Tesset's head rolled from side to side and then lifted, meeting Den's eyes.

"It wasn't enough," he mumbled, blood dripping from his mouth. "Thirty years of training, becoming my own king, and still, after all that, with everything I had"—a faint smile drifted over his lips—"I lost."

Den sneered and raised his arm, lifting Tesset's body high over his head.

"You lost the moment you called me master."

And with that, he slammed Tesset into the ground. Nico felt the impact through her boots. She didn't even realize she'd run onto the beach until she was falling to her knees at Tesset's side. He was lying on his stomach, his body half buried in the sand, perfectly still. Her hands flew to his face, turning his head, but the second she touched his skin, she knew.

Nico snatched her fingers away, letting his head fall back. It couldn't be. He couldn't be gone. Not like that. Not so quickly. Not Tesset. Not the man who'd stopped the demonseed with one hand.

But it was true. When she looked at him, she no longer saw a man of iron. She saw nothing but dullness, a spirit turned to dumb, dead meat. Choking back a sob, Nico moved away. This thing was not Tesset. She had seen much death in the small parts of her life she could remember, but she had never *seen* death, not like this, and her mind was scrambling to make sense of something a human soul was never meant to see.

"It's a waste, really."

Nico hadn't even heard Den move, but he was standing over her. She tensed, but the Warlord wasn't looking at her. He was frowning at Tesset's body like a child examining a broken toy.

"I'd thought for sure he'd be stronger after so long," he said bitterly. "Such a waste. Sorry, little girl." He patted Nico on the shoulder. "I guess I'll go and see if that swordsman can't give me a better run."

Nico's arm shot up and grabbed his hand, her fingers digging into the back of his palm. She felt him tense, and then she heard his voice, very low, right beside her ear.

"You don't want to do this," Den whispered. "I try to fight only strong people, but I will kill you if you get in my way."

Nico held her grip. "If you think I am weak," she whispered back, "you are the one who will die."

Den paused, and his eyes sparked with a new light. "I'd thought you were his daughter, maybe," he said, a smile spreading across his face. "But I was wrong. You were Tesset's student, weren't you?"

"He showed me the way to be my own master," Nico answered, ripping his hand off her shoulder.

Den's eyebrows shot up. "Is that so?" he said. "Well, then, as one free soul to another, let me give you some advice." He leaned in low, bringing his face level with hers. "Run away. You may think you want to try fighting me to reclaim your master's honor, but you should forget that. You can't beat me."

Nico gritted her teeth, her eyes boring into his. "No."

Den leaned back as Nico stood up. "I made a promise," she said, bracing her feet on the sand. "You will not pass this beach."

Den shrugged. "It's your death," he said, planting his own feet. "I just hope you can give me a better challenge than your master."

"He wasn't my master," Nico said firmly. "I have no master but myself."

Den smiled wide. "Good to see you learned better than he did." He beckoned. "Come, then. Let's see whose kingdom is greater. Yours or mine."

Nico didn't answer. Instead, she grabbed a handful of her coat at her chest. The moment her fingers touched the fabric, she opened her spirit.

"Cover us."

The words were scarcely out of her mouth before the coat obeyed. It sprang off her back, the black fabric expanding, pulling out every inch of the enormous lengths of cloth Slorn had woven into it. It grew and grew, spilling onto the sand behind her and rising overhead like a wave of night. Den held his stance, watching through narrowed eyes as the coat arched over his head. Moments after it started, the coat stopped, trapping Nico and Den inside a large, pitch-black tent of living cloth.

"Clever," Den's voice sounded from Nico's left. "But blinding me won't be enough."

"I didn't do it to blind you," Nico said, fading into the dark. "I did it because I don't want the world to see what I'm going to do."

"And what is that?" Den's voice was curious, not afraid.

Nico didn't answer. She slipped through the shadows until she was facing Den's back. She could see him clearly, but not with her eyes. Her coat was too well made for that. It blocked the light so completely that even her night vision was useless. She could still see with her other sight, though, and now that her normal vision was gone, the world of the spirits was clearer than ever.

Den hadn't moved since the dark had fallen. She could see him holding his breath, waiting for her to give herself away, but more than that, she could see *him* clearly for the first time, not his body, but the actual spirit that was Den. Generally, when she looked at people, wizards or the spirit deaf, the souls beneath their bodies looked jumbled and chaotic. Tesset was the exception. His soul had looked like metal, almost like the Heart's blade.

Den was completely different. Back in the light, she'd seen him as a fortress. Now, in the dark, she saw how much of an understatement that was. Den's body was a vault of power. Every part of him was perfectly aligned, every angle perfectly set. Strength flowed uninterrupted from his head to his arms to his feet, and when he shifted, everything in his body moved together in perfect unison. For a moment, Nico forgot the fight and simply stared in wonder. Looking at Den, she saw the pure essence of human potential, and with it, the truth of what it meant to be absolutely, completely in control.

"Well?"

Den's voice snapped her out of her gawking, and Nico shrank back reflexively before remembering he couldn't see her. But even as she thought it, Den looked over his shoulder and stared straight at her.

"Come," he said. "I'm getting bored."

Nico fled away through the dark, coming up on his side. Den was still facing the place where she had been, and Nico breathed in relief. Maybe his turn had been just a lucky guess, or maybe he could sense her, but it wasn't instant. Either way, he wasn't looking at her, at least for now. Nico clenched her fist. For now was good enough. All she needed was one good hit.

She exploded out of the shadows low to Den's right, her fist clenched as she flew toward his unguarded side. She was taking a cue from Tesset, aiming for his liver. Fortress or not, Den's body was still human, and no human could take repeated blows to the liver without feeling it. For a thrilling second, she felt her fist connect, and then things started to go wrong.

She could see the shock wave from her blow running through the orderly fortress of his spirit. The force rippled out from her fist, but rather than shooting through the muscle and hitting his liver as she'd intended, the blow began spreading and dissipating the moment it touched him. It all happened so quickly that Nico had to play the strike over in her mind before she realized Den had shifted his spirit the moment she'd touched him, spreading the shock out across his body. Even now, she could see the echoes fading. Every piece of him had taken its part, breaking her blow down to nothing.

She was still staring in amazement when Den grabbed her arm. He snatched her off her feet before she could react and brought her dangling up in front of him, his other hand grabbing her neck as surely as though he were the one who could see.

"I told you," he said, fingers digging into her throat. "Blinding me does nothing."

Nico gasped and tried to kick him in the groin with her dangling legs. He spoiled the blow with his knee, spirit moving instantly to absorb the shock just like before.

"And it's not just that I can hear you," he continued as though nothing had happened. "I can *feel* your killing intent."

He opened his hand, and Nico plummeted, crashing into the sand. The moment she hit, Den's boot was on her back.

"You should have run when I gave you the chance," he said, grinding his heel into her back. "If you don't even know that, then you have no hope of beating me."

Nico gasped in pain, bringing in more sand than air. Den's heel was like an iron spike on her spine, pressing so hard she saw bursts of color behind her eyes. But the dark was still her highway, and the moment her mind cleared enough to slip into the shadows, she sank into dark ground. Relief flowed over her as the pressure of Den's foot vanished from her back. She slipped sideways, coming up in the shadows behind Den as she looked down to survey the damage.

Nico froze in place, all pain forgotten. In the days since she'd first started to see as spirits saw, she'd never once looked at herself without her coat. Now, in the dark, with no coat and no normal sight to intervene between her and truth, she saw herself for the first time.

Above her, Den looked up from the sand where she had been, his face surprised. "Where did you go?" he whispered. "And why are you so afraid?"

Nico did not hear him. She'd forgotten all about Den, about the fight, about her injuries. All she could do was stare in horror as the demon's voice filled her mind.

Now you understand why the spirits panic when they see you?

She didn't. There was no way to understand what she saw inside her own body, beneath the frail mask of human spirit. The only way to describe it was darkness. Living, devouring, hungry darkness. And below that...

Why are you surprised? The demon's voice was like silk against her mind. *You've always known you were a monster.*

"Knowing's not the same as..." She couldn't say it.

Seeing? the demon finished, his smooth voice sharpening to a cutting edge. *I suppose that's true. Poor Nico, don't you wish now you'd taken my offer when you had the chance?*

Nico snarled, snapping herself out of her terrified trance with a burst of defiant rage. She flung open her soul, slamming the demon back into his prison. Across the shadows, Den stiffened and spun to face her. Nico didn't care. She fell panting to the sand, staring up at the blank darkness of her coat, desperately looking anywhere but at her body, if she could even think of that *thing* as her body anymore. But even as the thought of it filled her with fear, another voice spoke in her mind, a voice that sounded very much like Tesset's.

Horrible as it is, it's still your body, isn't it?

Nico blinked. Trembling, she raised her hand, holding it as close as she dared to her face. The blackness below her skin flowed like water. Below it, the shifting yellow eyes stared at her without blinking while the hungry mouths opened and closed in a way that made her stomach clench. Black claws scraped against the thin cage of her flesh, looking for a way out, and on her wrists where her manacles had once rested, she could see the faint outlines of black, jagged teeth waiting for any scrap of food.

Mixed with the liquid darkness, Nico could actually see her own heart pounding in terror in her chest, but she forced herself not to look away. This was her. Her body, her power, her life. She hadn't fought for so long and hard only to be afraid of it now.

Nico flicked her eyes to Den. He'd found the edge of her coat and was pressing his hands against it, looking for the edge. She could see the orderly flow of his spirit tensing. He was losing his patience. Soon he would rip the cloth and return them to daylight, and then there would be no way to stop him going up the beach. That wasn't acceptable. She'd told Josef she would stop him. But Nico was facing a very real dilemma. She couldn't beat Den, not as she was, not even when she had the dark to move through and he had nothing. That left only one path. She had to become stronger, become something Den couldn't stop. Nico looked down again at her own darkness, the clawed hands scraping against her flesh. "Become" was the wrong word, she thought with a grim smile. She already was a monster. All that was left was to embrace it. After all, the monster was hers. She'd ripped it from the demon of the Dead Mountain with her own hands. Now it would fight as she commanded, for it was a part of her, and she was the master of herself.

Before she lost her nerve, Nico looked away from Den and turned her focus inward, sinking down into the pit of her soul. The demonseed leaped to meet her with a vigor that turned her stomach, but she ignored the discomfort and opened her arms, pulling the creature in with a lover's embrace. Power, strong and addictive, flooded her mind. She took it all and held it as hard as she could, letting the slimy black water wash over her, the black teeth bite into her skin and become her own.

When Nico opened her eyes again, she was no longer afraid.

At the edge of her coat's shell, Den froze. He whirled, finding her instantly, but Nico didn't even try to run. After all, it wasn't her killing intent he'd used to find her this time. He was no longer fighting blind, for even a blind man couldn't miss her eyes glowing like lanterns in the dark. She spread her tainted spirit like claws, pushing the demon's fear forward. But Den did not flinch when the fear reached him, not even when she shoved it down his throat, and despite herself, Nico was impressed.

"Are you not afraid?" she whispered, wincing at the horrible sound of her own, two-toned voice.

"I have no need for fear," Den answered simply, looking her up and down. "You are a demonseed?"

"I am Nico," Nico said. "I am a monster, but I am also myself."

"A good answer," Den said, stepping into his stance. "I am also a monster. All men are who know no fear. So, monster Nico"—he grinned wide—"why don't you make me remember how it feels to be afraid?"

Nico returned his grin, her mouth opening wider than a human's should to reveal four jagged rows of black teeth, and vanished into the dark.

Den held his stance, waiting.

He didn't have to wait long. The first blow came from above, a black claw reaching down to grab his head, the razor-sharp talons hooking under his jaw. Den grabbed the hand with both of his, but before he could rip it away, another claw appeared from the ground and lashed up, digging into his leg above the knee.

Den grunted and kicked down, spinning sideways out of both claws. The moment he was free, he grabbed the claw from above and ripped Nico out of the shadows. The claw from the ground vanished as she landed in a crouch. The second her feet were on the ground, Nico sprang up, her body shifting back and forth between solid darkness and smokey shadow as she wrapped her arms around Den's shoulders, locking herself to him.

Den's hands went up immediately, but it was too late. She was clutched around his neck. Den froze, his fingers sliding over the black, stone-hard flesh of her arms.

"It's useless," he said, his voice tight and calm despite the pressure she was putting on his throat. "You can't eat me, not without my permission. I am the king of my soul."

"I know," Nico whispered, her dual-tone voice dry as dust. "But I'm not trying to eat you. The demon eats souls. I don't. I'm a human monster, just like you."

"Really?" Den sneered. "Then what are you trying to do?"

The darkness in front of him shimmered and Nico's face appeared, her golden eyes narrowing as she smiled wide. "Hold you still."

Den's eyes widened in surprise as Nico's hold vanished and he looked down to see her black claw buried elbow deep in his chest.

Den coughed, but he did not stumble. Instead, his hand shot out, grabbing for her throat. But his fingers passed through her body like water through sand.

"How," he whispered, hand falling limp at his side.

Nico looked down at her black arm buried in his chest. "Even fortresses have weak points," she said, her voice wafting like smoke. "Your ability to will your body to absorb any damage has held off the ravages of battle and age, but you're still human, Den, with a human's blindness. Blind, you built your fortress to defend against attacks from the outside. Attacks you could see. But in the dark, all shadows are mine, even ones inside your body." She wiggled her claws in his chest. "All I had to do was hold you still long enough to reach them."

Den bared his bloody teeth and began to laugh. He fell to his knees in the sand, still laughing as Nico's claw ripped free. His laughter dissolved into coughing as he collapsed onto his side, looking at her with fading eyes.

"I always knew this was how it would end," he wheezed. "I knew nothing human could kill me."

"You're wrong," Nico said, her glowing eyes narrowing. "I am still human."

"No," Den said, his voice trailing off as the last of his breath left. "You're not."

Not anymore.

"No!" Nico shouted, stepping away from Den, her body flashing between hard flesh and smokey shadow as she tried to push the demon back.

Oh yes, the demon answered, completely ignoring her efforts. *I told you. Every time you used your powers, I would come back. Every time you were weak, I'd be here. You just suffused your body into shadow to beat this man. How can you even dare to say you're still human?*

"*No!*" Nico screamed again, clutching her head between her claws. "I am my own master! My soul is my own!"

That may be, the demon said. *But that doesn't mean you're still human.* The voice paused. *Do you know how new demons are made, Nico?*

Nico clamped her mouth shut, but the demon went on anyway.

I can replicate myself forever through seeds, it said. *Over and over, always the same, little shoots of myself growing in fertile soil. But sometimes, through extraordinary pressure, a seed changes. It ceases to be a part of me and becomes something new. A new demon, a true demon, with its own ambitions and drives. If this was the world that was, the world before, I would now try to kill you. Predators can't abide competition, after all. But this isn't our world, is it? It's her world, and so I think I'll let you be.*

"Her who?" Nico snapped.

The demon laughed. *Our darling jailor, of course. You'll know her when she comes, but by then it will be too late. Maybe she'll actually manage to destroy you rather than just locking you under a corpse, as she did me. But trust me when I say this, little daughter, whatever plans Benehime has for you, the day will come when you would give anything to go back to the time when I was the biggest thing you had to worry about.*

"I doubt that," Nico muttered, pushing the demon's voice down, down, down until it was little more than a whisper.

You'll see, the demon said as he faded. *Talk to you soon.*

Nico slammed the boulder down with a rage she'd never felt before. She was standing in the field, panting as the cool air blew over her face. But even as she realized where she was, she knew something was wrong. Her field, the high golden field of her soul with its rolling hills and enormous sky, was dark. It was night, a cool, still night. Nico looked around in confusion and pictured the sun, the bright noon day that she'd created when she'd made this place.

No sun came. When she looked up at the sky, all she saw was darkness. Endless, endless darkness, and something else. She squinted. High overhead, something was moving against the black sky. A hand, she realized as her blood went cold. A clawed hand, scraping at the sky. From the second she saw it, she could not look away. The hand clenched in the dark above her, clawing faster, harder, until at last it grabbed a great fistful of the sky and, with a horrible, twisting motion, ripped it away.

Harsh, blinding light burned her to ash. Nico fell with a scream, eyes slamming open. She was back on the beach, lying in the sand with Eli standing over her. He was panting like he'd just run a marathon and his hands were gripping the black cloth of her coat, which he'd just torn down.

She blinked at him, confused. "What happened?"

Eli glanced at something beside her. "Looks like you won."

Slowly, painfully, Nico turned her head. Den's face lay a foot from her own, his dead eyes open and staring into hers.

"I won," she whispered.

"You did," Eli said, reaching toward her with her coat. "Now let's try to help you survive it."

Nico looked at him in confusion, and then, hesitantly, she glanced down at her body. Her eyes widened. She was covered in a slick, black liquid. The stuff oozed like hot tar, but it smelled coppery, and it was oozing out of her. Nico's breath caught in what was left of her chest. It was blood, black blood. *Her* black blood.

With a choked scream, Nico started to scramble away on instinct only to find she couldn't. Beneath the tarry slick of her blood, her arms were twisted and broken. So were her legs. She looked like a little ink-filled doll dropped from a great height and shattered on the stone. She didn't even feel pain as she stared at what the demon transformation had left of her body, not at first, and not for the next several seconds. But once it came, it consumed her. Shaking uncontrollably, she fell into the sand, gasping against her panic-frozen lungs as Eli knelt beside her.

She tried to say something, but her mouth wouldn't work. Eli wouldn't have heard her anyway; he was focused on her limbs. A blinding crack of pain hit her as he pulled them straight, wrapping each one as fast as he could with her coat. She focused on his face as she fought to stay conscious, trying not to think about why he looked so pale and scared.

"Josef is going to kill me," Eli muttered, pulling her coat tight.

That was the last thing Nico heard before the awakened cloth of her coat crawled over her face and she sunk at last into unconsciousness.

CHAPTER

22

The sun hung low over the island as the Oseran ships came around. The fleet was looking ragged. Every runner had arrows peppering its side. Many had dead rowers, struck by a lucky shot, and all the sailors were exhausted. Their tiny supply of clingfire was long gone, but three palace ships were now floundering in the blue water. The first was nearly completely under, her sailors streaming off in lifeboats, which the runners harried whenever they could. The second was burning merrily while the third was taking on water through an enormous gash in its side. Josef had just ordered the flagship to circle back for another strike when his captain shouted, "Sire!"

Josef looked to see the dour old sailor grinning like a boy as he pointed to a thin line of red-tinted signal smoke cutting the evening sky over the beach. Josef lurched forward, rocking the boat as he leaned into the water. Sure enough, the sharp tip of the coral ledge was now clearly visible below their keel.

"We did it," he said, falling back with a grin.

Behind him, the captain began to laugh.

They'd done it. It hardly seemed possible, yet the proof was right below them. They'd sunk only three ships out of a fleet of thousands, but it'd been enough. They'd held the Empress's palace ships over the reef for the two hours they'd needed. Now the tide was rushing out as they watched, bringing the deep-running palace ships ever closer to the rocks below.

"I wouldn't believe it if you told me!" the captain shouted, slapping his king on the shoulder. "We did it! Thirty minutes until this whole strand is nothing but ten feet of surf over coral. Those big hulkers won't even be able to turn around before they run aground."

"Give the signal," Josef ordered, laying the Heart on the deck beside him. "We're going home."

A whoop went up from the sailors, and they leaped into action. The ship jerked as the sail swung around, forcing Josef to duck or be conked in the head. He didn't mind. The moment he'd released the Heart, the exhaustion hit him. He collapsed gratefully on the deck, savoring the wonderful feeling of being flat. Although his body was sending him strong signals it never wanted to move again, he reached up one last time, grabbing the edge of the ship and hauling himself up for a look at the rapidly approaching shore. The crescent beach of the bay was shrouded in shadow as the sun sank behind the mountain, but there was still enough light for him to see what was there. Or, more worryingly, what wasn't.

There was no sign of Den, or Nico. The sand was sundered, and even this far away he could see the dark patches left by blood. Blood, but no bodies.

"What was that, sire?" the captain said.

"I said go faster," Josef grunted, falling back to the deck.

"Yes, sire," the captain said. "Fast as we can."

Josef nodded and lay still as the narrow flagship raced home across the retreating blue water.

The bay filled as the runners returned. Of the ninety-five ships, eighty-two had made it back. A far better number than Josef had expected, and mostly due to the runners' speed. The Oseran archers simply hadn't been able to keep up. All around him, men were hopping from ship to ship, hugging and shouting in joy as they roped in.

Josef's captain steered the flagship away from the crowded docks, beaching it instead. Josef hopped out the second they scraped bottom, sloshing through the water to the beach as he made a beeline for the narrow stair leading up the storm wall. Those sailors already on the beach moved respectfully out of his way, whispering in awe. Any other time, this change would have made him self-conscious, but now Josef was too preoccupied to notice. He reached the top of the storm wall and ran for the watchtower, throwing open the heavy door and climbing the stairs three at a time. Eli met him on the second landing.

Josef pushed straight past him. "How did it go?"

"Den got the worst of the fight, if that's what you're asking," Eli said, keeping right on his heels.

"This isn't the time to be clever," Josef growled. "Did she win?"

"Well, Den's dead," Eli said. "So is Tesset. Nico is alive, for the moment."

"If she's alive, she's staying there," Josef said firmly. "She's a survivor."

"I'm well aware of your confidence in her unkillability," Eli said. "But you really should listen a moment before you barge—"

Josef slammed open the door to the observation room and stopped cold.

"—in," Eli finished, coming to a stop beside him.

Josef said nothing. He just stared.

"I did all I could," Eli said softly. "But I'm not a doctor, and I couldn't get the actual doctors near her without her coat going on the defensive. I don't even know what happened in that fight. I've seen a lot of bloodied people, mostly you, but I've never seen injuries like—"

His voice dropped off as Josef moved away. Josef crossed the room and fell to his knees beside the small, black bundle lying on the floor against the wall.

Nico was completely wrapped in her coat, cocooned like a caterpillar. That much was normal after a big fight. What wasn't normal was the dark pool of thick black liquid seeping into the floor beneath her. Josef swallowed. Slowly, gently, he reached out, brushing the wet cloth with his fingers. The coat twisted away from his touch with a sound that reminded him of hissing, but the sound stopped as Nico's small, pale hand emerged from the coat's folds, her thin fingers reaching for his.

Josef gripped her hand, sucking in a breath when he saw the black stains on her nails. Her pale skin was mottled black and purple, and he could see the beginnings of larger wounds on her arm before it disappeared into her coat. A long, burning stab of guilt cut through him, and Josef winced, opening his mouth before he realized he had no idea what to say. He sat there a moment, clutching her fingers as he searched for the words.

"I'm sorry," he whispered at last.

"Don't be." Nico's voice was thin and muffled by the coat. "I kept my promise."

"You shouldn't have had to," Josef said. "This is my war."

"Your war is my war," she whispered. "You should know that by now."

"Well, you won't have to fight it anymore," Josef said, folding his hands over hers. "Rest, Nico. I'll win it from here."

"I know you will," she said, her fingers going slack.

Josef raised her hand to his lips for a moment and then carefully tucked her arm back into the coat. The cloth rustled, pulling Nico back into its protective swaddle. Josef stood and turned to see Eli hovering in the doorway.

"I'm sorry," he said. "I couldn't help her."

"You brought her here," Josef said bitterly. "That was more than I could do." He met his friend's eyes. "I'm going to win the war, Eli. No matter what, I'm going to win."

"I know you are," Eli said with a grin. "Why do you think I'm still here?"

Josef shook his head. "Come on," he said, starting for the door. "We're not done yet."

"Yes, your majesty," Eli said, his smile widening at Josef's murderous look as they jogged down the stairs.

Nara frowned at the gap left in the line of her palace ships, and her scowl only deepened as she turned to the man kneeling at her feet, his forehead pressed against the tile floor of her balcony.

"Well?" she said. "Did you crush those buzzing gnats holding up our assault? I would like to get close enough to launch the war spirits before we lose the entire front to whatever idiocy is going on at the front."

"The Oserans have retreated, Empress," the general said, pressing his head harder against the ground. "But we must pull back as well. The tide is going out. Your fleet will be stranded on the rocks if we do not retreat."

Nara looked away with a sniff. "I do not retreat."

"But, Empress," the general's voice trembled. "We've already lost three ships. If we do not retreat now, we could lose the rest of the first wave."

"General," Nara said, glaring down. "Do you know who I am?"

"You are the Immortal Empress," the man said, crouching lower. "Queen of all the world."

Nara lifted her chin. "And do you think that the queen of the world fears something as trivial as the tide?"

The general swallowed. "No, Empress."

"You must have faith, General," Nara said, opening her spirit.

The general shook visibly as the enormous pressure landed on him. "I believe," he whispered.

The Empress began to smile as she opened her spirit wider. When her power was roaring in her ears, she reached out, plunging herself into the current that was still waiting below her ships. The mob of water spirits screamed and thrashed as she grabbed it, but her will was absolute.

"The fleet moves forward," she said, her voice thick and resonant with power. "I don't care how many troops it takes. Beach the ships if you have to. We conquer the island by nightfall."

"Yes, Empress," the general said, crawling backward out of her presence all the way to the stairs before standing and running down to the command center to signal her orders to the fleet.

"Well?" Josef said, joining his admiral on the stone walkway above the bay. "How much longer?"

"Not long," said the admiral, dancing from foot to foot in his anticipation. "Tide's nearly out. There's no way they can escape now."

"Good," Josef said, nodding to the crowd of gawking sailors and guardsmen crowding the beach. "Get those men onto the cliffs. Once the ships hit the rocks and start taking on water, the crews are going to head for the shore. If they land, it'll be bad. No one fights harder than men with no retreat. We have to sink their boats before they reach the shore."

"Yes, sire," the admiral said. He saluted and started down the stairs, barking orders as he went. Josef stayed put, glancing at Eli as the thief stepped up beside him.

"You're growing more kingly by the minute."

"Save it," Josef grumbled, glaring at the distant shadows of the

palace ships. "We've bought some time, but if the Council reinforcements don't get here before the tide comes in again, that'll be
that. I can't sink the whole fleet by myself. All it'll take is one of
those ships making landfall and we'll be overrun."

"If it happens, we'll deal with it," Eli said firmly. "You've bought
us a reprieve for the moment. That's something to be—"

Eli stopped midsyllable, his face screwing up in a look of surprise.

Josef tensed. "What?" he said. Because Eli looking surprised was
never good.

"It's just—" Eli bit his lip. "I'm no sailor, but isn't the water supposed to be moving toward the *sea* when the tide goes out?"

Josef blinked and looked down. Sure enough, the ocean was
rushing into the bay, pushing the line of the surf back up the beach.

"Don't tell me the Empress can even change the tides," he
whispered.

"No," Eli said. "Look." He pointed, moving his finger back and
forth from the sea to the bay, tracing a faint line of darker, deep
running water running in through the Rebuke's protective cliffs.
"It's a current. She's pushing against the tide with a current."

Josef cursed and ran for the stairs. "Admiral!"

The admiral, already halfway down the storm wall on his way to
deliver Josef's orders, looked up. "Yes, sire?"

It would have taken too long to explain, so Josef jumped the
short wall onto the stairs and ran down himself, grabbing the admiral's shoulders and pointing the man at the sea. The admiral struggled a moment, and then his body went slack as a look of pure dread
crept over his face.

"Powers help us," he whispered.

Josef let him go. "What can we do?"

The admiral ran a trembling hand through his thin, gray hair as
he watched the ocean swell back up nearly to the storm wall's base.

"She's pushed us neatly back to high tide," he said, his voice despairing. "More than enough to get her ships over the reef. After that, it's a straight shot to us."

"You think she'll hit the Rebuke?" Josef said.

"Undoubtedly," the admiral said. "This is the most strategically valuable spot on this side of the island. It's also where our fleet is and a clear path to the city itself. She'd be a fool not to take this bay, and I very much doubt the Immortal Empress is a fool." The old man clenched his teeth. "We can't let her enter the bay. If they land a ship on us here, we're done."

"Can we take the fleet out again?" Josef said. "Sink the ships as they come in?"

The admiral shook his head. "It took you two hours to sink three ships. By the time you cut one down, we'll be overrun."

Josef cursed loudly. "So what do we do?"

The admiral licked his lips, but before he could answer, another voice spoke up.

"Abuse your advantages," Eli said, walking down the stairs to join them.

The admiral frowned, but Josef turned to face the thief. "Go on."

"This is a nice, deep bay," Eli said. "But those palace ships are ten times the size of the biggest Council freighter. They're heavy, loaded for conquest, and running deep. Even with the current lifting them, they'll have to enter the bay carefully to avoid scraping bottom. But raise that bottom a little, and you make a difficult task impossible."

Josef stared at him. "How am I supposed to raise the bottom of the sea?"

"Put something on it," Eli said, glancing pointedly at the ships filling the bay.

The admiral almost turned green. "You can't mean—"

"Are you suggesting I sink my fleet," Josef said over him. "My *only* fleet, to make a wall?"

Eli nodded. "That's exactly what I'm saying."

"*Are you an idiot?*" the admiral screamed.

"No," Eli said, crossing his arms. "But I might start to think you are if you can't see that your runners are no longer useful."

"Majesty!" the admiral cried. "You cannot listen to this madness." He flung out his hand toward the boats. "Those runners are fine, precision-crafted warships. You can't sacrifice our naval strength on one foolhardy gambit!"

"Actually, I don't see why not," Josef said, rubbing his chin. "Eli's right. Without clingfire, the runners are only good now for drawing fire and dodging between palace ships. Dodging doesn't win wars. If we can block the bay, we can buy time for the Council to arrive."

"But, sire," the admiral said, his voice cracking. "That fleet was your mother's pride!"

"And my mother would throw it away in a heartbeat if it served her country," Josef said. "We can't be sentimental if we're going to have a hope of surviving."

The admiral looked like he was about to cry. "If you sink the fleet, we'll be defenseless against the next naval attack."

Josef smirked. "Fight the sword at your throat, admiral, not the sword in the sheath. If sinking the fleet gives me the luxury of missing it later, I'll count that a victory. Man the runners, skeleton crews only, and tell the men to line them up at the mouth of the bay. I want everyone else to get a bow and get to the cliffs. This is now a siege."

The admiral clutched his head in his hands. "I can't believe this is happening."

"Believe it," Eli said, giving the old man a gentle push. "Off you go now. We don't have much time."

Too shocked to realize he was taking orders from the prince's layabout friend, the admiral nodded and ran down the stairs, calling orders in a mournful voice.

The sailors of Osera lived up to their reputation. Not fifteen minutes after the plan was hatched, the runners were moving out. Four men crewed each ship, rowing hard against the current until they reached the mouth of the bay. They worked quickly, throwing the wrist-thick docking lines from ship to ship. As one pair of men tied the lines, the other worked the anchor, dragging the chain back and forth across the seabed to catch the rocks. One by one, the boats linked together, forming a floating wall between the bay and the sea. When the ships were all tied in position, by rope to each other and by anchor to the ocean floor below, the sailors kissed the prows good-bye before pulling the bilge plugs. As the sea rushed in, the sailors jumped into the bay and swam for the trawlers waiting to take them to shore.

Josef watched it all from the cliffs where the royal guard and those sailors not tasked with sinking the fleet had positioned themselves with crossbows taken from the watchtower armory. The admiral was there as well, his face pale and drawn.

When the last ship had been scuttled, Josef examined the battlefield. The mouth of the bay was now a spiky wall of sunken ships. Each runner had been scuttled prow first, its iron-tipped nose shoved deep between the craggy rocks of the bay floor with its long body pointing up and its narrow mast stabbed into the water behind it like a brace. Even so, the wall of scrapped boats looked like little more than flotsam before the enormous palace ships.

"Will it work, you think?" the admiral whispered.

"We'll know soon enough," Josef said. "Are the archers ready?"

The admiral nodded. "Everyone's in position. The scuttle crews will get bows and get up to the cliffs as soon as they land."

"Good," Josef said. "Because the enemy's on its way."

The Empress's fleet had cleared the reef and was now plowing across the span of deep water that ran parallel to the coast. The front line of ships was already within striking distance of the sea cliffs, but the fleet slowed as it neared the island, turning off the Empress's current to form a ring around the mouth of the bay. Lights flashed on the decks as the ships signaled to each other, and then one of the palace ships from the circle's northern end broke off from the group and began slowly moving toward the wall of sunken ships.

"They'll stop," the admiral said as the palace ship crept toward the barrier. "They have to stop. They'll break their hulls and strand themselves if they don't. No admiral would waste a ship like that."

"And no woman would give up life as a princess and betray her homeland for the love of a ruler she's never met," Josef said bitterly. "Don't underestimate the Immortal Empress, admiral." Josef looked up, raising his voice as he grabbed his crossbow from the ledge. "Stations! Here they come!"

The order was scarcely out of his mouth when the enormous palace ship crashed into the sunken remains of the Oseran fleet.

The squeal of wood on wood echoed off the cliffs, followed by the horrible crunch of breaking timbers. At the mouth of the bay, the line of sunken ships was bowing, dragged inward by the momentum of the enormous ship. The water churned as the sunken runners plowed along the seabed, and then, with a great clang of metal on stone, the tangle of anchors and knotted chains reached the end of its slack. The line caught, and the palace ship jerked to a halt.

The bay held its breath as the ship stopped. On its deck, the soldiers were sliding, thrown off their feet by the sudden stop. Some fell hundreds of feet into the water below as the ship tilted with a great groan, its keel well and truly stuck in the wall of the sunken fleet.

A cheer went up from the cliffs and then died out almost as quickly as the prow of the palace ship began to shake. Josef squinted. It was possible the crash had broken something inside, but the soldiers on the deck weren't running with the sort of panic he'd expect from the crew of a damaged ship. He was still watching their movements for a sign of their plan when the prow of the palace ship fell forward.

The great pointed nose fell like an ancient tree, crashing into the bay with a splash that echoed off the cliffs. It bobbed once in the water before a network of ropes wrenched it tight. Josef bit back a curse. The prow hadn't broken. It was designed to fall, forming a launch ramp for the troop boats Josef could now see waiting inside the ship's enormous belly. The second the ramp was steady, the boats began to roll out, pushed by men carrying long wooden shields over their heads, their dark faces set in grim determination as they hauled the boats down the ramp and into the bay.

Three ships were in the water before Josef realized his army was gawking and not firing.

"Shoot!" Josef shouted, arching his neck to look up at the sailors on the cliffs. "*Now!*"

The men jumped at his voice, and at once a ragged volley launched from the cliffs. The short, black crossbow bolts flew from all directions, falling on the boats like rain. The enemy raised their shields over their heads, but it wasn't enough. Men fell screaming into the water with bloody splashes as the Oseran arrows struck true, but it did not stop the torrent of boats pouring out of the palace ship.

"Keep firing!" Josef shouted as he reloaded his own bow. "Don't let up!"

Wave after wave of bolts shot down from the cliffs, covering the enemy ramp in a bristle of wooden quills. The bolts struck hard,

hard enough to punch holes in the troop ships that were already in the water. But for every boat the Oserans sank, two more appeared from the palace ship's maw, sliding down the ramp into the bay whose blue water was now a sickly shade of purple.

"How many of the bastards are in there?" the admiral shouted.

"Too many," Josef said, tossing his empty quiver down and reaching for another. "But they're not the real trouble. Look."

The admiral followed Josef's gaze past the palace ship's open nose to its back, and his ashen face turned even grayer.

On the rear deck of the palace ship, ten men stood in a circle around a glowing sphere of iron and stone. The sphere grew brighter by the second, until it hurt Josef's eyes to look at. When it was as bright as a small sun, the men threw out their hands in unison and the glowing ball launched into the sky. It arced above the bay and started to fall, hurtling toward the watchtower with a high-pitched scream.

"War spirit!" the admiral cried. "Get a team down there!"

"No!" Josef shouted. "Keep firing! The war spirit is covered!"

The admiral stared at him. "Covered how?"

Josef nodded at the storm wall. "Time for that lazy bastard to do his part."

The admiral turned and nearly dropped his bow. Eli was standing on the storm wall, staring up at the falling war spirit with a calm smile as he unbuttoned his shirt. With each button, black smoke rose to curl around him, flashing with sparks. Overhead, the war spirit was picking up speed, its scream ratcheting up to a deafening wail even Josef could feel in his bones. Just before it crashed into the tower's tile roof, the fire over Eli's head exploded and an enormous, glowing hand snatched the war spirit out of the air.

Heat poured over the bay as Karon roared to life. He stepped out of the smoke, his great feet searing the stone of the storm wall. The lava spirit's glowing face was split in a wide grin as he hefted the war spirit in his hand and, after a windup, threw it back. The war spirit shot out of the lava giant's hand like an arrow. It flew screaming, leaving a streak of smoke behind as it barreled across the bay and landed with an enormous crash in the palace ship's hull.

The palace ship rocked under the impact, slamming into the seafloor with so much force Josef felt it through his boots. The Empress's soldiers screamed as their ramp tipped into the water, capsizing the launching ships and toppling their passengers into the bay. Up on the cliffs, an enormous cheer went up from the Oserans. Down on the wall, Eli held his arms up in answer.

"Stop cheering and keep firing!" Josef shouted. "We're still under attack and you're only puffing up his head!"

The men scrambled to obey, sending another rain of arrows down on the invading ships. The wizards on the palace ship were running madly now, too busy patching the hole from the returned war spirit to launch another. Meanwhile, the flow of soldiers from the open nose of the palace ships slowed to a trickle as the crews retreated to help deal with the damage. This left those already in the water unguarded as the Oseran arrows rained down like black hail, and for a moment, Josef almost believed they'd stopped the charge.

"Sire!" a voice shouted, shattering the illusion. "South!"

Josef turned just in time to see a second palace ship crash into the wall of the sunken fleet at the bay's southern tip. The crack of wood drowned out every other sound as the boat ground forward. This ship was going much faster than the first, cleaving into the bay in an attempt to break the barrier. But for all its power, the stubborn tangle of anchors held, and the enormous ship slammed to a stop, sending soldiers skidding off her decks.

Josef gave a triumphant shout. But even as cheers began to ring from the cliffs, the second ship's prow fell, and a fresh surge of soldiers poured into the bay.

"Don't stop!" Josef roared, firing his crossbow at the new boats. "Keep firing! Don't let them reach the shore!"

The sailors on the cliffs answered him with a rain of arrows. The bolts whistled as they flew. Some hit nothing but water, others landed in the heavy shields the enemy took shelter beneath as they pushed the line. A few lucky shots struck true, sending soldiers toppling out of boats. But with so many firing from the cliffs, those few lucky shots had been enough. Just barely. But now, as the second palace ship began disgorging its troops in earnest, the Oserans started to fall behind.

"Keep firing!" Josef shouted again, grabbing another quiver of bolts. "Focus on the ones in the water!"

He had just launched another bolt when he heard a crash above him, and Josef looked up to see Eli's lava spirit grabbing the edge of the cliff. Karon's glowing hands cut easily through the stone, carving out an enormous boulder. Down on the storm wall, Eli was shouting words Josef couldn't hear, pointing at the new palace ship. Karon nodded and hefted the boulder in his hand. He closed his fingers, firing the stone to a red-hot ember before launching it at the second ship.

The boulder struck true, hitting the palace ship's enormous tower of a mast. Josef covered his ears against the crack of shattering wood as the mast snapped and fell, its top plummeting into the deck below. This, plus the impact of the stone itself, was enough to crack the ship's keel against the seabed. The palace ship broke with a scream of wood, and then the air was filled with a rushing roar as the water began to gush in.

Josef screamed in triumph, raising his arm to Eli, who bowed in return, a huge grin on his face. Karon was grinning too as he reached out to cut another boulder from the cliff.

Nara clutched the railing of her balcony, glaring furiously at the enormous, glowing giant sinking her ships. Even at this distance, there was no mistaking the lava spirit for anything other than what it was, and that raised a new problem. No mere wizard could command the fire that ran through the heart of the world. The Oserans had a star fighting for them.

She clenched her teeth. What star would dare oppose her? She was no longer the favorite, but she close enough that it shouldn't matter. Even forgetting that, how could there be a star here when Benehime herself had ordered this island burned to the ground?

Nara paused, thinking quickly. Perhaps the Shepherdess didn't know? For all her power, she wasn't omnipotent. Maybe she wasn't aware that one of her stars had turned rogue? It wouldn't be the first. The Lady had been forced to put down the Great Bear not long before this. If a star was interfering with the invasion, the wise thing to do would be to call the Shepherdess and get her blessing before continuing, but Nara hesitated.

The Lady loved her as a conqueror, an Empress. An Empress ruled with absolute authority. An Empress rolled over everything in her path. An *Empress* did not run crying to the Shepherdess whenever trouble appeared. Nara pursed her lips. Until the Lady told her differently, the order to burn Osera stood. Whoever this star was, they would soon learn what it meant to challenge the soon to be recrowned favorite.

Smile returning, Nara opened her spirit again and sank down into the sea. This time, she ignored the great current, grabbing a smaller one instead. The current cried and begged, but it obeyed like all the others in the end. As it fled to do her bidding, Nara sat back on her couch to see what the star would do.

Josef didn't notice the admiral's absence until the old man returned, his face grim.

"Sire!" he yelled over the roar of snapping bows. "We're running out of bolts!"

"Can't be," Josef said, launching the last bolt from his quiver. "Finley had six months' worth laid up."

"Six months of normal fire," the admiral said. "Not for this."

Josef turned and looked, his heart falling. He hadn't had time to notice in the heat of battle, but the crate he and the other men on this part of the cliff had been using was empty. So was the crate it sat on.

"They're on the last box on the south side as well," the admiral said. "A runner just came asking for more. I had to turn him away."

"So there's nothing left?"

The admiral shook his head. "We emptied the tower armory as you commanded. Every last bolt was here."

Josef cursed and looked down at the bay. He could hear it happening already. The whistling roar of the bolts was shrinking, the light on the bay brightening as the rain of arrows began to dissipate.

"Send runners to the other cliff," he said, tossing his now-useless crossbow on the ground. "Tell the men to finish the bolts they have and get down to the wall."

"What can we do on the wall?" the admiral said. "We've a hundred royal guard left, but the rest of these men are sailors, not infantry."

"Then it's time to switch vocations," Josef said. "We've five hundred men here. That many of the enemy are lying facedown in the water already, and we haven't even made a dent in their numbers. But we've still got terrain on our side. If Eli's message got through, the Council fleet should be on its way right now. All we have to do is hold a little longer."

"If we go down there we'll be slaughtered!" the admiral shouted.

"We'll be slaughtered anyway!" Josef shouted back. "If you want roll over for it, be my guest, but I mean to die as an Oseran should: fighting."

And with that, he left the admiral gaping and stomped down to the storm wall.

Eli was waiting for him at the base of the cliff, though he didn't look as smug as Josef had expected. He was smiling, but his face was pale and his eyes were dark with exhaustion.

"You all right?" Josef said as the thief fell in beside him.

"Fantastic," Eli said.

Josef didn't buy it. "You look like you've been running for three days straight. If you can't keep it up, say something. I'd rather fight without a lava spirit than have it go out on me at a bad time."

"I can keep this up as long I have to," Eli said firmly, glancing up at the lava giant as it stepped aside to make room on the storm wall for the gathering troops. "It's just that there's not much for Karon to burn for energy here, so I'm having to feed him some of my own." He laughed. "It's disgustingly Spiritualist-like, actually. My only comfort is that Miranda isn't here to see it."

"Just don't push yourself," Josef said. "I can't have you and Nico down at the same time."

"Don't worry about me," Eli said, his voice suddenly serious. "Think of this as my chance to pay a little back for all the blood you've spilled for me."

"I don't reckon debts in blood," Josef said, reaching out to grab Eli's shoulder. "Watch yourself, thief."

"You too, king," Eli said, breaking off from Josef with a salute.

Josef shook his head and jogged over to join the soldiers.

The Oserans crowded the storm wall. The royal guardsmen were already in formation by the stair, but the rest of the men stood in loose knots, some still clutching their empty crossbows. They parted to make a path for Josef as he climbed onto the storm wall's lip and turned to face his army, such as it was.

"Listen up!" Josef shouted. "I'm not going to waste time with kingly speeches. All I'll say is this. We did our best to hold the enemy back, but it was never more than a dyke against the flood. Now we're up to our necks, and the only chance we have to stop the Empress from crushing this island and our lives under her feet is the stone under ours." He stomped hard on the storm wall. "We are not dead yet. Reinforcements are coming from the mainland even as I speak. Our job now is to buy those slow Council bastards time enough to get here. Fortunately, Osera herself is on our side. We've got a choke hold." He pointed at the narrow stair leading up from the beach. "We've got the sun at our backs, and we're forcing them to fight uphill. These are our weapons, and with them, we are going to hold this wall."

But even as he pointed out their terrain advantage, many of the men still looked doubtful. Some even looked like they were about to cry. Josef took a deep breath. The storm wall might be strong, but the men were a brittle barrier, easily broken. He was going to need them to be stronger if this was going to work, and so, with nothing left to lose and Eli too far away to hear him, Josef decided to throw it all in.

"Men of Osera!" he shouted, doing his best to infuse his voice with the deep, proud sincerity he remembered from his mother's speeches. "I've been a horrible prince to you my entire life, but though I might be your king for only another few minutes, I mean to make them count. As a swordsman, I learned that the two most dangerous enemies are the desperate man and the man defending his home. Right now, we are both. We are the worst enemy the Empress has ever met. We will hold this wall and make her remember the cost of fighting Osera!"

The cry that came when he finished made Josef jump. The men screamed with a fury he could feel to his bones, raising their blades as they did. Josef raised his sword in answer and shouted for them to get in position. The men scrambled to obey, the sailors lining up on the storm wall while the guard fell in around Josef at the top of the stair. The royal guard saluted their king as he passed, following Josef as he climbed down the stair until he was halfway between the beach and the top of storm wall. Here Josef stopped, planting his sword as the guard fell into formation behind him.

Down below, the first boats had made it to the shore. The enemy jumped into the surf with a blood-curdling scream, surging up the beach like a black tide. They hit the storm wall and began crowding into the bottleneck of the narrow stair. When the first enemies came in range, Josef stepped forward, swinging the Heart with a shout. Behind him, the Oserans answered with a scream that shook the stones of the storm wall itself.

"Eli," Karon rumbled, pressing his hand to the ground. "The rock says there are ships coming across the channel from the mainland."

"Please tell me it's the Council," Eli moaned.

"Sad showing if it is," Karon said. "Only two boats."

"I'd take a rowboat and a mule at this point," Eli said. "Meanwhile, you ready to give our swordsman some cover?"

"Sure," Karon said, grinning as he grabbed another boulder from the cliff. "Where do you want this one?"

"I'm thinking middle of the bay," Eli said, his voice breathy. Karon was pulling hard on him now. "Make some waves. See if we can't capsize a few boats."

"Easy enough," Karon said, firing the stone in his fist until it was red hot. But as he reached back to throw, a crash made them both jump.

Eli spun around, eyes wide as a spout of water erupted from the sea. It thrust from the bay like a spear, shooting up the storm wall straight at Karon. Eli threw out his hands, but the water was too fast, and he, exhausted, was too slow. The geyser of water hit his lava spirit full in the chest. Some of it hit Eli as well, and he gasped as the icy-cold shock took his breath away. This was no mere ocean water; it was a deep-sea current flowing full force, thrown up from the sea.

Karon fell as the water drenched him, screaming as his light went out. The ground trembled when he landed, and the impact threw Eli off his feet. He landed on the sandy ground by the road, tumbling hard. But before he was done falling, he was scrambling to his feet. Beside him, Karon's body was no longer glowing, but a black heap of steaming rubble. Eli rushed forward with a curse, plunging his hands into the hissing stone. It burned as he touched it, but not nearly as much as it should have. Cursing louder, Eli dug down, stabbing his spirit through the cooling rock as he dug toward Karon's molten core.

He caught it just in time. Eli tugged his hands out of the stone and pressed the lava spirit's flickering heart to his own chest. His skin burned when Karon touched it, but Eli had never welcomed the pain so much. He clenched his teeth and pushed harder, forcing the lava's heart into his own. Karon went without a sound, and, for a long moment, Eli knew he'd lost him. Then the lava's heat flashed as Karon's pulse merged with Eli's, and the burning heart began to beat.

Eli fell to the soaked ground, panting and clutching his burning chest. "Karon," he whispered. "Say something."

The silence stretched on.

"Please," Eli pleaded. "Please say something."

But the lava spirit didn't answer. Eli could feel Karon's heat in his chest, but it was so small, so fragile. Before he could panic further, Eli forced himself to stand. He teetered toward the watchtower, desperately searching for somewhere to collapse. If Karon was going to survive, he needed all of Eli's strength, which meant Eli couldn't have any of it for a while.

"Hang on," he whispered, pushing open the watchtower door. "I promised I wouldn't leave you, but that cuts both ways, you know? Don't go out on me now."

His only answer was silence as he pulled himself up the watchtower stairs.

Meanwhile, halfway down the storm wall, Josef met the first of the Empress's soldiers with a clash that echoed across the bay.

CHAPTER

23

Hold the line!" Josef screamed, swinging the Heart at the seething wall of soldiers.

The enemy covered the beach in a solid mass, but only a few could go up the stairs at a time. These Josef held off easily, but the enemy, realizing the obvious path was blocked, was now climbing the jagged stone of the storm wall itself.

"Spread out!" Josef shouted to the soldiers behind him. "Half left, half right! Knock them off as they climb. Don't let them reach the top!"

The orders were swallowed as he gave them, overwhelmed by the war cries of the enemy as they surged forward and the dying screams of his soldiers as they shot the last of their bolts at the climbers only to find that the enemy had bows of their own.

Josef swung again, knocking three enemy soldiers down the stairs with a curse. For every man he knocked down, two more popped up. The crashed palace ships were still vomiting up troops, and the bloody bay was full of boats. The storm wall was alive with the enemy. They swarmed the stairs, swarmed the wall; some were even climbing the cliffs themselves, pulling themselves hand over hand up the vertical stone toward the abandoned archer lines. Meanwhile, the Oseran sailors had spread themselves thin in an attempt to hold the storm wall. They screamed as they fought, their eyes wide with the wildness of men pushed past their limits. The only place the enemy sailors weren't attacking was the blackened stretch where Karon had stood, but the lava spirit himself was nowhere to be seen. Instead, a great pile of black stone blocked the storm wall, the boulders still and quiet. Josef knew little of wizardry and nothing about the link between Eli and the giant, but even he knew those dark, cold rocks were not a good sign.

Unfortunately, Josef had bigger worries than the lava spirit. As more and more soldiers began to climb the storm wall, the Oserans were starting to fold. The fragile line he'd drawn as their last stand was cracking. Any second now it would break completely and he would fail his mother one last time.

The Heart jerked in his hands, bringing him back to the fight in front of him. He could feel the blade thrumming against his fingers, and Josef blinked as the Heart's plan became clear in his mind. It was risky, but he trusted the Heart to know its own limits, and they had precious little else to call on. Decision made, Josef swung wide to scatter the enemy and then brought his sword back, holding the blade in front of him with both hands. Down the stairs, the Empress's soldiers hesitated, watching for the strike. When it didn't come, they surged into the opening, swords rising to cut him down. When they were a step away, Josef slammed the Heart into the stair. Iron hit stone with a resounding *gong*, and the weight of a mountain fell on the beach.

As far as he could see, the Empress's soldiers collapsed, slammed to the ground by the pressure. The Heart's force spread wider than Josef had ever seen. It filled the bay, sweeping the soldiers off the storm wall and crushing them into the hard sand below. Infantry boats sank into water pressed glassy by the enormous weight, and a sudden, deafening stillness descended. Even the Oserans were silent, staring down the storm wall at the prone bodies of the Empress's troops in dumb amazement.

Finally, a guardsman behind Josef snapped out of the trance, reaching out to press his shaking hand against the invisible wall of the Heart's weight. "Are they dead, sire?" he whispered, eyes wide.

Josef raised his head, careful to keep his hands on the Heart's hilt. "No," he said. "The ones forced underwater may drown, but no one will die from the pressure. I don't understand it myself, but my wizard friend says it's impossible to kill a human with spirit pressure alone."

The sailor blinked. "Spirit pressure?"

"Don't ask me," Josef said. "I don't do that wizard stuff." He looked over his shoulder, raising his voice. "Everyone!" he shouted. "Stop gawking! We're falling back to the watchtower."

"But we have no more bolts!" a sailor cried. "What are we going to do in the tower?"

"You want to stay out here?" Josef bellowed back.

The man didn't answer, and Josef took the chance to push the guards behind him up the stairs. "Get the wounded to the tower. The rest of you, prepare to hold the road. We'll fight these bastards for every inch!"

The men sprang into action, grabbing the wounded and dragging them back. They swarmed the watchtower, carrying their fallen comrades on their backs as they climbed the stairs. Those who could still fight gathered at the head of the road to the city and began piling barrels, empty arrow crates, anything they could find into a makeshift barricade.

Of the Oserans, Josef alone did not move. He watched his men climb the stairs, hands clenched around the Heart's hilt. Down in the bay, nothing stirred, but as the minutes ticked by, the Heart began to quiver against his palm. Josef gripped it harder and stood firm, trying to press his strength into the Heart as the sword had done for him so many times before. He didn't know if it worked, but the Heart held. Five minutes. Seven minutes. At ten minutes Josef knew as surely as though the blade had shouted that time was up. It was just enough. The sailor's retreat was finished. He was now alone on the stairs with the flattened invaders.

In one smooth motion, Josef ripped the Heart out of the step and turned to run, charging up the stairs toward the Oseran line. Behind him, the sword's weight vanished like mist, and the silent air filled with the angry, confused roar of the Empress's army as it got to its feet and began to give chase. Josef reached the top of the stairs and ran full-out toward the makeshift barricade. Yelling for his men to get out of the way, he jumped the piled barrels. The second his feet hit the dirt, he turned and took stock of their new position.

It was bad. Osera's primary defense on this side had always been the sea and the cliffs. Here, behind those walls, they had precious little. The tower with its thick stone and reinforced doors was safe, but the road was another matter. The wall of junk the soldiers had cobbled together wouldn't stop a charge, only delay it. After that...

Josef glanced over his shoulder. The road ran up the mountain behind him, through the shoddy neighborhoods of the eastern slope to the castle and the city beyond. A straight shot. Josef gritted his teeth. He could feel his men watching him, their eyes wide and terrified. Raising his sword, Josef forced himself to look confident. He wasn't sure if it worked. The men didn't look reassured, but they didn't run away either. That would have to be good enough, Josef decided. He wasn't his mother, after all.

"We hold here," he said, planting his feet firmly on the sandy road. "Get ready."

He felt the line tighten around him. The royal guardsmen moved to take the road's center, locking together in tight formation with their short swords ready. The sailors hovered at the edges, clutching their knives with wild-eyed intensity as the first enemy reached the top of the storm wall.

For a few seconds, it was just one man, and then the Empress's army poured over the wall. They came in a black wave, armor rattling like an avalanche, their raised swords gleaming in the last rays of the evening sun. When they opened their mouths to shout, the air itself seemed to thicken with the rage of their battle cry.

"Hold!" Josef shouted, but the command was lost in the enemy's roar. It didn't matter. His men were frozen in place by fear. They couldn't have moved now if they'd tried, not even to run. All they could do was bunker down and scream their last defiance as their death charged forward to crush them under a thousand booted feet.

Josef gripped the Heart. Even his sword couldn't beat so many, but he would hold as long as he could. The Heart weighed heavy in his hands, echoing his resolve. They would go down as a swordsman should, in glorious battle surrounded by the bodies of their enemies. But even as he braced for his final stand, Josef heard a cry that stopped him cold. It was a high-pitched shout, not panicked or afraid, but commanding. A woman's shout, and as it sounded, a great wave of water shot through the air above his head and landed on the charging army.

The wave swept the soldiers off their feet, washing them back over the storm wall and down to the beach in the space of a breath. Josef lowered his sword, staring dumbfounded at the now-clear storm wall. He was so shocked, he didn't even flinch as the lithe, silvery, canine shape sailed through the air and landed right in front of him.

Gin landed neatly and turned to flash Josef the smuggest, toothiest grin he'd ever seen, but the dog's grin was nothing compared to the haughty smile on his rider's face.

"Well, well," Miranda said, looking down on him from her ghosthound's back. "If it isn't Josef Liechten."

"Miranda," Josef said, leaning on his sword. "Took you long enough."

Miranda sniffed. "Is that any way to greet your savior?"

Josef shrugged. "Better late than never, I suppose."

She shook her head and turned Gin back toward the city. Josef moved to follow her and stopped, eyes wide. The road from Osera, which had been empty not a minute before, was now filled with the strangest creatures he'd ever seen. There were cats made of living wood, birds shaped from clouds, and even what looked like a long, flat snake made of mud. There must have been a hundred at least, each different, and each carrying a rider whose hands flashed with enormous, gaudy rings.

"Powers," Josef whispered. "What in the world is that?"

"*That* is your salvation," Miranda said proudly. "The Spirit Court comes to face the Empress."

"Lucky us," Josef muttered, taking a step back as the lead rider, an intense man mounted on an enormous jade horse, came to a halt beside Miranda.

"Who is this?" the man asked, looking Josef up and down.

"A criminal, Master Banage," Miranda answered. "But one on our side, for now at least."

Josef looked the old man over. So this was the Rector Spiritualis she was always going on about. He'd have to remind Eli to change his alias.

Banage arched an eyebrow at Miranda's introduction and then moved on to business.

"Miranda, with me," he said, dismounting. "The rest of you"—he looked over his shoulder at the waiting Spiritualists—"form a perimeter and wake the local spirits. This island is now under the Court's protection."

"Yes, Rector!" The shout rose from a hundred throats in unison, and the wizards began to dismount. One by one their creatures disappeared, flowing back to the rings on their riders' fingers. Josef noted that the Rector's own mount had vanished into the large oval of polished jade on his index finger. Banage didn't even seem to notice. He and Miranda were already walking toward the sea wall.

"Hold it!" Josef shouted, leaving his poor, shocked sailors standing dumb on the road as he ran after the two wizards. "What are you, crazy? There are a thousand soldiers down there!"

"Shoo," Miranda said. "Go back to the others. We've got it from here."

"Got what?" Josef yelled.

"Young man," Banage said calmly, not even looking at Josef as he walked. "A thousand soldiers are of little concern. Whom do you think you are dealing with?"

"A pair of suicidal idiots," Josef snapped back.

"I see only one of those," Miranda said, glaring at him.

Josef threw up his hands as Miranda and the Rector Spiritualis stepped out onto the edge of the storm wall. Gin sat down beside his mistress, tail lashing back and forth. Down on the beach, the enemy was regrouping. Soldiers from the boats were trading places with the men down the wall by Miranda's wave. Meanwhile, a mass was gathering at the wall's base with archers taking up position to cover the next push to retake the wall.

Josef cursed and reached to pull Miranda out of arrow shot at least, but she smacked his hands away.

"Just stand back," she said, raising her voice over Gin's growling.

Josef had a pretty nonkingly answer for that, but Miranda had already turned back to face the beach. She stood still a moment, feet pressed against the storm wall's edge, her red hair blowing in the sea wind like a painted archer target. Josef cursed, but before he could yank her down to safety, dog or no dog, Miranda held out her hand and a wave of water exploded into the air.

The torrent poured down the storm wall, sweeping it clean. It blasted the soldiers into the sand before turning like a snake and rushing down the beach until it reached the northern cliff. There it shot up again, defying gravity in a geyser of white spray to knock off the soldiers scaling the cliff face, shucking them from the stone like barnacles before turning back toward the beach, knocking those soldiers who'd tried to stand back onto their faces as it rushed to clear the southern cliff.

But while Miranda's water was sweeping the beach, the soldiers in the boats were on the move. Archers brought up their bows while those with shields gave them cover, and the air filled with the snapping of bowstrings. A volley of arrows launched from the water, whistling toward the two wizards on the storm wall's edge.

Josef moved on instinct, raising his sword. He couldn't cut all the arrows down, but maybe he could stop enough to keep the idiot wizards from getting themselves killed. But as he stepped into position, the Rector Spiritualis raised his arms, the ruby on his thumb glowing like a furnace. That was the last thing Josef saw before a blast of light drowned his vision.

A wave of blistering hot air caught Josef in the face. He stumbled away, cursing as he blinked against the swimming shapes the light had left on his vision. As his eyes cleared, he looked up to see a great ball of fire hovering in the air before Banage. Its edges burned like liquid gold, and its center was so bright Josef couldn't look at it. The fire roared and twisted like a living thing, the flames turning until they settled at last into the shape of a great, golden bird.

The bird opened its mouth, roaring like a furnace as it devoured the arrows. The shafts were consumed instantly, transformed into a harmless rain of ash that pattered at the Spiritualists' feet. When the last arrow had been consumed, the bird began to beat its wings. Each wing beat hammered Josef with a wall of heat, and with each flap, the bird grew larger until its fire filled the sky. The light was so intense now, Josef could barely see, but he could make out the shadow of Miranda crouching on the wall, her water surrounding her and her dog in a protective barrier against the heat. Banage, however, had no protection. He stood at the heart of the fire, a speck of black against the inferno. With a great sweeping motion, the Rector Spiritualis threw out his arms, shouting words that were instantly lost in the roar. The bird screamed in answer and fell, plunging down the storm wall in a river of fire.

For a moment the Empress's army just stood there, staring at the blinding bird. And then, in unison, the invasion force turned and fled. The men on the beach threw themselves into the water, scrambling over each other to get their heads below the waves as Banage's fire spirit swept over them. Everything the bird touched was consumed. Its heat was so intense it blackened the sand and boiled the surf. Those caught in its flames turned to ash in an instant while those who'd made it to the water began to scream as the bay itself became a scalding pot beneath the bird's heat.

Out in the deep water, the landing boats rocked as the soldiers fought to turn them back to the crashed palace ships, but the ships' men were pulling up the landing ramps in a desperate attempt to put anything they could between themselves and the fire. The men in the boats screamed curses, but their voices were drowned out by the roar of the bird as it flew low over the bay, sending the invaders leaping into the sea to avoid its fiery wings.

Josef stood on the wall, scarcely daring to believe his own eyes. Minutes ago he'd been prepared to die in Osera's last stand; now he was watching from safety as the enemy fell over themselves in desperate retreat. He cast an almost sheepish glance at the Spiritualists. Miranda was on her feet again, holding out her hand as her water spirit returned, the cold blue tide vanishing into her palm. Banage was standing beside her with his fingers pressed against the enormous ruby glowing on his thumb, eyes following his bird beneath brows furrowed in concentration.

When every one of the infantry ships had been capsized, the bird turned and flew back to the storm wall. It grew smaller with every foot before finally vanishing into Banage's ring with a puff of smoke. The Rector smoothed the stone with his fingers as the jewel's glow faded.

"How high can Durn lift the bay line?" he said, voice calm and quiet, as though he were discussing a change in his schedule.

Miranda flexed her hand as the last traces of water vanished into her skin. "Three feet?" she said. "Maybe a little more."

Banage nodded, moving his fingers from the ruby to a deep-green stone wrapped in delicate gold filigree on his thumb. "Three feet will be fine. Be ready on my mark."

Miranda nodded and closed her eyes. A second later, the storm wall began to rattle under their feet. Josef cursed, but Banage didn't even seem to notice. He was looking at the bay, eyes locked on the line of sunken ships.

"Steady," he said, clutching his ring as the closing prow of the last palace ship locked into place. "Now."

The heavy ring on Miranda's thumb lit up with a green flare. Far in the distance, over the screams of the panicking soldiers and breaking waves, Josef heard the sound of stone grinding. He followed it and found himself staring at the line of sunken ships. That line was now churning, the sea bubbling like a boiling pot. Josef squinted, leaning out over the wall to see what was happening below the water. In the end, however, it was the sound that told the truth. The bay filled with the groaning of stone as the line of scuttled ships began to rise from the water. Josef stepped back in awe, eyes wide as he looked at Miranda to see her clutching the enormous green stone on her thumb with her eyes closed, her face furrowed in deep concentration as sweat ran down her cheeks. Banage, however, was cool and collected. He stood steady, watching the rising line of ships, his fingers hovering over the green ring on his own thumb.

The grinding rumble went on and on until, at last, Miranda gasped and stumbled, catching herself on Gin as the green light faded. The moment her ring flashed out, Banage stepped forward, holding up his hand as his ring flashed to life, glowing like a green sun on his finger as the grinding of the stone gave way to a great creaking moan of splitting wood. Josef turned back to the bay, but he saw nothing. The sunken fleet was well out of the water now, resting on a line of exposed seabed. Even the two grounded palace ships were several feet higher, their front halves pushed up like matrons with their noses in the air. But that was all Miranda so far as Josef could tell. Banage was obviously doing something as well, but whatever it was, Josef couldn't see. He could hear it though, and he kept his eyes on the bay as the sound of splitting wood grew louder and louder.

Without warning, a wall of green erupted down the line of scuttled ships. It started at the edges where the bay met the cliffs, leaves exploding from the sunken runners as a line of oak trees sprouted from the raised seafloor. The trees spread across the bay like green fire, their canopies popping open like paper lanterns before Josef's eyes until a wall of dense foliage cut the bay off from the sea.

But as the trees' growth slowed, the sound of splitting wood grew louder than ever. Josef scowled, confused, and then a flash of motion pulled his eyes north, toward the first palace ship, and he gaped in disbelief. The grounded ship was moving, its enormous hull rising up as graceless as a bull on its hind legs. Soldiers slid off the decks as the front half of the ship's hull rose out of the water, pushed up by an enormous tangle of tree roots. The same thing was happening to the second palace ship on the other side of the bay. The tree roots dug under the ships' broad bottoms, forcing them up until their noses were in the sky. Finally, with one last, enormous crash, the two palace ships slid backward, off the roots, out of the bay, and into the ocean. They landed in the open sea with a crash, both ships slamming into the water and then sinking almost immediately as the ocean surged in through the shattered hulls.

But that was all Josef saw. The moment the palace ships were dislodged, the trees surged in. Huge oaks shot up like arrows to fill the gap, branches exploding from the trunks as the new canopies spread until the ocean was completely obscured behind a wall of solid green.

The men in the water, those who remained after Banage's fire bird, swam frantically to the line of trees and began to climb, picking their way through the branches and throwing themselves into the ocean beyond in a desperate attempt to escape. Banage watched their struggles with a smile before turning to Miranda.

"Well done," he said, helping her back to her feet. "I'm going to provide some cover. Lend me your mist?"

"Of course, Master Banage," Miranda said, reaching to touch one of her smaller stones. It flashed blue the second her fingers passed it, and Josef smelled the clean, predawn wetness of a mountain valley as a thick mist filled the air. Meanwhile, Banage rubbed his fingers against a white stone set in a thin band on his wrist, and a second smell, salty and cold, joined the first as a thick sea fog rose up from the bay. Fog and mist rose together, intertwining and expanding until the bay vanished beneath a thick, gray blanket. But the fog wasn't finished. It spread up the stairs, around the tower, and along the cliffs, spilling up the mountain toward the mainland. By the time Miranda and Banage finally stepped down from the sea wall, the entire island of Osera was shrouded in cloud.

"That should buy us a little time," Miranda said, glancing at Josef before her eyes darted to something over his shoulder. Josef turned to see his soldiers standing on the storm wall behind him, staring in amazement at the two wizards who, in a little under five minutes, had completely reversed Osera's fortunes.

"Not much time," Banage said. "The fog gives us cover, but they don't need to see to launch war spirits. Frankly, I'm surprised Osera isn't knee-deep in them already. We need to speak with Queen Theresa immediately." He turned to the gathered soldiers. "Who's in charge here?"

The men looked at each other, and then at Josef.

"I am," Josef said with a sigh.

"Don't be absurd," Miranda scoffed. "I don't know what kind of scam you people are running, but we don't have time for your games. Where's the queen?"

"In the palace," Josef said coldly. "Won't do you any good, though. Queen Theresa is dead. I'm king of Osera now."

Miranda's face went very pale. "If you think for one moment I'm going to buy that load of—"

"He's speaking the truth, ma'am," one of the soldiers interrupted, standing a little straighter.

Miranda blinked. "You've got to be *kidding*!" she roared. "Do you know who this man is? He's a wanted criminal! A thief! A bounty hunter, pride fighter, and right-hand man of the most notorious—"

"That'll be enough," Josef said, putting enough edge in his voice to ensure that it really was enough. Miranda snapped her mouth closed, but her scowl only grew deeper.

"How are *you* king?" she said at last.

"Because my mother was queen," Josef answered, turning around and walking toward the tower. "And as I said, she's dead. Now come on. If our time's limited, I don't want to waste it on things that don't matter."

Miranda and Banage exchanged a tight-lipped look and followed.

Down in the bay, hidden by the fog, the last of the Empress's soldiers climbed through the wall of trees and dove into the sea, swimming through the waves and toward the line of palace ships waiting on the other side.

CHAPTER
24

Banage stopped them at the foot of the tower to hear reports from the other Spiritualists, but Miranda was too enraged to listen. Josef Liechten? A king? Of *Osera*? It was absolutely impossible. This had to be one of Eli's scams. How he could trick an entire kingdom, queen included, Miranda had no idea, but she intended to find out. That thief could not be allowed to meddle with something this big.

By the time they entered the tower, Miranda had worked herself into a cold fury. For all his talk about not wasting time, Josef set a maddeningly slow pace. They climbed the winding tower steps carefully, stepping over the wounded as they went. The gristly scene only sharpened her rage. She wasn't sure how, but she was positive Eli was somehow to blame for all this. And while she couldn't actually pin the Empress's sudden appearance on him, she was absolutely sure Osera would have been in a better position to defend itself if he hadn't been here running whatever con he was running.

The stairs finally ended at a large watch room ringed with windows. There were wounded here too, but the half of the room overlooking the bay was clear, though the view of the bay itself was completely obscured by Allinu's mist and Banage's fog spirit. She could feel her mist straining to keep the island covered against the light of the setting sun and the stiff wind from the sea, and Miranda sent a small pulse of power down to Allinu's ring. The strain eased a bit, and she turned her full attention back to the task at hand.

A large table was set up under one of the bay-facing windows. Beside it, an older man in an officer's coat was waiting with a map, which he handed to Josef. Josef took it and leaned over the table, seemingly forgetting about them entirely. The older man looked stricken for a moment by Josef's indifference and then stepped forward, bowing before Banage.

"Rector Spiritualis," he said. "On behalf of all Osera, please let me thank you. You arrived in the nick of time."

Banage nodded. "It was our duty." He paused.

"Admiral Hawthorne," the man supplied in a hurried voice. "Commander of her majesty's navy. *His* majesty's now, of course," he corrected himself. "Though there's not much left of it."

"Wouldn't be *any* left if these two hadn't shown up," Josef said, standing. He looked Miranda in the eye, then Banage. "Thank you," he said, his voice surprisingly sincere. "I really thought that was the end. Thank you for the fog as well. Maybe it'll buy us enough time for the Council reinforcements to arrive."

"Don't count on it," Banage said. "Product of nepotism he may be, but Myron Whitefall's an experienced general. His objective is the preservation of the Council, not Osera. He won't waste time sailing troops out here when he can use your fall to buy the time he needs to fortify the continent."

Josef's face grew very dangerous. "If that's how it is, then why are you here?"

"Because we are not the Council," Banage said. "Much as some would like to claim otherwise, the Spirit Court is an independent body with its own priorities, and right now those include stopping the Empress's advance. If you are indeed king of Osera, then we are prepared to offer you our full cooperation toward that end."

Josef nodded. "What have you brought?"

Banage began to rattle off the Court forces—the number of Spiritualists, the capabilities of the spirits at their command, so on and so forth. Miranda stopped listening almost immediately and began scanning the room. There were many prone shapes lying in the dark around them. Miranda examined each of their faces, looking for the boyish, infuriating one. If Josef was here, Eli couldn't be far away. He was probably watching right now...

Even as the thought crossed her mind, she spotted a familiar shape. At the far edge of the room, a small bundle lay pressed against the wall. Miranda had spotted it only by chance, and even now, when she was turned to look straight at it, the bundle seemed to fade into the shadows. But nothing could hide the white, feminine, skeletally thin hand peeking through the folds. Miranda sucked in a breath. She'd know that hand anywhere. It was the same hand that had dug into Gin's back in Mellinor, and considering Josef was standing a few feet away, there was no doubt in her mind. It was Nico, and if she was there— Miranda's eyes jumped to the lanky soldier sitting slumped beside the demonseed, his unruly black hair falling down to hide his face.

"Eli Monpress!" she shouted, interrupting Master Banage midsentence. "Come out now. You're not fooling anyone."

Everyone turned in surprise to see what she was pointing at. Across the room, the slumped man heaved a long sigh and looked up.

"Nothing gets by you, does it?" Eli said.

Miranda ignored him, turning to the admiral. "That man is the thief Eli Monpress," she said. "He must be arrested at once."

The admiral stared at her, his face strained and white as paper.

"Lady Spiritualist," he said at last. "I fear you are mistaken. That is Lord Eliton Banage, best friend and adviser to King Josef Liechten of Osera."

For several seconds, Miranda was too shocked to speak.

"Banage?" she said at last. "Eliton *Banage*?" She turned back to Eli, who was on his feet by this point, neatly picking his way toward them through the lines of the wounded. "Of all the..." She almost couldn't find the words. "Slanderous, outrageous, *presumptuous*—" The list dissolved into enraged sputters. "How *dare* you try and hide behind the name of the most respected wizard on the continent! I don't care if we're at war or if the Empress is coming up the stairs as we speak, I'm taking this criminal in *right now*. Master Banage!" She turned to face her Rector. "I'll handle this. He won't..."

Her voice trailed off when she saw Master Banage's face. He was standing perfectly still, his eyes open so wide she could see the whites all the way around. He was staring at Eli like another man might stare at a corpse suddenly come to life.

"There is no slander," Banage said, his voice thin and almost trembling. "It's been a long time, Eliton."

"Fifteen years," Eli said, stepping up to stand beside Josef.

Miranda couldn't even speak. She just stood there, looking from Banage to Eli and back again. "Impossible," she whispered. "*Impossible*. There is *no way*—"

"Miranda," Banage said, his voice suddenly as sharp as a razor. "Go downstairs and command the front until I return."

Miranda blinked. "What?"

"Now," Banage snapped.

She stared at him stupidly as the command sank in. Then, without a word, Miranda obeyed. She turned and walked down the stairs, the click of her boots and the moans of the wounded the only sound in the tower. She didn't stop walking until she reached the edge of the sea wall. She stood on the precipice, staring out into thick fog, her mind whirring so fast she didn't even notice Gin until the ghosthound pressed his nose into her back.

"Eli is Master Banage's son." The words tumbled out of her before she could stop them.

"Really?" Gin said, sitting down beside her. "I always thought they smelled kind of similar."

"This has to be some kind of joke," Miranda went on as though she hadn't heard him. "Master Banage is a man of duty and integrity. I've never heard him tell a lie, and I don't even think he's capable of stealing. Eli is the most irresponsible, conniving, *sleazy* excuse for a wizard I've ever met. How can they possibly be related?"

"Morality isn't an inherited trait," Gin said, flicking his ears. "Look at things objectively and it's really not surprising. I mean, they're both dark haired, tall for humans, thin built, and powerful wizards."

Miranda didn't even want to go down that path, but now that Gin had put the idea in her head, her mind would not stop finding similarities. The way Eli and Master Banage both talked with their hands, for instance, or the particular way their eyes would narrow when they were angry. The little details kept coming, piling up until even her outrage couldn't overpower the mountain of evidence.

"Powers," she muttered, flopping against Gin. "Why didn't Master Banage just *tell* me?"

Gin snorted. "Can't blame him. Can you imagine anyone willingly owning that thief as a son?"

Miranda rubbed her eyes. "I don't even know anymore. I can't believe—"

She stopped when she felt Gin's paw nudge into her side. The ghosthound was looking over his shoulder. Miranda turned as well and saw one of the young Spiritualists, a girl whose name she couldn't remember, standing timidly several feet away with a look on her face that screamed, *I have an important message but I'm too shy to interrupt.*

Miranda sighed. "What?"

"Spiritualist Lyonette," the girl said, bowing low even though she and Miranda were technically the same rank. "Someone's approaching from the city."

"Someone?" Miranda said, frowning. "What kind of someone?"

"We're not sure," the girl said. "It's hard to see with the fog, but it looks like two people leading ten wagons."

"Two people leading ten wagons?" Miranda's scowl deepened, and Gin began to growl. "All right," she said, jumping off the wall. "Let me have a look." Because, really, how much stranger could this day get?

The girl smiled in relief as Miranda and Gin walked to the head of the road. Sure enough, squinting through the mist Miranda could just barely make out ten wagon-shaped shadows coming down the mountain with surprising speed. Gin raised his nose, sniffing the air in a loud huff.

Miranda waited impatiently. "Well?"

"You're not going to believe this," Gin said, lowering his head with a snort. "And you're not going to like it either."

"What?" Miranda said pointedly.

Gin told her, and he was right, she didn't like it one bit. Biting back a curse, she grabbed the Spiritualist girl and sent her up the stairs to warn Master Banage that things had, against all odds, gotten worse.

Eli hung back, keeping Josef between himself and Banage. The king and the Rector were talking strategy, something about leveraging Josef's ability to sink palace ships, but Eli was too distracted to pay much attention to the actual plan. The Rector's eyes never left Josef or the map, but Eli could feel the old man watching him without watching, just like he used to. Eli crossed his arms and glared pointedly out at the fog. He'd known the moment he decided to send Miranda the message that it would come to this. He didn't regret calling for help, even this beat asking Benehime for aid, but that didn't mean he had to like it.

He was staring as hard as he could at the blank, gray spot where the beach should be when he heard someone enter the room. He looked up to see a girl about Miranda's age, though with only a fraction of Miranda's rings, standing in the doorway. She bowed nervously and went straight for the Rector, whispering in his ear. Banage's already stern face fell into a deep frown as she spoke. When she finished he nodded and waved her away, turning to Josef with a dour look.

"It seems the Council is here."

"Council?" Josef said expectantly. "Troops?"

Banage shook his head. "I imagine troops are coming, but right now you'll have to content yourself with the Council's head wizard."

Despite his best efforts, Eli's breath caught.

Thankfully, Josef didn't notice. He was glaring at Banage, turning this latest development over in his head, looking for the trap. "I thought the Spirit Court split from the Council," he said. "That's what you told me."

"We have," Banage said. "But we face a common enemy. I should think you'd welcome the help."

"That depends on the help," Josef said.

"For that, you'll have to ask her yourself," Banage said, his voice cold. "The Court does not involve itself in her methods."

Josef looked at the Rector with a curious scowl, but he started toward the door all the same. He paused when he reached it, looking over his shoulder at Banage, who had not moved.

"Go ahead," the Rector said. "Eliton and I have things to discuss in private."

Josef's eyes darted to Eli, but the thief shook his head. It would have come to this sooner or later. Might as well be sooner.

Josef turned and started down the stairs, leaving Eli and Banage staring at each other. Thanks to the thick fog, the tower was very dark now. Eli could barely make out the wounded lying on the other side of the room. Banage, however, he could see clearly thanks to the light that was still emanating from his rings. Eli grimaced and looked away.

"If you're here to arrest me, don't bother," he said. "I'm under the king's protection. Last time I checked, Spiritualists don't break local laws."

"I'm not here to arrest you," Banage said quietly. "Though I am happy you remember some of the doctrine I tried to teach you."

"How could I forget?" Eli grumbled. "Sometimes I think you taught me to read only so I could study Spiritualist laws." He paused, waiting for Banage to start raging, but the room was more silent than ever. The quiet stretched on and on until Eli could bear it no longer. "You wanted to discuss things in private," he said, sitting on the edge of the table. "So discuss."

Banage took a deep breath. "Why didn't you come home that night?"

Eli didn't have to ask which night he meant. "I had no reason to," he said. "What was there for me to go home to? You didn't want me unless I was ready to be an obedient Spiritualist."

"That's not true," Banage said. "I was trying to teach you discipline. Responsibility. You were always powerful, and there are rules that—"

"Oh, yes," Eli said, surprised at how bitter his voice sounded. "How could I forget? You cared more for rules than you ever did for me."

"I was trying to teach you respect for the spirits!" Banage shouted. "Obviously, I failed. Look at you, a thief and a degenerate, using spirits for your own selfish purposes." He clenched his fists, his rings glowing brighter as his spirits reflected his anger. "When I think of what you could have been. What I could have made you—"

"I don't have to listen to this," Eli said, hopping off the table. "I freed myself from your expectations years ago, old man. If you're going to be disappointed in someone, save it for yourself. You were a terrible teacher and a miserable excuse for a father. If I didn't turn out the way you wanted, that's entirely on you."

Eli started to leave, but Banage moved to stand in his way. Eli reached out to push his father aside, but his hand stopped an inch from the old man's arm. Banage was looking at him with an expression Eli had never seen on his face before. If it had been anyone else, he would have said the old man was on the verge of tears.

"I am more disappointed in myself than you will ever know," Banage whispered. "When your mother refused to leave Whitefall's Council, I took you away from Zarin and tried to raise you as best I could. Every night since you vanished, I've been haunted by regret for all I could have done to prevent it. I've hated you, Eliton. I've despised you, blamed you, but I never, ever stopped loving you." His hands reached out, fingers trembling, to clutch Eli's shoulders. "The day I first saw your bounty poster was the happiest day of my life, because that was the day I knew you were still alive."

"And you sent your apprentice after me," Eli said.

Banage flinched. "I had to. Whatever you may think, I am responsible for you, as a father and as Rector. I could not let you go on abusing spirits and flaunting the rules of the Court."

Eli reached up and pried Banage's fingers off his arms. "I've never abused a spirit in my life," he said. "Ever. Ask Miranda, she knows. So would you, if you knew me at all."

"And you think for that I should just let you do as you like?"

Banage said, his voice growing heated again. "You're one of the most powerful wizards I've ever seen, and yet you insist on being a criminal. If you will not willingly accept the responsibility and self-control that power demands, then it is my duty to make you. If you want to throw your life away, that's your decision, but you can't be angry with me for doing my duty!"

"*Throwing my life away?*" Eli roared. "You finally find me after fifteen years and that's all you want to talk about? How I'm wasting my power as a wizard? *Powers*, father." He looked away in disgust. "All I ever wanted was for you to see that I was worthy of your interest. Me. Not my power as a wizard or my future as a Spiritualist. Just me, Eli, your *son*."

He glanced back out of the corner of his eyes, but Banage's face was sterner than ever. Eli sighed and shook his head. "Obviously that's too much for you," he muttered, pushing past Banage and stomping toward the door. "Next time you want to have a private chat, don't bother unless you've got something new to say."

"Wait."

Eli paused. He could hear Banage moving, but he didn't turn back. He didn't even want to look at the man anymore.

"Your mother is outside," Banage said, his voice strangely thick. "Will you say something to her?"

"No," Eli said, stomping down the stairs. "I have even less to say to her than I had for you."

If he'd looked back then, he would have seen Banage put his head in his hands, but he didn't. He ran down the stairs two at a time, ducking out at the second-to-last landing, the only landing that had a window. He wiggled through the narrow slit and dropped to the walkway along the sea wall, keeping the tower between himself and the gathered Spiritualists standing at the tower door. He could hear voices on the wind, Miranda's, Josef's, and another, a smoky, haughty voice from his memory. Eli stopped, nearly overcome by the memory of fragrant smoke. Then the wind shifted and the voices vanished. Free again, Eli walked to the very end of the sea wall and sat down in the crevice where the wall met the cliff. The fighting had been lighter here, and he was able to find a clean stretch of stone. The fog hid the ravaged battlefield, and staring into the blank grayness, he was almost able to forget where he was and why.

You should have known better, love.

Powers, Eli thought, closing his eyes as the voice filled his mind. Not now.

His ribs burned through his tattered shirt as Benehime's white arms snaked around him.

I don't even know why you stayed to talk, she whispered in his ear. *To Banage you're just another duty, another mess to put right. Did you really think it would be any different?*

Eli dropped his head. He hated Benehime's voice at the best of times, but he never hated it as much as when she spoke sense. "Good thing I didn't call the Spiritualists to go over ancient history," he muttered. "So long as Banage fights the Empress, I don't really care what he does with his private time."

Oh yes. He could hear Benehime's smile. *How goes the good fight? Not well, I'm guessing, considering the sorry state of your darling lava spirit.*

Eli set his teeth and said nothing.

He's going to die, you know, Benehime whispered. *Such a waste. I could save him, of course. Him, your swordsman, even your little demon. I could save them all, but oh—* She paused. *That's right. You're not going to ask for my help . . .*

Her voice trailed off, letting the words hang. In the silence, her finger slid across his chest to hover just on the edge of Karon's burn. The moments ticked on, but Eli didn't break his silence. Finally, Benehime sighed in his ear.

I'll be waiting, she whispered, her hands pulling back through her cut in the world. *And unlike Banage, who wants you to be something you're not, or Miranda, who just wants you to disappear, or even Josef, who wants you to save his kingdom, all I ask, all I've ever wanted, is your love. Come home, Eliton. Let me help you. Love me again as I love you and I'll give you everything—your lava spirit, your friends' lives, safety for this land, everything.*

Eli closed his eyes as the Lady's presence began to fade.

When you're ready, love, I'll be here. I'll always be here for you.

The words echoed in the fog, and then the Lady was gone. Eli closed his eyes as her pressure vanished, clutching his fingers against Karon's burn.

"I'm sorry," he whispered. "I'm so sorry. I'll find another way to save you. But you know I can't go back." He felt the water on his cheeks before he realized he was crying. He scrubbed his eyes fiercely and tried to look away, but everywhere he looked, he saw the ravages of war. The dead were little more than shadows in the fog, but he felt them just as he heard the terrified whispers of the spirits all around him, the moaning fear of the winds above, and though he knew it was his imagination, Eli could almost taste the reproach in their voices.

Eli bowed his head. "I'm sorry this is happening," he said, rubbing his eyes on his sleeves. "I'm sorry I *let* this happen. I'm letting everybody down. It's my fault."

And it was. It was his fault. His fault for thinking Benehime would actually be above starting a war over her stupid obsession. His fault for letting it continue. He could stop it right now. One more lie, that's all it would take. But...

"I'm sorry," he said, choking on the words. "I can't go back to her. I'm so sorry, so, so sorry, but I can't. *I can't.*"

The sob shook him this time, and Eli clenched as his burned chest seized. Despite the motion, Karon didn't move. Eli swore under his breath and let gravity slide him down the cliff and toward the cold, wet stone, curling into a ball on his side as the mist swallowed him whole.

Miranda stood at the foot of the watchtower with her arms crossed and her mouth set in a stubborn line. Gin stood beside her, growling deep in his chest as he kept his eyes on Sara and, more important, Sparrow, who was standing beside her. Sara stared right back, smoking her ever-present pipe in long puffs. Sparrow simply looked bored, lounging on the wagon with a sleepy expression like ghosthounds growled at him all the time. Of course, for most of the last two months, that had pretty much been the case.

Miranda ignored the flamboyant man completely, focusing on Sara, head wizard of the Council of Thrones, inventor of the Ollor Relay, and Eli Monpress's mother. Powers, she thought with a stifled groan, that explained so much. But at least it meant Eli came by his scheming honestly, most likely making it the only honestly gotten thing he possessed. She studied Sara as the wizardess took another puff of her pipe, trying to see what Master Banage had ever seen in the woman. Whatever it was, it must be long gone. Miranda had been ready to strangle her from the first moment they'd met.

The door of the tower creaked and she turned gladly to greet Master Banage. But it wasn't the Rector who emerged from the tower. It was Josef, and he did not look happy.

"What's all this?" he said, eyes moving up and down the spectacle gathered at his door.

"All this" was a line of wagons, the same wagons from the Council's assault on the Spirit Court Tower earlier that morning. Each was large enough to carry eight men with room to spare and filled with lumpy objects hidden beneath a cover of thick, tied canvas.

There were ten wagons in total, all identical, and none with a driver or animals to pull them. They rolled on their own, much like Slorn's wagons, though with wheels instead of legs. But these weren't like Slorn's wagons; Miranda was positive of that. One, Sara wasn't that nice, or a Shaper, and two, the wagons didn't move and fidget like Slorn's awakened creations did. These wagons followed Sara's instructions with a sluggishness that reminded Miranda more of bad puppetry than spirit work. Still, strange as this was, Miranda put it out of her mind. The threat, if there was one, wouldn't come from wagons that moved themselves but from whatever Sara was hiding under their cloth covers.

Sara met Josef with a smile, her eyes flicking to the enormous sword on his back. "You must be Josef Liechten, master of the fabled Heart of War. I hear you're king of Osera now. Congratulations, and my sincere condolences on the loss of your mother."

Miranda snorted. Sara didn't sound sincere at all. Fortunately, none of this seemed to faze Josef.

"Right," he said. "And why are you here?"

"To honor the Council's duty to Osera," Sara answered with a shrug. "And to offer a new weapon in the war against the Empress."

That got Josef's attention. "What have you got?"

Sara smiled. "You'll see for yourself as soon as the fog clears, which should be any moment now."

"What are you talking about?" Miranda said.

Sara looked surprised. "Can't you hear it, Spiritualist? Listen. The mist is straining. Something's pushing on it."

Miranda shifted her attention immediately to her mist, but Allinu felt fine. Nothing was different. Miranda frowned and pushed softly on the thread of power connecting them. The thread pushed back, but the push was weak and thin, and Miranda's breath caught.

"Allinu!" she shouted, looking up.

"Sorry, mistress," the mist whispered around her. "We're holding as best we can, but the Empress has a wind. I don't know how much longer we can keep this up."

"A wind?" Miranda scowled. "How big a wind?"

"Big enough to blow your mist away," Sara said, glancing up. "Look."

Miranda looked. Sure enough, she could see patches of the evening sky overhead.

"I'm sorry, mistress," Allinu whimpered. "We tried."

Miranda made a soothing sound and held out her hand. The mountain mist spiraled down, sinking into her ring with a sigh. Banage's fog was dissipating as well, and Miranda turned, staring out at the sea as the air cleared.

"Powers," she muttered, blinking against the strong, unnaturally steady wind from the sea.

Behind her, Josef added a more powerful curse.

Just beyond the line of trees and wrecked ships was a wall of palace ships. There were seven in all, pulled so close to each other that their crews could step from one boat to the next. Their decks were black with soldiers arranged in alternating lines, the first row kneeling, the next standing just behind them. All of them were holding larger versions of the curved bows the soldiers who'd invaded the bay had been carrying, and every bow was drawn. Miranda swallowed as the full force of what she was seeing hit her. Thousands of arrows, notched and drawn, and all of them pointed at the top of the storm wall where the Oseran forces were standing.

"Durn!" Miranda shouted, but her rock spirit's name was lost in the deafening snap of the bowstrings. A black wall of arrows shot over the bay. There wasn't time to duck, no time for Miranda to do anything except to raise her hands in a pathetic shield as the arrows whistled toward her.

When the arrows were close enough that Miranda could see the fletching, everything suddenly went black. She blinked in surprise and then winced at the thud of the arrows striking something solid and smooth. Miranda stepped back, and then she began to grin. Durn towered over her, a great stone wall covering a ten-foot-long span of the storm wall. She grinned wider and slapped her hand against the stone. "Thank you."

"Of course," Durn answered, his gravelly voice thick with pride.

Beside her, Josef lowered his sword. "Nice trick."

Miranda looked over her shoulder. By luck of where she'd been standing, Durn's wall had also sheltered the road, the door to the tower, and most of their forces. Outside the stone's reach, arrows lay everywhere. They stuck in the ground, lay broken on the stone, and a few were even embedded in the wooden shutters of the watchtower windows. Miranda swallowed. If Durn hadn't shielded them, that surprise attack might well have been the end. Back on the road, the sailors and Spiritualists stood in a stunned clump, their eyes glassy as everyone realized how close they'd come to death.

"They're notching another volley."

Josef's voice fell through the stunned silence like an iron weight. Miranda turned her head to see the swordsman at the edge of Durn's wall, peering out at the enemy.

"Get to cover!" she cried.

She didn't have to say it twice. Soldiers and Spiritualists scrambled for the safety of the tower's shadow. They used the broken arrows as markers, crowding into the lee of the tower where no arrows had landed. Sara, however, did not move. She stood calmly beside her wagons, and Sparrow stood calmly beside her, though his face was paler than usual as he kicked a stray arrow that had landed inches from his boot.

"They're not going to shoot again," Sara said when she caught

Miranda's alarmed look. "The arrows are just to keep us huddled. I'd get your Spiritualists back out here. The real attack is about to start."

"What do you mean?" Miranda said, crouching behind Durn. "How do you know?"

"I've fought the Empress before," Sara said, lifting her chin. "Look. Here they come now."

Miranda pressed her hand against Durn's surface. The stone softened under her fingers, letting her push a small hole through the wall, just enough to see that Sara was right. On the deck of the center palace ship, behind the line of archers, a circle of ten people stood around a ball of stone and metal. The circle of figures raised their arms, and the ball began to glow red hot. Miranda felt her mouth go dry. She'd never seen one before, but there was no question that the thing at the circle's center was one of the Empress's war spirits. But even as she recognized what she was looking at, the circle of wizards threw their arms toward Osera and the glowing ball launched off the deck. It flew through the air with a deep, wailing scream, leaving a trail of smoke behind it as it arced up and then down, straight toward Durn's wall.

Miranda ran back before she knew what she was doing, throwing out her hand as Mellinor surged out of her. The water flew up in a spout at the falling war spirit, and they collided midair in a burst of steam. A second later, she felt Mellinor's triumph echo through her as the jumble of metal and stone, now black and dripping, slammed to the ground at the watchtower's foot, followed by a shower of icy cold water.

Miranda held out her hand as Mellinor flowed back into her. "Good catch!"

"Don't celebrate yet," Mellinor said, his voice dire. "Look."

Miranda glanced back to see the war spirit stirring in its crater, and then the spirit began to unfold. Stone and iron shifted, forming four sturdy legs, a solid, low-slung body, and a broad, flat head with a great hanging jaw of sharp, steel teeth. The moment the transformation was complete, the war spirit rolled smoothly to its feet, steam rising as it started heating itself up again.

"Powers," Miranda muttered, raising her hands. Beside her, Gin fell to a crouch, claws ready. But before she could do more than ready her spirits, Josef stepped in front of her, sword out.

"I'll handle this," he said. "Get your wizards ready to stop the rest."

"The rest?" Miranda said, bewildered.

Josef nodded and jerked his head toward the water. Miranda turned, and her heart sank. The sky was full of smoke trails as countless red-hot spirits launched from the decks of the palace ships. Most were already flying high overhead to fall on the city behind them. Miranda could only watch in horror as the first one crashed into the mountain, landing in the houses on the eastern slope with an impact she felt through her boots.

But even as the first wave hit, more war spirits were launching. The second volley hit the palace itself. One struck the crumbling tower at the top, taking it clean off. Another crashed into the palace's eastern face, cracking the wall as it tore into the inner halls.

"Miranda," Mellinor whispered in her ear. She barely heard him. She was staring in horror as a war spirit crashed through the palace roof, shattering the floors below with a distant boom of pulverized stone.

"*Miranda!*" the sea spirit shouted.

She snapped out of it. "Right," she muttered, running for the lee of the tower where the Spiritualists were hiding.

"All of you!" she shouted, pointing to no one in particular. "Get to the city and get those spirits under control!"

The Spiritualists stared at her dumbly.

"Go!" she shouted again.

This time, they obeyed. The air was full of flashes as they called their mounts and took off toward the burning city, but Miranda didn't see it. She was already marching back toward Durn's wall.

"We have to stop those ships," she said. "Where's Master Banage?"

"Still in the tower, I think," Gin said, hunching down behind the stone spirit.

Miranda bit back a frustrated groan. "What's he doing? We need him."

"Don't know," Gin growled. "Look sharp, Sara's on the move."

Miranda snapped her head to see her dog was right. Sara had all ten of her wagons lined up along the edge of the storm wall. She and Sparrow were beside the first one, untying the canvas cover.

"What are you doing?" Miranda shouted, marching over.

"What does it look like?" Sara said, undoing the last knot with a snap of her fingers. "I didn't come here to enjoy the show. The war spirits that have already landed are more than enough to over-whelm your small force of Spiritualists. If we're going to save this island, we can't have them launching any more, which means we have to sink the ships."

"Sink the—" Miranda said, coming to a stop beside her. "How?"

"Same way you sink anything," Sara said. "Put a hole in it."

She flashed Miranda a thin smile and tugged the canvas aside. It slid off the wagon, revealing...Miranda wasn't actually sure. The wagon was full of straw and raw wool, like a packing crate, and nestled neatly in the padding were five black orbs. Each one was slightly larger than a man's head, perfectly round and as shiny black as a puddle of freshly spilled ink. The sun was well down now as evening shifted into night, but Miranda could see the orbs well enough thanks to the grim glow of the burning city behind her. The spheres glistened wetly in the fire light, and though she could hear nothing, something about the orbs made Miranda very uneasy.

"What are those?"

"You'll see soon enough," Sara said, picking one up.

The orb fit neatly between her small hands. As Sara rested it against her chest, Miranda swore she saw the orb's black surface tremble.

"Sparrow," Sara said, lowering the orb. "Ready yet?"

"Almost," Sparrow answered.

Miranda glanced up at his voice to see that he'd uncovered the next wagon. This one held no soft packing or strange orbs. Instead, the wagon contained a miniature catapult. The weapon was very cleverly made, with several different levels of tension to fit the most power into the smallest space. So cleverly made, in fact, that Miranda was only slightly surprised when it greeted Sara in a calm, professional voice.

"Hello, Sara. What is our objective today?"

Miranda gaped. "You brought an awakened catapult?"

"Of course," Sara said, placing the black orb in the small depression at the end of the catapult's arm. It didn't look big enough at first, but the catapult shifted as the sphere settled, moving the grain of its wood to hold the glassy ball neatly in place.

"Shaper-made," Sara said with a smile. "What's the point in slaving for the Council if you can't spend some money once in a while?"

Miranda stared at her, eyes wide. "Why do you need a Shaper-made catapult?"

"Because I put far too much effort into these to waste them on bad shots," Sara said dryly, running her hand over the orb. "We'll start with the center ship."

This last bit was directed at the catapult. It obeyed instantly, turning the wagon until it was pointed at the palace ship in the very center of the line. "Ready on your mark," it said, gears creaking as the arm wrenched back.

Sara held out her hand, checking the wind. The moment it fell slack, she gave the order.

"Fire."

The catapult slung, and the black orb flew silently through the air, vanishing almost instantly into the dark. Miranda held her breath, listening for... she wasn't sure. An explosion, perhaps. But all she heard was the slight, musical sound of glass breaking, so soft it was nearly hidden by the waves. But what followed couldn't have been hidden by anything. Miranda bent double, slamming her hands over her ears as the night began to scream.

CHAPTER
25

The scream was high and terrified. It cut through Miranda's skull, drowning out even her own thoughts. But horrible as the scream was, it was nothing compared to what Miranda saw out in the water. At the center of the Empress's line, the prow of the middle palace ship was gone. Not wrecked, not cracked, *gone*. The place where it had been was now solid darkness. No, Miranda squinted, not solid. It was more like a shadowy cloud, but there were glints inside it, tiny flashes of fast-spinning light.

The cloud crept down the ship, screaming as it went. The Empress's soldiers rushed forward, but when they reached the cloud, they vanished as well. After that, the soldiers turned and fled, running for the wizards at the stern of the ship. Miranda watched in horrified amazement as the shadow pushed forward, slowly consuming the enormous ship while a rain of sawdust and powdered metal fell like snow into the sea below.

When her body could move again, Miranda turned to Sara.

"What is that?"

"I should think you'd recognize it," Sara said, picking up the next orb. "I got the idea from your report."

"No," Miranda said, shaking her head. "It can't be."

"Of course it can," Sara said as she lovingly loaded the glassy black ball into the waiting catapult. "Clever idea, actually, compressing a sandstorm. So much power and destruction at your fingertips." She shook her head. "Only problem was the deadline. It's not like I can just make storms. What you see here is my entire stock. Now do you understand why I didn't want to risk them on a nonawakened launcher?"

Miranda was barely listening anymore. "You copied Renaud's glass storm?" she screamed. "*Are you out of your mind?*"

Sara gave her a sideways look. "It was very effective."

"It was *Enslavement*!" Miranda roared.

Sara winced. "Not so loud, if you don't mind." She turned to the catapult. "Next shot will take out the second-to-last ship on the left."

"Yes, Sara," the catapult said, dutifully turning itself.

"Hold that order!" Miranda shouted, grabbing the catapult with both hands. It stopped, confused, and Sara gave Miranda a cutting look.

Miranda was too angry to care. "Did you Enslave this storm?" she said, jabbing her finger at the ball loaded on the catapult's arm.

"No," Sara answered. "If I had, I could have gotten it down to the marble size you wrote about. The smaller size would have been more difficult to aim, however, so it wasn't necessary."

Miranda blinked in disbelief. "You didn't Enslave it because you were worried about size?"

"That and Enslaved spirits are far too unstable," Sara said. "Would you let go of my catapult?"

Miranda tightened her grip. "If you didn't Enslave these sandstorms, how did they get like this?"

Sara heaved an enormous sigh. "I understand this is difficult for a Spiritualist to comprehend, but there are more ways of being a wizard than servants and Enslavement. Sandstorms are nothing but sand and air spirits whipped together, a roving spirit brawl without any real kind of mind. All I had to do was lean on them a little, give them some firm direction. Stupid spirits take a strong hand."

"If all you did was lean on them, how did they end up as glass?" Miranda said hotly.

Sara shrugged. "I can lean fairly heavily, and they might have been a bit upset about it, but it's a sandstorm's nature to be upset. I only concentrated that anger, pressed them together into something a little more effective, and now I'm giving them an outlet." She shook her head at Miranda's furious expression. "Honestly, you're as bad as Etmon. There's no real harm done."

"*No real harm?*" Miranda roared. "You took an innocent spirit and pressed it so hard you changed its substance! It was a *sandstorm*, not a glass storm."

"An improvement," Sara snapped, but before she could say more, a crash echoed over even the sand's screaming, and they both looked up to see Banage barreling out of the tower. Relief rushed over Miranda like a cool wave. Banage's face was strangely drawn, his eyes red and sunken, almost like he'd been crying, though that couldn't be. But whatever had caused him to look that way was gone now, burned away by pure, unadulterated rage.

"*Sara!*" he bellowed, breaking into a run.

Sara rolled her eyes. "Here we go again," she said with a sigh. "Fire."

Pain exploded through Miranda's hand as the catapult obeyed, launching the next black orb into the night. Miranda followed it as long as she could, clutching her injured hand to her chest as the orb exploded and a new, equally horrible scream joined the first as the released glass storm enveloped the next palace ship.

That was when Banage reached them. He grabbed Sara by the jacket, nearly lifting her off her feet as he brought her up to face him. But before he could do more than sputter, he froze. After a second of confusion, Miranda saw why. Sparrow was standing right behind him, a long, slender knife pressed into the back of Banage's neck.

"Unhand the lady."

Miranda's hand moved in a flash, rings lighting up like lanterns as Gin snarled, but Banage moved first. He dropped Sara and stepped back. Sparrow lowered his knife and moved to Sara's side as she straightened her collar.

"That was very unlike you, Etmon," she said coldly.

Banage took a deep breath. "I find it hard to control my temper when I see the head of the Council wizards using Enslavement. I will see you hanged for this."

"I very much doubt that," Sara said. "We are at war, and my spirits are the only thing holding the line at the moment. But maybe you should ask the Oserans? I'm sure they'd love to die with you to save a few idiot storms."

"War or not, there are rules that cannot be broken!" Banage shouted. "Morals are not flexible. They don't change to fit your convenience. You never understood that, Sara." His arm shot out, finger stabbing at the cartful of orbs. "You will stop this at once, or so help me—"

"Or what?" Sara said. "You'll leave? Fine, go ahead. You're already a traitor to your country. What's one more?" She grabbed Miranda's shoulder, pushing her into Banage. "Run away," Sara said. "And take your little parrot with you. There's no room for idealists in war. I'd have thought you'd learned that years ago."

Banage didn't answer. Instead, he clenched his fist. As he did, Miranda caught a flash from the large, black stone on his ring finger, and the ground began to rumble. Sara's eyes widened, but even she didn't have time to react as an enormous stone hand exploded from the ground below the awakened catapult. The stone fingers, eight in all, closed over the wagon, crushing it instantly with a crash of splintering wood and a soft cry from the catapult as its launching arm snapped in two. Banage opened his palm, and the stone hand retreated back into the ground, leaving the whimpering catapult crooning over its broken arm.

For a moment Sara just stood there, mouth open, and then she turned on Banage with a cold fury that could have killed a weaker man. "That was bald treason."

"That was my duty as a Spiritualist," Banage said, setting his hands at his side.

Miranda stood beside him, grinning so hard her face hurt. But the joy was short lived. The screaming glass clouds on the palace ships were still going, but those ships without mad sandstorms were regrouping. On their decks, circles of wizards were moving in unison, and the decks of the ships began to glow. Miranda stepped back, swallowing against the fear that clenched her throat.

The palace ships' decks were full, absolutely full, of war spirits. They glowed like bonfires, waiting their turn as the wizards moved from spirit to spirit, launching them one after another until the sky was full of bright burning dots.

Their light was so bright Miranda could see the annoyance on Sara's face clearly.

"Well," she said, sticking her pipe between her teeth. "You've certainly done it now."

Banage ignored her and turned to Miranda, his face terrifying in the strange red light.

"Every spirit," he said softly. "Bring out every spirit you have."

Miranda nodded and closed her eyes, sinking immediately into the well of her soul. Her spirit opened with a roar. Beside her, she felt a wave of pressure as Banage's spirit opened as well. It was intense, but unlike an Enslaver's, Banage's spirit didn't press down on the connection she shared with her spirits. Instead, it buoyed them, power feeding on power as they stood together, spirits ready as the bright burning amalgams hurtled down.

"Empress," the general said. "That black weapon of theirs is powerful. We should pull back and continue the bombardment from a safe distance."

Nara heard him speaking, but she did not listen. He was just a distraction, a buzzing that interfered with what was truly important. She stood at the very edge of her balcony. Her spirit was open, though only slightly, and she was using it to reach out toward Osera. The island was burning merrily, a sight that should have pleased her, but she was focused on the dark below the fires, searching for a flash of white.

She could feel the Lady on the island. Feel her like the beloved Benehime was part of her own flesh. But where? And why? Nara clenched her teeth until she could taste her bitter anger. Why was the Lady on the island and not with her? Did it have to do with the star controlling the lava spirit she'd drowned earlier? And if so, why? Didn't the Shepherdess see who was winning?

"Empress?" the general said again, his voice hesitant.

"Why does she not answer me?" Nara growled. "Whom does she think this war is for?"

The general blinked. "Empress," he said timidly. "I'm afraid I do not under—"

Before he could finish, the Empress vanished. The general blinked, staring at the place where she had been, but nothing was left except the fading afterimage of a long, white line, hovering in the air.

At that same moment, Nara stepped onto the deck of her foremost palace ship, much to the terror of the soldiers. They jumped back when she appeared, raising their swords and then dropping them just as quickly to throw themselves on the ground.

"Empress!" The cry rose from hundreds of throats as the realization of who was standing on the deck spread through the ship. Everywhere, men stopped their attack and fell to their knees, pressing their heads to the deck.

Nara ignored them all. She stomped to the prow of the ship. Ahead of her, the swirling black madness of the storm blocked her view, screaming as it tore through the ship's nose. Irritated, Nara let a flash of her true nature show. The glass storm froze when it saw her, all anger gone. She dismissed it with a wave of her hand, and the black glass fell pattering to the water, disappearing into the dark sea below with a soft cry. Even before it hit, the Empress was walking forward. For anyone else, this would have been suicide. The raging glass had consumed the prow, leaving a sheer, hundred-foot drop to the sea below. But Nara was the Immortal Empress, a star of the Shepherdess, and the ship knew its place. Boards flew from the lower decks as she walked. They came from the outer hull, the railings, anywhere that was still stable. They piled on top of each other, forming a solid, if makeshift, ramp beneath her feet. When she reached the place where the end of the prow had been, Nara stopped. The boards creaked below her, stretched to the very edge of their ability to hold. Nara ignored the sound and leaned forward, toward the island.

She paused, listening, watching, seething. The feel of the Shepherdess was stronger than ever. Nara followed it as a dog follows a scent, reaching past her ships, across the bloody bay, and up the steep, rocky wall to the lone figure sitting with his back pressed against the cliff. She could see him in her mind as her will touched him—a young man, thin and gangly with shaggy, dark hair. He was hunched over, his arms wrapped around his knees, but she could feel the burning trace of the Shepherdess's touch all across his body, and the realization stabbed her like a sword in her gut.

"You," Nara whispered, her voice shaking with hatred.

What's wrong, Nara? The Lady's voice seemed to float on the wind. *Are you so surprised? You knew there was another star here, and I only have two among the humans.*

"Why is he here?" Nara roared, forgetting herself in her rage.

He's here because you're here, the Shepherdess whispered. *You said you would do anything to be first in my heart, Nara. Now's your chance. Fight for my favor. The boy has set himself up as defender of this island. Crush his forces and take it from him, and I will know once and for all who loves me best.*

"If you want a fight, I will give you one!" Nara shouted into the wind. "Watch me, Benehime! I will show you the difference between that boy and an Empress."

Her voice echoed across the water, but the only reply was the Lady's laughter, chiming like glass bells in the night.

"Captain!" the Empress shouted, looking over her shoulder. Sure enough, the captain was there, kneeling at the end of the makeshift plank. "Tell the wizards to prepare another volley and signal the fleet to ready the assault boats. We conquer this island within the hour."

"But, Empress." The man's voice was shaking. "The wizards on the shore—"

"Will mean nothing in a moment," the Empress finished for him, turning back to the front. "I am about to teach this land what it means to defy the Immortal Empress."

She heard the soft thunk of the captain's head on the deck as he bowed deeper still and assured her that her orders would be followed. Nara barely listened. Instead, she closed her eyes, reaching down into the well of her soul and giving her spirit a hard, sudden twist.

A ripple of power flew out of her, soaring silently over the dark sea, over the new-grown trees blocking the bay, over the bloody water and the forgotten bodies of her soldiers. Her will struck the island like a tidal wave, suffusing the land. All at once, the air was thick with the proof of who she was, *what* she was.

On the shore, the effect was immediate.

In the minutes before the Empress struck, the storm wall was still in chaos.

Miranda crouched panting against Durn's solid wall, Mellinor coiled around her in a rope of glowing water. Banage had his own stone spirit out and was holding the war spirit down with three granite shackles. The war spirit strained against his hold, its sharp claws rending enormous gouges in the road, but Banage's spirit held it firm. Now, it was Miranda's turn.

"Hit it high and hard!" Banage shouted, his voice straining. "We may not get another shot!"

Miranda closed her eyes, focusing on what she was about to do next. "Durn?" she whispered, accompanying the whisper with a surge of power. "Mellinor?"

"Ready," Durn said behind her.

Mellinor just tightened the spinning of his water, forcing it to race faster and faster.

That was all Miranda needed. She shot up, pushing off the dirt as she threw out her arm, throwing all her power along with it. At the same time, Durn surged forward, joining her power and riding with it. Mellinor joined a moment later, sharpening his water to a swirling point at the end of Durn's sharpened fist.

The power from the three of them, Durn, Mellinor, and Miranda, hit the trapped war spirit at the same time, and it screamed as Durn's fist, sluiced with Mellinor's water, dug into the tangle of metal and stone at its center. The spirit's body flashed red hot, boiling Mellinor's water away, but this just made the attack worse. Water, stone, and steam now forced their way into the Empress's war spirit like a drill, tearing everything in their path until, with a deafening shriek, the war spirit's head and front left leg fell to the ground, ripped from its body by the sheer force of her blow.

Miranda flopped to the ground, gasping with relief. Durn and Mellinor fled back to her, and she welcomed them with open arms. She was beaming with pride, but as she opened her mouth to shout her joy, the ground shook.

She scrambled back, raising her hands against the blast of heat as the war spirit tore itself to its feet, breaking through the granite rings of Banage's stone spirit. She heard Banage cry out somewhere in the dark, but she didn't have time to look for him. Her eyes were on the war spirit as it teetered on its three remaining legs, its headless torso listing sideways as its metal began to glow red hot yet again.

"These things are impossible to kill."

Miranda glanced to see Gin beside her with Banage on his back. The Rector Spiritualis hopped down and moved to Miranda's side, clutching the cloudy-gray gem that had been his stone spirit's black ring.

"He'll be fine with time," he said before Miranda could ask. "Dunerik is nothing if not resilient."

"None of us will be fine if we don't find a way to make these things stay down," Gin growled. "Even that pigheaded idiot's still fighting."

Miranda could only guess the dog was referring to Josef. She didn't have a look to spare for the swordsman, but the constant clang of metal on stone from the walk in front of the tower told her everything she needed to know. If the Heart of War couldn't carve these monsters... She clenched her teeth, forcing the thought from her head before it could finish. No point in going down that path. She'd do better to stay focused on the spirit in front of her.

The war spirit was burning full tilt now, and the heat pouring off it was enough to make Miranda's hair crackle. It moved slowly backward, its three feet taking small, careful steps toward the pulverized remains of its head and fourth leg.

"It's trying to put itself back together," Miranda said, sending a pulse of power to Durn. "I want a pillar underneath it. Shoot it up, we're going to knock the head and the leg into the bay."

But as she gave the order, she realized something was wrong. The surge of power she'd sent down the thread that connected her stone's spirit to her own had reached its destination, but Durn had not answered. A cold cringe of fear curled in her stomach, and Miranda looked to see Durn standing behind her, still as the ground under their feet.

"Durn," she said again, adding a little force to her voice.

"I can't," the stone whispered, his voice full of fear. "We're too late."

"Too late?" Miranda asked, but even as the question left her lips, the wall of power crashed into her. Miranda gasped as the enormous weight forced her to her knees, and she wasn't alone. Every one of her spirits had gone perfectly still. Even Gin was on the ground, facing the bay with his head on his paws, almost like he was bowing.

"Durn's right," her hound whined, pressing his nose into the dirt. "We took too long. She's here."

Miranda didn't have to ask whom they meant. Straining against the power, she lifted her head just enough to see the palace ships. She didn't know what she was looking for, what to expect, but she knew the Empress the moment she saw her.

She was smaller than Miranda would have thought, narrow boned and pale, her black hair piled in an elaborate knot on top of her head. Her golden armor shone brighter than her war spirits, but it was not the brightness that drew Miranda's gaze, nor was it the fact that the woman was standing on a seemingly impossible line of wooden boards stretching out from the palace ship's destroyed prow. What drew Miranda's attention was the same thing that drew the attention of everything in the bay, large and small, awakened or asleep. It was power. Pure, unadulterated, undeniable power radiated from the woman like light from a lamp. Even as a blind human, Miranda could almost see it burning, and her heart began to sink.

"That's it then?" she said, almost laughing at the absurdity. "We've lost."

"We never had much chance to begin with," Banage replied. "We set ourselves against a star, after all."

Miranda did laugh then, a dry, humorless sound of utter disbelief. Across the bay, those palace ships that still had prows began to lower them. The moment the ramps hit the water, ships laden with troops began to pour out. Hundreds of ships, thousands, more ships than Miranda could count, all rowing toward the bay.

The Empress watched her ships with haughty pride. Miranda was too far to see her expression, but she didn't have to. The woman radiated triumph as a fire gives off heat. With a great sweeping motion, the Empress swung her hand down and the wall Durn had raised across the bay tore itself apart. Trees and ship hulls flew in every direction as the seafloor rent itself to let the Empress's boats pass.

For one endless moment, Miranda could only watch as the Empress, with one motion, undid all the ground they'd gained that day. Despair like she'd never felt filled her mind as the boats began to pour into the bay. Despair so thick, so overwhelming, she didn't hear Mellinor the first time he spoke.

"I said let's go," he said again, his voice surging through her mind like a deep current.

"But she's a star," Miranda whispered. "She has the will of the

Shepherdess. We can't stand against her. Nothing in the world can. That's what the Shaper Mountain said."

"No," Mellinor said. "Nothing in the world *will*. There's a difference between can't and won't." As he spoke, Mellinor's voice shifted, and Miranda could hear the echo of the enormous sea who'd spoken to her in the dark throne room so long ago. "I am the Great Spirit of the inland sea," he boomed in her mind. "I am still myself, with my own mind and my own soul, and I have no love for the stars or their White Lady. Any one of them could have freed me from Gregorn's prison, but they didn't. They left me to rot and madness in a pillar of salt for *four hundred years*." Mellinor's voice was racing with rage now, and Miranda could feel his power flowing through her, filling her.

"You have shown me more care and protection in the last year than my Shepherdess ever did," Mellinor said finally. "If you're not ready to roll over and give up like the rest, then I am with you, mistress."

Miranda put her hands to her face to stop the tears flowing down her cheeks. "Thank you," she whispered. "If we can try, we must. But how?"

Mellinor told her, and Miranda fell still. It was dangerous, very dangerous. It also went against everything she stood for as a Spiritualist, sworn to keep her spirits from harm. But as she turned it over in her mind, something flinched inside her, snapped like a bone being set into place, and she knew what she had to do.

She turned on her heel and started to run. Gin, still bowing, didn't follow. Banage called her name, but Miranda didn't look back. She kept running, feet pounding across the ruined paving as she ran along the storm wall's edge, straight toward Josef.

CHAPTER

26

Josef clutched the Heart of War, blinking against the sweat that dripped into his eyes. In front of him, the metal-and-stone creature hovered over its two severed legs, still not dead. Josef lifted his wrist to his face, rubbing the sweat and dirt away as best he could. This was taking too long. Cutting the Empress's war monster was easy, but keeping it down was another story, and he was getting tired.

Tired was, as Eli would say, the bedrock of understatement. He was exhausted. His fight with Adela, becoming king, sinking the ships, defending the beach, and—his mind grew dark—the death of his mother, it was all adding up. He'd been fighting in one way or another since midmorning, and now this. He watched as the war creature rolled back to a defensive position, its severed legs already crawling back toward its body. He had to finish this quickly and go help the Spiritualists with the others before the whole island was overrun. Assuming, of course, it wasn't already.

He glanced up at the city. The mountain above him glowed like a sunset. Everywhere he looked things were burning and falling. Even at this distance he could hear the screams of the people, now his people, as they tried to fight the fiery monsters destroying their homes. Rage built up in his chest, but before he could give in to it, the Heart grew heavy, calling his attention back to the fight at hand. Josef obeyed, letting everything else fall aside as he focused on the war spirit, which was nearly finished pulling itself back together. The Heart's hilt pressed against his sweaty palms, pulling him forward, urging him to finish it now, while they still could.

Josef obeyed. He lunged forward, letting the sword's weight pull him into a low sweep. The Heart caught the war spirit's left front leg just as it reattached, and the war spirit opened its great, steel-toothed mouth in what Josef could only guess was a scream of pain. Sometimes being spirit deaf had its advantages.

The Heart jerked in his hands, and Josef refocused. He was beneath the creature now. The blasting heat dried his sweat instantly, baking his skin hard. Josef coughed at the reek of smelted metal, but before he could flee between the creature's legs to cool, dark safety, the Heart jerked again. Josef nodded and shifted his stance, turning with the Heart as the sword flew up to strike the monster's exposed, red-hot belly.

The black blade cut upward, slicing through the glowing metal like a razor through snow. The war spirit jerked above him, a belated dodge, but it was no use. The Heart was lodged at the center of its great, lumbering torso. But Josef was now at the limit of his reach. He stood on his toes, fully extended below the writhing creature with the Heart buried to the hilt in its body. He had no leverage to continue the blow up or strength to knock the spirit over. So he did the only thing he could. He planted his feet and brought the sword down in an arc in front of him.

The Heart cut cleanly down and burst free with an explosion of heat as the war spirit's torso tore open. The spirit was thrashing now, and Josef rolled away before one of those writhing legs could skewer him by accident. The second he was clear, Josef spun to face the monster again. The war spirit was on the ground now, rolling and thrashing as it tried to pull its split torso back together. The Heart of War shook in Josef's hands, but Josef didn't need to be told twice. He darted forward, dodging the spirit's thrashing metal legs as he swung the Heart over his head with both hands. Then, gritting his teeth, he swung it down.

The first blow slammed the spirit to the ground. The next drove it into the stone. Josef swung the Heart as hard as he could, shivering with power as the black blade came alive in his hands, hammering the war spirit into the stone of the storm wall with the weight of a mountain. Finally, on the tenth stroke, the war spirit lay still.

Josef fell backward, nearly dropping the Heart as he gasped for air. In front of him, the Empress's monster lay at the bottom of the crater left by the Heart's rage, beaten beyond any recognition. Stumbling, Josef pushed himself up, ears still ringing with the fading power of his sword. Because of this, he didn't hear the woman yelling until she standing right beside him.

"What?" he shouted, turning to see Miranda. She looked terrible, clothes ripped and stained, hair bedraggled and clinging to her sweaty, soot-streaked face. She also looked determined, and that worried him. In his experience, Miranda looking like that meant something terrible was about to happen.

"I need you to cover me down to the beach," Miranda said, her voice exasperated, as though she'd already said this many times.

Josef blinked. "The beach? Why?" He looked over the storm wall and winced. Apparently that crash he'd heard earlier had been more than just the war spirits. Something had punched through the wall that protected the bay. The water was full of boats now, some with their soldiers already out and wading toward the shore.

"Forget it," he said, turning away. "The beach is a lost cause.

Fight the battles you can win. We should regroup at the top of the stair and—"

"No." Miranda's voice was determined. "I'm not going down there to fight the soldiers. I need you to protect me from them so I can get to the water."

"The water?" Josef said. "What are you going to do in the water?"

Miranda lifted her head stubbornly. "I'm going to do my best to save your people."

Josef ran a hand through his sweaty hair. "Where's that dog of yours? Can't he do it?"

"No spirit can help me with this," Miranda said, shaking her head. "The Empress is a star. That's why I need you."

Her words made no sense, but then most wizard talk made no sense to Josef, so he didn't bother asking for an explanation. Instead, he leaned back and studied her face. She looked as she always did: utterly determined, completely implacable. Powers, it would probably be more work to fight her off than to fight for her. And who knew? Maybe her plan, whatever it was, would be what they needed. He glanced at the dead war spirit lying in the crater beside them. Anything would be more effective than hammering down the rest of the Empress's metal monsters one at a time.

"All right," Josef said, jogging toward the stairs. "How much time do you need?"

"Not much," Miranda said, running beside him. "Success or failure, I have a feeling it'll be over soon."

Josef paused when he reached the top of the stairs. Down below, the first line of soldiers had just reached the sand. He hefted his sword, leaning forward. "Let's go."

He didn't wait for her reply before he charged. The soldiers on the beach were focused on their landing, pulling the boats in and watching the air for arrows. They didn't see him coming until it was too late. He half fell, half ran down the storm wall and landed in the sand swinging. The Heart's power sang through him, washing away his tiredness. His first blow tossed the closest soldier into the cliffs, his next threw two more into the water. The fourth man had time to draw his blade, but the steel shattered the second it met the Heart's black edge, and he went flying as well, slamming into the boat he'd been in the middle of hauling onto the sand.

Josef moved in a circle, swinging the Heart back and forth like a scythe to clear a small stretch of beach. The moment the opening was made, Miranda rushed into it. She ran straight for the water, wading in until it reached her knees. As she splashed into the dark bay, Josef could see more water pouring out of her. Beautiful, glowing blue water cascaded from her outstretched hands, falling into the waves lapping at her knees. It was so beautiful, the shimmering, glowing water mixing with the black surf, that Josef nearly lost his arm to a well-aimed stroke. He cursed and resumed swinging, sending the enemy scuttling back. But even as he drove them off, more came. Hoards of black-armored soldiers jumped from their boats, swords drawn. Josef was panting now. He could feel the fatigue in his muscles now even with the Heart's power roaring through him. That was a bad sign. Even the greatest awakened sword had limits, and he was fast approaching them.

"Spiritualist!" he shouted as the Heart broke another sword. "Whatever you're going to do, do it quickly!"

If Miranda answered, he didn't hear. He caught a glimpse of her as he came back around. She was kneeling in the bay, her face inches from the lapping waves. The glowing water was gone, but he could still make out a small, shimmering line of it running from her out into the bay. That was all he saw before he had to turn back to the fight. He cursed louder than ever, forcing his tired muscles to keep moving, keep fighting. Whatever that fool girl was doing, he hoped she was as right as she always seemed to think she was.

That was his last conscious thought before he abandoned himself to the fight completely.

Miranda knelt in the bay, her fingers digging into the sand below the water. The bay was freezing cold, but she didn't feel it. Battle raged all around her, but she didn't hear it. All her focus, all her attention, everything she was flowed with Mellinor as he pushed out to sea.

When the inland sea had first told her what he meant to do, she'd balked. After all, it was the threat of being sent to the sea that had driven him to accept her as his mistress in the first place. Sending him there now violated the core of their Spiritualist pact, yet Mellinor had insisted, and Miranda, having no other options, had agreed, but only if they did it right.

She'd made their plan clear as Josef had led the way to the beach. The sea was a mass of unruly water spirits, too large to have names or souls of their own. Any water spirit, even a great one like Mellinor, would be torn apart if he entered the sea on his own. But he wasn't on his own. Miranda was with him, and her spirit would act as a wall to protect him against the pounding currents. So long as they kept in physical contact, she should be able to pour enough strength into Mellinor to keep him together long enough to do what needed to be done. Or that was the theory, anyway.

"Just stay with me, Miranda," Mellinor whispered, his voice trembling up the thin tendril of water that connected them as he rushed across the bay. "Don't leave the water, no matter what."

Miranda nodded and opened her spirit wider, reaching out with everything she had. She'd never been this close to a spirit. Her mind seemed to blend with Mellinor's, and suddenly she could feel the ocean all around her as though she *were* Mellinor. When it happened she nearly fell forward at the shock, sputtering as she took in a great mouthful of bitter seawater. But the burning taste was far away. She was flying with Mellinor through the water, clinging to him as the sea tried to rip them apart. Water pounded her from all directions, cold and sharp and filled with tiny, babbling voices. They pushed her, pulled her, beat her soul like a drum as they tried to break through her and join Mellinor's water with their own, but Miranda would not let go. She clung to her inland sea with everything she was, her will an iron wall around him as they pushed out of the bay.

The moment they entered the open sea, a current hit them at high speed, sending both Miranda and Mellinor reeling.

"Hold tight!" Mellinor cried, clinging to her as they tumbled with the stampeding water. "Don't let go!"

Miranda didn't. She held on, wrapping herself in and through Mellinor's spirit until she could no longer tell where she ended and he began. After a few moments, Mellinor righted them and they started upward again, cutting through the churning water like an arrow.

This tied together with her inland sea, Miranda could almost see the currents. They reminded her of flocking birds—great packs of water spirits moving as one, screaming with a million voices. They rushed Mellinor whenever he came near, and Miranda felt each tiny spirit strike her like a needle shot at high speed. Any one alone would have been nothing, but there were thousands of them, hundreds of thousands, and they would have torn her apart had Mellinor not been whispering in her mind.

"You're doing fine," he said, his own voice strained so thin she could hardly make it out. "Just a little farther."

"It's horrible." Miranda didn't realize she was crying until the sob strained her chest. "How can anything survive here?"

"It can't," Mellinor said bitterly. "At least, water can't. Right now, with me, you're as much water as human. That's why you can feel it." A tremor of fear ran through her, and she realized she was feeling an echo of Mellinor's terror. "The sea tears us all apart," he whispered. "It is the horrible end that awaits all water that loses its shore. Now do you see why I was so thankful when you saved me from being sent here by Monpress?"

"If I'd known what it was like, I'd have killed him before I let him send you here," Miranda whispered back.

"Glad it didn't come to that, then," Mellinor said. "Prepare yourself, we're here."

"Here?" Miranda whispered. It felt like any other place in the water.

"Yes," Mellinor said. As he spoke, Miranda could feel the slick, heavy weight of the wood as though she'd hit it with her own back. She looked up, seeing as though she were standing inside Mellinor. Great, black shapes loomed overhead, their edges outlined by the shifting, distorted torchlight. They were below the palace ships.

"I'm going to need to take over a very large amount of water to do this," Mellinor said. "More than I can take on my own, even if I weren't in the sea. This is the most crucial point, Miranda. I'm counting on you to hold me together. Whatever happens, do not leave the water. If you step out of the sea, our connection will weaken and I won't be able to hold together. Do you understand? Do not move, no matter what."

Back in her own freezing body, surrounded by the clanging of swords, Miranda dug her hands deeper into the sand, lying in the water with only her head still above the waves.

"I won't move," she whispered, ignoring the taste of salt that filled her mouth as she spoke. "So long as I can, until I die, I will never, ever abandon you."

"I believe you." Mellinor's voice seemed to flow through her, filling her completely. "Here we go."

Miranda saw what happened next two times, one far away through her own human eyes, the other from Mellinor's perspective as though she were floating at the center of his water. Mellinor was spreading out below the boats, pulling the tiny sea spirits into his own flow. They screamed as he ripped them from their currents, and then fell silent as they were absorbed. His water grew and grew, spilling off in all directions until Miranda could feel the entire sweep of the Oseran island against her body. Mellinor's spirit was straining now, thinning, and she strained as well, holding him together. Finally, just before they both broke, Mellinor stopped taking in water. For a moment he hung there, a vast sea inside the ocean. And then, with a great, undulating roar, he surged upward, taking Miranda with him.

The palace ships began to creak. From her body in the surf, Miranda was dimly aware that the fighting around her had stopped. Everyone, even Josef, was staring across the bay as, with a great groan of creaking wood and the sea's own moaning, the line of the Empress's palace ships lurched to the left.

The ships tilted in unison as Mellinor's sea surged beneath them in a great, vertical wave. Sailors scrambled as the decks turned sideways. Some managed to grab the railings in time; others were not so lucky. Miranda felt them splash into the sea as though they were landing in her own body, but she paid them no mind. Only one body mattered.

From both her perspectives, she looked up at the woman standing on the long plank at the prow of the center palace ship. The Empress stood steady even as her ship tilted beneath her, but her head was turned down toward Mellinor. That was all the warning Miranda got before the Empress's spirit hit them.

The force of the Empress's will knocked Miranda's breath out. It landed on the sea like an iron, crushing Mellinor's wave beneath a wall of immovable, unconquerable power. The sea flattened, its surface pressed glassy smooth by the Empress's will. As the wave vanished, the palace ships crashed back to the water, bobbing back and forth as they righted themselves. The Empress smiled haughtily and turned back to the island, already confident in her victory, and had Mellinor been alone, a simple spirit, it would have been a victory indeed. But he was not alone, and his spirit was not only water. Miranda's will ran through him like a steel net, holding him together even as the Empress pressed him down, for, immortal as she was, powerful as she was, the Empress was still human, and she was still subject to the one immutable law of wizardry: One human spirit cannot control another.

"Go!" Miranda shouted, scrambling to get her head above water as the wave from the palace ship's landing washed over her. "Now!"

Mellinor answered with a roar, and his water surged upward with four hundred years of pent-up rage. This time, though, the wave did not move the boats. It rose in a solid whip of high-pressured water, flying straight for the Empress.

Now it was the Empress's turn to be surprised. She whirled around, her face open with shock as Mellinor crashed into her. The lance of water shattered her golden armor, knocking her off her perch like a bird shot off a treetop. For one glorious moment, the Empress plummeted toward the water, Mellinor's wave rising to meet her with a roar of victory. And then, just as quickly, everything changed.

Seconds before she hit the water, a wind howled down from the sky to catch her. The Empress bounced on the cushion of air and then shot up, riding the wind back to her ship. She landed on the deck and fell to her knees, clutching her chest as the scales of her golden armor fell around her like rain. Down in the water, Mellinor roared with frustration, but Miranda lay still, watching from both viewpoints as red blood covered the Empress's hands.

Their blow had hit. The Empress was wounded, but even as the rush of victory sent her head swimming, Miranda saw the Empress stand. She straightened up, tossing her sundered golden armor to the deck. Her chest was covered in bright red blood, but even as Miranda saw it, the wound began to heal. The edges of the Empress's broken skin glowed blinding white, closing up as Miranda watched. The blood vanished, leaving her pale skin clean and whole. In a matter of seconds, the Empress's wound was completely gone.

Mellinor's rage caught Miranda by surprise. The Great Spirit exploded from the sea, flying over the ship to strike the Empress again. Miranda clung to the water, throwing everything she had into Mellinor's blow, but this time, the Empress was ready.

She raised her hand, and Mellinor's wave stopped as though it had hit a wall. Mellinor screamed in fury, pounding on the Empress's barrier with every drop of water he'd absorbed. Miranda screamed with him, pouring herself into the attack. They were so close she could see the Empress's face less than a foot from their water, her ancient, dark eyes shifting away to look...

Miranda gasped, bringing in a lungful of water as her perspective shot back to her own human body. She coughed and blinked the burning seawater out of her eyes as she raised her head. She couldn't see anything, but even at this distance she could feel the Empress staring at her. A spike of terror plunged into her mind as Mellinor's voice washed through her.

"Hide, Miranda!" he screamed. "Hide!"

But it was too late. Across the water, the Empress raised her arm, the one that wasn't holding Mellinor back, and flicked her finger. The second the motion was complete, the sand below Miranda exploded.

The force blew her backward, ripping her from the water and sending her flying through the air with such power she couldn't even move her limbs to flail. She landed hard in the sand, rolling up the beach until she struck the sharp stones at the base of the storm wall. For a moment the world went completely black. She could feel nothing, hear nothing, and then, with a deafening roar, it all came back. Josef was standing over her, the great, black, bloody blade of the Heart glistening in his hand. He was knocking the soldiers back without looking, shouting at her to get up. Miranda stared at him, literally struck dumb. She couldn't make sense of what was happening, but she felt empty, like something was missing.

Then, in one, cold, horrible moment, she realized she could no longer feel Mellinor.

She scrambled away from Josef, running all out toward the bay. Soldiers grabbed for her, but she kicked them aside, scrabbling on her hands and knees through the sand until she reached the water at last. She threw herself into the surf, slamming her body beneath the cold waves. Her soul roared open as she submerged, reaching out until her mind was on the edge of breaking. She yelled Mellinor's name, screaming with her spirit and her voice until both were raw. She screamed again and again, taking in great gulps of seawater with each shout, but it was no use. Nothing answered.

Hands closed on her shoulders, pulling her out of the surf. She fought wildly, writhing in the man's iron grip even as she recognized Josef's voice telling her to calm down or they wouldn't get out of here alive. But she didn't want to calm down, she didn't want to get out alive.

"No!" she shrieked. "Let me go! I promised! *I promised I wouldn't leave him!*"

Josef ignored her. She fought as he dragged her out of the water, but her punches and kicks bounced off him. He tucked her under one arm and ran for the stairs, keeping the Heart high in his free hand, ready to swing. He didn't have to. The enemy was keeping their distance now, unwilling to engage him even when he was burdened with a hysterical woman. Perhaps it had something to do with the dying men lying scattered across the sand. Whatever it was, Miranda didn't care.

"You don't understand," she screamed, the words broken by sobs. "I let him go. I left the water! *I failed him!*"

"That may be," Josef said, charging for the stairs. "But we're still alive, though not for long if you don't stop fighting me."

Miranda went limp, her body flopping in his grasp. She was sobbing violently now. She couldn't help it. She'd poured too much of herself into Mellinor, and what she had left was barely enough to keep her lungs working, let alone stop the tears.

She was still crying uncontrollably when the force hit her, but it wasn't until Josef stopped that she recognized what it was. After all, she'd felt the Empress's spirit just moments before, but that strength, strong as it was, was nothing compared to the wave of pressure that rolled over her now.

All around them, the soldiers were dropping to their knees, pressing their foreheads into the sand. The beach grew silent as everything went still. The fighting on the wall above them silenced as well, and Miranda got the feeling that if she could somehow climb up to look at the city of Osera, she'd find that even the fires had stopped burning. With the sole exception of the waves lapping on the shore, everything in the world seemed to have gone still, and in that stillness, the Empress spoke.

"Osera," she called, her voice clear and ringing through the air. It came from every direction, filling Miranda's ears with its hated smugness. Slowly, painfully, Josef turned them, and Miranda found herself looking out at the sea she never wanted to see again and at the woman standing in midair above it.

"You have fought bravely," the Empress said, standing on a swirl of wind above her ship. "I admire strength, but the time for fighting is over. You have lost. Your army is broken, your wizards defeated, your city burning. Put down your weapons and surrender, and I may be merciful."

"She's got to be kidding," Josef said, though his voice was quiet. "Oserans don't surrender."

There was no way she could have heard him, but the Empress answered in the most effective way possible. She opened her spirit fully.

Miranda seized up as the true power of the Shepherdess's star struck her. Even Josef gasped, his arm clutching painfully around her waist. But it wasn't just the spirit pressure. Out over the water, the Empress had begun to glow. Light shone through her skin, filling her body until she glowed like the morning, but brightest of all, brighter than the sun, brighter than anything Miranda had ever seen, was the mark on the Empress's chest. The moment she saw it, Miranda knew exactly what it was and what it meant.

Bow down.

The Empress's voice echoed through Miranda's mind, through the very fabric of the world, and as it faded, the world obeyed.

The soldiers around them were already bowing, but now the sand under their knees joined them. All along the island, the spirits were lowering themselves before the Empress. The winds bowed, the stone bowed, even the fires shrank back in obedience, burning low before the star. Even the spirit deaf felt her presence. Oseran soldiers fell to their knees without knowing why, their spirits obeying on instinct alone. Only the wizards remained standing. Up on the storm wall, Banage clutched his rings, staring at the Empress in astonishment and growing terror. Even Sara had lost her jaded expression. She was looking about in open amazement, her eyes wide as she watched the world change itself to honor the Empress.

Miranda's own spirits were bowing as well. She could feel them pressing on their rings, but she barely noticed it. The enormous pressure of the Empress filled her mind, impossibly bright, impossibly glorious, and strangely familiar. Miranda clenched her teeth, forcing her mind to work. She knew this feeling, this light. She'd felt it before. Suddenly, the memory came back clearly, her kneeling in King Henrith's throne room floor beside Nico and Josef's bodies with Gin at her back, staring in amazement that she was not dead while all around her pressure just like this thrummed through the air. And at its center, walking through the ruined hall that bowed only for him, crushing Mellinor's fury with only his presence...

Before she could think about what she was doing, Miranda yanked herself from Josef's grasp and bolted for the stairs. The swordsman didn't seem to notice. His attention, like everything else's in this corner of the world, was on the Empress.

Miranda ran as she had never run before. She clambered up the stairs and hit the top of the storm wall running, dodging the bowing war spirits as she charged the watchtower door. She banged it open and threw herself at the stairs. They were empty now, and a distant part of her mind realized that the common soldiers had had the sense to move the wounded when the war spirits arrived. Good, she thought bitterly, less for her to trip on. She was taking the stairs three at a time now, her lungs heaving as she pushed herself with all her might.

She hit the door to the upper room like a battering ram, and it slammed open. She wasn't sure how she'd known he would be there. Maybe some tiny part of Mellinor still remained, pointing her toward him. Whatever had led her, it had been right. The man she had come for was standing by the window, staring out across the silent beach at the Empress. He didn't even have the good grace to jump when she came in. He just turned slowly, mouth opening to say something.

Miranda didn't give him the chance. She charged him, barely aware of what she was doing as her fingers dug into his shoulders and slammed him into the wall beside the window. He let her, his body going limp under her hands.

She was shaking so hard she could barely keep her grip. Her mind was choked with loss, guilt, failure, and blinding anger, all mashing together until she could no longer form coherent thoughts. When she opened her mouth, the words came out in a trembling, ragged sprawl.

"You're one of them, aren't you?" she whispered. "You're a star."

Eli leaned back against the wall without a sound. Behind him, the Empress's fleet started forward yet again.

CHAPTER

27

Eli stared down at Miranda, ignoring the pain as her fingers dug into his shoulders.

"You are, aren't you?" Miranda said again, her voice quaking. "I saw you, back in Mellinor. It all makes sense now. I never understood how you could get spirits to listen just by talking to them. Why no spirits would ever tell me about you after you left. I knew you had to be something special, something more than just a wizard. Now I see. Nothing can disobey you, can it? You just give an order and your Shepherdess will—"

Eli's anger exploded without warning. He lunged forward, yanking her hands off his shoulders. "That's not how I work and you know it!" he yelled, his voice raw.

Miranda stepped back in shock, and then her face flushed red as her anger rose to match his. "Shut up and answer the question! Are you a star or not?"

"Oh, *fine*," Eli said through clenched teeth. "You win. I'm a bleeding star. Cover that with sugar and eat it, if it makes you happy."

"*Makes me happy?*" Miranda roared. "You're a *star*. What are you doing, hiding up here while—" Her voice began to quiver, and she took a shuddering breath. "If you're really a star, how did any of this happen? You knew the Empress was coming. You *knew* it would be like this. I thought Josef was your friend. How could you let this happen to his country?" She flung out her arm, pointing at Nico's bloody bundle, still lying exactly where he'd laid her this afternoon. "How could you let *any* of this happen? What kind of a coward are you?"

Eli swallowed against the guilt she was hammering down his throat. "I tried to make them leave," he said lamely.

"Tried to make them leave?" Miranda shouted, shaking with rage. "How selfish can you be? Don't you see that this is bigger than your little gang? An entire country is falling, and the continent is next. Hundreds of men have lost their lives today, and—"

She cut off, and Eli winced as tears began to pour down her face. Powers, she'd lost one of her menagerie, hadn't she? He hoped it wasn't the dog. She really would rip his head off if she lost her dog. But though he steeled himself for the worse, her answer still hit him like a punch in the gut.

"Mellinor," her voice broke as she said the spirit's name. She looked at him, her eyes so full of hatred Eli couldn't help but hate himself along with her. "My spirit is *dead*, and it's *all your fault!*"

Eli cringed as her voice hit him and bumped into the wall behind him. She had him cornered. There was nowhere to run.

"Everything is your fault," she said, her voice breathy and raw. "You could have stopped this at any time, couldn't you? Mellinor wouldn't have had to fight, wouldn't have had to die if you weren't hiding in here like a filthy, selfish *coward who won't lift a finger to*—"

Eli moved in a flash. He dropped, reaching out with both hands. The first grabbed her head to hold it still; the second covered her mouth, stopping her voice.

"That's enough," he said.

Miranda tore away from him and lashed out with her fist. Her swing caught him by surprise, and he didn't have time to move before her punch landed in his ribs, her sharp rings digging into his skin. He let her go, falling back with a grunt as he clutched his side. Miranda stood over him, panting as she raised her fist again.

"That's not nearly enough," she said. "I can't believe you're Master Banage's son. You have all the power in the world, but you're too selfish to use it for anything other than taking what other people have worked for. You know nothing of duty. You don't even know what it means to be a responsible wiz—"

"Shut up!" Eli shouted. The anger in his voice shocked them both. Eli stared at her a moment and then dropped his head to his hands. "Powers, Miranda, do you think I *wanted* this? I never wanted to be a star. Look at the Empress. Does that look like the kind of power it does the world any good to have?" Eli shook his head. "I hate it. I hate the way the world turns over and shows its belly to that woman. I hate the way everyone has to dance on her string, even the Immortal Empress. I've spent my whole adult life trying to get away from her, to make my own way on my own power. To make my life *worth* something, even if it's just a bounty."

"You think your bounty makes you worth something?"

Eli sucked in a tight breath. He couldn't see her face from where he was sitting, but he didn't have to. He could feel her disgust bearing down on him like a weight.

"It's nothing," Miranda said. "Less than nothing. All that matters is action, Eli Monpress. If you're sitting on your power, if you let Mellinor die just to keep your *self-worth*. If you're going to let the Empress put her boot on every spirit on this continent all to save your *pride*, then you are even worse than I thought you were."

He heard the floor creak as she turned away.

"You're not worth a drop of Mellinor's water," she said, her voice thick with hatred and loss. "But what more could I expect from a thief and a con artist and a selfish, irresponsible—"

The list went on and on, and Eli sat on the floor and took it. He couldn't even argue with her anymore. She was right. He could have stopped this. He could have saved her spirit, saved Josef's men, saved Karon, saved everything, but he hadn't. He'd sat there and let it happen all because he couldn't stand to go back. Couldn't stand to let that woman win.

But I have won, love.

Eli sucked in a breath. He shouldn't have been surprised, he thought bitterly. Of course she would be here. She was always here.

I told you I'd win in the end, Benehime said. He could feel her now, kneeling beside him just on the other side of the veil that separated the spirit's world from her white nothing. *After all your valiant efforts, this is your reward, known forever far and wide as the man who doomed a continent to keep his pride.* She made a tsking sound. *You've let everyone down—your father, Josef, Nico, even Miranda, who never expected you to be anything more than a thief. But I'm different. I will always treasure you, darling star. I love you more than anything else in this sad, tiny world.*

The skin of his ear began to tingle as Benehime's lips pressed against it through the veil. *Look at the wizard girl. Her loss is already suffered, but hers can be the last. You can still save things. All you have to do is stop being stubborn. Give in, embrace your position as the favorite again, and you can be the hero.* Her voice fell to a shivering whisper. *Come home to me, Eliton, and everything will be put right. I swear it.*

And just like that, Eli gave up.

He stood in one smooth motion, and Miranda stumbled back, surprised out of her tirade.

"What do you think you're doing?" she shouted, glaring at him with red-rimmed eyes.

Eli didn't answer. He stomped past her, shrugging off her hand when she tried to grab him. He kicked open the watch room door and started down the stairs. The boards creaked as Miranda started to follow him, but Eli didn't look back. He kept his eyes straight ahead as he clattered down the tower steps and burst through the door at the bottom into the silent, bowing world.

The door to the watch room slammed shut with a crash that made Miranda wince. She stood there panting, too exhausted to chase the thief down the stairs but too furious to give up. As a compromise, she went to the window, reaching it just in time to see Eli emerge from the bottom of the tower. He walked across the storm wall and down the stairs in quick, angry steps. The world was silent around him, every spirit cowering before the might of the Empress, but Eli paid it no mind. He hit the beach with a stomp and kept walking, stepping over the kneeling bodies of the soldiers. When he passed Josef, Miranda thought she saw him slow, but then he was moving again as fast as ever, marching toward the sea.

Miranda caught her breath when he reached the surf. The waves were still lapping despite the Empress's pressure, but the moment Eli's boot touched it, the ocean froze. Miranda blinked at the deathly silence that descended on a shore where the sea had gone completely still. The water stood motionless as far as she could see. Even the great breakers on the horizon were frozen midcrest. Overhead, the air was perfectly still as well, the winds holding their breath as Eli walked forward, striding across the smooth water like it was stone.

When he reached the center of the bay, Eli stopped. He folded his arms across his chest and glared up at the towering wall of palace ships. High overhead, the Empress looked down at him with a haughty sneer. In that whole, still world, they were the only two who moved.

"Well, well," the Empress said. "The rat emerges."

Miranda blinked. The Empress hadn't raised her voice, but Miranda could hear her as clearly as though the woman were standing beside her.

"Come to meet my challenge at last?" the Empress continued, drawing a shining sword from the scabbard at her hip. "Come then, boy. I'll show you who is truly worthy of the Lady's favor."

"Nara." Eli said the name like an insult. "You want her? Take her. Love her for another eight centuries. But this?" He pointed his thumb over his shoulder at the shore. "This land is mine. Go home. No one wants you here."

"I am not yours to send away," the Empress hissed. "You claim this land? Fight to keep it. The Shepherdess has no love for the weak."

Eli tilted his head to the side. Miranda could feel the impatience radiating off him even at this distance, but Eli didn't answer the Empress's challenge. He just stood there, staring up at the woman with a smile so defeated it made Miranda's chest ache. And then, without warning, he opened his spirit.

Eli's power exploded out of him. It filled the beach, filled the sky, and swept over the Oseran mountains to fill the channel behind them. It expanded and expanded, pressing down so hard Miranda had trouble breathing. And then, at its center, a light brighter than any Miranda had ever seen broke like the sunrise.

All at once, the world, already bowed in homage to the Empress, turned its back on her and prostrated itself before Eli. Miranda clutched the window's edge, staring in amazement. She'd seen this once before, in Mellinor, but the scale was totally different now. Everything Eli's spirit touched woke, and every spirit that woke praised him. The sea flattened to glass below his feet and the winds circled him in supplication. On the island, the mountain woke and began to tremble, the very rock bowing in obedience. The sand on the beach swelled in reverence, burying the soldiers in its eagerness to show its respect, and even the stones of the tower were singing praises. Their song was little more than a buzzing under her fingers, but its meaning was clear. Miranda stood perfectly still, her eyes so wide they hurt. She had been amazed when the Empress opened her spirit, but this was so much more. Terrifyingly more.

When she found her voice at last, the question was a whisper, more air than sound. "What is he?"

For a moment nothing answered, and then Durn, sturdiest and calmest of her spirits, spoke.

"He is the favorite."

Miranda caught her breath, trying to remember where she'd heard that term before, but too many new things were tumbling through her head and she couldn't make it all fit together. It didn't matter though, for in the next moment, something happened that put everything else out of her mind.

Out on the glassy sea, the Empress fell as the wind abandoned her. She landed on the deck of her palace ship, crashing into the wood with an impact that made Miranda wince. For a moment the woman lay stunned, and then the Empress curled into a ball, burying her head in her hands as she began to weep. Down on the water, Eli, barely visible beneath his own light, shook his head in disgust and raised his arms.

All along the Empress's fleet, from horizon to horizon, white lines began to appear in the air. They fell like unraveling thread, the long, white slits growing until they were as large as the monstrous ships themselves, one for each boat. Miranda swallowed as the sea filled with white. Until this moment, she hadn't actually realized just how large the Empress's force was. The sight almost made her laugh. How had the Council ever thought it could win?

A few seconds after they appeared, the white lines stopped growing. For one breathtaking moment they hung in the air beside the ships, each a shining, pure white beacon. Their light lit up the night, each line reflected in the beautiful, still water below. Tears pricked Miranda's eyes as the scene the Shaper Mountain had shown them flashed again through her mind—the night sky lit up with a million lights, the things called stars. Unbidden, her eyes drifted up. The sky looked as it always had, enormous and black, the crescent moon hanging almost sulkily just above the horizon. She'd never thought of the sky as empty, but now, compared to the beautiful lights below, Miranda couldn't see it as anything but.

Below the blank curve of the night sky, Eli stood before the endless lights, the brightest of them all. He looked around at the white lines, almost like he was counting, and then, with a careless motion, he brought his arms down. In that one movement, the white, glowing lines vanished, taking the fleet with them.

Miranda rubbed her aching eyes, but when she opened them again, the view was the same. The ocean stretched out to the horizon, dark and empty. Of the Immortal Empress's innumerable fleet, not a single ship was left.

Down on the glassy water, Eli's light was the only one left. Without meaning to, Miranda found herself leaning forward, drawn to his light. But as she stretched for a better look, she saw that Eli was staring back, his eyes pinned on hers despite the distance. She smiled at him, a great, relieved grin. Five minutes ago she'd been ready to kill him. Now he'd just done the impossible and saved them all. But Eli didn't return her smile. He glared at her, his face bitter and drawn as another light flashed beside his.

Two white lines appeared on either side of Eli's head. They fell to his shoulders, shimmering in the night as his own light faded. A second after they appeared, two white arms emerged, long and perfect and glowing like white fire. They reached out, folding around

Eli's neck until they were almost choking him in their embrace. Eli winced as though in pain, but his eyes never left Miranda's. She stared at him, confused, and then she saw his mouth move.

It wasn't like earlier. She couldn't hear him now. Actually, she wasn't sure if he was making a sound or just mouthing the words. But his lips were expressive as always, and she could see the words plainly even at this distance.

Hope you're happy, he mouthed. *Good-bye.*

And then the white arms pulled him back, and Eli vanished without a sound.

Darkness fell with a physical force as his light snuffed out, leaving the world blacker than anything Miranda had ever seen. She could dimly hear a familiar sound repeating in the distance, but it took her several seconds to realize it was the waves lapping on the beach. The wind howled gently over the tower, a land breeze moving out to sea, carrying with it the smell of fire and smoke, but the sounds of battle were gone. As her eyes adjusted to the new dark, she looked down at the beach to see the Empress's soldiers standing dumbly. Several simply dropped their swords in the sand and sat down, too stunned by the defeat of their Empress and the disappearance of their fleet to do anything more. In their midst, Josef stood and began rounding them up, calmly announcing that the war was over.

Miranda wasn't sure how long she stood there. Half an hour, maybe more. She certainly didn't know when Nico joined her, but as she turned at last to go downstairs she found the girl standing at the window beside her, staring out at the dark sea with her coat wrapped around her shoulders.

Miranda winced and backed away. Nico looked terrible. Her pale skin was mottled with bruises all the way to where it vanished beneath her coat. Dried blood caked her hair, and both her eyes were blacked. Her expression, however, wasn't one of pain, but of dread. Miranda hovered a moment, unsure what to do, and then Nico spoke.

"The light woke me up," she whispered, her voice fragile and raw. "Where's Eli?"

Miranda bit her lip, trying to think how best to answer. After several moments, she settled on the truth.

"I think he's gone."

Nico licked her lips, but she didn't move. Miranda didn't move either. They just stood there, side by side, staring into the dark, looking in vain for what was no longer there.

ACKNOWLEDGMENTS

Thank you to Lindsay, whose edits, observations, and refusal to pull punches made this book five times what it was when I first gave it to her. Also, a huge thank-you to the hardworking people at the Watkinsville Jittery Joe's. You are all coffee-making saints. Thank you for letting me take up the corner chair indefinitely.

extras

orbit

meet the author

Alyssa Alig

RACHEL AARON was born in Atlanta, Georgia. After a lovely, geeky childhood full of books and public television, and then an adolescence spent feeling awkward about it, she went to the University of Georgia to pursue English literature with an eye toward getting her PhD. Upper-division coursework cured her of this delusion, and she graduated in 2004 with a BA and a job, which was enough to make her mother happy. She currently lives in a 1970s house of the future in Athens, Georgia, with her loving husband, overgrown library, elfish son, and small, brown dog. Find out more about the author at www.rachelaaron.net.

introducing

If you enjoyed
THE SPIRIT WAR,
look out for

SPIRIT'S END

The Legend of Eli Monpress

by Rachel Aaron

At eleven, Eliton Banage was the most important thing in the world, and he knew it.

Wherever he went, spirits bowed before him and the White Lady he stood beside, Benehime, beloved Shepherdess of all the world. In the two years since the Lady had found him in the woods, he had wanted for nothing. Anything he asked, no matter how extravagant, Benehime gave him, and he loved her for it.

She took him everywhere, to the wind courts, to the grottoes and trenches of the seafloor, even into the Shaper Mountain itself. All the places Eli had only dreamed about, she took him, and everywhere they went, the spirits paid them homage, kissing Benehime's feet with an adoration that spilled over onto Eli as well, as it should. He was the favorite, after all.

For three happy years, this was how Eli understood the world.

And then, the day before his fourteenth birthday, everything changed.

It began innocently. He'd wanted to go to Zarin, and Benehime had obliged. It was market day and the city was packed, but the crowds passed through them like shadows, unseeing, for Eli and the Lady were on the other side of the veil, that silk-thin wall that separated the spirits' world from Benehime's. As usual, Eli was walking ahead, showing off by slipping his hand through the veil to snitch a trinket or a pie whenever the shadows of the merchants turned away. He was so fast he could have done it without the veil to hide him, but Benehime had ordered he was never to leave the veil without her explicit permission. It was one of her only rules.

He'd just pulled a really good snatch, a gold and enamel necklace. Grinning, he turned to show it to Benehime, but for once she wasn't behind him. Eli whirled around, necklace dangling from his fingers, and found the Lady several steps back. She was perfectly still, standing with her eyes closed and her head cocked to the side, like she was listening for something. He called her name twice before she answered. He ran to her, giving her the necklace, and she, laughing, admired it a moment before throwing it on the ground and going on her way.

This was how it usually went. Benehime hated everything humans made. She said they were like paintings done by a blind man, interesting for the novelty but never truly worth looking at. Eli had long since given up asking what she meant. Still, she liked when he gave her things, and making her happy was the most important thing in his life.

She stopped twice more before they made it to the main square. By the third time, Eli was getting annoyed. Fortunately, her last pause happened only a dozen feet from his goal—the Council bounty board.

"Look!" Eli shouted, running up to the wall of block printed posters. "Milo Burch's bounty is almost a hundred thousand now!" He stared at the enormous number, trying to imagine what that much gold would look like. "He's like his own kingdom."

Benehime woke from her trance with a laugh. *Come now,* she said, stepping up to join him. *You saw five times that much in the gold veins under the mountains just last week.*

"It's not *about* the gold," Eli said, exasperated. "It's about being someone who's done things. *Big* things! Big enough to make someone else want to spend that much gold just to catch you." He took a huge breath, eyes locked on the swordsman's stern face glowering out of the inked portrait. "What kind of man must Milo Burch be for his head to be worth that much money?"

Who knows, Benehime said with a bored shrug. *Humans have so many laws.*

"I'm going to have a wanted poster someday," Eli said, fists clenched. "And a bounty. The biggest there's ever been."

Nonsense, love, Benehime said, taking his hand. *What would you do with such a thing? Besides*—she kissed his cheek—*no one could ever want you more than I do. Now come, it's time to go home.*

"But we just got here!" Eli said, trying to tug his hand away.

Before he'd finished his sentence, they were back in Benehime's white nothing.

Now, she said, sitting him on the little silk bed she'd ordered the silkworms to spin just for him. *Wait here and don't move. I have to take care of something, but I won't be long.*

Eli glared. "Where are you going? And why can't I come with—"

Eliton.

Benehime's voice was sharp, and Eli shut his mouth sulkily. She smiled and folded her hands over his.

I'll be back soon, she whispered, kissing his forehead. *Wait for me.*

Eli squirmed away, but the Lady had already vanished, leaving him alone in the endless white. He sat down with a huff and began picking at his pillow with his fingernails while he counted the seconds in his mind. When he'd sat just long enough to be sure she was really gone, Eli reached out with a grin and tapped the air. At once, a thin, white line appeared. It fell through the empty space, twisting sideways as it opened into a hole just wide enough for him to crawl through. Grin widening, Eli leaned forward and slipped through the veil after the Shepherdess.

She was easy to follow. Everywhere the Shepherdess went, the world paid attention. All he did was follow the trail of bowing spirits. The first few times he'd tried this she'd caught him easily, but Eli had learned over the past few months that if he kept himself very quiet, Benehime didn't always see him. And so, keeping himself very still and very silent, Eli slipped through the world until he saw the Lady's light shining through the veil. He stopped a few feet away, lowering himself into the dim shadows of the real world before opening the veil just wide enough to peek through.

What he saw on the other side confused him. When the Lady had left so suddenly, he'd thought for sure she was going to some spirit crisis. A flood maybe, or a volcano. Something interesting. But peeking through the tiny hole, he didn't see anything of the sort. Benehime was standing in a large, dirty study, her white feet resting on a pile of overturned books. In front of her, a thin, old man sat on a single bed. The sheet was thrown back as though he'd gotten up in a hurry, but his eyes were calm as he faced the Shepherdess, his large jeweled rings burning like embers on his folded hands.

Eli frowned. Why was Benehime visiting a Spiritualist? She disliked the stuffy, meddling wizards even more than he did. Yet the man was almost certainly a Spiritualist. No one else wore jewelry that gaudy. And the study they were standing in was clearly the upper level of a Spiritualist's Tower. It looked just like his father's, Eli thought, though Banage would never let his room get so cluttered. He never allowed anything to fall short of his expectations, the old taskmaster. Eli glowered at that, but before he could fall into thinking about all the things his father had done wrong, the old Spiritualist spoke.

"You're her, aren't you?" he said, his voice full of wonder. "The greatest of the Great Spirits?"

I am no spirit.

Benehime's voice was so cold and cruel it took Eli several seconds to recognize it. She leaned over as she spoke, bending down until her eyes were level with the old man's. Her presence saturated the air, cold and heavy as wet snow, but the man didn't even flinch.

Who told you?

"Doesn't matter now," the Spiritualist said, waving his hand, his rings glittering with terror in the Lady's harsh, white light. "You're here, and I have questions."

Typical human arrogance, Benehime said, crossing her arms. *To think I would answer your questions.*

"If we are arrogant, it is you who made us so, Benehime," the old man said, his voice growing every bit as sharp and cold as hers. "We are your creation, after all. Or, should I say, your distraction."

Benehime sneered, her beautiful face twisting into a terrible mask. *It seems the whispers of treason were grossly understated. I came here to silence a spirit who didn't understand my very simple doctrine of silence and find a full-blown rebellion. Tell me, human, when those spirits who've stupidly thrown their lot in with you were spilling my secrets, did they also tell you that the price for such knowledge was death?*

"And what do I have to fear of death?" the Spiritualist said. "I am old, my life well lived. I have spent sixty years in duty to the spirits. I consider it an honor to die asking the questions they cannot."

With that, the old man pushed himself off the bed. He creaked as he stood, rings burning on his fingers as his spirits poured their strength into his fragile old limbs. When he spoke again, his voice was threaded with the voices of his spirits.

"What is on the other side of the sky, Shepherdess?" he asked. "Why is it forbidden to look at the hands that scrape the edge of the world? Why do the mountains ignore the claws that scrape their roots? What secret horror do the old spirits hide from the young at your order? What are you hiding that is so dangerous that speaking of it, or even just looking its way, is cause for death?"

His voice rose as he spoke, and by the time he finished, he was shouting, yet his calm never broke. The Spiritualist's soul filled the room, its heavy power steady and tightly controlled. His spirits clung to it, cowering in their master's shadow from the Shepherdess's growing rage. By this time, Eli could feel the Lady's cold fury seeping through the veil itself, but when she spoke at last, it was a question.

Why do you care? she said. *Even if I told you the truth, you couldn't do anything with it. Why waste your life on knowledge that means nothing?*

Eli held his breath. Benehime wasn't talking to the man but to the trembling spirits on his fingers. Even so, it was the Spiritualist who answered.

"I ask because they want to know," he said, raising his rings to his lips. "And while you may control my spirits utterly, you cannot control me, and you cannot control the truth."

The Shepherdess bowed her head, and Eli leaned forward. Anger flashed in him. If this man had made his Lady cry, he'd... He was still figuring out what he would do when a sound rang through the still room. It was musical and cold, colder than anything he'd ever felt, and Eli realized the Shepherdess was laughing.

Do you know how many times I've been told that? She giggled, raising her head with a smile that made Eli's blood stop. *You think you're the first to demand answers? Please. I've been Shepherdess for nearly five thousand years now. I can't even remember how many times one of you has asked me those same questions, but I've never, ever answered. And do you know why, little wizard?*

For the first time since she'd arrived, the Spiritualist was speechless.

Let me tell you something about spirits, Benehime whispered, reaching out to trace the old man's jaw. *Spirits are panicky, stupid, and willfully ignorant. They knew what was on the other side of the sky, and they chose to look away and say nothing, to let the truth be lost in the press of time. They chose safety. They chose ignorance. The only one who didn't get a choice was me.*

She sighed deeply, trailing her fingers down the old man's neck to his sunken chest, tapping each rib beneath his threadbare nightshirt. *You want the truth, Spiritualist?* she said, her white eyes sliding up to lock on his dark ones. *I'll tell it to you. The truth is your precious spirits don't want to know what's out there, because if they did, their panic would tear them apart.*

"I don't believe you," the Spiritualist said, though his voice was far less sure than before. "The spirits deserve—"

The spirits deserve exactly what they have, Benehime snapped back, anger cutting through her voice like an icy wire. *This is their world, created for them, and its rules, my rules, are for their protection.*

As she finished, her hand slid into the old man's chest. Her white fingers parted his skin like a blade, and the old Spiritualist gasped in pain. He would have fallen to his knees had Benehime's hand not been in his chest, lifting him up until his face was an inch from hers.

That may not have been the answer you thought you were dying for, she whispered. *But that's the problem with demanding the truth, Spiritualist. It doesn't always come out as you'd like.*

With that, she slid her hand out of his chest and the old man fell. His body changed as he plummeted, growing thinner, the skin shriveling. Eli pressed his hand over his mouth to keep from screaming as the old man, now little more than a skeleton, hit the ground and crumbled to dust. His rings hit a second later, the gold and jewels landing on the wooden floor with hollow clinks. Benehime shook her hand in disgust, and the Spiritualist's blood fled from her skin, leaving her fingers clean and white. When her hand was purified to her satisfaction, she reached down to pick up the largest of the Spiritualist's rings, a great onyx band the size of Eli's thumb.

The spirit began to sob the second Benehime touched it, and she silenced its blubbering with a sharp shake.

You, she said. *See what you've done? This is your fault, you know. Why did you tell him?*

The ring did not speak. Benehime scowled, and her light grew brighter. Even through the veil, the pressure of her anger was enough to make Eli's ears pop. He watched in horror as the ring shook. Just when he was sure it was about to shake itself apart, the ring spoke one word.

"No."

Benehime arched a thin white eyebrow. *No?*

"I'm not afraid of you, Shepherdess," the black stone whispered. "No, not Shepherdess. Jailor, for that's what you really are. You say you're our provider, but our wizard gave us more than you ever have. He fought for us, fought to learn the truth, and you killed him for it."

Benehime's white eyes narrowed. *You want to share his fate?*

she said. *You're a strong stone, Durenei. Bow and beg forgiveness, and I may yet overlook this transgression.*

The ring trembled in her hand, but its voice was stone when it spoke at last. "I hold true to my oaths and my master," it whispered. "And I will never bow to you again."

Benehime's face closed like a trap as she clenched her hand in a fist, crushing the ring with a snap of breaking metal. The stone spirit gave one final cry, and then Benehime opened her hand to pour a thin stream of sand onto the floor.

After that, the Shepherdess didn't offer her forgiveness again. She stepped forward, stomping her bare, white foot on the Spiritualist's rings. She crushed them one after another. Each one died with a soft cry, and when her foot lifted, nothing was left but dust. When they were all destroyed, the Shepherdess snapped her fingers.

The veil rippled, and Eli tensed, ready to run, but she wasn't calling him. Instead, a white line opened and the Lord of Storms stepped through to stand beside the Shepherdess. He looked around as he entered, and his face settled into an even deeper scowl when he saw the piles of dust on the floor.

Erase this man and his spirits from the world's memory, the Shepherdess said, waving at the dust. *I don't know his name, and I never want to.*

The Lord of Storms folded his arms over his chest. "That's not my job."

The words were barely out of his mouth when the Shepherdess's arm shot out, her white fingers grabbing his throat.

I've had enough insurrection for today, she whispered. *You are my sword. I made you, and you will do whatever I ask. Do I make myself clear?*

"Yes, Shepherdess," the Lord of Storms whispered around her hold.

She released him with a disgusted sound and turned away, walking toward the center of the tower. The entire world was silent around her, holding its breath. When she reached the middle of the room, she stopped and held out her arms. When she brought them down again, the tower fell with a sigh. Great stone blocks crumbled to sand as Eli watched. Books fell to dust. Wood splintered to nothing. The spirits died without a sound, too terrified even to cry out. Within a few seconds, Benehime and the Lord of Storms were floating in the empty air above a dusty clearing, all that was left of the Spiritualist's two-story tower.

I'll leave the rest to you.

"Yes, Shepherdess," the Lord of Storms said, but the Lady was already gone. She vanished like the moon behind a cloud, leaving the night darker than ever. The second she was gone, Eli fled as well, scrambling through the veil to beat her back home.

He barely made it, winking into place on his pillow just as she appeared. She looked for him at once, and he beamed back at her as always, but his heart was thudding in his chest. She was the same as always, white and beautiful, but when Eli looked at her, all he could see was her foot coming down, her hand leaving the dead man's chest.

What's the matter, love? she whispered, sinking onto the pillow beside him. *You're shaking. Are you cold?*

Not trusting his voice, Eli shook his head. Benehime sighed and pulled him into her lap. Eli cringed from her touch before he could stop himself, and Benehime froze.

Never pull away from me, she said, her voice cold as glacier melt. *You love me.*

"I love you," Eli whispered automatically, letting her move him as she liked. They sat like that for a while, tangled together, and then Benehime spoke.

Always remember, love, she whispered, kissing his hair, *the world is a horrible place without gratitude or understanding. No matter how hard you work, you will never be thanked and you will never be loved. But we will always be together, darling. I will always love you, and you will always love me. Now, tell me you love me.*

"I love you," Eli said again.

Benehime nodded and pulled him closer, crushing him against her chest until he could barely breathe. *Whatever happens, darling*—she kissed him again and again—*whatever comes, remember, I am all that matters in the world for you. I am your hope and your salvation. Love me forever and I will raise you up when all others are cast off. Though the world may end, no harm shall ever come to you. I swear it.*

Eli nodded, letting the White Lady kiss him, but even as her lips landed again and again, all he could think of was her face, cruel and unrecognizable as she crushed the Spiritualist's onyx ring in her fist. And it was at that moment, in the space between one kiss and the next, that Eli knew things could never be the same again.

After that night, Eli knew no peace.

Nothing changed at first. He continued as always, following Benehime wherever she needed to go, entertaining her when she was bored, telling her he loved her whenever prompted like a little parrot. But he didn't mean it, not anymore.

Now that he'd seen the truth once, he saw it all the time—the cruel shadow that lay behind her smile. The way she held him just a hair too tight. The faint threat in her voice every time she told him to say he loved her. But worst of all were the spirits. Before, when they'd trembled in front of Benehime, he'd thought it was awe. He now saw it for what it really was: pure terror. He would stand beside her as she dealt with the spirits, hating every second of it. Hating her for being that way. Hating himself for not seeing it sooner.

It hurt to think how childish he'd been, how naive. He'd thought he was important, standing beside her, having spirits bow to him as they bowed to her, but he was nothing but a shadow, an afterthought of their fear. It made him sick. Living with his father in the tower, the spirits had been his friends. They'd been kind to him when Banage had driven all kindness out in the name of discipline, and this was how he repaid them? Following their tyrant around, lapping up her attention like a little lovesick dog?

The truth of it ate at him. Everything she did now—the forced kisses, the constant promises she wrung out of him—it made Eli furious. Made him feel used and helpless and disgusting, but what could he do? Benehime was always with him. She didn't sleep, only sat beside him while he did. She never let him out of her sight, save for those times she vanished mysteriously. Eli didn't follow her anymore. He'd seen as much of her true nature as he cared to, but even if he had taken those chances to open a hole and escape, she would find him. Assuming the spirits didn't report him at once, she'd told him many times that his soul shone like a beacon. All she had to do was look at her sphere and pick him out. No, if he wanted to escape for real, for good, he would have to convince Benehime to let him go. Of course, he had about as much chance of that as of convincing gravity not to pull him down, but Eli was never one to let impossibilities stand in his way.

Eight months later, he finally came up with a plan. He spent another month refining it, and yet another being the best possible boy Benehime could ever ask for. Finally, when the plan was firmly cemented in his mind and Benehime was in the best mood he could manage, Eli sprang.

They were in the jungle far, far south of the Council Kingdoms. Eli had suggested the place because he knew the Lord of Storms hated the hot, muggy weather and he'd needed as few variables as possible. They were perched in the branches of an obliging tree, their feet dangling lazily in the air. Eli had suggested the spot himself, and he was using the tree's flowers to make Benehime a crown. The Lady watched, her face beaming with love at the seemingly spontaneous show of affection.

The moment he laid the crown on her head, Eli said the words he'd been rehearsing to himself for the past eight weeks.

"Do you remember the story you told me once," he said, his voice perfectly casual, "about when you first found Nara?"

Don't speak her name, Benehime said, adjusting her crown with loving fingers. *She's forgotten, my treasure. Only you matter now.*

Eli smiled his best bashful smile and pushed a step further. "Yes, but do you remember how you gave her a wish?"

Benehime laughed and drew him into her lap. *Is that where this is going?* she said, kissing his cheek. *Do you want a wish, too, love? Silly boy, you know I'll give you whatever you want.*

"It's not so much a what as something I want to do," Eli said, reaching into the pocket of his beautiful white shirt and taking out the folded piece of paper he'd so carefully snitched the last time they were in Zarin.

Benehime's smile faded as Eli spread the paper across their laps. It was a wanted poster for Den the Warlord. His terrifying face glared up at them, daring anyone to try for the enormous number written in block capitals below him: five hundred thousand gold standards.

What is this?

"You remember just before my birthday?" Eli said. "When I said I wanted to be on a wanted poster? Well, I've been thinking about it more and more lately, and I think I'm ready."

Benehime leaned back to stare at him, her white face genuinely confused. *Ready to do what?*

"Get on a poster," Eli said. "I've decided. I want to be a thief. Not just any thief, the world's greatest thief!"

Love, Benehime said patiently. *If you want something, I'll give it to you. You don't have to steal.*

"It's not about wanting anything," Eli said. "It's about being the best. Bounties are a measurement: The bigger the bounty, the better you are at whatever you did. Den was the best betrayer, and his face is known across the Council Kingdoms. Milo Burch was the best swordsman, and now he's worth more dead than some nobles see in a lifetime. Den's bounty alone is five hundred thousand gold! One hundred thousand would buy you a good-sized kingdom. How many people can say 'I'm worth five kingdoms'?"

Benehime sighed and pulled the flower crown from her head. Her brows were furrowed, a bad sign. She was losing interest. Eli licked his lips. He'd have to play this next part just right.

"I'm going to beat that," he said, grabbing her hand. "I'm going to be the best thief ever. I'm going to steal everything worth stealing. I'm going to be famous all over, and I'm going to get the biggest bounty ever, twice as big as Den's. That's my wish. I want to earn a bounty of one million gold."

It was the biggest number he could think of. Across from him, Benehime shook her head.

You have the silliest ideas, she said. *Why would you want to be a thief?*

"Because stealing's the only thing I'm good enough at," Eli said, smiling as he raised his hand.

Benehime blinked. Eli was holding the flower crown that, a second before, had been safely grasped in her now empty hands. Suddenly, she began to laugh, reaching out to ruffle Eli's dark hair with her white fingers.

I can't deny you anything, she said. *All right, tell me what I have to do to get you your poster.*

Eli took a silent breath. This was it.

"That's the thing," he said, leaning into her touch. "If the bounty's going to mean anything, I have to earn it myself."

The laughter vanished from Benehime's eyes.

Eli's hands began to shake, but he kept his attention locked on the Lady. If he couldn't finish this now, he would never escape. "I want to find a thief to teach me," he said, enunciating each word to keep his voice from trembling. "I'll learn and—"

Enough. Benehime's voice had changed. It was cold now, and sharp as a razor. *Do you think you can outsmart me?*

Eli began to sweat. "I never meant—"

I may not pay much attention to the affairs of humans, but even I know you're setting up an impossible situation. A million gold? From stealing? You'd have to steal everything of value on the continent.

Eli swallowed. "I—"

You think I can't see what you're doing? Benehime's voice dripped with disgust as she took the crown from Eli's hand and threw it on the ground far below. *I've known for some time now that you were changing, Eliton. You tried to hide it, but I know you better than anyone. I knew you were growing distant. The Lord of Storms tried to warn me. He said you'd change, that you'd turn on me. He told me to make you immortal at the beginning, when you were still a child. But I wanted to wait.*

Her hand rose to his chin, delicate white fingers running down the line of his jaw. *I wanted to let you grow into your true potential,* she whispered. *To learn how to truly appreciate what you have here. I trusted that you would choose me above all else, as I chose you, and this is how you repay my faith? A transparent ploy?*

"It's not a ploy!" Eli lied.

Of course it is, Benehime said, slapping his face lightly. *You know as well as I do you could never earn a million gold. You thought I was ignorant of things like money and bounties, and you meant to play on that ignorance, getting me to agree to let you run off in pursuit of an impossible goal. Let me guess, the next part was that you'd return to me once you earned your bounty and we'd be together forever, right?*

Eli winced before he could hide it. She'd seen straight through him. The woman sitting across from him now was not the Benehime he knew, but the true Shepherdess—ruthless, cruel, and very, very dangerous. His heart began to pound as the hand on his cheek slid down to his throat, the slender fingers moving to press gently on his windpipe.

Come, dear, she whispered. *Don't look so afraid. I still love you more than anything. In fact, I like you best when you're being sneaky. But we'll have no more of this leaving talk. You're mine. My pet. My comfort. My favorite. Now, come and make me another crown and we'll forget all about this idiocy.*

She lowered her hand and Eli gripped his neck, rubbing the bruised skin. If he'd been older, more experienced, he would have dropped the subject and started picking flowers for a new crown, but he was young. Young and desperate, and as he watched what could be his last chance at freedom vanishing before his eyes, he could not help making a final, desperate grab.

"You're wrong," he said softly.

Benehime froze, her white body perfectly still. *About what?*

"I wasn't lying to you," Eli answered. "I do want to become the world's greatest thief, and I can earn a million gold bounty. You told me I could have whatever I wished for. That's it. I want the chance to prove you wrong."

Benehime sighed. *Now you're just getting desperate, love. The only way you could possibly earn a million gold bounty is if I helped you.*

"You're wrong!" Eli said, speaking his mind for the first time since the night she'd killed the Spiritualist. "I don't need your help. I'm not your pet. I'm a wizard and the best thief around. I can earn a million gold on my own."

Don't be stupid, Benehime said. *You think you're some kind of savant thief because you've snatched a few trinkets? The only way you got any of it was because I let you open the portals and steal through the veil. Part of growing up is learning to face the truth, Eliton, and the truth is that you're nothing without my favor. Just a charming boy with quick hands. How could something so small possibly be enough to earn a million gold?*

Eli swallowed against his pounding heart. "Want to bet?"

Benehime scowled. *What?*

"I'll make you a deal," Eli said, speaking quickly before he lost his nerve. "Give me the chance to prove I wasn't lying before. Let me go learn to be a thief and try to earn that million gold bounty on my own skills. If it really is impossible, if at any point I have to ask for your help, then you win. I'll come back to you and be everything you want me to be. But if I'm right, if I get a million gold without your help, then you have to let me go free."

Benehime leaned in until she was so close Eli could feel her cold breath on his skin. *Why*, she whispered, *would I ever take a bet like that? I hold all the cards. Why should I take a risk?*

"Because if you don't, then there's no point in letting me grow up," Eli said, his voice trembling. "You said you wanted me to learn to appreciate you, right? How can I do that if I never experience life away from you? If you keep me here, then you'll never know if I'm lying when I say I love you, because I've never had the chance to experience life without your love." He lurched forward, closing the tiny gap between them so that their foreheads pressed together. "Let me go," he whispered, staring into her cold, white eyes. "Let me try it on my own. If I fail, then I'll have learned how much I need you and I'll never, ever try to run again. And if I do somehow succeed, then I've proven that I love thieving more than I love you, and that sort of man isn't worthy of being your favorite anyway."

I decide who is worthy of my favor, Benehime said, but Eli could hear the consideration in her voice. Behind the blank wall of her white irises, he could almost see her thinking it over, testing the angles, looking for her edge.

She must have found it, for the Shepherdess leaned in and kissed him. It was a hard kiss, crushing his lips against her burning skin, but when she leaned back, the distance between them felt final. Real.

I always did like you best at your most defiant, she said, smiling. *Very well, you've got your chance. But I'm warning you, Eliton, I will hold you to every letter of our deal. You have to do it all yourself, no using my power, no showing your mark. And the moment you get in over your head, the second you have to ask me for help, you belong to me. Forever.*

"Fair deal," Eli said, a smile spreading over his face. "But you should know better than anyone how stubborn I can be."

Benehime almost laughed at that, but caught herself at the last moment. She reached up, resting her white hands on his shoulders. For a moment, Eli thought she was going to pull him into a hug, but then, without warning, she pushed him.

He toppled off the tree, falling fifteen feet before landing on his back in the wet cushion of leaf litter at the tree's base. The impact knocked the wind out of him, and for several moments all he could do was gasp for air. When his lungs finally started working again, he sat up with a groan, looking around at the endless forest. Overhead, the tree branch was empty. Benehime was gone.

He froze a moment, waiting for her to say something. But the forest was silent. Then, like someone opened a door, the sounds came roaring back as the spirits recovered from the Shepherdess's presence. Eli sat in the muck, trying to get himself to believe what his senses were telling him. Benehime was gone. His gambit had worked. He was free.

He stood up with a whoop that echoed through the forest, and for ten minutes he danced like an idiot, bouncing off the trees in celebration of his glorious, glorious freedom. The white world was gone; everywhere he looked he saw color. Spirits buzzed all around him, their noises calm and without fear, and Eli fell to the ground, greeting them with pure joy. The spirits, alarmed at this wizard who was suddenly shouting at them, clammed up immediately, but Eli was too happy to care.

After almost half an hour of this, he realized he'd better get going. He had a bounty to earn, and he couldn't do that in the middle of nowhere. Brushing the leaves off his white clothes, Eli reached out to tap the veil and make a door to somewhere useful.

He caught himself a second before the cut opened. Oh no, it wasn't going to be that easy. No using the Shepherdess's gifts, that was the deal, and Eli would stick to it if it killed him. They were enemies in the game now, and if she got even an ounce of leverage on him, she would push on it with everything she had, just as Eli would. Now that he was still, he could almost feel her waiting on the other side of the veil, watching him, urging him to make a mistake, to give her something she could use.

With a sly smile, Eli drew his hand back and slid it into his pocket. He picked a direction almost at random and began to walk through the forest, whistling as the evening rain began to fall.

Giuseppe Monpress, the greatest thief in the world, had retired to his northern retreat for a little well-earned rest and to plan his next heist. He was just sitting down to his first dinner in solitude, a splendid roast duck with shallots and an excellent bottle of wine he'd lifted from the Whitefall family's private cellar, when he heard a knock on his door.

Monpress froze. This was one of his most secure hideouts. He was high in the Sleeping Mountains, deep in bandit country. But he had an understanding with the local gang, and anyways, bandits didn't knock. He swirled the wine in his glass, considering his options as the knock came again, louder this time.

With a long sigh and a sip from his glass, Monpress decided he'd better answer it.

He pushed his chair back and walked to the door, grabbing his dagger from the mantel, just in case. The knock was sounding a third time when Monpress opened the door and glared down at his most unwelcome visitor.

It was a boy. Monpress pegged him at a young fifteen. He was scrawny and short for his age with untrimmed black hair and a face that was too likable to mean any good. He was dressed in rags, his feet shoved into ill-fitting shoes that were far too thin for the half foot of snow on the ground, and he looked as if he hadn't had a good meal in weeks. But, hungry as he must have been, the boy didn't even glance at the succulent duck sitting on the table. Instead, he looked Monpress straight in the eye and flashed him what the boy probably considered a deeply charming smile.

"Are you Giuseppe Monpress?"

Monpress leaned on the door, framing the duck behind him with his crooked arm, just to be cruel. "That depends on you," he said slowly. "Unless you can give me a very compelling reason why you know that name, you can think of me as your death."

To his credit, the boy's smile didn't falter. "I heard from a reliable source that Giuseppe Monpress was the greatest thief in the world, so I set off to find him. Took me the better part of a month to pin him down to this part of the mountains, but I couldn't get an exact location, so I've been checking each likely valley."

"Impressive," Monpress said. "And what were you going to do when you found him?"

The boy straightened up. "I'm going to ask him to take me as an apprentice."

"I'm sorry you've wasted your time, then," Monpress said. "Giuseppe Monpress doesn't take apprentices."

"Since only Giuseppe Monpress would know that, I think you've answered my question," the boy said. "And I can assure you, Mr. Monpress, that you'll take me."

Despite himself, Monpress began to chuckle. "And why is that?"

"Because I'm going to be the greatest thief in the world," the boy said proudly. "And because, if you don't take me, I'm going to sit on your doorstep until you change your mind."

Monpress smiled. "Assuming, for the moment, that you're right, you can hardly expect the greatest thief in the world to be trapped by a boy at his door. What will you do when I give you the slip?"

"Find you again," the boy said with a shrug. "As many times as I need to."

"I see," Monpress said. "Why are you so determined, if I may ask?"

The boy looked insulted. "I told you," he said. "I'm going to be the greatest thief in the world. You don't get to the top by apprenticing yourself to amateurs."

"So you're serious about just sitting there?" Monpress said.

"Absolutely," the boy said, and then, to prove his point, he sat down on the icy step, propping his legs up in Monpress's door. The position only helped to highlight how pathetically thin he was, and Monpress felt a tiny twinge of pity. Fortunately, it was easily quashed.

"Well," he said, stepping back. "Then I hope you have a lovely night."

He held just long enough to see the boy's smile begin to crumble before he shut the door in his face.

Nodding at a job well done, Monpress slipped his dagger into his belt and returned to the table. As he sat down in his chair, he braced himself for a racket as the boy began to demand to be let in, but none came. Except for the howl of the wind outside, the cabin was silent. If Monpress hadn't just shut a door in his face, he'd have never known the boy was outside.

He glanced sideways at the shutters, rattling in their grooves as the storm blew back up, and then back down at his rapidly cooling dinner. He'd just raised his knife and fork to carve the duck when the wind gave a low, mournful howl. Giuseppe rolled his eyes and set his silverware down with a sigh. He stood up and marched over to the door. Sure enough, the boy was sitting on the doorstep just as Monpress had left him, only his black hair was now full of snow.

"Change your mind?" the boy said, looking up.

"Not as such," Monpress said. "Happy as I would be to let you sit out there until you starved, it seems that my conscience is heavy enough without a boy's life weighing on it. I'm not agreeing to anything, mind you, but since it's clear you're the suicidally stubborn type, you might as well come in and eat."

The boy grinned from ear to ear and rushed inside so fast Monpress was nearly knocked off his feet. The boy sat down in Monpress's chair and began devouring the duck like he'd never tasted food in his life. The thief sighed and walked over to rescue his wine before it too disappeared into the boy's maw.

"What's your name?" he said as he spirited his drink to safety.

"Eli," the boy gasped between bites.

Giuseppe frowned. "Eli what?"

The boy shrugged and kept eating. Monpress sat down with a sigh, sipping his wine as he watched the boy reduce his fine roast duck to bones. The child was cracking them to suck the marrow when he caught Giuseppe looking.

"What?" he said, shoving a leg bone into his mouth.

"Nothing," Monpress said. "Just trying to shake the feeling that I've let my doom in by the front door."

"I wouldn't fret about it too much," Eli said. "I was planning to come down the chimney once you'd banked the fire anyway." He flashed Monpress a smile before spitting out the bone in his mouth and reaching for another. "When do we start training?"

Monpress drained his glass and poured himself another. He briefly thought about continuing his denials, but he was rapidly running out of energy to fight the boy's seemingly endless optimism. "Tomorrow morning," he said, taking a long drink.

Eli's eyes widened, and his face broke into an enormous grin. "What am I doing?"

"Fetching a cask of whiskey from my stash up the mountain."

Eli's face fell dramatically. "*Whiskey?* Why?"

"Because, if you're going to be staying here, I'm going to need it," Monpress said. "Finish your supper. I think a speck of duck still exists."

Eli gave him a skeptical look before turning back to the far more important task of making sure no bit of duck flesh escaped his attack.

Outside the little cabin, far from the cheery light of the little fire, the white shape of a woman vanished into the deep drifting snow.

VISIT THE ORBIT BLOG AT

www.orbitbooks.net

FEATURING

BREAKING NEWS
FORTHCOMING RELEASES
LINKS TO AUTHOR SITES
EXCLUSIVE INTERVIEWS
EARLY EXTRACTS

AND COMMENTARY FROM OUR EDITORS

WITH REGULAR UPDATES FROM OUR TEAM,
ORBITBOOKS.NET IS YOUR SOURCE
FOR ALL THINGS ORBITAL.

WHILE YOU'RE THERE, JOIN OUR E-MAIL LIST
TO RECEIVE INFORMATION ON SPECIAL OFFERS,
GIVEAWAYS, AND MORE.

imagine. explore. engage.